"You are," Sir Anthony said, "a curious mixture. You'd no suspicion of it?"

She laughed. "None, sir, upon my word."

"A babe in our midst," he remarked thoughtfully. "And yet—not a babe."

"I told you, sir, that I have been about the world a little."

"You must have spent a prodigious time touring Europe," he said pensively.

"I don't know why you should think so, sir. I made the Grand Tour."

"You must have made it a very extended one to have seen so much," Sir Anthony pointed out gently.

"You forget, sir, a great part of my life was spent abroad with my parents."

There was a slight pause. The gentleman was looking straight between his horse's ears. "What a very tender age at which to have seen so much!" he remarked blandly.

The mare bounded forward under a spur incautiously driven home. "Sir," said Prudence, "for some reason I don't guess you seem to hold me in suspicion." It was a daring move, but she could see no other.

Up went the straight brows in sleepy surprise. "Not at all. Why should I?"

"I have no notion, sir."

Praise for

GEORGETTE HEYER

"For sheer escape reading, with no pretensions of any kind, this reviewer recommends Georgette Heyer!"
—*Milwaukee Journal*

"I love her wit, her marvelous use of language, her complex, often quirky characters, her sense of place and the sheer Englishness of her stories."
—*New York Times* bestselling author Mary Jo Putney

"[Georgette Heyer] transports her readers to a world where passion and manners collide, with entertaining and often humorous results."
—Award-winning and bestselling author
Teresa Medeiros

GEORGETTE HEYER

THE MASQUERADERS

With a foreword by
Anne Stuart

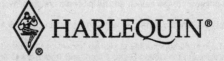
HARLEQUIN®

TORONTO • NEW YORK • LONDON
AMSTERDAM • PARIS • SYDNEY • HAMBURG
STOCKHOLM • ATHENS • TOKYO • MILAN • MADRID
PRAGUE • WARSAW • BUDAPEST • AUCKLAND

Special thanks and acknowledgment are given to
Anne Stuart for her contribution to the
foreword for *The Masqueraders*

ISBN 0-373-83606-6

THE MASQUERADERS

Copyright © 1928 by Georgette Heyer

Foreword copyright © 2004 by Harlequin Books S.A.

Visit us at www.eHarlequin.com

Printed in U.S.A.

THE
MASQUERADERS

Foreword by
Anne Stuart

Anne Stuart

has been a published author since the age of
seven, a troublemaker since she was born and
a high priestess at the altar of Georgette Heyer
since she first read her. She's written over fifty
books in numerous genres, including romantic
suspense, Regency, historical romance, gothic
romance and series romance, and she's currently
celebrating her thirtieth year as a published author.
She has won the prestigious Romance Writers of
America Lifetime Achievement Award, appears
regularly on bestseller lists and currently writes
romantic suspense and historical romance for
MIRA Books.

FOREWORD

I went into my home office, climbed on top of the sofa that's usually covered with clean laundry waiting to be folded, and reached for the top shelf, balancing precariously. The entire room is filled with built-in bookcases, and the books crammed in them are arranged with no rhyme or reason. Except for the top two shelves in the left-hand corner by the French doors. That's where La Grande Georgette resides in pristine splendour, alphabetic order, most of them in duplicate and triplicate, since Georgette Heyer is someone to read and reread until the paperback begins to fall apart.

They were all there, of course, though I will occasionally lend them out to my trusted friend Maria. Every mystery, including the divine *Behold Here's Poison* with the delicious Randall, the Amiable Snake. Every historical, from the faintly tedious to the fascinating reappearance of old friends in *Infamous Army*. And of course, every romance, the Regencies and the Georgians, the comedies and adventures, the delicious heroes and clever, brave heroines.

The Masqueraders was up there, of course, in a place of honour. It had a pale blue cover, with an idiotic picture of a gentleman in a Prussian uniform with lace cuffs and a Victorian lady with a late 1960s hairstyle snuggling. This for the ultimate tale of Georgian-era cross-dressing! The once-white pages are now a pale yellow, rather like a soft tea rose, and the musty smell of aging paper is a fine perfume to a connoisseur like me.

The cover price was seventy cents for an edition that was published in 1969, though it was written in 1929. How many books are still in print seventy-five years after they're written? How many books do we still have thirty-five years later, despite marriages, moves, children and the various complications of life? Georgette Heyer remains sacrosanct, to be carried with me wherever I decide to live, be it Princeton or New York City or the hills of Vermont.

It was probably the fourth or fifth book of La Grande Georgette's that I'd read, and it has a slightly different tone from the majority of her works, one that I cherish. It's set in an earlier time (just after Bonnie Prince Charlie's rebellion or, as Anne Stuart would assure you, the failed attempt to put the true king on the throne of England). The Merriot siblings have been drawn into the fray by their charming, extraordinary father, and it has ended badly, with the two of them wanted for high treason. So there was no help for it—

handsome, brave, slender Robin takes on the clothes and wigs and manners of a diminutive woman, while tall, strapping Prudence makes a creditable young man, and together they arrive in London, following orders from their maddeningly mysterious father.

Of course they each find someone to fall in love with even before they arrive in the city, which presents somewhat of a problem, since Robin's beloved assumes he's a woman and Prudence's chosen, Sir Anthony the Mountain, would normally believe young Peter Merriot was simply a friendly young lad in need of a mentor. Sir Anthony, being wise and observant beneath his unruffled exterior, knows exactly who and what Prudence is, and while his sense of honour keeps his behaviour impeccable, he has fallen in love as well, and the smouldering passion is unmistakable.

I've always been a sucker for masquerades. For people pretending to be lost heirs, for lost heirs pretending to be someone else, for men disguised as women, women disguised as boys, tricksters and shape-shifters playing their various games. *The Masqueraders* is undoubtedly the finest cross-dressing delight since William Shakespeare, a rare, unexpected treat.

There are wicked villains, of course, including the odious Mr Markham. There are kidnappings and blackmail and mysterious highwaymen and midnight rescues and sword fights aplenty. And above all there is the Old Gentleman, the Merriots' father, as mischievous, troublemaking, and wickedly delightful a character as was ever devised.

The language is arch, stylized and terribly funny, in the way that only La Grande Georgette could carry off. When I was young I wanted to grow up to be a cross between Georgette Heyer and Mary Stewart. I ended up being no such thing, but that doesn't keep me from curling up with a copy of *The Masqueraders,* or *Devil's Cub,* or *These Old Shades,* or *Venetia,* or… I could go on and on. On a rainy afternoon, when your heart is breaking, there's no greater gift than to reimmerse yourself in the delightful world Georgette Heyer created. It is delicious comfort of the most basic kind—La Grande Georgette's work is a treasure beyond price.

One I offer unto you, perhaps with Prudence's shy, placid smile, or Robin's daring grin. Or most likely the Old Gentleman's naughty, mischievous laugh. *The Masqueraders* is a wicked delight, worth more than its weight in gold, and I envy any of you who get to enjoy it for the first time.

Anne Stuart

THE
MASQUERADERS

CHAPTER ONE

A lady in distress

IT HAD BEGUN TO RAIN an hour ago, a fine driving mist with the sky grey above. The gentleman riding beside the chaise surveyed the clouds placidly. 'Faith, it's a wonderful climate,' he remarked of no one in particular.

The grizzled serving man who rode some paces to the rear spurred up to him. 'Best put up for the night, sir,' he grunted. 'There's an inn a mile or two on.'

The window of the chaise was let down with a clatter, and a lady looked out. 'Child, you'll be wet,' she said to her cavalier. 'How far to Norman Cross?'

The serving man rode up close to the chaise. 'Another hour, ma'am. I'm saying we'd best put up for the night.'

'I'd as soon make Norman Cross,' said the gentleman, 'for all it's plaguily damp.'

'There's an inn close by, as I remember,' the servant repeated, addressing himself to the lady.

'*En avant*, then. Produce me the inn,' the lady said. 'Give you joy of your England, Peter my little man.'

The gentleman laughed. 'Oh, it's a comforting spot, Kate.'

The inn came soon into sight, a square white house glimmering through the dusk. There were lights in the windows, and a post-chaise drawn up in the court before it.

The gentleman came lightly down from the saddle. He was of medium height, and carried himself well. He had a neat leg encased in a fine riding boot, and a slender hand in an embroidered gauntlet.

There was straight-way a bustle at the inn. An ostler came running; mine host appeared in the porch with a bow and a scrape and a waiting man sped forth to assist in letting down the steps of the chaise.

'Two bedchambers, for myself and my sister,' said the gentleman. 'Dinner, and a private room.'

Consternation was in the landlord's face. 'Bedchambers, sir. Yes—on the instant! Polly, the two best bedchambers, and fires to be lit in them!' A serving maid went scuttling off. 'Sir, the private room!' Mine host bowed, and spread a pair of deprecating hands. 'But this moment, sir, it was bespoken by a lady and a gentleman travelling south.' He looked slyly, and cast down his eyes. 'But they stay only for dinner, sir, and if your honour and the lady would condescend to the coffee-room—? There's never a soul likely to come to-night, and 'twill be private enough.'

There was a rustle of skirts. My lady came down from the chaise with a hand on her servant's shoulder.

'The coffee-room or any other so I get out of this wet!'
she cried, and swept into the inn with her cavalier
behind her.

They found themselves straight in a comfortable
large room. There was a table set, and a wood fire
burning in the hearth. A door led out into a passage
at the back, where the stairs rose steeply, and another
to one side, giving on to the taproom.

A trim girl in a mob cap brought more candles, and
dropped a shy curtsey to the lady. 'If you please, my
lady, should I take your ladyship's cloak? Your ladyship's abigail…?'

'Alack, the creature's not with me!' mourned
Madam Kate. 'Take the cloak up to my chamber,
child. So!' She put back the hood from her head, and
untied the strings round her throat. The cloak was
given to the maid; Madam stood up in a taffety gown
of blue spread over a wide hoop. She wore her fair
ringlets *en demie toilette,* free from powder, with a
blue ribbon threaded through, and a couple of curls
allowed to fall over her shoulder. The maid thought
her a prodigiously lovely lady and bobbed another
curtsey before she went away with the cloak.

My lady's brother gave his three-cornered hat into
his servant's keeping, and struggled out of his greatcoat. He was much of his sister's height, a little taller
perhaps, and like enough to her in appearance. His hair
was of a darker brown, confined demurely at the neck
by a black riband; and his eyes showed more grey than

blue in the candlelight. Young he seemed, for his
cheek was innocent of all but the faintest down; but
he had a square shoulder, and a good chin, rounded,
but purposeful enough. The landlord, following him
into the coffee-room, was profuse in apologies and
obeisances, for he recognised a member of the Quality.
The lady wore a fine silk gown, and Mr Merriot a
modish coat of brown velvet, with gold lacing, and a
quantity of Mechlin lace at his throat and wrists. A
pretty pair, in all, with the easy ways of the Quality,
and a humorous look about the eyes that made them
much alike. The landlord began to talk of capons and
his best burgundy, and was sent off to produce them.

Miss Merriot sat down by the fire, and stretched one
foot in its buckled shoe to the blaze. There was a red
heel to her shoe, and marvellous embroidered clocks
to her silken stockings. 'So!' said Miss Merriot. 'How
do you, my Peter?'

'I don't melt in a shower of rain, I believe,' Peter
said, and sat down on the edge of the table, swinging
one booted leg.

'No, faith, child, there's too much of you for that.'

The gentleman's rich chuckle sounded. 'I'm sufficiently substantial, in truth,' he remarked. He drew out
his gold and enamelled snuff-box from one of his huge
coat pockets, and took a pinch with an air, delicately
shaking the ruffles of lace back from his wrists. A ruby
ring glowed on one of his long fingers, while on the
other hand he wore a big gold seal ring. A smile crept

up into his eyes, and lurked at the corners of his mouth. 'I'd give something to know where the old gentleman is,' he said.

'Safe enough, I'll be bound,' Madam answered, and laughed. 'It's the devil himself, I believe, and will appear in London to snap his fingers under the noses of all King George's men.'

'Fie, Kate: my poor, respected papa!' Mr Merriot was not shocked. He fobbed his snuff-box and put it away. A faint crease showed between his brows. 'For all he named London—egad, 'tis like his impudence!—it's odds he's gone to France.'

'I don't permit myself to hope too much,' said Miss Merriot, with a smile at once dreamy and a little impish. 'He'll be there to lead us another of his mad dances. If not…I've a mind to try our own fortunes.'

'In truth, I've a kindness for the old gentleman,' said Mr Merriot pensively. 'His dances lead somewhere.'

'To lost causes.' There was a hint of bitterness in the tone.

Mr Merriot looked up. 'Ay, you've taken it to heart.'

'Not I.' Kate jerked a shoulder as though to shake something off. 'We went into it—egad, why did we go into it?'

'Ask the old gentleman,' said Mr Merriot, the slow smile creeping up again. 'He had a loyal fervour, belike.'

Kate drew down the corners of her mouth. 'It's a pleasing image. He meant it for a *beau geste,* I dare swear. And we? Well, I suppose we went willy nilly into the net.'

'I don't regret it. The old gentleman meddled in Saxe's affairs, but we came out of that net.'

'That was in the nature of adventuring. This—' Kate paused. 'Bah, I hate lost causes! It was different.'

'For you?' Mr Merriot lifted an eyebrow. 'Did you want the Prince, child?'

'We fought for him while it lasted. He had the right. But now it's over, and the Butcher's made a shambles of the North, and there are those who have died on Tower Hill, while we—we try our fortunes, and the old gentleman weaves us a fresh net. I believe I'll turn respectable.'

'Alack, we were made for sobriety!' said Mr Merriot.

Came the landlord, and a serving maid with dinner. Covers were laid, and a cork drawn. Miss Merriot and her brother sat down to fat capons and a generous pasty. They were left presently toying with sweetmeats and their wine. The maid bore off all that remained of the capons through the door that led into the passage. The door was left ajar and allowed a glimpse of another door, across the passageway. From behind it came the sound of a lady's voice raised in protest.

'I won't, I tell you!' it said. 'I won't!'

There came the sound of a deeper voice, half coaxing, half bullying; then the lady cried out again, on a hysterical note of panic. 'I won't go with you! You sh-shan't elope with me against my will! Take me home! Oh please, Mr Markham, take me home!'

Miss Merriot looked at her brother. He got up, and went unhurriedly to the door, and stood listening.

The man's voice was raised now in anger. 'By God, Letty, you shan't fool me like that!'

Following on a crash from behind the closed door as of a fist banged on the table, came a choked, imploring murmur.

'No!' barked the man's voice. 'If I have to gag you, to Gretna you'll go, Letty! D'you think I'm fool enough to let you slip through my fingers now?'

Mr Merriot turned his head. 'My dear, I believe I don't like the noisy gentleman,' he said calmly.

Madame Kate listened to a cry of: 'My papa will come! I won't marry you, oh, I won't!' and a faint frown was between her eyes.

There came the sound of a coarse laugh. Evidently the gentleman had been drinking. 'I think you will,' he said significantly.

Miss Merriot bit one finger nail. 'It seems we must interfere, my Peter.'

Peter looked rueful, and drew his sword a little way out of the scabbard.

'No, no, child, put up!' said Madam, laughing. 'We know a trick worth two of that. We must have the fox out of his earth, though.'

'Stay you there,' said her brother, and went out into the courtyard, and called to John, his servant.

John came.

'Who's the owner of the post-chaise, John?' inquired Mr Merriot.

The answer was severe. 'It's a Mr Markham, sir, running off to Gretna with a rich heiress, so they say. And the lady not out of her teens. There's wickedness!'

'John's propriety is offended,' murmured Miss Merriot. 'We will dispose, John, since God seems unwilling. I want a stir made.'

'Best not meddle,' said John phlegmatically. 'We've meddled enough.'

'A cry of fire,' mused Mr Merriot. 'Fire or footpads. Where do I lie hid?'

'Oh, are you with me already?' admired Kate. 'Let me have a fire, John, or a parcel of daring footpads, and raise the ostlers.'

John fetched a sigh. 'We've played that trick once before. Will you never be still?'

Mr Merriot laughed. 'It's a beauty in distress, John, and Kate must be up and doing.'

A grunt only was vouchsafed, and the glimmering of a grim smile. John went out. Arose presently in the courtyard a shout, and a glow, and quickly uproar.

'Now I wonder how he made that fire?' said Miss Merriot, amused.

'There's a shed and some straw. Enough for John.

Well, it's a fine stir.' Mr Merriot went to the window. 'Mine host leads the household out in force. The wood's so damp 'twill be out in a moment. Do your part, sister.' Mr Merriot vanished into the deserted tap-room.

Miss Merriot added then to the stir by a scream, close followed by another, and a cry of '—Fire, fire! Help, oh help!'

The door across the passage was burst open, and a dark gentleman strode out. 'What in hells name—?' he began. His face was handsome in the swarthy style, but flushed now with wine. His eye lighted on Miss Merriot, and a smell of burning assailed his nostrils. 'What's the noise? Gad, is the place on fire?' He came quickly into the coffee-room, and received Miss Merriot in his unwilling arms. Miss Merriot neatly tripped up her chair, and with a moan of 'Save me!' collapsed onto Mr Markham's chest.

He grasped the limp form perforce, and found it a dead weight on his arm. His companion, a slim child of no more than eighteen, ran to the window. 'Oh, 'tis only an old shed caught fire away to the right!' she said.

Mr Markham strove to restore the fainting Miss Merriot. 'Compose yourself, madam! For God's sake, no vapours! There's no danger. Damnation, Letty, pick the chair up!'

Miss Letty came away from the window towards Miss Merriot's fallen chair. Mr Markham was tightly

clasping that unconscious lady, wrath at his own helpless predicament adding to the already rich colour in
his face.

'The devil take the woman, she weighs a ton!'
swore Mr Markham. 'Pick the chair up, I say!'

Miss Letty bent to take hold of it. She heard a door
open behind her, and turning saw Mr Merriot.

Of a sudden Miss Merriot came to life. In round-
eyed astonishment Miss Letty saw that lady no longer
inanimate, but seemingly struggling to be free.

Mr Merriot was across the floor in a moment.

'Unhand my sister, sir!' cried he in a wonderful
fury.

Miss Merriot was thrust off. 'God's Life, 'twas herself—' began Mr Markham, but got no further. His
chin came into sudden contact with Mr Merriot's
sword hilt, nicely delivered, and Mr Markham fell
heavily all amongst the table legs.

'Oh, neatly done, i'faith!' vowed Miss Merriot.
'Down like an ox, as I live! Set the coach forward,
Peter, and you, child, upstairs with you to my cham-
ber.'

Miss Letty's hand was caught in a firm clasp. Quite
bewildered she was swirled away by the competent
Miss Merriot.

Miss Merriot's brother put up his sword, and went
out into the court. John seemed to rise up out of the
gloom to meet him. 'All well, sir?'

Mr Merriot nodded. 'Where's the dear gentleman's chaise, John?'

John jerked a thumb over his shoulder.

'Horses put to?' inquired Mr Merriot.

'Ay, they're ready to be off. The men are in the taproom—it's dry they are after the great fire. There's an ostler to the horses' heads.'

'I don't want that ostler there,' said Mr Merriot. 'Drive the chaise past Stilton, John, and hide it somewhere where the gentleman won't find it too soon.'

'Hide a chaise and horses, is it?' John growled.

'It is, John,' said Mr Merriot serenely. 'Tell that ostler that I want a horse saddled on the instant. One of our own, if need be. I shall set the dear gentleman after you, John. God speed you.'

'Ah, it's a mad couple you are!' said John, but he moved away to where the lights of the chaise shone. Mr Merriot heard him give the order to the ostler, and offer to hold the horses' heads. He heard the ostler run off towards the stables and himself turned back into the coffee-room smiling placidly.

Miss Merriot had come downstairs again and was standing by the fallen Mr Markham calmly surveying him. 'Well, child, is it done?' she asked.

The clatter of horses and the rumble of wheels on the cobbles answered her. John was off; they heard the chaise roll away down the road to London. Miss Merriot laughed and dropped her brother a mock curtsey. 'My compliments, child. It's you have the head, indeed. Now what to do for the poor gentleman? Water, my Peter, and a napkin. Observe me all solicitude.' She sank down on to the floor, and lifted Mr Markham's head into her lap. Mr Merriot was chuckling again as he handed her the water, and a napkin.

The landlord came hurrying in, and stared in horror at what he saw. 'Sir—madam! The gentleman's coach is off! Oh law, madam! The gentleman!'

'Off is it?' Mr Merriot was interested. 'Tut, tut! And the lady in it, belike?'

The landlord's jaw dropped. 'Ay, that would be it! But what's come to the gentleman, sir? Good lord, sir, never say—'

'The poor gentleman!' said Miss Merriot, holding a wet napkin to Mr Markham's brow. ''Twas the drink turned the head on his shoulders, I dare swear. An accident, host. I believe he won't die of it.'

'A warning to all abductors,' said Mr Merriot piously.

A gleam of understanding shot into the landlord's eyes. 'Sir, he'll be raving mad when he comes to.'

'A warning to you, good fellow, not to be by,' said Mr Merriot.

There was significance in Mr Merriot's voice. It occurred to mine host that the less he knew of the matter the better it might be for himself, on all sides. He went out discreetly at what time Mr Markham gave vent to a faint groan.

Mr Markham came slowly back to consciousness,

and opened heavy eyes. He did not at once remember much, but he was aware of a swollen jaw-bone which hurt him. A cool hand was placed on his brow, and something wet was laid on his sore chin. He rolled his eyes upwards, groaning, and saw a fair face bent over him, framed in golden ringlets. He stared up at it, trying to collect his bemused wits, and vaguely it seemed to him that he had seen that face before, with its fine, rather ironical blue eyes, and its curiously square chin. He blinked, and frowned in the effort to pull himself together, and saw the delicate mouth smile.

'Thank God you are better!' came a cooing voice. 'I have been in an agony! Dear sir, pray lie still; 'twas a cruel blow, and oh the misunderstanding! Peter, a glass of wine for the gentleman! There, sir, let me but raise your head.'

Mr Markham allowed it, perforce, and sipped at the wine held to his lips. Some of the mists were clearing from his brain. He raised himself on his elbow, and looked round.

'Oh, you are much better!' cooed the voice. 'But gently, sir. Don't, I implore you, overtax your strength.'

Mr Markham's gaze came to rest on a flowered waistcoat. He put a hand to his head, and his eyes travelled slowly up the waistcoat to Mr Merriot's grave face. Mr Merriot was on one knee, glass of wine in hand; Mr Merriot looked all concern.

Recollection came. 'Burn it, you're the fellow—'

Mr Markham's hand went to his jaw; he glared at Peter Merriot. 'Did you— By God, sir, did you—?'

'Let me help you to a chair, sir,' said Mr Merriot gently. 'In truth you are shaken, and on wonder. Sir, I cannot sufficiently beg your pardon.'

Mr Markham was on his feet now, dizzy and bewildered. 'Was it you knocked me down, sir? Answer me that!' he panted.

'Alas, sir, I did!' said Mr Merriot. 'I came in to find my sister struggling, as I thought, in your arms. Can you blame me, sir? My action was the impulse of the moment.'

Mr Markham was put into a chair. He fought for words, a hand still held to his jaw. 'Struggling? she flung herself at me in a swoon!' he burst out.

Miss Merriot was kneeling at his feet, napkin in hand. Mr Markham thrust it aside with an impotent snarl. 'You have the right to be angry, sir,' sighed Miss Merriot. ''Twas all my folly, but oh sir, when the bustle started, and they were crying fire without I scarce knew what I did!' Her fair head was bent in modest confusion. Mr Markham did not heed her.

'Blame you? blame you? Yes, sir, I can!' he said wrathfully. 'A damnable little puppy to—to—' Words failed him; he sat nursing his jaw and fuming.

Mr Merriot said haughtily:—'You're heated sir, and I believe excusably. I don't heed what you say therefore. I have asked your pardon for a mistake—understandable, I contend—that I made.'

'Puppy!' snapped Mr Markham, and drank off the rest of the wine in the glass. It seemed to restore him. He got up unsteadily and his hot gaze swept round again. 'Letty!' he shot out. 'Where is the girl?'

'Dear sir, indeed you are not yourself yet!' Miss Merriot laid a soothing hand on his arm. 'There is no girl here save myself.'

She was shaken off. 'No girl, you say?' roared Mr Markham, and went blundering towards the room across the passage. 'Letty!' he shouted. 'Letty, I say! Hell and damnation, her cloak's gone!' He came back, his face dark with rage and suspicion, and caught at Mr Merriot's straight shoulder. 'Out with it! Where is she? Where have you hidden her? You don't trick me, my fine sir!'

Miss Merriot, hovering watchfully, cast herself between them, and clung to her brother. 'No, no!' she cried. 'No swords, I do beseech you. Sir, you are raving! There is no girl here that I have seen.'

Mr Merriot put his sister aside. 'But wait!' he said slowly. 'As I remember there was a lady in the room as I came in. A child with black hair. My sister was overwrought, sir, and maybe forgets. Yes, there was a lady.' He looked round as though he expected to see her lurking in some corner.

'Damme, it won't serve!' cried out the infuriated Mr Markham, and went striding off to the door that led into the taproom, calling loudly for the landlord.

Mine host came quickly, with an uneasy look in his

face. In answer to Mr Markham's furious query he said nervously that in the scare of the fire someone had driven off with his worship's chaise, and he doubted but that the lady was in it.

Mr Markham swung round to face Peter Merriot again, and there came a red light into his eyes, while his hand fumbled at his sword hilt. 'Ah, you're in this!' he snarled.

Mr Merriot paused in the act of taking snuff. 'Your pardon, sir?' he asked in some surprise. 'A lady gone off in your post-chaise, and myself in it? I don't understand you, sir. Who is the lady, and why should she go off so? Why, it's churlish of her, I protest.'

Mr Markham seemed undecided. 'It's no business of yours,' he said savagely. 'But if I find 'twas you did it.—Which way did the chaise go?'

'To—towards London, sir,' nervously answered mine host. 'But 'tis only what Tom says. I didn't see myself, and indeed, sir—'

Mr Markham said something between his teeth at which mine host cast a horrified glance at Miss Merriot. The lady appeared to be unmoved. 'Saddle me a horse at once! Where's my hat?'

Light dawned on Mr Merriot. 'Egad, it's a runaway, Kate. Faith, sir, it seems my—er—impetuosity was indeed ill-timed. A horse, of course! You should be up with the chaise soon enough. A horse for the gentleman!' Mr Merriot swept out into the court, bearing mine host before him.

'It's ready saddled, sir, but Tom says the gentleman ordered it half an hour since,' said the puzzled landlord.

'Saddles and ready, eh? Then see it brought round to the door, for the gentleman's in a hurry.'

'Yes, sir, but how came it that the horse was bespoke when the gentleman was a-laying like one dead?'

'Bespoke? A ruse, man, a ruse, and your man in madam's pay very like. Best keep your mouth shut. Ah, behold the bereft gentleman!'

Mr Markham came stamping out with his hat rammed over his nose, and managed to hoist himself into the saddle with the assistance of two scared ostlers. He gathered the bridle up, and turned to glare down upon Mr Merriot. 'I'll settle with you later,' he promised ferociously, and setting spurs to his horse dashed off into the darkness.

Miss Merriot came out to lay a hand on her brother's shoulder. 'The dear gentleman!' she remarked. 'Very well, child, but what next?'

CHAPTER TWO

Arrival of a large gentleman

BROTHER AND SISTER went back into the coffee-room. As they entered by one door a little figure tiptoed in at the other, and stood poised on one two as if for flight. 'Has he gone?' breathed Miss Letitia.

It was Peter Merriot who went forward and took the lady's hand. 'Why, yes, child, gone for the moment,' he said, and led her to the fire.

She raised a pair of big pansy-brown eyes. 'Oh, thank you, sir!' she said. 'And you too, dear madam.'

Miss Merriot flushed slightly, whereat the humorous look came into Peter's eye again. He looked down at Miss Letty gravely enough, and pulled a chair forward. 'Sit down, madam, and let us have the story, if you please. I should desire to know how we may serve you.'

'You have served me,' vowed the lady, clasping her hands in her lap. 'My story is all folly, sir—wicked folly rising out of the most dreadful persecution.'

'You shock me, madam.'

Miss Merriot came to the fire, and sat down beside

the little lady, who promptly caught her hand and kissed it. 'I don't know what I should have done without you!' she said fervently. 'For I had quite made up my mind I didn't want to go to Gretna Green at all. You see, I had never seen him in his cups before. It was a terrible awakening. He became altered altogether once we were out of London, and—and I was afraid—a little.' She looked up blushing. 'At home when I saw him he was so different, you see.'

'Do I understand, my dear, that you consented to elope with the gentleman?' inquired Miss Merriot.

The black curls were nodded vigorously. 'I thought it would be so romantic,' sighed Letty. She brightened. 'And so it was, when you hit him,' she added, turning to Peter. 'It was positively marvellous!'

'Did you elope with him for the romance of it?' asked Mr Merriot, amused.

'That, and because of my papa,' said Letty. 'And because of being bored. Oh, have you never known, ma'am, what it is to be cooped up, and kept so close that you are ready to die of boredom?'

'In truth, I've led something of a rover's life,' said Miss Merriot. 'But continue, child.'

'I am an heiress,' announced Letty in tones the most lugubrious.

'My felicitations, ma'am,' bowed Mr Merriot.

'Felicitations! I wish I were a pauper, sir! If a man comes to the house my papa must needs imagine he is after my money. He said that of Gregory Markham.

And indeed I think he was right,' she said reflectively.
'Ma'am, I think fathers are—are the veriest plague.'

'We have suffered, child,' said Miss Merriot.

'Then, ma'am, you will feel for me. My papa puts
a hateful disagreeable woman to be my duenna, and I
am so guarded and sheltered that there is nothing
amusing ever happens to me, in spite of having been
brought to town. Add to all that, ma'am, Sir Anthony
Fanshawe, and you will see why I had come to the
pitch of doing anything only to get away!'

'I feel we are to deplore Sir Anthony, Kate,' said
Mr Merriot.

'It is not that I am not fond of him,' Letty explained.
'I have always been fond of him, but conceive, ma'am,
being required to marry a man whom you have known
all your life! A man, too, of his years and disposition!'

'I perceive in you a victim of parental tyranny,
child,' said Miss Merriot. 'We consign Sir Anthony to
perdition.'

Letty giggled at that. 'Oh, never, ma'am! 'Tis a
model of prudence and the virtues! And thirty-five
years old at the very least!'

Mr Merriot flicked a speck of snuff from his sleeve.

'And to escape this greybeard, hence the young
Adonis yonder, I suppose?'

Miss Letty hung her head. 'He—he was not very
young either, I suppose,' she confessed. 'And I have
been very silly, and wicked, I know. But indeed I
thought him vastly more entertaining than Tony. You

could not for your life imagine Tony excited, or in a scrape, or even hurried. And Gregory said such pretty things, and it was all so romantic I was misled.'

'The matter's plain to the meanest intelligence, madam,' Mr Merriot assured her, 'I discover in myself a growing desire to meet the phlegmatic Sir Anthony.'

His sister laughed. 'Ay, that's to your taste. But what's the next step?'

'Oh, she goes with us along to London. Pray, ma'am, may we know your name?'

''Tis Letitia Grayson, sir. My papa is Sir Humphrey Grayson of Grayson Court, in Gloucestershire. He is afflicted with the gout. I expect you may see him by and by, for I left a note for him, and he would be bound to find it.'

'We await his coming, then,' said Miss Merriot. 'It solves the matter. My Peter, bespeak a bedchamber for Miss Grayson.'

A confiding hand was slipped into Kate's as Mr Merriot strolled away to the door. 'Please will you call me Letty?' said Miss Grayson shyly.

Mr Merriot made an odd grimace at the panel of the door, and went through into the taproom.

Mine host had barely recovered from his very natural bewilderment at finding that the supposed fugitive was still in his house when there came the sound of a chaise bowling at a rare speed along the road. It drew up at the inn, and in the light of the lamps Mr Merriot saw his servant jump down. He pursed his lips in a soundless whistle. 'This should be papa,' he said pensively. 'Your fourth room will be wanted, host.' He went back into the coffee-room to find that Miss Letty was at the window already, peering out.

'Your papa, as I believe,' announced Mr Merriot.

'I am afraid it is,' agreed Miss Letty. 'Yet with the gout plaguing him so much—oh lud! As I live, 'tis Anthony!'

Miss Merriot threw her brother a comical look. 'And so your desires are fulfilled, child. We are all impatience, Letty.'

Mr Merriot stood by her chair, and took snuff. The door opened to admit a large gentleman, who came in very leisurely.

'Lud, it's a mammoth!' said Miss Merriot, for her brother's private ear.

'Oh, are you jealous?' he retorted.

The large gentleman paused on the threshold and put up his quizzing-glass, through which he blandly surveyed the room. He was a very large gentleman indeed, with magnificent shoulders and a fine leg. He seemed rather to fill the room; he had certainly a presence, and a personality. He wore a tie wig of plain brown, and carried his hat under his arm. The hilt of his sword peeped out from between the folds of his greatcoat, but in his hand he held a cane.

'The gentleman would appear to be annoyed,' murmured Mr Merriot, looking at the lines about the newcomer's mouth and square jowl.

'La, my dear, how can you say so?' marvelled Miss Merriot, seeing the large gentleman's grey eyes calm and bored. She rose with an air, and swept a curtsey. The gentleman must not be allowed to dominate the room thus. It seemed he had the way of it. 'Make your leg, child,' she threw over her shoulder at Peter. 'We are under observation.'

The sternness about Sir Anthony's mouth vanished. He smiled and showed a row of very even white teeth. He bowed with easy grace. 'Madam, your most obedient! Sir, yours!'

Mr Merriot took Miss Letty by the hand. 'Permit me to restore to you Miss Grayson, sir,' he said, ignoring an indignant protest from the lady.

Sir Anthony showed no desire to receive Miss Grayson, who looked him defiantly between the eyes. He smiled still, but he did not offer to take her hand. 'You should be whipped, Letty,' he said pleasantly.

Miss Grayson flushed. ''Deed, sir, and did you bring your cane for that purpose?' she demanded.

'No, my dear, but I should be happy to benefit you that far.'

Peter Merriot was amused, and permitted his chuckle to be heard. 'Faith, it's a stern suitor.'

'You are—very rude—and—and—and hateful!' declared Miss Grayson, outraged.

Sir Anthony laid down his cane and his hat, and began to take off his greatcoat. As one who had no further interest in Miss Grayson he took out his snuff-

box, unfobbed it, and held it out to Mr Merriot. His
hand was very white and finely shaped, but it looked
to have some strength. 'Sir,' said he, smiling sleepily
for all his grey eyes were alert beneath their rather
heavy lids, 'you will permit me to thank you on behalf
of my friend, Sir Humphrey Grayson, for your services
to his daughter.'

Mr Merriot helped himself to a pinch of snuff. Grey
eyes met grey; the humorous look played around Mr
Merriot's mouth. 'Lud, here's a solemnity!' he said. 'I
am Miss Grayson's servant to command.'

Miss Grayson forgot her dignity. 'Tony, 'twas wonderful! His sword was out in a trice, and I thought he
was about to run that odious Markham right through
the body, but just as it was too monstrously exciting
for words the point seemed to flash upwards and the
hilt caught Markham on the chin.' She demonstrated
with a small fist to her own pretty chin. 'He went
down like a stone,' she ended dramatically. Her glance
fell on Miss Merriot by the fire. 'And Miss Merriot
too was splendid, Tony, for she pretended to swoon
in Markham's arms.'

Mr Merriot looked down at his sister something
quizzically. 'My dear, I eclipse you,' he murmured.
He turned again to Sir Anthony. 'Thus we mourn our
departed suitor. Now where did you find my man
John?' He began to pour wine, and handed one glass
to the large gentleman.

'At Stilton,' Sir Anthony replied. 'Just before I saw

my friend Mr Markham. He was endeavouring to hide a chaise and horses which—er—aroused my suspicions. He was induced to confide in me.'

Mr Merriot looked meditatively at that square handsome face. 'I wonder why?' he said, for he knew his John.

A singularly attractive smile crossed Sir Anthony's face. 'My charm of manner, sir, I believe,' he said.

There came a laugh from Miss Merriot. 'I begin to have a kindness for the large gentleman,' she remarked to the room at large. 'And you met the so dear Mr Markham, sir?'

'Hardly, madam. I had rather say I saw the so dear Mr Markham pass me in a cloud of—mud, I believe.'

'I wonder, did he see you?' Miss Merriot's eyes were bright with laughter.

'I am almost persuaded that he did,' said Sir Anthony.

'Then I take it we are not to expect his return?' Miss Merriot cocked a knowing eyebrow.

'I hardly think so, madam,' said Sir Anthony placidly.

Miss Merriot looked at Miss Grayson. 'Why, child, I like the large gentleman, I protest,' she said. 'Pray, sir, have you dined?'

'So far I have not had the time, madam, but I have reason to hope the landlord is preparing dinner for me at this moment.'

Mine host himself came in most opportunely then,

with the serving maid behind him, carrying a loaded tray. A fresh cover was laid, a roasted chicken placed before Sir Anthony, and a fresh bottle uncorked.

'You permit, madam?' Sir Anthony bowed towards Miss Merriot.

'Pray, sir, be seated. You will be ravenous.'

'I confess I hate to miss my dinner,' said Sir Anthony, and began to carve the chicken. 'There is something of me to maintain, you see,' he added, with a twinkle, and a glance cast down his noble bulk.

Miss Grayson cut in on Miss Merriot's laugh. 'Food!' she ejaculated scornfully, and tapped an impatient foot. Sir Anthony paid no heed. 'Well, Tony, you are come nigh on a hundred miles to rescue me, as I suppose, and now have you nothing at all to say but that you have missed your dinner?'

'That thought has been absorbing me for the last twenty miles,' said Sir Anthony imperturbably.

'And me in peril!' cried the affronted Miss Grayson.

Sir Anthony raised his eyes from the chicken and looked coolly across at her. 'Oh, were you in peril?' he inquired. 'I came merely to put an end to an indiscretion, as I thought.'

'Peril! At the hands of such a Monster!' Miss Grayson was indignant. 'I wonder, sir, that you need ask.'

Sir Anthony poured wine for himself and Mr Merriot. 'My dear Letty,' said he, 'you have so frequently assured us that Mr Markham is a model of all the virtues that I did you the honour to respect your judgement.'

Miss Grayson turned scarlet, and looked as though she were about to cry. 'You didn't, Tony! You are just being—disagreeable. And he's not a model of virtue! He is an odious brute, and—and so are you!'

'Tut, child, the gentleman's hungry, and will be the better for his chicken,' said Mr Merriot.

'I am not a child!' flashed Miss Grayson, and was off in a swirl of skirts to Miss Merriot's side. From the shelter of Miss Merriot's arm she hurled a tearful defiance. 'And I would sooner go to Gretna with that Monster than marry you, Sir Tony!'

Sir Anthony remained unmoved. 'My dear Letty, if this piece of absurdity was to escape my attentions, believe me it was not in the least necessary. So far as I am aware I have never asked you to marry me. Nor have I the smallest intention of so doing.'

This pronouncement brought Miss Grayson's head up from Kate's shoulder. In round-eyed astonishment she gazed at Sir Anthony, busily engaged with the wing of a chicken.

'I have to suppose,' said Miss Merriot sharply, 'that the gentleman is an original.'

Mr Merriot turned away to hide a laughing face. 'These family arrangements—!' he said.

'But—but Papa says—' began Miss Grayson. 'Why, Tony, don't you *want* to marry me?'

'I do not,' said Sir Anthony.

Miss Grayson blinked, but she did not seem to be offended. 'Why don't you?' she asked with naïve curiosity.

At that Sir Anthony looked up, and there was a twinkle in his eyes. 'I suppose, Letty, because my taste is at fault.'

'Well!' Miss Grayson digested this in silence. She disengaged herself from Kate's arm, and went slowly to the table. Sir Anthony rose at her approach, and received one little hand in his large one. 'Tony, will you tell Papa?' she asked.

'I have told him, my dear.'

'How did he take it?' asked Miss Grayson anxiously.

'Philosophically, child.'

'I am so glad!' said Miss Grayson, with a relieved sigh. 'If you don't want to marry me, Tony, I can go home with a quiet mind. And I can even forgive you for being so disagreeable.'

'And I,' said Sir Anthony, 'can finish my dinner.'

CHAPTER THREE

My Lady Lowestoft

MISS MERRIOT called 'Come in!' to a scratching on the door. Came Mr Merriot into the big bedroom, and walked across to the fireplace where Kate stood. Mr Merriot cocked an eyebrow at Kate, and said:—'Well, my dear, and did you kiss her good-night?'

Miss Merriot kicked off her shoes, and replied in kind. 'What, are you parted from the large gentleman already?'

Mr Merriot looked into the fire, and a slow smile came, and the suspicion of a blush.

'Lord, child!' said Miss Merriot. 'Are you for the mammoth? It's a most respectable gentleman, my dear.'

Mr Merriot raised his eyes. 'I believe I would not choose to cross him,' he remarked inconsequently. 'But I would trust him.'

Miss Merriot began to laugh. 'Be a man, my Peter, I implore you.'

'Alack!' sighed Mr Merriot, 'I feel all a woman.'

'Oh Prue, my Prue, it's a Whig with a sober mind! Will you take it to husband?'

'I suppose you will be merry, Robin. Do you imagine me in love on two hours' acquaintance? Ah, you're jealous of the gentleman's inches. Said I not so?'

'My inches, child, stand me in good stead. I believe it's the small men have the wits. My compliments on the sword-play.'

'At least the old gentleman taught me a trick or two worth the knowing,' placidly said the lady, and pulled up her coat sleeve to show a stained shirt. 'The last glass went down my arm,' she said, smiling.

Her brother nodded. 'Well, here's been work enough for an evening,' he remarked. 'I await the morrow. Give you good-night, child, and pray dream of your mammoth.'

'In truth I need a mammoth to match me,' said Madam Prudence. 'Pray dream of your midget, Robin.'

She went away humming a snatch of an old song. It was apparent to her that her brother frowned upon the morrow, but she had a certain placidity that went well with her inches, and looked upon her world with calm untroubled eyes.

The truth was she was too well used to a precarious position to be easily disturbed, and certainly too used to an exchange of personality with Robin to boggle over her present situation. She had faith in her own wits: these failing her she had a rueful dependence on

the ingenuity of her sire. Impossible to tread the paths
of his cutting without developing an admiration for the
gentleman's guile. Prudence regarded him with affection, but some irony. She admitted his incomprehen-
sibility with a laugh, but it did not disturb her. She
danced to his piping, but it is believed she lacked the
adventurous spirit. Now Robin might fume at the mystery with which the father chose to wrap himself
about, but Robin enjoyed a chequered career, and had
an impish dare-devilry that led him into more scrapes
than the old gentleman devised. Withal he surveyed
the world with a seriousness that Prudence lacked. He
had enthusiasms, and saw life as something more than
the amusing pageant Prudence thought it.

It seemed he had taken this last, unlucky venture to
heart. To be sure, he had had a closer view of it than
his sister. She supposed it was his temperament made
him enthusiastic for a venture entered into in a spirit
of adventure only, and at the father's bidding. She remembered he had wept after Culloden, with his head
in her lap at the old house in Perth—wept in a passion
of fury and heartbreak, and dashed away the tears with
an oath, and a vow that he hated lost causes. To Prudence it was a matter of indifference whether Stewart
Charles or German George sat the throne; she suspected her sire of a like indifference, discounting heroics. They were swept into this rebellion for—God
knew what cause; they were entangled in its meshes
before they knew it. That was Mr Colney's way. He

made a fine speech, and it seemed they were all Jacobites. A year before they were entirely French, at Florence; before that there was a certain gaming house at Frankfort, whose proprietor of a sudden swept off his son and daughter to dip fingers in a pie of M. de Saxe's making.

French, German, Jacobite—it was all one to Prudence. But this England was different. She conceived a fondness for it, and found it homelike. Doubtless it was the mother in her, that big, beautiful, smiling creature who had died at Dieppe when Robin was a child.

She remarked on it to Robin next morning, before their departure for London.

Robin laughed at her; he was busy with the painting of his face. 'Lord, my dear, you're the very picture of English solidity,' he said. 'Do you ride with the mountain?'

'So I believe,' said Miss Prudence. Her eyes fell on John, packing away Master Robin's razors. 'La, child, have you shaved? And you with not a hair to your chin!'

This drew a grim smile from the servant. 'You'd best have a care, the pair of you,' he said. 'We're off to put our heads in a noose. The gentleman with the sleepy eyes sees things, I'll warrant you.'

'What, do you shy way from the mountain?' Robin said. 'I might engage to run in circles round it.'

The man looked upon his young master with rough affection. 'Ay, you're a cunning one, Master Robin, but the big gentleman's awake for all you think him so dull.'

Prudence sat saddle-wise across a chair, and leaned her arms on the back of it. Chin in hand she regarded John, and said lazily: 'Where's the old gentleman, John?'

There was no expression in the stolid face. 'I've lived with him more years than you, Miss Prue, and I don't take it upon myself to answer that.'

'How long have you lived with him, John?'

'Since before you were born, mistress.'

Robin put down the hare's foot, and got up. 'Ay, you're devilish close, a'n't you, John? Maybe you know what he'll be at now?'

'Maybe I do, maybe I don't,' was all the answer vouchsafed him. 'What's to be your ladyship's dress to-day?'

Robin came down to the coffee-room twenty minutes later in a dimity gown and pink ribands. The hood was cast aside in favour of a straw hat with ro-settes, and more ribands, but Prudence, very sober in fawn breeches, and a coat of claret-coloured cloth, carried a fine mantle over her arm, which was presently put about Madam Robin's shoulders.

Miss Letty was agog to be off. They set forward in good time, Robin and the lady seated demurely in the chaise, with the seeming Mr Merriot and Sir Anthony riding a little way behind, for escort.

There were questions, of course: Prudence was pre-

pared for them and knew no faltering. She spoke of a
home in Cumberland—it seemed remote enough—and
of the Grand Tour. Sir Anthony had made it: that went
without saying. They conversed of foreign towns am-
icably and safely. Prudence displayed a remarkable
knowledge of places; indeed she had the greater part
of Europe in her memory, as it were, and an intimate
acquaintance with haunts unfrequented by the fairer
sex. Once she saw the straight brows rise, and tranquilly awaited developments.

'You've seen a vast deal for your years, Master Peter,' said Sir Anthony.

'They number twenty, sir,' she replied. If the truth
be told they numbered twenty-six, but she looked a
stripling, she knew. 'But I lived abroad with my parents some years before my mother's death. She could
not support the English climate.'

Sir Anthony bowed politely, and desired to know
where Mr Merriot might be found in London.

'My sister is to visit my Lady Lowestoft, sir,' Prudence answered. 'I am her escort, and I believe her
ladyship will give me a lodging. Perhaps you are acquainted with her?'

'Faith, all the world knows Lady Lowestoft,' said
Sir Anthony. 'If she denies you, or you grow tired of
the petticoats, my dear boy, you may command a lodging with me at any time.'

Prudence flushed in sudden surprise, and looked
sideways at the gentleman. This was unexpected; it

seemed Sir Anthony was developing a kindness for her. She thanked him gravely, and learned that he owned a house in Clarges Street.

They came to London in the dusk. Prudence sat straight enough in the saddle, but she owned privately to fatigue. It was necessary to restore Miss Letty first to her father, where also they left Sir Anthony. The lateness of the hour was pleaded as an excuse for not entering the house with Miss Letty, but Miss Merriot promised to wait upon her as soon as might be. The chaise drove on to Arlington Street, and drew up at my Lady Lowestoft's door.

Prudence came down out of the saddle with a sigh of relief. Robin touched her shoulder. 'Bravely done, child. Journey's end now.'

'A halt,' Prudence amended. 'No doubt we'll ha' done with our travels when we get to heaven.'

My lady's black page it was that ushered them into my lady's withdrawing room. This was a spacious apartment, resplendent with gilt and yellow brocade. My lady, it seemed, had a taste for the new French furniture. The page went away to carry Mr and Miss Merriot's names to his mistress, and Miss Prudence looked round with a comical grimace. 'Faith, it seems my Lady Lowestoft is the same Thérèse de Bruton,' she remarked.

The door was opened, and swiftly shut again behind a lady who came in with a swirl of a silk gown over an enormous hoop—a lady with black eyes like slits in a thin, vivid face, a powdered wig, and many jewels. She stood with her back to the door, her hand still on the knob, and as she looked sharply from one to the other of her visitors the narrow black eyes narrowed still more, and her face was all alive with laughter. 'Eh, but which is the man of you, my little ones?' she demanded.

Prudence made her bow. 'So please you, madam.'

My lady came to her with quick jerky steps. 'Never! Do I not know thee, my cabbage? Eh, Prue, my dear!' She cast her arms about Prue's large person, and kissed her on both cheeks. Robin fared the same, but returned the caress with greater alacrity than his flushing sister. Prudence had never a taste for stray kisses.

'And the *bon papa,* my children?' cried my lady, holding a hand of each.

'There, madam, we suppose you to have the advantage of us,' Robin said.

She looked a query, with her head tilted birdlike to one side. 'Ah? What's this? You have no news of him?'

'In truth, madam, we've mislaid the old gentleman,' Prudence said. 'Or he us.'

My lady burst out laughing again. 'I would you had brought him! But that was not to be expected. Yes, he wrote to me. I will tell you—ah, but you are tired! You must sit down. Take the couch, Miss Merriot— *tiens,* that is not a name for my stupid tongue!—Prue, my angel, some chocolate, yes? Marthe shall make it herself: you remember Marthe, no?'

'Egad, is it the same fat Marthe,' Robin said. 'I drank her chocolate in Paris, ten years ago!'

'The same, my cabbage, but fatter—oh, of an enormity! you would not believe! To think you should remember, and you a little *gamin*—not more than fourteen years, no? but the wickedness even then! And again in Rome, not?'

'Oh, but it was my Lady Lowestoft, then, at the Legation. We—what were we? Sure, it must have been the Polish gentleman and his two sons. There had been some little fracas at Munich, as I remember.'

This made my lady laugh again. She was off to the door, and sent her page running with orders to Marthe.

'So the old gentleman wrote to you, madam?' Prudence said. 'Did he say he would send us?'

'Say? Robert? *Mon Dieu,* when did he in all his life say what one might so easily comprehend? Be sure it was all a mystery, and no names writ down.'

Prudence chuckled. 'Egad, we may be sure of that. But you knew?'

'A *vrai dire*. I might guess—since I too know Robert. Ah, he might count on me, he knew well! It is this rebellion, not?' She sank her voice a little, and her bright eyes were keen as needles.

Robin put a finger to his lips. 'To be frank, ma'am, I believe I'm under attainder.'

Her very red lips formed on O, and she wrinkled

up her nose. 'Chut, chut! He must then put your head in a noose too?'

'Why, madam, to say sooth we were not loth. Prudence lay snug enough at Perth.'

My lady beamed upon Prudence. 'I had thought you in the thick of the fight, my child. It is well. But since it ended, where have you been? *Voyons,* it is many months since it is over, and you are but just come to me!'

There came that bitter look of brooding into Robin's eyes. It was Prudence who made answer. 'Robin was fled to the hills, my lady. I waited snug enough, as he says.'

'To the hills?' My lady leaned a little forward. 'With the Prince, no?'

Robin made an impatient movement. The cloud did not lift from his brow. 'Some of the time.'

'We heard rumours that he had gone. It is true?'

'He's safe—in France,' Robin said curtly.

'The poor young man! And the *bon papa*? Whither went he?'

'Lud, madam, do you ask us that?' laughed Prudence. 'In France, maybe, or maybe in Scotland still. Who knows?'

The door opened, and the page let in fat Marthe, a tray in her hands. It was a very colossus of a woman, of startling girth, and with a smile that seemed to spread all over the full moon of her face. Like her mistress, from one to the other she looked, and was of a sudden smitten with laughter that shook all her frame like a jelly. The tray was set down; she clasped her hands and gasped: 'Oh, la-la! To see the little *monsieur habillé en dame!*'

Robin sailed up to her and swept a practised curtsey. 'Your memory fails you, Marthe. Behold me—Prudence!'

She gave his arm a playful flap. '*My* memory, *alors*! No, no, m'sieur, you are not yet large enough to be mademoiselle.'

'Oh, unkind!' Robin lamented, and kissed her roundly.

'Marthe, there is need of secrecy, you understand?' My lady spoke urgently.

'*Bien, madame;* I do not forget.' Marthe put a finger to her lips. '*Tenez,* it must be myself to wait always upon the false mademoiselle. I shall see to it.' She nodded in a business-like fashion. 'John is with you yet?'

'Be very sure of it,' Robin said.

'All goes well, then. No one need suspect. I go to attend to the bedchambers.' She went off with a rolling gait, and was found later in Robin's room, twitting the solemn manservant.

CHAPTER FOUR

Mistress Prudence to herself

FROM MY LADY LOWESTOFT much might be learned of Society and Politics. She moved in the Polite World, and made something of a figure in it, for she had sufficient wealth, some charm, and a vivacity of manner that was foreign and therefore intriguing. There saw withal a shrewd head on her shoulders.

She was a widow of no very late date; indeed she had interred Sir Roger Lowestoft with all decency little more than a year back, and having for a space mourned him with suitable propriety she had now launched upon a single life again, which promised to be very much more entertaining than had been the married state. It must be admitted Sir Roger was little loss to his lady. She had been heard to say that his English respectability gave her cramp in the soul. Certainly she had been a volatile creature in the days of her spinsterhood. Then came Sir Roger, and laid his sober person, and all his substantial goods at her feet. She picked them up.

'I am no longer so young as I was, *voyez vous*,' she

had said to her friends. 'The time comes for me to range myself.'

Accordingly she married Sir Roger, and as an Ambassador's lady she conducted herself admirably, and achieved popularity.

She was ensconced now in her house in Arlington Street, with fat Marthe to watch over her, a monkey to sit in the folds of her skirts, as Fashion prescribed, and a black page to run her errands. She entertained on the lavish scale, her acquaintances were many, and she had beside quite a small host of admirers.

'You understand, these English consider me in the light of an original,' she exclaimed to Prudence. 'I have an instant success, *parole d'honneur!*'

She was off without awaiting the reply, on to another subject. Conversationally she fluttered like a butterfly, here, there, and everywhere. She had much to say of the late executions: there were upflung hands of horror, and some pungent exclamations in the French tongue. She spoke of his Grace of Cumberland, not flatteringly; she had a quick ripple of laugher for his ugly nickname, and the instant after a brimming pair of eyes when she thought how he had earned it. Blood! England must needs reek of it! She gave a shudder. But there must be no more executions: that was decided: no, nor risings either. All that was folly; folly the most outrageous. *Peste,* how came the Merriots in so forlorn a *galère?*...

They sat alone at the dinner-table; the lackeys had

withdrawn, and even the little black page had been
sent away. Prudence answered my lady, since Robin
sat silent. 'Oh, believe me, ma'am, we ask ourselves!
The old gentleman had a maggot in his brain belike.
A *beau geste,* I am persuaded; nothing else.'

'But stupid, my child, stupid! There was never a
hope. Moreover, we do very well with little fierce
George. Bah, why plunge all in disorder for a pretty
princeling?'

'He had the right.' Robin spoke sombrely.

'*Quant à ça,* I know nothing of the matter, my little
one. You English, you chose for yourselves a for-
eigner. *Bien!* But you must not turn against him now.
No, no, that is not reasonable.'

'By your leave, ma'am, not all chose him.'

She flashed a look at him. 'Eh, so he had you under
his spell, the bonnie prince? But you—no, my cabbage, you are no Jacobite at heart. A spell, no more.'

'Oh, I am nothing at all, ma'am, rest you content.
I meddle no more in the affairs of princes.'

'That is wise,' she approved. 'This time you escape.
Another time—who knows?'

He laughed irresponsibly. 'As to that, my lady, I
don't count myself safe as yet.'

His sister's serenity was ruffled momentarily. She
looked with some anxiety towards my lady, who bent
towards her swiftly, and patted her hand.

'Ah, no more of that! *Au fond,* you do not like to
see blood flow, you English. It is thought there has

been blood enough: the tide turns. Lie close, and all blows over. I am certain of it—*moi qui te parle!*'

Robin made a face at his sister. 'The creature must needs play the mother to me, madam.'

'Madam, behold my little mentor!' Prudence retorted. 'Give you my word I have my scoldings from him, and not the old gentleman. 'Tis a waspish tongue, egad.'

Talk ran awhile then on the vagaries of Mr Colney. My lady must needs speculate upon his whereabouts; his dutiful children could not permit themselves to indulge in the optimism of hazarding a guess. Sufficient for them that he had named London as a meeting-place: wherefor behold them here, in all obedience.

My lady professed alarm; Prudence cracked a nut. My lady was urgent to know the nature of Mr Colney's business in the late rebellion; her queries were met by a humorous quirk of the eyebrow, and a half shrug of the shoulder. *Eh bien* then, might he with safety show himself in town? Had he not, in effect, been conspicuous up there in the North?

It was Robin who said with a laugh:—'Lud, ma'am, and did you ever know him when he was not conspicuous? It has been dark intrigue for him, here and there—a go-between, as I take it. What does one know of him? Nothing! But I'd wager my last guinea he has his tracks well covered.'

My lady reflected on the likelihood of this, but it was evident that she continued to feel some trepidation at the thought of *ce cher* Robert coming to London, which was, in fact, the lion's den.

Prudence smiled. 'My lady, he has very often informed us that "I contrive" might well stand for his motto, and, faith, I believe him.'

"'I contrive,'" mused my lady. 'Yes, that is Robert. But it is the motto of the Tremaines.'

'The more like the old gentleman to appropriate it,' said Robin. 'Who are the Tremaines?'

'Oh, one of your old families. They are Viscounts of Barham these many years, you must know. The last one died some few months since, and the new one is only some cousin, I think, of name Rensley.'

'Then our poor papa can have his motto,' said Prudence.

She had a mind to learn something of Sir Anthony Fanshawe, and drew the trend of the talk that way. There was no word spoken of Miss Letty and her indiscretion: Sir Anthony had been chance-met on the road—also one Mr Markham.

My lady wrinkled her brow at the last name; it was plain she did not count Mr Markham amongst her friends. More closely questioned, she said that he was a man of *mauvais ton,* a great gambler, and received at an astonishing number of houses, for no reason that she could perceive unless it were his friendship with my Lord Barham.

'There you have two people of no great breeding,' ran her peroration. 'Have naught to do with either, my children. Both are counted dangerous, and both are rogues. Of that I am convinced.'

'And Sir Anthony?' said Robin, with a quizzical look at his sister. 'Is that another rogue?'

My lady found this infinitely amusing. 'The poor Sir Tony! To be sure, a very proper gentleman—well born, rich, handsome—but fie! of an impenetrability. Ah, you English!' She shook her head over the stolidity of the race.

'He displays already a most fatherly interest in my little sister, ma'am,' Robin said solemnly. 'We are like to be undone by it.'

'Robin must have his jest, my lady.' Prudence was unruffled. 'I believe I am not a novice in the art of simulation. I don't fear Sir Anthony's detection.'

'My dear, he does not see a yard before his own nose, that one,' my lady assured her. 'Fear nothing from him. You will meet him at my rout to-morrow. All the world comes.'

There was no more talk then of Sir Anthony, but he came again into Prudence's mind that night when she made ready to go to bed. She came out of her coat—not without difficulty, for it was of excellent tailoring, and fitted tightly across her shoulders—and stood for a while before the long mirror, seriously surveying herself. A fine straight figure she made: there could be no gainsaying it, but she found herself wondering what Sir Anthony, of the lazy speech and sleepy eyelids, would make of it. She doubted there might be too great a love of the respectable in the gentleman. She placed her hands on her slim hips, and looked, without seeing, into the grey eyes in the mirror. Sir Anthony refused to be banished from her mind.

Respectable! Ay, there was the sneering epithet of a vagabond for an honourable gentleman. It was tiresome of the man, but there was that in his face inspired one with trust, and a disinclination to simulate. One could not imagine the large gentleman descending to trickery and a masquerade. So much the worse for him, then, if he found himself ever in a dangerous corner. One might give the masquerade an ugly sounding name: call it Deceit; no good ring to that. Or call it the pitting of one's wits against the world's; that had a better smack.

The fine mouth showed a tendency to curl scornfully. One's wit against the world was well enough; one's wit against a single fellow creature, not so good. The one was after all a perilous losing game, with all to risk; the other savoured a little of the common impostor. Sir Anthony would be friendly; unpleasant to think that one could show but a false front.

She caught herself up on the thought, turned away from the mirror, and began to untie the lace at her throat. Egad, she was in danger of turning sentimental because a large gentleman looked on her with kindness. A sentimental country, this England: it awoke in one a desire for security.

The neckcloth was tossed on to the table, and a soft

chuckle came. Ludicrous to think of security with Mr
Colney for sire. She reflected ruefully that her father
was somewhat of a rogue; disreputable even. A gaming house in Frankfort, forsooth! She had a smile for
that memory. Hand to mouth days, those, with herself
in boy's clothes, as now. The old gentleman had
judged it wisest, and when one remembered some of
those who came to the gaming house one had to admit
he had reason. A dice box in one pocket, and a pistol
in the other, though! Proper training for a girl just
coming out of her teens! A mad life, egad, but there
had been much to recommend it. One had learned
something, after all. Sure, only to live with the old
gentleman was an education: one owed him a deal, but
if one desired to enter into a life of security his very
existence must prove a bar.

She perceived in her thoughts a tendency to edge
round to the contemplation of Sir Anthony, and judged
it time to have done. Dimly she could see difficulties
ahead; characteristically she dismissed them with a fa-
talistic gesture. Time enough to ponder them when
they presented themselves.

She pulled the heavy curtains back from the bed,
and of habit slipped a little gold-mounted pistol beneath her pillow. She climbed into the big four-poster,
and very soon lay lightly asleep. Not the dark future,
nor Sir Anthony would be permitted to disturb Prudence's repose, though fleetingly both might enter into
her dreams. After all, one could not be mistress of
one's thoughts in sleep.

CHAPTER FIVE

Sir Humphrey Grayson waits upon Mr Merriot

THE MORROW BROUGHT Sir Humphrey Grayson early
in the forenoon to wait upon Mr Merriot. The message
was brought Prudence in my Lady Lowestoft's boudoir, where she sat in converse with her hostess. The
exigencies of his toilet still kept Robin above stairs;
his sister had left him to the lacing of his corsets, an
operation conducted by John and accompanied by
some of the young gentleman's choicer oaths.

My lady, upon the news of Sir Humphrey's call
being brought, was all agog with curiosity. She had
no notion the Merriots held other acquaintance than
herself in town, and desired to be told how they were
known to Sir Humphrey, who, to be sure, led something of the life of a recluse.

Prudence mentally consigned Sir Humphrey to perdition: it seemed he would be an added complication.
The fewer people to know of Miss Letty's escapade
the better for that sprightly lady, but Prudence reflected that there were mysteries and secrets of her
own enough to keep close without the addition of an-

other's. She evaded my lady's questions. She claimed
no acquaintance with Sir Humphrey, but believed Sir
Anthony Fanshawe had solicited his kindness on her
behalf. My lady was left to make what she could of
this; Prudence went downstairs to the room looking
out on to the street that was used for morning callers.

There arose at her entrance a tall thin gentleman
with stooping shoulders and a limp. He wore the powdered wig of Fashion, but neglected to paint his face.
The brown eyes, not unlike Miss Letty's own, held
some trouble. He had the look of a man prematurely
aged by ill-health.

The gentleman bowed to Mr Merriot, leaning the
while on his cane. Mr Merriot returned the bow and
was swift to pull forward a chair for the visitor. 'Sir
Humphrey Grayson, I believe? Sir, you honour me.
Will you not be seated?'

A certain grimness about Sir Humphrey's mouth
vanished as his glance took in Mr Merriot. The young
gentleman had a great air of Fashion, but practised
what Sir Humphrey had come to believe an old-
fashioned courtesy towards the elder generation. He
took the chair offered, with a passing reference to a
gouty foot. There was a slight squaring of the bent
shoulders: it was evident this elderly gentleman had
little relish for his visit. 'Mr Merriot, I believe you
must know the reason of my being here,' he said
bluntly. 'Let me be plain with you. My daughter has
put me in your debt.'

A stiff-backed old man; one must perforce pity the hurt to his pride. Prudence made swift answer. 'Why, sir, I protest, there is no need for such talk! Do me the favour of letting a very trifling service be forgot!'

There were further signs of thaw. 'Bear with me, Mr Merriot. You must do me the honour of accepting my very heartfelt thanks for your rescue of my daughter.'

'Why, sir, there is nothing to all this. My part was played but a bare half-hour before Sir Anthony came upon us. He would have settled the business as quickly had I let be. Pray let us not speak of it! I am happy to have been of service to Miss Grayson. Or thank my sister, sir, whose quicker wits devised the little plot.'

Sir Humphrey permitted himself to smile, and to incline his head. 'I do indeed desire to render my thanks to Miss Merriot. My foolish daughter can talk of naught else but that same plot. At least allow me to compliment you on a tricksy piece of sword-play.'

Prudence gave her rich chuckle. 'An old ruse, sir, but useful. I trust Miss Grayson finds herself none the worse for her adventure?'

'Rest assured, sir, my daughter is incorrigible.' But a reluctant smile went with the words.

'Why, sir, it's a child, after all, with a child's desire for a romantic venture.'

'It might have led to a most damaging scandal, Mr Merriot.'

Prudence discerned some anxiety in Sir Humphrey's

eye, and made haste to reassure. 'All fear of that must be at an end with you sir; of that I am certain. None save Sir Anthony and ourselves can know aught of the matter.'

There was again a bow. 'My daughter should count herself fortunate in meeting so discreet a friend in her trouble,' said Sir Humphrey.

This punctilious grandeur became oppressive. Prudence conceived the happy thought of sending a message up to Robin. Sir Humphrey professed himself all desire to lay his compliments before Miss Merriot. Black Pompey was sent running to Robin's chamber, and in a little while Robin came, all powdered and patched and scented; a fair vision in pale blue taffety. No girl, Prudence thought, could appear lovelier.

There was a curtsey, a few gliding steps towards Sir Humphrey, and a delicate hand held out. Sir Humphrey bowed low over it, and a faint crease crept between Prudence's brows. It seemed to her unseemly that the old courtier should kiss her graceless brother's hand. She met Robin's dancing eyes of mischief with a look of some reproof. Robin sank into a chair with a bellow of stiff silks. 'Sir Humphrey, this is too kind in you, I protest! Miss Letty spoke of your love of seclusion. There was no need for this visit. No, no, sir, you shall not thank me for the other night's work!' A fan was spread, but a laughing pair of eyes showed above it. 'Spare my blushes, sir! Conceive me fainting in the arms of the Markham! Oh lud!'

Prudence might retire into the background; Robin had the situation well in hand. She sat down on the window seat, and was at leisure to admire her brother's adroitness. For some reason he seemed bent upon the captivation of Sir Humphrey. Prudence could guess the reason. Faith, more complications brewing. But it was unseemly again that Robin should ogle so elderly a gentleman. Lord, what a clever tongue the child had!

Indeed, talk ran merrily between the two in the middle of the room. Robin seemed to have the knack of inducing a stiff-necked sire to unbend. Within ten minutes he might count Sir Humphrey very much his friend, and dare even to touch lightly on the subject of Miss Letitia's indiscretion. There came no rebuff: only a word or two sufficient to show the worried state of Sir Humphrey's mind.

Robin put by the fan of painted chicken-skin. With a pretty air of coaxing and of deference he cooed softly: 'An impertinence in me to speak of the matter at all, dear Sir Humphrey. Forgive me!' He was assured of Sir Humphrey's forgiveness, nay, more, of his attention. 'Well, well!' Madam Kate smiled confidentially upon him. 'I own to some few years more than the child can boast, I believe. Perhaps I may whisper a word or two.'

Sir Humphrey begged the favour of Miss Merriot's advice. Prudence, by the window, was forgot. There was no doing anything; she could but sit by while

Robin became as outrageous as the fit prompted him. Lud, but they were plunging deeper and deeper into the morass!

Robin was dropping dulcet words of advice into a father's ear. Let him not coop Miss Letty up so close; sure, it was a high-spirited child only in need of a little amusement. Too young?—Oh, fie, never think it! Take her out into the world; let her make her curtsey to Society. By no means take her back to Gloucestershire; that were fatal. So it went on, somewhat to Prudence's amusement. Robin had a mind to pursue the acquaintance, then? Snared by a pair of pansy-brown eyes, ecod!

The amusement fled before the next words. Sir Humphrey made bold to solicit Miss Merriot's kindness for his daughter. His sister was, perhaps, not an enlivening companion for so frivolous a child as his Letitia. He should think himself more than ever in her debt if Miss Merriot would take Letty a little under her wing.

'Now how to escape that?' thought Prudence.

But it seemed that Robin had no desire to escape the imposition. There were professions of the utmost willingness; he pledged himself to wait upon Miss Grayson the very next day.

'The rogue!' thought Prudence, and said it aloud as soon as Sir Humphrey had taken his ceremonious leave of them.

Robin laughed, and dropped a mock curtsey. Surely the devil was in the boy to-day.

'Lord, child, let us be serious. What are you pledged to now?'

'To be a friend to the little dark beauty. I'm all alacrity.'

'It's evident.' His sister spoke dryly. 'I believe it won't serve, Robin.'

Robin raised one mobile eyebrow. 'What's this? You've nervous qualms, my Peter? Faith, I thought there were no nerves in you. I stand in no danger of discovery that I can see.'

'None, child. You're incomparable,' Prudence said frankly. 'You've more female graces than ever I could lay claim to, even in my rightful petticoats. I believe my sense of propriety is offended.'

Came a flash into the blue eyes, and a head thrown up a little. 'Oh, do you doubt me? *Merci du compliment!*'

Prudence was unmoved. 'Ay, that's the old gentleman in you. It's a fine gesture.'

The chin came down; the mouth tightened a moment, then relaxed into a laugh. 'You'd enrage a saint, Prue. Well, let us have it.'

Memories of the night's reflections chased one another across Prudence's mind. 'It's trickery. You become an impostor.'

'I became one when I entered first into these

damned uncomfortable clothes, child. Are you answered?'

Impossible to put those hazy ideas into verbal form. 'I suppose so,' said Prudence slowly. 'Do you know, I begin to dislike myself?'

Robin looked at her, then put an arm about her waist. 'Well, say the word. I'll take you to France, and we'll ha' done with all this.'

'You're a dear, Robin. No, I chose this road, and we'll stay.'

'I've a notion it may lead to some end. Play it out, my dear. Trickery it is, but we harm none.' Prudence looked sceptical. 'Oh, you are thinking of the Grayson child! Never doubt me.'

'I don't doubt you. But she thinks you are a woman, and there are things she may say you should not be hearing.'

'Do you think I cannot stop her? 'Tis I shall lead the talk. Be at rest, Prue.'

'And if she discovers the truth?'

'I don't fear that.'

There seemed no more to be said. 'We brave it to the end, then. Well, I'm content.'

CHAPTER SIX

The polite world receives Mr and Miss Merriot

MY LADY LOWESTOFT made no idle boast when she declared that all the world might be seen at her rout that evening. The world, as she knew it, was the Polite Society of the day; and Polite Society chose to venerate her ladyship. She had the felicity of seeing her salons filled to overflowing. Downstairs there were refreshments laid out in the dining-room; angel cakes, and ratafie; strange French concoctions and some of the late Sir Roger's best Burgundy; sweetmeats of every known variety and French champagne, sparkling in the glasses, to go with them. There was a card room also, spacious enough to hold some few tables with comfort. Those who wished might escape from the chatter and the scraping of the fiddles in the saloons above, to seek a little quiet diversion here with a dice-box. My lady was fond of all games of chance herself, but her duties as hostess kept her to-night in the main rooms, where people came and went, gathered into knots for conversation, separated again to greet a new arrival, or lent an indulgent ear to the fiddlers scraping away at the back of the room.

Robin, in his character of Miss Merriot, was kept near my lady. He had chosen to array himself in shades of rose pink. A necklace lay on the white skin of his chest, and a bracelet enclasped one rather sinewy arm. If there could be found aught whereat to cavil in his appearance it must be those arms. They lacked the dimpled roundness necessary for beauty. Elsewhere no fault could be detected. The fair hair was piled on top of his head, lavishly powdered, and decorated with a jewelled ornament; the face below was pink and white as any girl's, with blue eyes dreamy under delicately pencilled brows, and a nose many a reigning toast might envy. A black riband round the throat served to emphasise the creamy whiteness of the skin; the waist, thanks to John's lacing, was trim enough, and the foot peeping from beneath the hem of a flowered petticoat sufficiently small to escape notice. Maybe it was fashioned on the large size for so dainty a lady, but a high heel disguised a possible fault.

There could be no fault found either in his deportment. Standing a little back from the crowd, Prudence watched him with a critical eye. He had several times before donned this woman's garb, but never for so long a stretch. She had coached him to the best of her ability, but well as she knew him could still fear some slip. She had to admit knowledge of him was deficient

yet. Sure, he might have been born to it. His cursteys
were masterpieces of grace; the air with which he held
out a hand to young gallants so consummate a piece
of artistry that Prudence was shaken with silent laughter. He seemed to know by instinct how to flirt his fan,
and how to spread his wide skirts for the curtsey. Apparently he might be left safely to his own devices.
His sister withdrew her gaze from him, reflecting that
she would give much to hear what he was saying to
the beautiful Miss Gunning standing beside him. If the
spirit of mischief did not carry him away there was
naught to be feared in his bearing. Prudence turned
away, and came upon my Lady Lowestoft, in gay talk
with Mr Walpole, who, since he lived so close, was
naturally a late comer.

My lady manoeuvred the elegant Mr Walpole away
from Prudence's vicinity, and disposed of him at
length to his dear friend Gilly Williams, who, with Mr
Selwyn, seemingly but half awake, stood talking by
the fire.

My lady came rustling back to the door, for there
were guests still ascending the stairs. To Prudence,
under her breath, she said: 'I take him away, so! Of
an inquisitive disposition, my cabbage! You would not
believe! I feared he might pry too close…. Ah, madame!' She curtseyed to a new arrival, and, a moment
later, was exchanging witticisms with my Lord March,
that saturnine peer.

A gentleman but lately introduced to Prudence sug-

gested a hand at picquet. She looked calmly at this
gentleman and professed herself all readiness. It took
her no more than a minute to reach the conclusion that
she was to be a lamb for the fleecing. Well, the gentleman should see.

There were several men in the card room, some few
dicing, some talking idly beside, and one party engaged in a hand of lansquenet. Prudence sat down with
Sir Francis Jollyot at a table away from the door, and
assented placidly to his proposed stakes. They seemed
large, but she had played for larger, and was in no
wise perturbed.

''Tis a game I'm devilish partial to,' Sir Francis
observed. 'You play it much, eh?'

'A little, sir,' Prudence said and displayed hesitation
over the question of her discard. Across the table Sir
Francis smiled in infinite good-humour. He had played
with young gentlemen from the country before, and
foresaw a profitable evening. When the game was over
he condoled with Mr Merriot on his ill-fortune, and
proposed a fresh one. Prudence accepted most cor-
dially. She perceived a greater skill at picquet in herself than in her smiling opponent. Played carefully this
game of turning the tables on the wolf would be amusing. With no less hesitation in her demeanour, but with
much less folly in her discards, she won the game. She
was complimented on the cards she had held, and embarked upon the third encounter.

'A reverse!' commented Sir Francis gaily. 'I hardly

thought you would keep a guard to that Queen in the last hand, throwing the King of Hearts.'

The crease showed between Prudence's brows. 'Did I throw my King? You played out your cards so fast, you see, I scarcely…' She left the end of her sentence to be understood. Sir Francis thought that he did understand, and sorted his hand with a smile ill concealed.

There came a fresh arrival into the room, and paused a while in the open doorway. This gentleman was very large, with wide shoulders under a coat of maroon velvet, and a strong, handsome face. Under heavy lids his eyes fell on Prudence and rested there.

'Why, Fanshawe! I had thought you were out of town. Someone told me you had gone down to Wych End.' Mr Troubridge, standing nearby, stepped closer to Sir Anthony, and offered his snuff-box. 'What are you looking at? Oh, my Lady Lowestoft's protégé! By name Merriot, and seemingly a pleasant youth. That face should captivate the ladies.'

'It should,' Sir Anthony replied. 'Jollyot wastes no time, I see.'

Mr Troubridge laughed. It was after all, no concern of his. 'Oh, trust Jollyot! By the way, young Apollo has a prodigious fine sister. Have you seen her? One of your fair beauties. She's above stairs in the withdrawing room.'

'I've been presented.' Still Sir Anthony's eyes dwelt on the unconscious Prudence. 'Up from the country, are they? Now, neither has the look of it. Our young gentleman yonder'—very slightly he indicated Prudence with a movement of his quizzing-glass—'has all the air of a town beau.'

'Very modish, to be sure. He'll have need of keen town wits if he plays with Jollyot.' Mr Troubridge smiled a little, and looked towards the picquet table.

Prudence sat sideways at it, an arm laid along it, and one shapely leg stretched out before her. She wore a coat of dull gold brocade, with the skirts very full and stiffly whaleboned, and the great cuffs turned back to the elbow. There was much foaming lace at throat and wrists, and a jewelled buckle was placed above the black riband that confined her powdered locks in the nape of her neck. She was looking at the cards held in one hand, her face expressionless. There was a patch set at the corner of the firm mouth, and one high up on the cheek-bone. Her other hand, with a glowing ring on it, lay lightly on the arm of her chair. As though conscious of the gaze upon her, she looked up suddenly, straight at Sir Anthony. A tinge of colour rose in her cheeks; involuntarily she smiled.

'Oh, do you know him?' asked Troubridge, surprised.

'We were introduced above stairs,' Sir Anthony answered, with a fine disregard for the truth, and went across the room to Prudence's side. 'Well met, my dear boy.' His hand pressed on Prudence's shoulder to prevent her rising. 'No, do not permit me to interrupt.'

At the sound of that lazy, pleasant voice a faint frown crossed Sir Francis' face. He acknowledged Sir Anthony's greeting only by a curt nod, and declared a point of five.

Sir Anthony stood still behind Prudence's chair, and in silence watched the play through his eye-glass. The stakes had been raised at each new game; at the end of this one Sir Francis was most strangely a heavy loser. Either the young sprig from the country had played the game a-many times before, or else the Providence who guides the hands of novices had exerted herself most prodigiously on Mr Merriot's behalf. Sir Francis was disinclined to believe Mr Merriot an adept: he had not the manner of it.

Sir Anthony moved at last, and spoke before Jollyot could suggest yet a fourth game, 'Will you take a hand with me, Merriot?'

'I should be pleased, sir.' Prudence swept the little pile of guineas to one side.

There was nothing for Sir Francis to do but to go elsewhere. He gave up his seat to Fanshawe, and trusted he might have an evening with Mr Merriot some time in the near future.

'Why, sir, I shall count myself fortunate,' said Prudence.

Sir Francis moved away to a group of men by the

window. Prudence turned to find Sir Anthony shuffling the pack. 'Will you name the stakes, sir?' she said.

'What you will,' Sir Anthony replied. 'What were they with my friend, Jollyot?'

She told him indifferently enough.

'Do you make it a rule to play for so large a sum?' blandly inquired Sir Anthony.

'I make it a rule, sir, to play for whatever sum my opponent suggests,' was the quick answer.

The heavy lids lifted for a moment, and she saw the grey eyes keen. 'You must needs have faith in your skill, Mr Merriot.'

'In my luck I have, Sir Anthony.'

'I felicitate you. I will play you for the half of Jollyot's stakes.'

'As you please, sir. Will you cut?'

It would not do to show a change of front now that the large gentleman had watched her at play with Sir Francis. Prudence fumbled a little at the cards, and displayed a beginner's uncertainty. Sir Anthony seemed to be engrossed with his own hand, but as she hesitated once more over the five cards of her discard he glanced up, and drawled: 'Oh, spare yourself the pains, my dear boy! I am no hawk.'

Prudence fenced cautiously; she was not quite sure what the gentleman would be at. 'The pains of what, sir?

'Of all this dissimulation,' said Sir Anthony, with a

disarming smile. 'I must suppose you were taught to play picquet in your cradle.'

Almost she gasped. It seemed as though John had reason when he said that large gentleman was awake for all his sleepiness. She laughed, and forebore to evade, judging her man with some shrewdness. 'Nearly, sir, I confess. My father has a fondness for the game.'

'Has he indeed?' said Sir Anthony. 'Now, what may have induced you to play the novice with my friend Jollyot, I wonder?'

'I have been about the world a little, Sir Anthony.'

'That I believe.' Leisurely Sir Anthony looked at the three cards that fell to his minor share. 'It seems you lost no feathers in that bout.'

She laughed again. 'Oh, I'm an ill pigeon for plucking, sir! I declare a point of five.'

'I concede it you, my fair youth.'

'A quarte may perhaps be good?'

'It depends, sir, on what heads it.'

'The King, Sir Anthony.'

'No good,' Sir Anthony said. 'I hold a quarte to the Ace.'

'I am led to believe, sir, that three Kings won't serve?'

'Quite right, my dear boy; they must give way to my three Aces.'

This was all in the grand manner. Prudence chuckled. 'Oh, I've done then! My lead, and I count six, sir.'

The hand was played. As the cards were gathered up Sir Anthony said: 'I take it so shrewd a youth stands in no need of a friendly warning?'

Certainly the enigmatic gentleman was developing a kindness for her. 'You're very kind, sir. I do not know why you should be at this trouble for me.' It was spoken with some warmth of gratitude.

'Nor I,' said Fanshawe indolently. 'But you are not—in spite of those twenty years—of a great age, and there are plenty of hawks in town.'

Prudence bowed. 'I shall take that to heart, sir. I have to thank you.'

'Pray do not. Plucking pigeons has never been a favourite pastime of mine.... Well, I concede your point, but I claim a quinte and fourteen Queens, besides three Kings. Alack for a spoiled repique! Five played, sir.'

The game came presently to an end. 'Very even,' said Sir Anthony. 'Do you care to honour me at a small card party I hold on Thursday evening?'

'Indeed, sir, mine will be the honour. On Thursday and in Clarges Street, I think?'

Sir Anthony nodded. He beckoned to a lackey standing near, and sent him to fetch wine. 'You will drink a glass with me, Merriot?'

'Thank you, a little canary, sir.'

The wine was brought; one or two gentlemen had

wandered towards the table, and stood now in converse there. Sir Anthony made Mr Merriot known to them. Prudence found herself pledged to ride out next morning in the Park with a chubby-faced young gentleman of a friendly disposition. This was the Honourable Charles Belfort, who combined a passion for dice with almost phenomenal ill-luck, but managed to remain cheerful under it.

'Well, Charles, what fortune?' Sir Anthony looked up in some amusement at the young profligate.

'The same as ever. It always is.' Belfort shook his head. 'Bad, very bad, but I have a notion that my luck will turn to-morrow, at about eight o'clock.'

'Good Gad, Bel, why at eight?' demanded Mr Molyneux.

The Honourable Charles looked grave. 'Angels told me so in a vision,' he said.

There was a shout of laughter.

'Nonsense, Charles, they were prophesying your entry into a spunging house!' This was my Lord Kestrel, leaning on the back of Fanshawe's chair.

'You see how it is, sir'—Belfort addressed himself plaintively to Prudence.—'They all laugh at me, even when I tell them of a visitation from heaven. Irreligious, damme, that's what it is.'

There was a fresh outburst of mirth. Through it came Sir Anthony's deep voice, full of friendly mockery. 'You delude yourself, Charles: no angel would visit you unless by mischance. Doubtless a sign from the devil that he is about to claim his own.' He rose, and picked up his snuff-box. 'Well, Merriot, I must do myself the pleasure of making my bow to your sister. Upstairs, when I was there, she was surrounded.'

'I'll lead you to her, sir,' said Prudence readily. 'At nine in the morning, Mr Belfort: I shall be with you.'

Sir Anthony went out on Mr Merriot's arm. Half-way up the broad stairway he said: 'It occurs to me you may be in need of a sponsor at White's, my dear boy. You know you may command me. May I carry your name there?'

So she was to become a member of a club for gentlemen of quality? Egad, where would it all end? No help for it: the large gentleman overwhelmed one. She accepted gracefully, and then with a hesitancy not un-pleasing in a young man looked up into the square face, and said diffidently:—'I think you go to some trouble for me, Sir Anthony. From all I have heard I had not thought to find so much kindness in London.'

'There are any number would do the same, boy— my friend Jollyot, for instance. But you had better take me for sponsor.'

'I do, very gladly, sir.'

They came into the withdrawing room, where the crowd had dwindled somewhat. Robin was easily found, talking to an exquisite of advanced years. From the looks of it he was receiving some extravagant compliments. Prudence could not but applaud inwardly the

pretty modesty of the downcast eye, and the face
slightly averted.

Over his fan Robin saw them. He rid himself of his
elderly admirer with some adroitness, and came rustling forward. 'My dear, I vow I am nigh to swooning
from fatigue!' he told Prudence. He swept a curtsey
to Sir Anthony, and flashed him a dazzling smile.
'Give you good even, sir. I saw you a while back, but
there was such a press of people then!'

Sir Anthony's lips just brushed Robin's hand. 'All
gathered about Miss Merriot,' he said gallantly.

'What, with the beautiful Miss Gunning in the same
room? Fie, sir, this is flattery! Peter, of your love for
me, procure me a glass of negus.'

Prudence went away to execute this command;
Robin sat down with Sir Anthony upon a couch. When
Prudence returned with the wine it seemed as though
a good understanding had been established between
them. Robin looked up brightly. 'Sir Anthony tells me
he is to steal you from me on Thursday, my Peter.
Thus are we poor sisters imposed upon!'

'I want also to sponsor your Peter at White's,
ma'am,' Sir Anthony said, smiling. 'Thus still more
are you imposed upon.'

'Oh, these clubs! This means I shall see nothing of
the creature.' Miss Merriot put up her fan to hide her
face from Sir Anthony, in feigned indignation. So, at
least, it appeared, but behind the fan that mobile eyebrow flew up for Prudence's benefit, and the blue eyes

brimmed with laughter. It was done in a trice, and the fan shut again with a snap. 'Your kindness to Peter is much greater than your consideration for his poor sister, sir!' she rallied Fanshawe.

'Why, as to that I offer my apologies, ma'am. I stand somewhat in both your debts.'

'Ah, let's have done with that!' Prudence said quickly. 'There is no debt that I know of.'

'Well, let us say that what you are pleased to call my kindness is naught but a seal to what I hope is a friendship.'

'I'm honoured to have it so, sir,' Prudence said, and felt the colour rise, to her annoyance.

The large gentleman had a mind to befriend her, and there was no help for it. and was one glad of it, or sorry? There was apparently no answer to the riddle.

CHAPTER SEVEN

A taste of a large gentleman's temper

THE MORNING'S RIDE sowed promising seeds of a new friendship. The Honourable Charles had an engaging frankness; he kept no secrets from those admitted into the circle of his acquaintance, and it seemed probable that his life might be an open book for Prudence to read if she had a mind that way. With admirable dexterity she steered all talk into channels of her own choosing. She was certainly not squeamish, but half an hour spent in the company of the expansive Mr Belfort was enough to show that the greater part of his reminiscences was calculated to bring a blush to maiden cheeks. Prudence maintained an even complexion, and had sense enough to think none the worse of him for all his lurid confidences. Sure, they were not meant for a lady's ears.

The ride at an end, it was Charles and Peter with them; they might have been blood brothers. Prudence acquiesced in it, but grimaced to herself when she reflected that it had been in her mind to lie close in London. Evidently this was not to be. But there was nothing to be feared from Mr Belfort: the disguise was deep enough to hoodwink a dozen such rattlepates.

She came back to Arlington Street to find Robin posturing above a bouquet of red roses. Robin achieved a simper. 'Behold me, my Peter, in a maidenly flutter!'

Prudence put down her whip and gloves. 'What's this?'

'My elderly admirer!' said Robin in an ecstasy, and gave up a note. 'Read, my little one!'

Prudence gave a chuckle over the amorous note. 'Robin, you rogue!'

'I was made to be a breaker of hearts,' sighed Robin.

'Oh, this one was cracked many times before!'

Robin tilted his head a little; the merry devil looked out of his limpid blue eyes. 'I've a mind to enthrall the mountain,' he said softly.

'You won't do it. He's more like to unmask you than to worship at your shameless feet,' Prudence answered.

'Oh? Here's a change of front, by my faith! Unmask me, is it? Now why?'

'John was right. The gentleman's wide awake for all we think him so dull.'

'So?' Robin awaited more. She told him of the incident at cards the night before. He listened in silence, but shrugged a careless shoulder at the end. 'I don't see a great deal to that. Easy enough to see your game if he stood at your elbow. Did you fleece the wolf?'

'Some fifty guineas. We may stand in need of them if this is to continue long. But Sir Anthony—' she paused.

'You're bewitched. What now?'

'I believe we shall do well to preserve a strict guard before him.'

'As you please, but I think you rate a mountain's intelligence too high. Consider, my dear, how should any man suspect what is after all the very light of improbability? Why should so wild a surmise so much as cross his brain?'

'There is that, of course. Plague take the man, he must needs load me with favours!'

Robin laughed. 'He takes you to White's, eh? Some little matter of a card-party too, I think?'

'On Thursday, at his house.'

Robin folded pious hands. '"I believe my sense of propriety is offended,"' he quoted maliciously.

The shot glanced off her armour. 'You've none, child, rest assured.'

Robin let be at that, and went off to make ready for a call on Miss Grayson. My Lady Lowestoft's town chaise bore him to the house, and a lackey in sombre livery ushered him into the withdrawing-room.

An elderly lady arose from a chair near the fire, and dropped a stately curtsey. Before Robin could return the salute Miss Letty bounced out of her chair and came running towards him. An embrace was clearly offered; Robin withstood temptation, and held out his hands. Miss Letty's were put into them, and so he kept her at arm's length.

'My dear, dear Miss Merriot! I have so hoped you would come!' Letty cried.

The elder Miss Grayson spoke an austere reproof 'Letitia, your manners, child!'

Robin swept a curtsey to the lady. 'Why, ma'am, I beg you'll not chide her. I should be flattered indeed to receive such a welcome.'

'I fear, ma'am, our Letitia is a sad madcap,' Miss Grayson said. 'Pray will you not be seated? My honoured brother told me we might expect the pleasure of this visit.'

Miss Grayson's honoured brother at that moment made his entry and stayed some little while in converse with Miss Merriot. When he went out again he took his sister with him. Robin enjoyed an hour's tête-à-tête with Miss Letty, at the end of which time the lackey came in to announce the arrival of Mr Merriot to fetch his sister.

Mr Merriot must come in, Letty declared. Her greeting was scarcely less warm than had been her greeting to Robin. Sir Humphrey, reappearing, was cordial enough, and had to endure a rapturous hug from his daughter upon his announcement of an invitation but this instant received from my Lady Dorling, for a masked ball. My Lady Dorling begged the pleasure of the Misses Grayson's company, and Sir Humphrey said that Letty might go.

Would Miss Merriot be there?—Miss Merriot could not answer with certainty.

'I wonder, will Miss Merriot be there?' Prudence said when they sat together in the coach.

'Don't doubt it, child. A masked ball.... Well, we shall see.'

There was that in the tone which made Prudence look up sharply. 'What devilry's afoot?'

Robin's eyes mocked from beneath long lashes. 'You would give much to know, would you not?' he taunted.

Prudence declined to encourage this spirit in her brother. 'What's the upshot *là-bas?*' she inquired. The jerk of her head might be supposed to indicate the direction of the Grayson abode.

'Letty's to appear in Society. My doing.'

'And the Markham?'

'I'm somewhat at a loss. I might gather a word here and there, you understand: not many. I take it there's a dead-lock. All Sir Humphrey's concern is to keep the affair dark. Wherein I am to suppose Fanshawe with him.'

'There's to be no meeting?'

'What, are you in a flutter?' Robin gibed.

'As you see,' was the placid rejoinder.

'Ay, you're a cold-blooded creature, a'n't you? There's to be no meeting. I had thought it might easily be arranged, but it seems the Markham is an ambitionless creature, and lacks the desire to meet your mountain. There was some little talk of Fanshawe's swordsmanship.' He pursed his lips. 'As to that, I crave leave to cherish doubts.'

'They say he's a swordsman?'

'So I was given to understand. It's my belief the English don't understand the art. There's some mobility required. Do you see the mountain on the skip?' He laughed gently. 'With pistols I will believe him an expert. It's a barbarous sport.'

Prudence frowned. 'You would say there can be no meeting for fear of the Markham making a disclosure?'

'I apprehend the matter runs something after that fashion.'

'Faugh! It's a very cur.'

'Certainly, child, but curs may snap. I need not tell you to step warily, I suppose.'

'I stand in some danger of being called out, you think? I shall be all conciliation. It's possible the dear soul may himself step warily. That blow in the coffee-room—a child's trick, egad!—would make pretty telling.'

'Just, my dear, but run no risks. There are pitfalls on all sides.'

'You do perceive them, then? I've trod no trickier maze. And we plunge deeper and deeper.'

'There is flight open to us if need arise. I console myself with that thought.'

Prudence crossed one leg over the other. 'And the old gentleman?'

'Oh, the devil take him! This is in part a maze of his making. Have you considered it?'

'Of course. There should be word from him soon. I suppose we are to be swept back to France to await the next mad freak.'

'You don't want that?' Robin looked sideways.

'I'm in love with respectability,' said Prudence lightly.

There was a teasing word ready, but Robin forbore to utter it. This change in his sister promised to complicate things still further. Not a doubt of it, the mountain had caught her fancy, but there could be little hope of a happy ending. Gentlemen of Sir Anthony's stamp did not marry daughters of—egad, the daughter of what was she? There was no saying, but 'rogue' might serve as a general term. Cast off the old gentleman, and all his wiles. A shabby trick, that: she would never hear of it. Nor would they be in much better case. A girl must have some parentage, after all.

They came back to Arlington Street to find Sir Anthony himself paying his duty to my lady. It appeared he had come to fetch Mr Merriot to White's, hard by in St. James's. He bore Prudence away with him; she felt herself powerless to resist.

There was quite a sprinkling of people gathered at

White's, and amongst them was Mr Markham in conversation with a sandy-haired gentleman of some forty years. Prudence caught the sound of a name, and looked again with some interest. So the sandy gentleman was the new Lord Barham, of whom Lady Lowestoft had warned them? Certainly there was no great good to be observed in the heavy jowled face. She remembered some snatches of Belfort's talk that morning. There was a suspicion, so the Honourable Charles hinted, that Barham's methods of play were not quite impeccable.

Mr Molyneux came in, and had a pleasant greeting for Sir Anthony and his companion. After a moment Lord Barham walked across to say something to Mr Molyneux, who made Prudence known to him.

My lord stared upon the stranger and slightly inclined his head. It was evident that his lordship had no intention of wasting civilities upon an unknown gentleman; he turned a broad shoulder, and made some idle observation to Sir Anthony.

Fanshawe looked sleepily through his eyeglass: it was wonderful what an air of lazy hauteur the large gentleman could assume. 'You lack finesse, Rensley,' he said in a bored voice. 'I see my friend Devereux by the window, Merriot. Let me present you.'

My lord flushed angrily. As she followed in Fanshawe's wake Prudence heard him say to Markham:—'Who's that cockerel Fanshawe's befriending?'

Mr Markham's reply was lost to Prudence, but she

had seen the scowl on his face when he had first perceived her. But a little while later he came up to her,
and exchanged a greeting, and a smile had taken the
place of the scowl. Prudence liked it no better; she had
a notion Mr Markham meant mischief. There was not
a word spoken of the disastrous meeting on the road
to Scotland; all was politeness and affability. Upon the
approach of Sir Anthony, however, Mr Markham fell
back.

Prudence came through the ordeal of this visit to
White's with flying colours, and through a dozen other
such ordeals, as the days passed. At Sir Anthony's
card party she played at faro, and cast dice, and her
luck held. She had to witness the gradual collapse under the table of more than one gentleman, but her host
maintained a perfect sobriety. Prudence admired the
hard head of the man. The Honourable Charles could
still stand, but his legs were uncertain under him, and
he showed a disposition to tell a long and obscure
story to anyone who could be got to listen. Prudence
walked back to Arlington Street in the dawn, accompanied part of the way by Mr Devereux, who hung
affectionately on her arm, and professed, between hic-
cups, an everlasting friendship.

There were other card parties to follow this; a visit
to Ranelagh Gardens; a rout party, and later, my lady
Dorling's masked ball. My lady had sent cards to Mr
and Miss Merriot for this event: it promised to be one
of the largest parties of the season.

'Do you go, Sir Anthony?' Prudence asked, at Belfort's card party.

'I suppose I must,' Sir Anthony answered. 'These balls are a plaguey nuisance. I've a mind to go down to my house at Wych End after this one. Do you care to bear me company?'

She was at a loss for a moment, but her wits never deserted her for long. 'Why, sir, it would give me much pleasure, but I believe my sister has some claims on my company.'

'She might be induced to spare you for a week,' Sir Anthony suggested.

'You tempt me, sir, but no, I think I must refuse. There are some engagements binding me besides.'

Sir Anthony raised his eyebrows a moment. 'You're very positive about it,' he remarked.

She looked up. 'I offend you, sir,' she said directly.

'By no means. But I wonder why you will not come?'

'It is not "will not," Sir Anthony. I would like above all things to join you, but as I have said—'

'To be sure: those engagements,' nodded Sir Anthony, and turned away.

Prudence was left to stand alone in the middle of the room. She felt curiously forlorn, for it was evident Sir Anthony was not pleased.

Belfort called to her to come and throw a main with him. She moved across to his table, and out of the corner of her eye saw Sir Anthony sitting down to faro by the window. There was no getting near him after that; she became a prey to Lord Barham, who deigned to recognise her, and was conscious of a protective influence withdrawn. She was forced to play with my lord, and she lost rather heavily, and knew the reason. Escaping at length, she engaged on a hand at picquet with the optimistic Jollyot, and presently took leave of her host, complaining of the headache. The serious grey eyes travelled towards the faro table somewhat wistfully; Sir Anthony looked up.

There was a hard look on his face; he met the grey eyes coolly, and Prudence saw the fine mouth unsmiling. She turned aside to the door, and heard his deep voice speak. 'Oh, are you off, Merriot? Stay a moment, I'll bear you company.'

Five minutes later they were descending the steps into the street, and Sir Anthony drawled:—'How came you out of that bout with Rensley, my fair youth?'

'Badly,' Prudence replied evenly. She misliked the ironic note in the gentleman's voice.

'The pigeon lost some feathers, eh?'

'At least the pigeon played fair, sir!' said Prudence rather tartly.

'Softly, softly, my child! Do you say that Rensley cheated?'

Prudence flashed a glance upwards into that inscrutable face. 'Do you think he would not cheat a pigeon, sir?'

'No, little man, I thought that he would.'

She bit her lip. 'You're scarcely just to me, sir.'

'What, because I would not scare away an ogre from the nursling? Experience harms none, child.'

'I think you wanted to show me, sir, that I was at the mercy of all once away from your side,' said Prudence plainly.

'And are you not?' Sir Anthony inquired.

'There is perhaps a trick or two up my sleeve yet, sir. But why should you desire to demonstrate thus to me?'

'A further step in your education. You should thank me.'

The imperturbable voice exasperated one. Was there no coming to grips with the man?

'I think you are not entirely honest with me, Sir Anthony.'

'Expound, my sage. Wherein am I dishonest?'

She said steadily:—'You are angry with me for refusing to go with you to Wych End. I don't complain that you left me to Lord Barham. Indeed, I had rather you stood aloof, for I have no claim on you, and I believe I may take care of myself. But when you say that what you did was to educate me, sir, you are at fault.'

'What I did, then, was done out of spleen, you think?' Quite unruffled was the voice.

'Was it not, Sir Anthony?'

There was a slight pause. 'I have an idea I don't suffer from an excess of spleen,' Fanshawe said. 'Shall we say that my rendering you up to the wolf was a punishment for churlishness?'

This was coming to grips with a vengeance. Decidedly it was not well to cross the large gentleman. One felt something of a midget.

'I am sorry that you should think me churlish, sir.' She discovered that her voice sounded small, and rather guilty, and made an effort to pull herself together. 'I think you misunderstand the reason of my refusal to go to Wych End.' That was no sooner said than she wished it unsaid. God knew where it might lead.

'I don't consider myself omniscient,' said Fanshawe, 'but I am under the impression that life in town is more amusing than life at Wych End.'

She perceived the trend of the matter. Ay, here was a pretty tangle. It was, after all, an honour for an unknown young gentleman to be invited to stay with the great Sir Anthony Fanshawe. Her excuse had been lame; in a word, she must appear cubbish. And how to retrieve the false step? 'You are under a false impression, sir.'

'I am, am I?'

'I know very well, sir, that I am unduly honoured by your proposal, but I have been taught that it is a greater rudeness to ignore previous engagements than to refuse a flattering new invitation.'

'You have that wonderfully pat,' admired Sir Anthony. 'Pray let us forget the matter.'

'So long as I do not stand in your black books,' Prudence said tentatively.

There was a laugh, and a hand on her shoulder. 'I confess, I have an odd liking for you, young man. You are absolved.'

Ridiculous that one should feel a weight removed from one's mind. Prudence decided to say nothing to Robin of the matter, dreading his mirth.

CHAPTER EIGHT

The Black Domino

MY LADY LOWESTOFT stole up to the door of Prudence's chamber, threw a swift glance round to see that no one was by, and went in, firmly shutting the door behind her. Prudence sat before her dressing table, haresfoot in hand. She looked round to see who came in so unceremoniously. 'Fie!' she said, and turned back to the mirror.

'My reputation if any one saw me!' said my lady, and sat down in a swirl of purple silk. She carried a strip of velvet in one hand, and a purple domino hung from her shoulders. She put up the velvet to her face. 'So! Am not I *intrigante,* my dear?'

'Very, ma'am. You always are, masked or not.'

'So they say,' nodded my lady. 'Oh, la-la! we're very fine to-night, not?'

Prudence smoothed the crimson silk sleeve of her coat, and smiled a little. 'My *pièce de résistance,* ma'am.'

'Oh, you look very well. That goes without saying.

But what a wardrobe! The *bon papa* finds himself in affluent circumstances now?'

'Up and down, my lady. There seemed to be money enough when I saw him last.' Prudence pressed a patch on to her cheek with expert fingers. 'Are you for setting forward? I'll go see if Robin's dressed.' She picked up the crimson domino from the bed, and her mask and hat with it, and went out.

Robin's voice desired to know who it was that scratched on the door. Prudence answered, and heard him say: 'Oh, enter, my dear.'

She went in humming a snatch of song. It died on her lips at what she saw, and she shut the door rather quickly. In place of the lady she expected to find there stood in the middle of the room a slim, lithe young figure in satin small clothes, and a cambric shirt. The fair hair was powdered thickly, and tied back with a black riband in the neck; the white throat was hidden by a lace neckcloth which fell under the chin in deep ruffles down the shirt front. If Robin made a pretty girl, he was beyond doubt a very handsome young man.

'Robin, are you mad?' said Prudence quietly.

In the background, shaking out the folds of an elegant coat, John growled: 'Ay, you may well ask, mistress. It's taken leave of his senses he has.'

Robin laughed out. 'My poor John! I shall be the death of you yet.'

'You'll be the death of yourself, sir, and well you know it.'

Prudence came further into the room. 'What mischief now?'

'Madam Prude! I salute you. No mischief, nor any madness either.'

'I'm not so sure. Pray will you be serious?'

He held the mask over his eyes. 'What, shall I be known?'

'There's to be an unmasking at supper. What then?'

'At the supper hour—farewell, Robin!' He blew an imaginary kiss from the tips of his fingers, and tossed the mask on to a chair. 'Don't play the spoil sport, sister mine.'

She shrugged. 'It's to jeopardise your life for a pair of brown eyes.'

'It's to play with fire for the sake of romance, and when have we done aught else? Get you into a hoop and petticoats, and play with your mountain.'

'Ah now, will you ha' done, sir?' John put down the coat, scowling. 'You'll do no such thing, Miss Prue!'

'Not I. Robin, one single mischance, and you're sped.'

'My dear, you grow fearful of shadows. Let be. To-morrow I shall be again the demure Miss Merriot.'

Prudence knew too well that demon of perversity to attempt further argument. My Lady Lowestoft's voice begged permission to enter. Prudence turned, and opened the door. 'Oh, come in, ma'am, here's a piece of mad folly for you to see.'

My lady came in all curiosity, and gave a little shriek of laughter at sight of Robin. *'Mon Dieu, mon Dieu,* you *vaurien!'* she said. 'This is to go a-wooing, no? Don't tell me! Me, I know well!'

'It's to run a thousand dangers,' said Prudence. 'The devil's in him, I believe.'

Robin was busy fixing a diamond pin in the lace at his throat. 'I pledge you my word I run no risk, Prue. The waistcoat, John.'

'Hé, but this is adventure!' cried my lady, her eyes sparkling. 'You are anxious, my Prue? But no! Who should suspect? He may vanish before the unmasking, and Marthe shall be on the watch to let him into the house. It will all go well, I promise you.'

'Madam, you're a jewel!' Robin told her, struggling into his coat. He shook out his ruffles, and gave his neckcloth a twist. 'I am myself again.'

My lady surveyed him critically. *'Du vrai,* you are a very pretty young man,' she said. *'N'est-ce pas,* Prudence?'

'Something undersized,' amended Prudence, with her slow smile.

'Prue can only admire a mammoth, ma'am,' said Robin. His eyes ran over his sister's large frame. 'Well, perhaps she has reason.'

Thus it was that midway through the evening a slight gentleman in a black domino begged my Lady

Dorling to present him to a little lady in a pink domino, seated against the wall by an austere spinster.

Lady Dorling said laughingly: 'What shall I call
you, sir, for indeed the mask baffles me?'

White teeth showed in a dazzling smile. 'You shall
say that I am *l'Inconnu,* madam.'

She was delighted. 'Miss Pink Domino should feel
Romance at hand on such an introduction. Why, it's
the little Grayson child.' She led the Black Domino
up to the Pink one, and smilingly said: 'My dear, may
I present a partner to you for the minuet? He has no
name that I can find—only *l'Inconnu.* See if he will
tell you more.' She rustled away on the words, leaving
Miss Letty looking wonderingly up at the unknown.

He stood bowing deeply before her, one hand holding a point-edged tricorne over his heart, the other laid
lightly on the hilt of his dress-sword. The black domino fell all about him in silken folds; the velvet mask
through which his eyes glittered strangely baffled recognition.

Miss Letty made her curtsey, still gazing into the
Unknown's face.

'Mademoiselle will bestow her hand on me for this
dance?'

There was something faintly familiar in the elusive
voice. 'I may go, Aunt?'

The elder Miss Grayson gave reluctant consent.
Masked balls, where strange gentlemen with fanciful
sobriquets might claim introductions were not to her

taste, but there was no help for it. Miss Letty went away on the Unknown's arm.

'I have an odd feeling I know you, sir,' she confided, looking up with a child's smile. 'Please tell me, do I?'

He shook his head; she thought his smile intriguing beyond words. 'How should you know *l'Inconnu*, mademoiselle?'

This was Romance indeed. 'But you know me, do you not?' They were dancing now, and she asked the question as she sank to the curtsey.

They came together again. 'Ah, that is another matter entirely,' said the Black Domino.

She pouted. 'And you won't tell me! So many people I've guessed; oh, at once! There is Tony, for instance.' She nodded towards a massive figure in a grey domino. 'There is no mistaking him, to be sure. And I think I know which is Mr Merriot. I thought that lady in the blue domino was his sister, but of that I am not sure. Do you know, sir?'

'No, mademoiselle, but then I do not want to know. I am content to have found Miss Grayson.'

She blushed, and turned away her head.

'I offend Miss Grayson?' the Unknown said softly.

No, she was not offended. Only—only it was so very strange not to know who he was.

'My name you would not know if I told it,' he said. 'Why spoil a perfect hour?'

Her lips were a little parted. 'A perfect hour!' she echoed. 'Is it perfect, sir?'

'For me at least, Letitia.'

'But—but you must not call me by my name!' she said. Yet she did not sound angry.

'Nor tell you that I came only to dance with you?'

'D-did you, sir?'

He nodded. 'But, of course. Didn't you guess it, Letitia?'

'No, oh no! How should I? And—and you use my name again, sir.'

'But then it is such a pretty name,' he pleaded. 'Make me free of it for one night!'

'It is like an adventure,' she said. Behind the mask her eyes were like stars.

'An adventure, or a dream.' He led her out of the dance, away to an alcove behind great pots of flowers.

'Not a dream! Oh no, for then I should wake up, and I do not want to. I want to see your face at the unmasking.'

'You won't see it, Letitia; I shall remain the Unknown.'

She sat down on the couch placed in the alcove. 'But you will have to unmask, won't you? Everyone must.'

He smiled, and shook his head. 'To unmask would be to kill Romance, Letitia.'

She was doubtful. 'Would it? But how shall I know you again if I do not see your face to-night?'

'Ah, but will you want to know me again? Or will you not regret the perfect hour?'

'No, I am sure I shall not. And of course I shall want to know you again. Shall you not want to know me?'

'Always, but I have you in my dreams, Letitia.'

She blushed adorably. 'Do you know, that is the very prettiest thing anyone has ever said to me,' she confided. 'But I would like—I mean, I do not want to live only in your dreams. Shan't you wait upon my papa?'

The white teeth showed again in a smile of some mischief. '*L'Inconnu* never waits upon papa,' he said. 'You will remember me only as a Black Domino.'

Her face fell. 'I shan't see you again?'

'Yes, you will see me—perhaps.'

'And know you?'

He hesitated; then laughed, and stretched out his hand. 'When you see that ring again, Letitia, you will know that I have come once more.'

She looked down at the ring on his little finger, a curious piece of wrought gold in a fantastic design. 'Only by that?'

'Only by that.'

'But—' she considered awhile. 'You might forget to wear it,' she pointed out.

'I shall not forget.'

She sighed. 'It is all so mysterious. I fear perhaps it is just a game, and I shan't ever see you again.'

He quoted a Spanish proverb.

'Oh, are you foreign?' she exclaimed, as though that explained all.

'No, child, but I have been much in foreign lands.'

'How exciting!' she said. 'Tell me about it.'

But a large figure stood in the entrance to the alcove, and a pleasant voice said: 'Mistress Pink Domino, will you give your hand to a Grey one?'

L'Inconnu came to his feet, and bowed gracefully. 'I surrender you,' he said. 'But only for a little while.'

Sir Anthony held out his arm to Miss Grayson, and looked curiously at the Black Domino.

Miss Grayson went reluctantly, saying over her shoulder: 'I believe you will disappear.'

'I shall claim you again, be very sure.'

'Who in the fiend's name may that be?' said Sir Anthony.

'I don't know, Tony. He is just called *L'Inconnu*, but he knows me and I have a feeling I have met him. You don't know, either?'

'I haven't a notion, my dear. I am not quite sure that I approve of unknown gentlemen.'

Her eyes pleaded. 'Oh, don't, don't tell Aunt, Tony!' she begged. 'Truly, I am not being indiscreet.'

'You don't contemplate an elopement with the mysterious stranger?' he asked teasingly.

'Tony!'

'I beg your pardon,' he bowed solemnly.

'That was prodigiously ill-natured, Tony.'

'Never say so, my dear.'

'I have a very good mind not to dance with you now.'

She was conducted promptly to an antechamber, where there were refreshments spread. 'An excellent mind,' said Sir Anthony. 'I was never a good dancer. A glass of ratafie?'

She laughed. 'It's too bad of you, Tony!'

'My dear, it would be worse if I stood up with you, I assure you. My forte lies in fetching food and drink for my partners.'

She sat down, perforce. 'Well, a little ratafie, then. I do not intend to go near Aunt again all the evening. She may scold as much as she likes afterwards.'

Sir Anthony poured two glasses of wine. 'She's absorbed in euchre, child; you need have no fear. I drink to your very good health.'

Letty sipped at the wine, and dimpled haughtily. 'You might drink to my eyes, Tony.'

'No doubt I might,' he said, but showed no disposition to do so.

Letty looked meditatively up at him. 'I wonder whether you will *ever* say pretty things?' she said, aggrieved.

'Not to you, minx.'

'I know that. But to someone else?'

'My dear, I doubt I haven't the aptitude for it. I will tell you if ever I discover it in myself.'

'I don't suppose you will. Tell me, I mean,' said Letty with a flash of insight.

'There's no knowing. I'm to understand your ear's been tickled with pretty speeches to-night?'

She spread out her fan, and began to trace the pattern on it with one rosy-tipped finger. 'I shan't tell you that, Tony.'

'You need not.' Sir Anthony smiled a little. 'It leaps to the intelligence.'

'But don't you think, Tony,' said Letty sweetly, 'that it would be very wonderful if no one had said pretty things to me?'

Sir Anthony regarded her calmly. 'You bid fair to become a rare handful,' he remarked. 'And that is all the compliment you'll have from me.'

'I am very glad I am not going to marry you,' said Letty frankly. 'You would not suit me at all. Perhaps you'll marry my dear Miss Merriot instead.'

'Withhold your felicitations awhile,' he replied. 'The event is not imminent.'

'I expect you're agog to be off to claim her hand for the dance,' nodded Miss Letty sapiently.

Sir Anthony set down his empty glass. 'I shall have to curb my impatience, then,' he said. 'She's not here.'

'Oh, is she not? I quite thought that was she in the blue domino. Who told you?'

'My Lady Lowestoft. She is kept at home with the migraine, as I believe.'

Letty was all concern. 'Oh, poor Miss Merriot! But

Mr Merriot is here, isn't he? In the crimson domino?
Yes, I thought so.'

'To say truth, it was he set me on your track. He
told me he had sought you for the minuet only to find
you spirited away by a man in a black domino.'

This brought the Unknown back to mind. 'I would
like to return to the ballroom, please,' said Letty decidedly.

But it was Mr Merriot who claimed her hand, and
led her into the quadrille. Letty went with a good
grace, but looked eagerly about her. The Unknown
was nowhere to be seen, yet at the end of the dance
he seemed to spring up out of the ground, as it were,
and stood confronting Mr Merriot with that tantalising
smile curling his lips. 'The lady is promised to me.'
he said; there was a faint note of mockery in his voice.

'On the contrary,' said Prudence. 'The lady is
mine.'

Really, a masked ball was a most fascinating entertainment. Miss Letty clasped her hands in the folds of
her domino, and waited breathlessly.

The hilt of a sword was thrust slightly forward.
'Why, I would meet you for the honour of holding her
hand,' said the Unknown. 'But she shall choose.' He
turned, and offered an arm. 'Madam, will you walk?'

She looked beseechingly at Prudence. 'Mr Merriot,
I have to choose *l'Inconnu* because I am a female, and
they say the silly creatures love a mystery.'

Prudence laughed and bowed. 'I retire from the lists, then, cruel Pink Domino.'

'Besides,' said Letty coaxingly, 'your crimson and my rose go vilely together, sir!' She threw a smile over her shoulder as she went off, threading her way through the throng of people.

'Bereft, my Peter?'

Prudence started, and turned to face Sir Anthony, standing at her elbow, 'Robbed, sir, by a man in a black domino. I chose the wrong colour, and Miss Grayson won't stay to clash with my crimson.'

'So the mysterious stranger filches the lady from you. Too bad, my dear boy. Come and drown your sorrows in claret.'

Out on the terrace, under a starry sky, the Unknown raised Miss Grayson's hand to his lips, and held it there a long moment. She shivered a little, and her eyes widened.

'Take off the mask!' He spoke little above a whisper. 'Oh—no!' she said, and drew her hand away.

'Ah, don't deny me!' An arm slid round her shoulders, and deft fingers sought the mask's string over her ear.

'You—you must not!' Letty said faintly, and put up her hand to stop his against her hair.

But the string was untied, and the mask fell. Her hand was caught and held; she lay back against the Unknown's shoulder, and felt his other hand gently forcing up her chin.

It must surely be a mad dream from which she would awaken soon. She looked up and saw only glittering eyes behind the blackness of the mask, and the hint of a smile in the moonlight. The arm tightened about her shoulders; the hand beneath her chin pressed more insistently, and the Unknown bent his head till his lips found hers.

The spell held for a moment; then she quivered, and made a fluttering movement to be free. The Unknown sank on one knee, and lifted the hem of her gown to kiss. 'Forgive me!' he said. 'I may never have the chance again, Letitia.'

She stood poised for flight, but his words kept her still. Half timidly she stretched down her hand to him. 'Oh, do not!' she said. 'I think we are both mad to-night.'

He came to his feet, and stood holding her hands between his. 'But you will remember.'

'I shall see you again?' It was a forlorn petition.

'Who can say? This I promise: if ever you are in danger, or in need of a champion you will see me, for I shall come to you then.' He stood for a moment, silhouetted by the silver light against the deep blue sky; then once more he bent, and, turning her hand upwards, pressed a kiss into the palm. '*Adieu, ma belle;* you will not forget.'

He moved swiftly to the low parapet that walled the terrace in; looked over an instant, and placing his hand on the top, vaulted lightly over, down into the silent garden a few feet below.

She ran forward, and peered over the low wall. There was no one in sight, but she thought she heard an echo of his *adieu* borne back to her on a soft wind.

CHAPTER NINE

Mohocks abroad

IT SEEMED ROBIN WAS well satisfied with the night's work; his sister visited him as he lay sipping his chocolate in bed next morning, and cocked a quizzical eyebrow. Robin smiled sweetly, but volunteered no confidences. He went to call upon Miss Grayson later in the day, but although Letty was delighted to see her dear Kate, she was a little abstracted, and had but a few words to say of the ball. Yes, it had been very amusing; she wished Kate had been there. Yes, she had danced with a number of gentlemen. It was a pity Mr Merriot had chosen to wear crimson.

Robin went off with a smile playing about the corners of his mouth. He was constrained to drive out visiting with my Lady Lowestoft, and went, smothering a yawn.

Prudence—she was beginning, she thought, to feel more of a man than a woman—strolled round to White's, and found Mr Walpole there reading the 'Spectator'. Mr Walpole was graciously pleased to exchange a few words; he had a small flow of tittle-tattle at his tongue's tip, and announced his intention of retiring to Strawberry Hill. He protested that these late nights in town were harmful to his constitution. He raised supercilious brows at the sight of Mr Markham entering the room, and retired once more behind the 'Spectator'.

Mr Markham bowed to Prudence, and went to write letters at a table against the wall. Prudence stood talking to one Mr Dendy, and was presently tapped on the shoulder.

'Here's your man, Devereux!' said the voice of Sir Francis Jollyot.

Mr Devereux came up with his mincing gait. ''Pon my soul, so 'tis!' He swept a leg, flourishing a scented handkerchief. 'I am but this instant come from Arlington Street, where they told me you had walked out. I have to beg the honour of your company at a small gathering I have a mind to hold to-night. A little game of Chance, you understand.' He held up a very white finger. 'Now don't, I implore you, *don't* say me nay, Mr Merriot!'

Prudence smothered a sigh. 'Why, sir, I confess I had purposed to spend this evening with my sister,' she began.

'Oh, come now, Merriot!' expostulated Jollyot jovially, 'you must not deny me my revenge!'

'To be sure, I live in a most devilish outlandish spot,' said Mr Devereux mournfully. 'But you may take a chair: you know you may take a chair. 'Pon rep, sir, I do positively believe an evening spent at home is vastly more fatiguing than a quiet card-party. 'Pon my honour, sir!'

There was nothing for it but to show polite acceptance.

Mr Devereux was wreathed in smiles. 'To tell you the truth, sir, I've had a devilish ticklish task to find anyone free to-night,' he said naïvely. 'Fanshawe's engaged; so's Barham. Molyneux goes out of town; Selwyn's in bed with a trifling fever.'

Over against the wall Mr Markham stopped writing, and raised his head.

'I'm overwhelmed by the honour done me,' said Prudence ironically.

The irony went unperceived. 'Not at all, my dear Merriot. Oh, not in the least! I shall see you then, at five? You can take a chair, you know, and be there in a trice.'

'As you say, sir. But I think I have not the pleasure of knowing your address.'

Mr Devereux simpered elegantly. 'Oh, a devilish inconvenient hole, sir! I've apartments in Charing Cross.'

'Ah yes, I remember the street now,' Prudence said. 'At five o'clock, sir.'

Mr Devereux beamed upon her, and airily waved one languid hand. '*Au revoir,* then, my dear Merriot. You will take a chair, and suffer not the least inconvenience in the world. An evening at home—oh no, ecod!' He drifted away on Jollyot's arm, and the rest of his sentence only reached Prudence as a confused murmur.

Mr Markham went on with his writing.

Prudence walked slowly back to Arlington Street, and remarked to Robin, on his return, that she was in danger of wearing herself away to skin and bone.

Robin was bored. 'Heigh-ho, would I were in your shoes! All this female society gives me *mal-à-la-tête*.'

'Give you my word these card-parties and drinking bouts will be the death of me.'

Robin swung an impatient foot. 'Does it occur to you, my dear, that events have not transpired precisely as they were planned?' he inquired with a rueful look.

'It has occurred to me many times. We meant to lie close.'

'Oh!' My Lady Lowestoft was arranging flowers in a big bowl. 'But the *bon papa* planned it thus, my children. I was told to present you to the world.'

'Egad, we owe it to the old gentleman, do we?' said Robin. 'I might have known. But why?'

'*Seulement,* I think he judged it wisest. You escape remark this way. That is true, no?'

'I suppose so. But the impropriety of Prue's conduct—oh lud, ma'am!'

'Consider only the impropriety of your own, my child!' chuckled my lady.

'I do, ma'am, often. But as regarding this charming

réunion to-night, Mistress Prue, you'll be pleased to take a chair, and eschew the Burgundy.'

'Behold the little mentor!' Prudence bowed to him. 'Rest you content, my Kate.'

The evening was like a dozen other such evenings. There was dinner, and some ribald talk; cards, with the decanter passing from hand to hand, and the candles burning lower and lower in their sockets. Prudence made her excuses soon after midnight. Her host rolled a blear eye towards her, and protested thickly. Prudence was firm, however, and won her way. A sleepy lackey opened the front door for her, and she stepped out into the cool night air.

The street was deserted, but she knew a chair might be found at Charing Cross, a few score yards away. She swung her cloak over her arm, and walked in that direction, glad of this breath of clean air after the stuffiness of the card room.

It may have been that never quite dormant watchfulness in her that warned her of danger. No more than fifty yards up the street she felt it in the air, and checked her pace slightly. There was a shadow crouched in an embrasure in the wall a few steps further on—a shadow that had something of the form of a man. She slid a hand to her sword hilt, loosening the blade in the scabbard. She must walk on: no use turning back now. A little pale, but steady-eyed as ever, she went forward, her fingers closed about the sword hilt.

The shadow moved, and behold! there were two other shadows springing up before her. There was a flash of steel as she wrenched the sword free from the scabbard, and for a moment the shadowy figures held back. The moment's hesitation was enough to allow her to get her back against the wall, and to take a sure grip on the cloak over her left arm. Then there was a hoarse murmur, and the three rushed in on her with cudgels upraised.

Her rapier swept a circle before her; the foremost man jumped back with a curse, but the fellow to the right sprang in to aim a vicious blow at Prudence's head. The rapier shot out, and the point struck home. Came a gasp, and a check: the cloak, unerringly thrown, descended smotheringly over the wounded man's head, and there was at once a tangle of cloth and hot oaths.

Prudence made lightning use of this momentary diminution in the number of her assailants, parried a blow aimed at her sword arm, sprang sideways a little, and lunged forward the length of her arm. There was a groan, and the sword came away red, while the cudgel fell clattering to earth.

She was breathless and panting; this could not last. Even now the third man had got himself free of the cloak, and was creeping on her with it held in his hand. She guessed he meant to catch at her blade through it, and her heart sank. She thrust shrewdly at the man before her, and staggered under a blow from a cudgel on her left. She was nearly spent, and she knew that a few moments more must end it.

Then, from a little way down the street came a shout, and the sound of a man running. 'Hold them, lad, I'm with you!' cried the newcomer, and Prudence recognised the voice of Mr Belfort.

He fell upon her assailants from the rear, and there was swift and bloody work done. With a howl the man Prudence had first wounded went running off down the street, one hand clipped to his shoulder. His flight was a signal for the other two to follow suit. In another minute the street was empty, save for Prudence and the Honourable Charles.

Mr Belfort leaned panting on his sword, and laughed hugely. 'Gad, see 'em run!' he said. 'Hey, are you hurt, lad?'

Prudence was leaning against the wall, dizzy and shaken. The shoulder which had sustained the blow from the cudgel ached sickeningly. With an effort she stood upright. 'Naught. A blow on the shoulder, no more.' She swayed, but mastered the threatened faintness, and bent to pick up her cloak. Her hand shook slightly as she wiped her sword in its folds, but she managed to smile. 'I have—to thank you—for your prompt assistance,' she said, trying to get her breath. 'I rather thought I was sped.'

'Ay, three to one, blister them,' nodded Mr Belfort. 'But white-livered curs, 'pon my soul. Not an ounce of fight in 'em. Here, take my arm.'

Prudence leaned gratefully on it. 'Just a momentary breathlessness,' she said. 'I am well enough now.'

'Gad, it must have been a nasty blow!' said Mr Belfort. 'You are shaken to bits, man. Come home with me; my lodging is nearer than yours.'

'No, no, I thank you!' Prudence said earnestly. 'The blow—struck an old wound. I hardly heed it now.'

'Tare an' 'ouns, but that's bad!' cried Mr Belfort. 'Really, my dear fellow, you must come to my place and let me look to it.'

'On my honour, sir, it's less than naught. You may see for yourself I am quite recovered now. I shall not trespass on your hospitality at this hour of night.'

He protested that the night was young yet, but not to all his entreaties would Prudence yield. They walked on together towards Charing Cross, the Honourable Charles still adjuring Prudence at intervals to go home with him. 'By gad, sir, these Mohocks become a positive scandal!' he exclaimed. 'A gentleman mayn't walk abroad, damme, without being set upon these days!'

'Mohocks?' Prudence said. 'You think they were Mohocks, then?'

'Why, what else? The town's teeming with 'em. I was set on myself t'other day. Stretched one fellow flat!'

Prudence thought of the words she had caught as she had come up to the embrasure. A rough voice had growled: 'This is our man, boys.' She said nothing of this, however, to Mr Belfort, but assented that without doubt the men had been Mohocks, intent on robbery.

'A good thing 'twas I left Devereux's rooms directly after you,' said Mr Belfort. 'But that Burgundy, y'know—demned poor stuff, my boy! There was no staying longer. How a man can get drunk on it beats me. Look at me now! Sober as a judge, Peter! Yet there's poor Devereux almost under the table already.'

They parted company at Charing Cross, where Mr Belfort saw Prudence solicitously into a chair. She was borne off west to Arlington Street, and set down safely outside my lady's house.

A light burned still in Robin's room. Sure, the child would never go to bed until she was come home. She went softly in, and found Robin reading by the light of three candles.

Robin looked up. 'My felicitations. You escaped betimes.' His eyes narrowed, and he got up. 'Oh? What's toward, child? he said sharply, and came across to Prudence's side.

She laughed. 'What, do I look a corpse? I was near enough to it. But there are no bones broken, I believe.'

The beautifully curved lips straightened to a thin line; Prudence saw her brother's eyes keen and anxious. 'Be a little plain with me, child. You've sustained some hurt?'

'No more than a bruise, I think, but oh, Robin, it hurt!' Again she laughed, but there was a quiver in her voice. 'Help me to come out of this coat; 'tis on my left shoulder.'

The shoulder was swiftly bared and an ugly bruise disclosed. There came a soft curse from Robin. 'Who did it?'

'Now, how should I know? Charles spoke of the Mohocks.'

Robin was searching on his dressing table for ointment, and came back to her with the pot in his hand. As he smeared the stuff lightly over the bruise, he said remorsefully: ''Tis I who was at fault. I should have seen to it you had my lady's chaise out.'

'Oh, no harm done, as it chances. But there were three of them and I was all but sped. Then Charles came running up, and there was an end of it.' She slipped her shirt up again over her shoulder. 'Thanks, child. I would you had seen my sword play. I am sure it did you credit.' She paused and looked at the guttering candles. Her tone changed, and became serious. 'I have a notion they were creatures of Markham's set on to beat me.'

'Markham's?' Robin set down the ointment.

'I know of no one else with a grudge against me. They were not common Mohocks.' She told him what she had heard.

He strode to the window and back again, frowning. 'I think this is where we make our bow,' he said at last.

'Devil a bit!' was the cheerful response. 'For the

future I shall remember to take a chaise; that's all there is to it.'

'I had rather see you safe in France.'

'I won't go.'

He raised an eyebrow. 'Oh, do you turn stubborn?'

'As a mule. We go down to Richmond with my lady to-morrow, and the Markham may think that I've gone into retirement on account of my mauling. He should be satisfied. I await the old gentleman, for I've a curiosity to see what his game is.' She got up, and stretched her long limbs, wincing at the pain of her bruised shoulder. 'Get you to bed, Robin.' She went out, yawning.

They were gone on the morrow down to my lady's house at Richmond. My lady was loud in her exclamations of horror at what had befallen Prudence, but Prudence could chuckle now that all was over, the while Robin sat in frowning silence. His petticoats began to irk him.

Mr Markham heard of the affair at White's, from the lips of Mr Belfort. He professed himself all concern, but his friend Lord Barham, drawing him aside, said with a snigger: 'So that's a score settled, eh, my buck?'

'It's not,' said Mr Markham curtly, and scowled.

'Gad, I'd give something to know what you have against the young sprig!' said his Lordship. 'It's a conceited puppy, ecod! I've a mind to give it a trouncing myself.'

Mr Markham saw Sir Anthony Fanshawe, idly
twirling his quizzing-glass, and rather testily requested
his noble friend to guard his tongue. Sir Anthony continued blandly to survey the pair. Mr Markham strode
off, rather red about the gills.

Sir Anthony turned to Mr Belfort, standing in a circle of his acquaintances. 'Well, Charles, have you
been fighting with the devil's emissaries?' he said genially. 'What's this I hear of Mohocks?'

'Three of them, right in the middle of town, if you
please!' said Mr Belfort. 'Thunder an' turf, but it's a
crying disgrace! I'm saying to Proudie here that measures ought to be taken.'

Sir Anthony took out his snuff-box, and shook back
the ruffles from his hand. 'Oh, were you attacked?' he
inquired.

'Not I. 'Twas young Merriot they set upon, as he
came off from Devereux's last night.'

The strong hand paused for a moment in the act of
unfobbing the snuff-box. The sleepy eyes did not lift.
'Indeed?' said Sir Anthony, and awaited more.

'Three to one, the ruffians, and lucky I chances
along, for the lad's not over strong in the sword arm,
I take it. Game enough, but he was soon blown.'

'He was, was he?' Sir Anthony took snuff in a leisurely fashion. 'And—er—was he hurt?'

'A blow on the shoulder. It seemed to knock him
pretty well endways. But he said something of an old

wound there, which would account for it,' said Belfort, feeling that some excuse was needed.

'Ah, an old wound?' Sir Anthony was politely interested. 'Of course. That would, as you say, account for it.'

'There's naught to be said against the lad's courage,' Belfort assured him. 'Game as a fighting cock, pledge you my word. I was all for taking him off to my lodgings to attend to his shoulder, but no, he'd none of it!'

'He refused to go with you, did he?' Sir Anthony flicked a speck or two of snuff from his sleeve.

'Oh, wouldn't hear of it! Naught I could say was to any avail. He would be off home, and have no fuss made.'

'Very creditable,' said Sir Anthony, stifling a yawn, and strolled away to meet my Lord March, just come in.

CHAPTER TEN

Sudden and startling appearance of the old gentleman

AT RICHMOND, in the pleasant house with its gardens running down to the river, Sir Anthony was one of my Lady Lowestoft's visitors. He rode out to pay a morning call, and was fortunate enough to find my lady and her two guests at home.

Sir Anthony indicated Prudence's stiff shoulder with a movement of his quizzing glass. 'So you must needs go brawling about our streets, little man?'

There was a quick contraction of Robin's brows. He looked up to find the sleepy gaze upon him, and straightaway achieved a shudder. 'Oh pray, sir, don't speak of it!'

'You should keep him closer tied to your apron strings, ma'am,' said Sir Anthony, and began to talk of the state of the roads. But upon my lady's going out of the room he broke off to say: 'Have you any idea that it was Markham's men set upon you, young man?'

'Some little suspicion of it,' Prudence admitted. 'I shall be more wary in the future.'

'It's a vengeful creature.' Sir Anthony crossed one leg over the other. 'I believe you would do well not to go abroad unaccompanied at night,' he said, and fell to twirling his eyeglass by its riband.

He presently took leave of them, and rode off back to town. Robin said with a laugh: 'Oh, it's all solicitude! The benevolent mammoth!'

'Lord, must you still be jeering!' Prudence demanded and left him rather abruptly.

They returned to Arlington Street at the end of the week, arriving on the day of her Grace of Queensberry's rout, whither they were bidden. They went in state in my lady's town chariot, and my lady regaled them on the way with some highly entertaining details of my Lord March's private life.

Her Grace's salons were large enough to accommodate even the crowd that assembled at her house that evening. There were bright lights in sparkling chandeliers, and many heavy scented flowers, and over all the hum of gay chatter. Her Grace stood at the head of the stairs to receive her guests, and had the felicity of knowing that my Lord March, her son, was adorning the rout with his unaccustomed presence.

My lord was in excellent spirits, and stayed for at least an hour in the big withdrawing rooms. After having done his duty there so nobly, he retired to the card rooms for a spell, in search of a little relaxation.

Robin's elderly admirer found him out, and showed an ardent desire to know more of him. Prudence left him, murmuring compliments into one bashful ear.

It was quite late in the evening when there came a slight stir about the doorway, and Prudence had returned to Robin's side, ousting the elderly beau. She stood now behind his chair, Sir Raymond Orton a few paces from her, and my Lady Lowestoft, laughing immoderately at something Mr Selwyn was saying to her, not far distant.

Some late comer, it appeared, was arriving; a knot of ladies gathered near the door gave way, and Prudence could enjoy a clear view.

Two gentlemen came in, and stood for a moment looking round. One of these was my Lord March; the other was a slight, elderly gentleman with arresting grey eyes, a nose inclined to be aquiline, and thin, smiling lips. He was magnificently attired in puce satin, with embroidered waistcoat. His wig must surely have come straight from Paris; his shoes, with their jewelled buckles, had preposterous high red heels to them; the cut of his coat spoke the most fashionable tailor of the day in every line. There was the hint of a diamond in the lace at his throat, and on his breast he displayed several scintillating foreign orders. He stood very much at his ease, his head slightly inclined to hear what my Lord March was saying, and one thin white hand delicately raising a pinch of snuff to a finely chiselled nostril.

Prudence's hand found Robin's shoulder, and gripped hard. Robin looked up, and she felt him stiffen.

The old gentleman's eyes travelled slowly round the room the while he listened to my Lord March; rested a moment on Miss Merriot's face, and passed on. Her Grace of Queensberry came forward to welcome the newcomer, and he bent with great courtliness over her hand.

Robin turned in his chair. 'I am dreaming. I must be dreaming. Even he could not dare—'

Prudence was shaking with suppressed laughter. 'Oh, it's the old gentleman himself, never fear! Lud, might we not have expected something after this fashion?'

'Arm-in-arm with March—covered with jewels—all his misbegotten orders—gad, it beats all! And who the devil does he pretend to be now?' Robin sat fuming; he could not admire this last freak of his sire. 'Of course, we're sped now,' he said in a voice of gloomy conviction. 'This will land us all in Tyburn.'

'Oh, my dear, he's incomparable! You have to admit it.' Prudence saw Mr Molyneux advancing, and hailed him. 'Pray, sir, who is the magnificent stranger but just arrived?'

'What, don't you know?' cried Mr Molyneux, shocked. 'Ah, to be sure, you've been out of town this last week. That stranger is the greatest romance we've known since Peterson ran off with Miss Carslake.' He laughed at Robin. 'All the ladies are in ecstasies over it, I assure you. It appears, you see, that the grand gentleman is the lost Viscount. One thought such things only happened in fairy tales.'

Robin sank back in his chair; seeing him incapable of speech; Prudence said faintly: 'Indeed, sir? And—and who is the lost Viscount?'

'Fie, fie, what ignorance! And the thing's the jest of town!—but you have been at Richmond: I forget that. Why, none but Tremaine, my dear boy, of course!—Tremaine of Barham! Surely you must know that!'

Some dim recollection of my Lady Lowestoft's talk flitted across Prudence's memory. 'I didn't know there was a lost Tremaine, sir,' she said.

'Good Gad, not know of the Barham claim?' This was Mr Belfort, who had wandered up to them. 'Why, this is the lost black sheep appeared to filch the title from Rensley. It's a famous jest, and Rensley's as sour as a lemon over it.' He laughed delightedly at the thought of the deposed lord's discomfiture.

'But what's his claim?' persisted Prudence.

'Oh, that! To be sure, no one remembered his existence in the least, but it seems he's a brother of old Barham, who died a month or two back. Odd, a'n't it? *I* never heard of any brother, but it was all rather before my time, of course. Anyway, Cloverly was telling me he has all the papers to prove he's the man, and a fine romantic story it all is. A jolt for Rensley, though!'

'Does Rensley acknowledge him?' Prudence found strength to inquire.

'As to that, Rensley's lying low, I take it, but I believe he told Farnborough he was sure his cousin was dead, and that this man had stolen the papers. But Rensley would take that tone, y'know.' Mr Belfort perceived a friend close by, and was off to greet him.

'And what do you make of that?' said Prudence calmly in her brother's ear.

Robin shook his head. 'It's the most consummate piece of impertinent daring—gad, it beats our masquerade!'

'But how can he carry it off? And for how long?'

'And why?' Robin demanded. 'It's senseless! *Why?*'

'Oh, the old love of a fine dramatic gesture. Don't we know it? It's to rank with the time he played the French Ambassador in Madrid. And he came off safe from that.'

'But this—this is England!' Robin said. '*Cordieu,* will you but look at him now?'

The magnificent gentleman was bowing before Miss Gunning. Well they knew that flourish of a laced handkerchief. Egad, but he had all the airs of a Viscount, or of a Duke for that matter. A large figure came up with him; the new Lord Barham gave Sir Anthony

Fanshawe two fingers to clasp. Sir Anthony stayed but to speak a few words, and then walked leisurely away.

Came a gasp from my Lady Lowestoft's direction. My lady sprang up. '*Mon cher* Robert!' she cried, and held out her hands. Volubly she explained to Mr Selwyn that this dear gentleman had long been known to her.

'Thérèse!' My Lord Barham kissed both her hands. 'I have the supreme felicity to find you!'

'Faith, it's an ecstatic old gentleman!' The voice came from behind Prudence. Sir Anthony Fanshawe had come round the room to her side.

'I'm to understand it's a lost viscount, or some such matter?' Prudence took snuff with an air of unconcern.

'Quite so. The last of the Tremaines it appears. Offspring don't so far materialise.'

My Lady Lowestoft was bearing down upon them with a hand on Lord Barham's arm. '*Mon cher,* I must present to you some dear young friends of mine,' they heard her say. 'It is a Mr and a Miss Merriot, who are staying with me for a space.'

'I am enchanted to meet a friend of my Thérèse!' his lordship declared, and was straightway presented to Miss Merriot.

Robin arose, and spread out his skirts; as he rose from the curtsey he extended a hand right regally, and gazed limpidly into the face of his sire.

My lord bowed deeply over the hand, and, looking up, bestowed a glance of admiration upon Miss Merriot's fair countenance. 'But charming!' he said. 'Charming, I protest!'

It was Prudence's turn now, and she made my lord a leg. Deep down in the grey eyes the twinkle lurked. 'I am honoured, sir,' she said.

My lord bowed slightly, as became a man of his years and rank, and smiled with delight upon Mr Merriot. Indeed, a most affable old gentleman. He turned to compliment my lady on having two such enchanting friends to stay with her, and promised himself the pleasure of waiting upon her in the morning. With yet another bow to Miss Merriot he walked away with my lady on his arm.

'I am entirely overpowered,' complained Sir Anthony, and sat him down beside Robin.

Robin tilted his head speculatively. 'Something of a foreign air,' he mused. 'Do you agree, sir?'

'Something of an oppressive air I find it,' answered Sir Anthony, with a chuckle.

'My lady seems to know him very well,' remarked Prudence, and went away to glean what information she could.

Accounts varied, but it seemed my lord had quarrelled violently in his youth with his father, and taken himself off to France with a low-bred bride of his own choosing. Since that day he had never been heard of, until suddenly, soon after the death of his elder brother, he descended on the town in a blaze of magnificence. Prudence expressed surprise that he had not

shown himself upon the death of his father, but the
answer to that was ready. There were rumours that
there had been little love lost between the brothers:
the remarkable gentleman had chosen to remain in obscurity.

She could obtain no more certain information, and
returned with her gleanings to Robin. My Lady
Lowestoft was ready to go home; they greeted her proposal with relief, and were borne off under her wing.
My Lord Barham, seeing them go, waved his hand,
and said: '*A demain!*' most gallantly.

Not until they were safe inside the coach did my
lady give way to the mirth that was consuming her.
But then she lay back against the padded cushions and
laughed till the tears ran down her painted cheeks.

Robin regarded her gloomily. 'Ay, it's a rare jest,
ma'am.'

'It is—it is altogether *magnifique!*' she gasped. 'It
is a *coup* the most superb! Not even I dreamed of
anything so superb!' She sat up and dabbed at her
eyes. '*Voyons,* was there ever such a man? I myself
am ready to believe him to be Lord Barham. What an
air! What effrontery! *Mon Dieu, mon Dieu,* I have not
been in such an agony of laughter since he stole the
Margrave's mistress!'

'That's a tale I don't know,' said Prudence. 'I perceive that a hurried flight to France awaits us.'

'But no, but no! Why, my cabbage? He proves himself the lost vicomte, and who is to know more?'

'Oh, it's simple!' said Robin dryly. 'But there is always the possibility of the true viscount's appearance.'

'How, my child? We see the *bon papa* with all the papers. The real viscount is dead, of course! How else could Robert have the papers?'

'Good God, ma'am, do you put it above the old gentleman to steal them from a live man?'

'There's more to it than that.' Prudence's calm voice broke in. 'A counterfeit for a day, a week, a month is very well, but even the old gentleman can't maintain it for ever. Rensley won't be satisfied with a few documents. There'll be traps set, and others of no one's setting into which he is bound to fall. Consider, ma'am, what it means suddenly to become an English peer with estates, and a large fortune! The thing's not so easily done, I believe.'

'There's also the little matter of the late fracas in the North,' said Robin. 'Certain, he discards the black wig, and the French accent, but there must be information out against him.'

'My children, I have faith in him!' her ladyship declared. 'He is as I have said—*magnifique!*'

CHAPTER ELEVEN

My Lord Barham in Arlington Street

WHEN the black page announced my Lord Barham next morning both Mr and Miss Merriot were with my lady in the morning-room. My lord was ushered in, very *point-de-vice*, with laced gloves, and a muff of miniver, and a long beribboned cane. The muff and the cane were given into the page's charge; the door closed behind this diminutive person, and my lord spread wide his arms. 'My children!' he exclaimed. 'Behold me returned to you!'

His children maintained an admirable composure. 'Like Jonah cast up out of the whale's belly,' said Robin.

My lord was not in the least put out of countenance by this coolness. 'My son!' He swooped upon Robin. 'Perfect! To the last detail! My Prudence!'

Prudence submitted to a fervent embrace. 'Well, sir, how do you do?' she said, smiling. 'We perceive you are returned to us, but we don't understand the manner of it.'

He struck an attitude. 'But do you not know? I am Tremaine. Tremaine of Barham!'

'Lud!' said Robin. 'You don't say so, sir!'

He was hurt. 'Ah, you do not believe in me! You doubt me, in effect!'

'Well, sir'—Prudence sat on the arm of Robin's chair, and gently swung one booted leg to and fro—'We've seen you as Mr Colney; we've seen you as Mr Daughtry; we've even seen you as the Prince Vanilov. You cannot altogether blame us.'

My lord abandoned his attitude, and took snuff. 'I shall show you,' he promised. 'Do not doubt that this time I surpass myself.'

'We don't doubt that, sir.'

My lady said on a gurgling laugh: 'But what will you be at, *mon cher?* What madness?'

'I am Tremaine of Barham,' reiterated his lordship, with dignity. 'Almost I had forgot it, but I come now into my own. You must have known'—he addressed the room at large—'you who have watched me, that there was more to me than a mere wandering gamester!'

'Faith, we thought it just devilry, sir,' Prudence chuckled.

'You do not appreciate me,' said my lord sadly, and sat him down by the table. 'You lack soul, my children. Yes, you lack soul.'

'I concede you all my admiration, sir,' said Prudence.

'You shall concede me more still. You shall recognise a master mind in me, my Prudence. We come to the end of our travels.'

'Tyburn way,' said Robin, and laughed. 'Egad, sir, you've a maggot in your head to venture on such a piece of folly!'

The old gentleman's eyes glinted. 'Do my schemes go awry, then? Do I fail in what I undertake to do, Robin my son?'

'You don't, sir, I'm willing to admit, but you break fresh ground now, and I believe you don't know the obstacles. This is England.'

'Robin acquires geography!' My lord smiled gently. 'It is the land of my birth. I am come home, *enfin*. I am Tremaine of Barham.'

'And pray what are we, sir?' inquired Robin, with interest.

'At present, *mes enfants*, you are Mr and Miss Merriot. I compliment you. It is admirable. I see that you inherit a part of my genius.' He kissed his finger-tips to them. 'When I have made all secure you are the Honourable Robin, and the Honourable Prudence Tremaine.'

'Of Barham,' interpolated Prudence.

He looked at her affectionately. 'For you, my beautiful Prue, I plan a great marriage,' he informed her magnificently.

'A Royal Prince, belike?' said Prudence, unimpressed.

'I will choose from an older house than this of Hanover,' my lord said grandly. 'Have no fear.'

Robin looked at his sister. 'My dear, what to do?' he said helplessly.

'Leave all to me!' commanded my lord. 'I do not make mistakes.'

'Except in the matter of Royal Princes,' said Robin, with meaning.

'Bah! I forget all that!' The past was consigned to perdition with a snap of thin fingers. 'It might have chanced otherwise. I seized opportunity, as ever. Do you blame me for the Rebellion's failure?'

Prudence shook her head. 'Ah, sir, you should have been put at the head of it,' she mourned. 'The Prince would be at St James's to-day then.'

My Lord was forcibly struck by this view of the case. 'My child, you have intuition,' he said seriously. 'You are right. Yes, beyond all doubt you are right.' He sat lost in meditation, planning, they knew, great deeds that might have been.

They exchanged glances. My lady sat by the window, chin in hand, raptly gazing upon the old gentleman out of her narrow eyes. There was nothing to do but to wait for him to come out of his trance. Robin sat back in his chair with a shrug of fatalism; his sister continued to sling one booted leg.

My lord looked up. 'Dreams!' he waved them aside. 'Dreams! I am a great man,' he said simply.

'You are, sir,' agreed Prudence. 'But we should like to know what you plan now.'

'I have done with plans and plots,' he told her. 'I am Tremaine of Barham.'

There seemed to be no hope of getting anything more out of him. But Prudence persevered. 'So you have told us, sir. But can you prove it to the satisfaction of Mr Rensley?'

'If Rensley becomes a nuisance, Rensley must go,' my lord declared, with resolution.

'Murder, sir?'

'He will disappear. I shall see to it. It need not worry you. I arrange all for the best.'

'I wonder whether Mr Rensley will see it in that light?' said Prudence. 'Does he acknowledge you, sir?'

'No,' admitted his lordship. 'But he fears me. Believe it, he fears me!'

Robin had been sitting with closed eyes, but he opened them now. 'I grant you this much, sir: you are to be feared.'

'My Robin!' My lord flung out a hand to him. 'You begin to know me then!'

'I've a very lively fear of you myself,' said Robin frankly. 'Give me audience a moment!'

'Speak, my son. I listen. I am all attention.'

Robin looked at his finger-tips. 'Well, sir, the matter stands thus: we've a mind to turn respectable, Prue and I.' He raised his eyes. His father's expression was one of courteous interest. 'I admit we don't see our

way clear. We wait on you. To be candid, sir, you
pushed us into the late Rebellion, and it is for you to
extricate us now. I've no desire to adorn Tyburn Tree.
We came to London under your direction; we stayed
for you here, according to the plan. True, you have
come as you promised you would, but in a guise that
bids fair to compromise us more deeply still. We don't
desert you: faith, we can't, unless we choose to go
abroad again. But we've an ambition to settle in England. We look to you.'

The old gentleman heard him out in smiling silence.
At the end he arose. 'And not in vain, my children. I
live but to settle you in the world. And the time has
come! Listen to me! I answer every point. For the
Rebellion, it is simplicity itself. You cease to exist.
You vanish. In a word, you are no more. Robin Lacey—it was Lacey?—dies. Remains my son—Tremaine of Barham! I swept you into the Rebellion it's
true. In a little while I have but to stretch out a hand,
and you are whisked from all danger. Have patience
till I make all secure! Already I announce to the world
the existence of a son, and of an exquisite daughter.'
He paused. Applause—it was clearly expected—came
from my lady, who clapped delighted hands. His eyes
dwelt upon her fondly. 'Ah, Thérèse, you believe in
me. You have reason. Not twice in five hundred years
is my like seen.'

'The world has still something to be thankful for,'
sighed Robin. 'It's all very fine, sir, and I had as lief

be Tremaine of Barham as Robin Lacey; but how do you purpose to arrive at this promised security?'

'That I do not as yet know,' said his lordship. 'I make no plans until I see what I have to combat.'

'You realise there's like to be a fight, sir?'

'Most fully. There are maybe some few will know me from foreign days. Those I do not fear. They are less than nothing.'

'And,' interrupted his son, 'there may be also some few will know you from Scottish days. What of them?'

'They too are less than nothing,' said my lord. 'Who would dare to seek to expose me?' He laid stress on the last word; it seemed fitting. 'What man knows me among the Jacobites whom I do not know? Not one! I have some papers in my possession make me dangerous beyond the power of imagination.'

'Jacobite papers?' said Robin sharply. 'Then burn them, sir! You are not, after all, Mr Murray of Broughton.'

My lord drew himself up. 'You suspect me of infamy? You think that Tremaine of Barham turns informer? You insult me! You, my son!'

'Egad, sir, let us have done with heroics. I'm to suppose you keep your papers for some purpose.'

'You may consider them as a Sword of Damocles in case of necessity,' said my lord. 'There is only one thing that I fear. One little, significant scrap of paper. I shall overcome the obstacle.'

'Paper? You've set your name to something? Where is it?' demanded Robin.

'If I knew, should I fear it?' my lord pointed out.

'It seems to me, sir,' said Prudence slowly, 'that there is a Sword of Damocles poised above your head as well.'

'There is, my child. You perceive that I conceal nothing. But it is my fate to be victorious. I shall contrive.'

The grey eyes widened. '"I contrive,"' said Prudence softly. 'Do you know, sir, you puzzle me.'

'It has ever been my motto,' the old gentleman pointed out triumphantly. 'It is the word of the Tremaines. Consider it, my daughter! Consider it well! I take my leave of you now. You will find me in lodgings at Half Moon Street—close by my loved ones. I have come, and your anxieties are at an end.'

'It is in my mind that they are only just beginning,' said Prudence ruefully.

My lady got up to lay a hand on his lordship's sleeve. 'You do not take possession of your fine town house yet, no?' she inquired.

'In time, Thérèse, in good time. There are legal formalities. I do not trouble myself with lawyers!' This was once more in the grand manner. My lord beamed upon his children. 'Farewell, *mes enfants!* We meet again later.' He kissed my lady's hand, and was gone with a click of red heels on the wood floor, and the wave of a scented handkerchief.

CHAPTER TWELVE

Passage of arms between Prudence and Sir Anthony

THEY WERE LEFT TO STARE at one another. My lady showed an inclination to laugh. 'Well, my children? Well?' she demanded.

'I'm glad you think so, ma'am,' bowed Prudence.

'Oh, what's to be done with the man?' Robin said impatiently.

Prudence walked to the window, and stood looking out into the sunny street. Her voice held some amusement. 'My dear, I take it the question is rather what he will do with us.'

'Can you make head or tail of it?'

'Not I, faith.'

'Ay, you preserve your placidity, don't you?' Robin said.

She laughed. 'What else? If we fall, why then, we must. I see no way of preventing it. Alack, I haven't the trick of coaxing the old gentleman into sense.'

'There is no way. We're treading another of his mazes, and the devil's in it that we've no choice. For myself, if the old gentleman would be a little plain with us I'm willing enough to play this game out. But I would know where I stand. We ply him with questions, and what answer have we? Why, that he's a Tremaine of Barham, forsooth! What to do with a man who can say naught but what is assuredly a lie?'

'I think he believes it,' Prudence remarked, twinkling.

'Of course he believes it! He always believes in his own inventions. I'll swear therein lies his success. Lord, it's a wonderful old gentleman!'

My lady brushed her hand lightly across the table's polished surface. She looked curiously at her young friends. 'But you—you do not believe it?'

'Hardly, ma'am.' Robin shrugged. 'Do you?'

'Me, I know nothing. Would he embark on it, do you think if there were not some truth behind?'

'Ma'am, you've heard him. He belies himself omnipotent.'

'There's the motto.' Prudence spoke reflectively.

'I don't set great store by that. He may have had this in mind many a long day.'

'How?' She turned her head.

'We don't know when he came by these documents he holds,' Robin pointed out. 'As I see it he may have met the real Tremaine any time these forty years. When did Tremaine die? Or if he lives yet when had the old gentleman those papers from him? I believe this may have been deep laid.'

'Ah, so do not I!' Prudence came back into the

room. 'His genius lies in grasping opportunity at a moment's notice. I'll swear this was not in his mind when he swept us into the Rebellion.'

Robin was silent, puzzling over it. Came the page to announce Sir Anthony Fanshawe. Sir Anthony had called to fetch Mr Merriot to ride out past Kensington with him. Prudence went off, and my lady's black eyes twinkled merrily.

'That is a romance, not?' she said.

Robin caught back a sigh. 'I don't see the happy ending, ma'am.' He got up and began to pace the room. 'I wish I saw my way,' he said, pausing. He bit one finger-tip, frowning.

Her ladyship watched him. 'You stand by the *bon papa,* yes?'

'It seems likely. I see no other hope of a fair conclusion. This is to risk all for the slim chance of gaining all. Well, it has ever been our way. I might be off to France, taking Prue with me. That's the safe road. I can fend a path for us both. But it's the end to her romance.'

'And to yours, *mon enfant,*' said her ladyship softly.

'Perhaps. That does not signify so much. I was, after all, born to this game. But Prue's not. She hankers now after the secure life, wedded to the mountain, I suppose. It's a pretty coil.' He resumed his pacing. 'I've thought on all this, ma'am. I don't see the way to compass it, for the mountain's a respectable gentleman, and we—well, to be plain, we're adventurers.

Now comes the old gentleman, in a preposterous guise, and—egad, it's a forlorn hope, but the only one that I can perceive. If he can brave it out—why then, the Honourable Prudence becomes a fitting bride for an even greater man than the great Sir Anthony.'

She nodded. 'That's certain. Me, I do not see so very much to fear.'

'I see a multitude of things, ma'am, and one more clearly than all the rest. He admitted himself there was somewhere a document bearing his name. If I but knew who holds it!' He broke off, and compressed his lips.

'You think you could obtain it, my child?'

There was a confident little laugh. 'Let me have but wind of it!' Robin said.

'I shall see you yet as the heir of Barham,' my lady prophesied, and went off to send out the cards for her next evening party.

Along the road to Kensington Prudence rode by Sir Anthony's side, and talked idly of this and that. Sir Anthony rode a big raw-boned chestnut, and sat his horse well. The brute had tricksy manners, but he seemed to know his master, and responded to the slightest movement of the strong hand on the bridle.

Prudence herself had horsemanship. The bay mare from my lady's stable chose to curvet all across the road, in a playful endeavour to throw her off. She swayed gracefully to the mare's buckings, humoured her a little, and brought her up alongside her chestnut companion.

Sir Anthony sat easily in the saddle, watching her, a hand laid lightly on his hip. 'She's a little fresh,' he remarked.

Prudence leaned forward to pat the mare's neck. 'Playful. There's no vice.'

The mare reared up as though to protest against this reading of her character, and of a sudden all the indolence left Sir Anthony. He bent swiftly forward, and caught the mare's bridle close to the bit before Prudence knew what he would be at. The mare was brought down by a man's iron hand, but her rider sat unshaken.

Now, what possessed the man to do that? 'She doesn't throw me so easily, sir,' Prudence said gently.

'As I see.' Sir Anthony pricked onward. 'In all, you puzzle me, boy.'

Prudence studied the road ahead. 'I do, sir?' she said. 'I don't know why I should.'

The heavy-lidded eyes rested on her profile for a minute. 'Don't you?' said Sir Anthony.

A pulse began to beat rather fast in her throat. She waited.

'You are,' Sir Anthony said, 'a curious mixture. You'd no suspicion of it?'

She laughed. 'None, sir, upon my word.'

'A babe in our midst,' he remarked thoughtfully. 'And yet—not a babe.'

'I told you, sir, that I have been about the world a little.'

'It may be that. Was all this junketting about by yourself, I wonder?'

She was being cross-examined. One must step warily. 'There was usually a friend with me,' she answered indifferently.

'You must have spent a prodigious time touring Europe,' he said pensively.

'I don't know why you should think so, sir. I made the Grand Tour.'

'You must have made it a very extended one to have seen so much,' Sir Anthony pointed out gently.

'You forget, sir, a great part of my life was spent abroad with my parents.'

'Ah, to be sure!' he nodded. 'No doubt many of your experiences were gained then.'

'Yes, Sir Anthony.'

There was a slight pause. The gentleman was looking straight between his horse's ears. 'What a very tender age at which to have seen so much!' he remarked blandly.

The mare bounded forward under a spur incautiously driven home. 'Sir,' said Prudence, 'for some reason I don't guess you seem to hold me in suspicion.' It was a daring move, but she could see no other.

Up went the straight brows, in sleepy surprise. 'Not at all, my dear boy. Why should I?'

'I have no notion, sir.'

They rode on in silence for a little while. 'Shall we have the pleasure of seeing your respected father in town?' inquired the tiresome gentleman.

'I believe not, sir.'

'Why, I am sorry,' said Sir Anthony. 'I confess I have an ambition to meet the begetter of so worldly wise a youth.'

'No doubt my father would surprise you, sir,' said Prudence, with truth. 'It's a remarkable old gentleman.'

'No doubt he would,' agreed Fanshawe. 'I find that life is full of surprises.'

For a moment grey eyes met grey. 'The sudden appearance of the lost Viscount, for instance,' said Prudence lightly.

'Precisely. And the no less sudden appearance of the Pretender not so long back.'

So that was the gist of the matter, was it? Prudence drew in her breath.

The lazy voice continued. 'And—when one thinks of it—the sudden appearance of the Merriots.'

'Oh, that! Sudden to you, I make no doubt, but believe me it was not sudden to us. My sister was in a fever of anticipation for weeks before.'

The danger point seemed to be past. Sir Anthony preserved a thoughtful silence.

'You did not go down to your house at Wych End after all, sir,' remarked Prudence at length.

'No, little man. I changed my mind since your company was denied me.'

She flushed, and looked up frankly. 'I wonder that you should so greatly desire my company, Sir Anthony.'

He stroked the chestnut's neck with the butt of his whip, and smiled a little. 'Do you?' he said, and turned his head. 'Now why?'

Faith, when he let one see them the gentleman had most understanding eyes.

'Well, sir'—Prudence looked demure—'I have a notion you think me an escaped rebel.'

'And if you were,' said Sir Anthony, 'must I necessarily deny you my friendship?'

'I believe you to be a good Whig, sir.'

'I hope so, little man.'

'I took no part in the late Rebellion, sir.'

'I have not accused you of it, my dear boy.'

The horses dropped to a walk. 'But if I had, Sir Anthony.... What then?'

'You might still rest assured of my friendship.'

There was a warm feeling about her heart, but he did not know the full sum of it, alack.

'You are very kind, Sir Anthony—to an unknown youth.'

'I believe I remarked to you once that I have an odd liking for you, little man. One of these strange twists in one's affections for which there is no accounting.

If I can serve you at any time I desire you will let me know it.'

'I have to thank you, sir.' She could find no other words.

'You may perhaps have noticed, my dear boy, that my friends call me Tony,' he said.

She bent to fiddle with her stirrup leather, and her reply was somewhat inarticulate. When she sat straight again in the saddle she showed a heightened colour, but it might have been due to the stooping posture.

CHAPTER THIRTEEN

Encounter at White's

FAR FROM EXHIBITING a disposition to seek any sort of seclusion, such as might be supposed to become a gentleman waiting upon so large a claim, the new Lord Barham showed himself abroad whenever opportunity presented itself. It was quite impossible for anyone living in polite Society to be long ignorant of his lordship's existence: he was a most prominent gentleman. His stature might lack something in height, for he was after all but a small man, but this was more than compensated for by the overwhelming personality of the man. He had but to enter a room for every eye to turn involuntarily in his direction. It was not in his dress that this distinctiveness lay, though that was always gorgeous; it was not even in his carriage, however haughty that might be. It was thought to lie in the arresting quality of his eyes: if he looked at one, one was straightway conscious of no little magnetism.

Discussion concerning him was rife; his children had to listen to all manner of conjectures and rumours, and derived therefrom some amusement, and some alarm as well.

He had his supporters; in the ranks of the ladies they were numberless. Who, pray, could like that coarse Rensley? The ladies knew nothing of claims, or legal matters, but they were sure this gentleman had all the air of a great man, and was far more fitted to be a Viscount than that odious Rensley.

Amongst the men opinions were varied. There were those who said he had the look of the Tremaines, and there were others who could see no resemblance. Foremost of these was old Mr Fontenoy, who had some recollection of the lost Tremaine as a boy. He said that the lad he had known was a frank, impetuous youth, and could by no means have developed into the incorrigible actor this fellow showed himself to be.

But opposed to Mr Fontenoy stood my Lord Clevedale, that jovial peer, who claimed also to have known young Tremaine. He could very easily imagine that the hotheaded boy might easily change into the present figure as the years went by. He claimed old acquaintance with Lord Barham, and was accepted with rapture. To be sure, the Viscount seemed to remember very little of those bygone days, but then my Lord Clevedale's memory was also a trifle hazy. It was all so many years ago—thirty at least, his lordship believed, for young Tremaine had run off to the Continent when he was scarce a day more than eighteen.

No one set much store by Mr Rensley's stout refusal

to acknowledge his supposed cousin. Naturally Rensley would fight. The trouble was to know how to address poor Rensley. One could not have two Viscounts of the same name, but until the lawyers had done ferreting out information, and quibbling over documents the new lord had no claim to any title at all, and Rensley might continue to hold it, as he held the estates and the houses. Yet for some reason—it must again lie in that magnetic eye—the newcomer was everywhere addressed as Lord Barham, while his less forceful relative sank back into undistinguished esquiredom.

It was thought to augur well for the authenticity of my lord's claim that he made no demand on the estate. An impostor, so it was argued, would have been sure to try to get money advanced him from the lawyers. But his lordship had put forward no such suggestion; nor did he show any desire to oust Rensley from the town house in Grosvenor Square until all should be satisfactorily proved. The ladies thought this showed a sweet disposition in the old gentleman; the gentlemen wagged solemn heads, and did not know what to make of it.

When my lord made his stately way in at the sacred portals of White's club there were one or two gentlemen muttered darkly of effrontery. But the mutterings died down; my lord became a member of the club. No one quite knew the man responsible for this; it was Sir Anthony Fanshawe who said with a deep chuckle that he believed they might see my lord's proposer in my lord himself. Several gentlemen were quite indignant when the full force of this suggestion dawned on them, but there was no movement made to eject his lordship. He was accepted, perforce, and it had to be admitted that in spite of some foreign extravagancies of manner, his *ton* was all that it should be, and his general bearing a fine mixture of stateliness and affability.

But there was no denying the man was a puzzle. No one could remember ever to have heard him announce, pointblank, that he was in very truth what he claimed to be. It was recollected that naturally no one cared to ask him this ticklish question, and this was thought by some to extenuate this omission on his part. But others felt that an honest claimant should have an open way with him. Instead of offering any proof to Rensley, and the world at large, of his identity he seemed content to remain an enigma until the lawyers should have done. Lord Clevedale considered this attitude to be a point in the old gentleman's favour, but Mr Fontenoy shook his head, and said it was not at all in keeping with the character of young Tremaine.

There was some discussion also as to the ticklish point of my lord's social position while the matter stood in abeyance, but in the end it was decided, no one quite knew how, that he was to be received. In this the ladies may have had something to say, for they frankly doted on his lordship. So the old gentleman paraded the town, and became immersed in social engagements. His children met him almost every day at some house or other, and it was observed that his lordship was developing quite an affection for these young guests of his dear friend, Lady Lowestoft.

Sir Anthony saw fit to twit Prudence on the growing intimacy, one late afternoon at White's. They were standing in the card-room, Sir Anthony but just come in, and Prudence having risen from a faro table.

She had her answer ready. 'Oh, it's quite an amusing old *roué*!' she said, with a startling lack of respect for so near a relative. 'He comes to visit my lady, and ogles my poor Kate.'

'And how does Miss Merriot take that?' inquired Sir Anthony, nodding across the room to Mr Belfort.

'With equanimity, sir. I tell her she's like to lose her heart to the old gentleman. Pray, is he married, do you know?'

'I should have thought you would be more likely to have the answer to that,' was the unexpected rejoinder.

'I, sir?'

'My Lady Lowestoft should know, surely,' said Sir Anthony in mild surprise.

She bit her lip. Fool, to make so stupid a slip! A sure sign her nerves were not so steady as they had been. She proceeded to smooth over the slip. 'Oh, we know he had a wife once,' she said. 'But she has been dead these many years. He says nothing of a fresh marriage, but I believe he does not tell my lady all.'

There was a movement behind them. They stood a little in front of the door, and they turned now to see my Lord Barham came in on the arm of Lord March.

'Ah, my dear Fanshawe!' said the old gentleman. 'And my young friend Peter Merriot! You behold me fresh from the fatigues of a full hour with my perruquier.' He put up his arm, and surveyed the room through it. 'Now where, where is my good friend Clevedale?'

Clevedale himself came up. 'Well, Barham, what's this? You're half an hour late, and here am I waiting on you.'

My lord flung up his hands. 'The perruquier! I crave ten thousand pardons, my dear Thomas! But the exigencies of the perruquier! Had it been anything else in the world the claims of picquet had held me adamant. But adamant, my dear Thomas! My tailor, even, I would despatch to the devil. But a perruquier! You absolve me: you have to absolve me!'

Clevedale laughed. 'Gad, what foppery! Oh, I hold you excused. God send I never see you bald. Come off to my table. I've held it in the teeth of Molyneux this half-hour.' He bore my lord off to a place near the window.

'I wonder, doesn't he find that manner a thought fatiguing to maintain?' said Sir Anthony meditatively.

'Clevedale?' Prudence looked inquiringly.

'No, my innocent: the new Viscount.'

Mr Belfort came over to them. 'Tony, here's Dev-

ereux wants to play at lansquenet, and all the world's
bent on faro. Will you and Merriot join us? The devil's
in Devereux that naught else will do for him. But the
poor fellow's feeling plaguily low to-day: he's had bad
news, y'know.' Mr Belfort nodded profoundly. 'One
must try to cheer him, so I'm pledged to find a four
for lansquenet. Always plays lansquenet when he's in
trouble, does Devereux.'

'Pray, what's the nature of his trouble?' Prudence
asked solicitously.

'Oh, cursed bad news, my boy! That old aunt of his
from whom he has expectations has rallied, and they
say she'll last another ten years. Poor old Devereux,
y'know! Must try and raise his spirits.'

So with this praiseworthy intention they went to
play lansquenet with Mr Devereux.

There entered a few minutes later Rensley, in company with his friend Mr Markham. Mr Markham
looked heated; Mr Rensley was scowling. The truth
was he had been somewhat testy with his satellite, and
there had been a slight altercation. Mr Rensley refused
curtly an invitation to join a faro party, on the score
of his being promised to Markham. The pair sat down
to picquet at a table close to Mr Belfort's.

It fell to Mr Markham to deal, while Rensley looked
sourly round the room. His glance fell upon my Lord
Barham, likewise engaged on picquet. He uttered a
strong expletive beneath his breath, and glared angrily.
My lord, catching sight of him, waved a white hand,

which salutation Mr Rensley did not return. 'Damn the fellow, he's no more my cousin than you are!' he said, addressing Mr Markham.

Mr Markham was still feeling ruffled. Rensley was always quick of temper, and one bore outbursts of anger from a rich viscount. But if Rensley was going to lose his wealth and his title his friend Markham had no intention of bearing his ill-humour with complacency. 'Gad, man, let be!' he said shortly. 'You've said little else for the past hour. Do you take all five cards?'

Rensley sorted his hand rather sullenly, and took time over his discard. A well-known voice smote Mr Markham's ears: 'Don't despair, Devereux! She may die of an apoplexy yet!'

Mr Markham looked sharply round, and found that Mr Merriot was seated close at hand. He bowed politely, but his brow was black as he faced Rensley again.

Rensley saw, and smiled disagreeably. 'Ay, the young sprig from the country's here, Gregory. Ecod, I believe the lad's worsted you in some encounter! Eh! man? Now what did he do to you, I wonder?'

'That puppy!' Mr Markham flushed. 'I could break him across my knee!'

'Well, why don't you?' asked Rensley. 'You talk a deal, the Lord knows!'

Markham laid down his cards. 'Not to you for much longer, sir, I warn you!' he said.

'Oh, play to my lead, man, play to my lead! Gad, but you'll admit you'd try the patience of a saint with your prating of having seen that—that impostor somewhere, and not knowing where! Why can't you think?'

My Lord Barham rose from his table across the room, and stood for a moment talking to March. One or two men gathered around them, after a moment a dice-box was produced, and March cast the dice on the table. Heads were bent over it; there was a laugh, and a murmur of speech, and my Lord Barham swept up the dice.

Mr Markham chanced that moment to look up. He saw my lord shake back his ruffles, and with eyes growing gradually wider he saw him throw the dice with a curious flick of the wrist.

Mr Markham was in the act of dealing, but his hand with three cards in it stayed poised in mid-air, and he continued to stare across at my lord, his jaw slightly dropped.

'What's to do now?' demanded Rensley. 'Gad, have you remembered,' he added eagerly.

'That man—why, fiend seize it, he's no more than a common gamester! Of course I know him! Thunder and turf, he's no viscount. He used to keep a gaming-house in Munich! The instant he cast the dice it all came back to me. Know him! I've played in his house a dozen times.'

It seemed the dice had been cast for some special stake only. My lord was coming slowly across the

room with March and Clevedale, laughing gently at
something March said in his ear. He paused a moment
by the lansquenet table, and complimented Sir Anthony on his play. 'So few people nowadays understand the art!' he sighed. His smiling glance fell on
Rensley's face. He came to the other table, still leaning
on Clevedale's arm. 'My cousin! I salute you!' he said.

Mr Rensley's chair scraped along the boards as he
sprang up. 'Damn it, don't call me cousin!' he said
loudly. 'You're no more than a cursed gamester!'

There fell a sudden hush, for Rensley's voice carried through the room. Heads were turned; there followed a buzz of whispering. One of his companions
fell a little away from my Lord Barham. My lord continued to smile. 'Oh!' he said. 'Who told you that?'

Markham put down the pack of cards. 'I've visited
the gaming-house you used to keep in Munich,' he
said.

My lord looked at him with interest. The whole
room awaited breathlessly his reply. It came as a complete surprise to every man there. 'Then that must have
been where I met you!' he said in the tone of one
making an agreeable discovery. 'I thought your face
familiar from the first.'

At the lansquenet table Sir Anthony gave a low
laugh. 'Faith, I begin to have a liking for the old gentleman!' he said.

'You admit it, do you?' Mr Rensley felt his words
fall lamely upon expectant ears.

'Admit what?' said my lord, puzzled.

'Why—damme, that you've kept a common gaming-house!'

My lord's hand was raised. 'No!' he said emphatically, and a sigh went round the room. His next words dispelled relief. 'Never in all my life have I kept anything that was common! You insult me by the suggestion.'

There was a low ripple of laughter. People were gathering about that corner of the room, eager to hear what might be the issue.

'No use to play with words, fellow. That won't serve,' Rensley cried angrily. 'Have you kept a gaming-house?'

The old gentleman took snuff. 'I have kept at least a dozen, my dear Rensley,' he said, with perfect composure. He looked again towards Mr Markham. 'I am not entirely satisfied,' he mused. 'Are you sure you never had lessons in fencing from me, sir?'

There was a gasp. All play was at an end in the card-room. My Lord March burst out laughing. 'Gad, Barham, have you been a fencing-master, too?' he exclaimed.

The old gentleman shut his gold snuff-box with a snap. 'My dear March,' he said haughtily, 'there is nothing I have not been!' He looked again at Mr Markham. 'Are you quite sure I did not give you lessons in fencing? Let me think a moment! Yes, I had an establishment in Rome once, and—yes, yes, another in Turin!'

'It's quite possible, no doubt,' sneered Mr Markham. 'I don't trouble to remember all my fencing instructors.'

'Then of a certainty you are not a pupil of mine,' said my lord. 'Me you could never forget. For those whom I taught are masters of fence. It goes without saying. I am incomparable. I have no equal in the art!'

Again March broke in. 'I'd give something to hear the story of your life, Barham!' he said, hugely entertained.

Rensley flushed. 'His name's not Barham!' he said furiously. 'He's the impostor I always said he was!'

March froze to instant haughtiness. 'He has at least the advantage of you in the matter of good manners, Rensley,' he said.

Public opinion veered round in favour of the old gentleman.

'It's very, very deplorable,' Mr Devereux said, with a mournful shake of the head. 'But he might be all these damned bourgeois things and still remain Tremaine of Barham.'

'You're pleased to give him countenance, my lord, but you shall see him exposed!' Rensley snapped.

'But expose me!' cried the old gentleman, and threw wide his arms. 'I am here to answer you. Who then am I?'

'Good God, am I to know who you are?' exclaimed

Rensley. 'But you are not Tremaine! Why, you couldn't tell me a thing about the family that's not known to the whole world!'

'Ay, that's a challenge. He must answer that!' whispered Sir Raymond Orton.

'I can at least tell you, cousin, that a portrait of me hangs in the pink salon at Barham. A very damnable likeness of me as a child, taken with my late lamented brother,' said my lord softly.

'A hit!' Mr Belfort confided to Prudence. 'That's a hit!'

She sat in an attitude of negligent attention, an arm flung over the back of the chair, and her calm face inscrutable. She nodded, and was conscious of Fanshawe's eyes upon her.

Rensley banged his fist down on the table. 'It's not the pink salon!' he declared. 'There is no pink salon!'

Mr Belfort was of the opinion that this was a bad check.

'In my day,' said his lordship, undisturbed, 'it was pink.'

'Faugh, what do you know of it? You're trying to brazen it out with a bare-faced lie!'

Mr Fontenoy spoke grudgingly. 'There was a pink salon,' he said. 'Lady Barham used it.'

My lord swept round to face him. 'Ah, you remember then?' he said eagerly. 'A pink salon in the west wing! There was an oriole window, and my mother's broidery table set there!' He became rapt in reminiscences.

This produced a sensation. Mr Belfort thought the old gentleman scored a decided hit there.

Rensley was discomfited for a moment, but recovered. 'Oh, you've been in the house in your youth! That's all there is to that. You were a groom there, I dare swear, and you got into the house!'

Mr Belfort wagged a solemn head. 'Ay, that's a possibility, y'know.'

My lord's eyes glinted. Very sweet was his voice, dangerously sweet. 'It's more than you can claim to have done, my dear cousin,' he said gently. 'I'll swear you never set foot in it till my brother died!'

Rensley's jaw dropped; he grew purple in the face. 'Damn your impudence!' he spluttered.

Lord March interposed. 'Enough of that. Did you set foot in it, Rensley?'

The old gentleman was indignant. 'Certainly he did not!' he said, before Rensley could reply. 'There was never a Rensley dared show his face on our land! What had *we* to do with them?' Almost he snorted.

His daughter's eyes widened a little; Mr Belfort sniggered.

Rensley bit back a hot answer. Came a look of cunning into his face. 'So you never met me when we were boys, my Lord Barham?' he said.

'Only once,' said my lord. He dwelt lovingly on a

pleasant memory. 'How hard I punched your nose then,' he said dreamily.

There was a roar of laughter, hastily suppressed. Mr Rensley strode to the door. 'Don't think I've done with you, my fine gentleman!' he said savagely, and slammed out of the room.

The old gentleman smiled affectionately upon the assembled company. 'Very like an encounter I had once with a Margrave,' he said pensively. 'I was acting as one of his lackeys at the time.'

'Take an' 'ouns, a *lackey*?' gasped Clevedale.

'Certainly,' said my lord, with some hauteur. 'Why not? There was a lady in the case.' He smoothed a wrinkle from his satin sleeve. 'She was the Margrave's mistress,' he remarked.

Quite a number of people drew nearer. March thrust his arm in my lord's, and walked away with him. 'Let's hear that tale, Barham,' he said. 'Which Margrave?'

CHAPTER FOURTEEN

My Lord Barham becomes mysterious

THE OLD GENTLEMAN was left undoubtedly a victor; there could be no gainsaying it. Poor Rensley came off badly from a battle of wits. The world shook its head sadly over the startling disclosures of my lord's past history, but it was prepared to look indulgently on those shocking lapses. Had his lordship betrayed only the faintest sign of discomfiture, shown the slightest shame, the world might have decided to turn a cold shoulder on him. But my lord was far from showing either shame or discomfiture. So far, indeed, that his attitude was one of pride in his chequered career. He carried all off with a high hand. He said majestically that there was nothing he had not done, and such was the power of the man's eye that the world began to perceive clearly that he had nothing at all to be ashamed of.

There was also the attitude of my Lord March to be considered. March seemed to be in no doubt of the old gentleman's identity, and there were few who cared to set themselves up in opposition to my lord.

If the newcomer was good enough for March, he was certainly good enough for the rest of the world, but there were one or two far-seeing people who began to realise that the new viscount had wormed himself into the graces of society so completely, and so cleverly that it would be quite extraordinarily difficult (in the event of his claim falling to earth) to turn him out without loss of dignity to oneself.

His lordship made not the smallest attempt to conceal his lamentable past: his attitude gave one to understand that whatever he chose to do must of necessity become straightway a creditable performance. In fact, not the lowest of vocations could demean this grand gentleman.

It was considered then that to be sure, if one had the good fortune to be born a Tremaine one might do most things with impunity. Certainly it was a pity to have dragged that noble name in the dust, but after all one had to take into account that the old gentleman had been cast off penniless when little more than a boy. That must stand for his excuse.

As for Rensley, his attack had been ill-judged, and he had taken many shrewder blows than he had dealt. Not a doubt of it that March was right when he said that the old gentleman had the advantage of him in good manners. A number of people remembered that they had said at the outset that there was very little breeding to Rensley, cousin to the Tremaines though he might be. Viscount or no viscount, the old gentleman had great polish, and he showed himself perfectly at ease in the politest of company.

My lord had something to say on the matter himself when he took a dish of Bohea with my Lady Lowestoft next day. He smiled benevolently upon his daughter, leaning over the back of a couch, and said triumphantly: 'You saw me! You, my daughter, had the privilege of seeing a master mind at work! I felicitate you.'

Prudence gave her deep chuckle. 'I knew a few moments' dread, sir, I confess.'

He brushed that aside. 'Never again make that mistake. I am invincible. Observe the subtlety of my methods! I achieve a miracle.'

My lady gave a piece of angel cake to the monkey nestling at her feet. 'You told them, then, *mon cher*? You admitted the past?'

'They hung on my lips,' his lordship said dramatically. 'They waited breathlessly to hear what I would say. As always I became the centre, the dominating presence.'

My lady twinkled. 'And you said?' she prompted.

'I said, Thérèse, that I had kept a dozen gaming-houses. No other man alive would have dared. But I swayed them—I, Tremaine of Barham!' His admiration of the deed held him silent for a moment, but he went on. 'They perceived that I could play the lackey and still keep my prestige. It is true! It is very true.'

My lady gasped. 'And they condoned it? They sup-
ported you?'

'It was not for them to condone what Tremaine
might choose to do,' said my lord, with hauteur. 'They
applaud me now. I achieve the impossible.'

'He *is* a great man,' my lady said to Prudence. 'You
must admit it.'

'Oh, I do, ma'am, believe me.'

My lord tapped the lid of his snuff-box with one
polished finger-nail. 'Even that large gentleman, that
ponderous baronet, that sleepy-eyed Sir Anthony Fanshawe, who looked askance at me—even he concedes
me admiration. I win all to my side. It could not be
otherwise.'

'Indeed, sir, he said he had begun to conceive a
liking for you,' nodded Prudence.

My lord accepted this with a gracious inclination of
the head.

His daughter continued with a hint of seriousness in
her tone. 'Yet I think you would be well advised, sir,
not to seek too great an intimacy with that same large
gentleman.'

'My Prudence, it is he, and all the rest, shall seek
intimacy with me,' his lordship said majestically.

'That's as maybe, sir, but I have some friendship
with Sir Anthony, and I say beware!'

He shook his head, but it was more in sorrow than
in anger. 'Still you do not sufficiently appreciate me,'
he said.

'It's conceivable, sir, you don't sufficiently appreciate the large gentleman.'

My lady smiled. 'Ah, my cabbage, you have a too great opinion of *ce gros* Sir Anthony! He sees no further than the end of his nose.'

'You're mistaken, ma'am. He sees more than the rest of them put together.' She hesitated. 'He watches me. That I know. Something he suspects: not much, but a little.'

My lady looked incredulous. 'Not you, my child? But no!'

'Oh, not that! Well, who lives may learn. But I've warned you, sir.'

'The little Prudence!' My lord smiled affably. 'So cautious!'

'You named me Prudence, sir.'

He was inclined to suspect a hitherto unperceived foresight in himself. 'And wisely! A premonition. I must surely have known.'

'But to return, *mon ami*!' My lady clasped her hands in her lap. 'Society adopts you, then, in spite of all?'

'Again you observe the subtlety of my methods! Consider, my Thérèse! Consider how I become one of the select circle! It is fitting. I am at last in my proper milieu.' He looked kindly at his daughter. 'I shall carry you with me, my child. Have no fear. You shall be established—you and Robin.' He became aware of Robin's absence. 'But where is my son? Where is the beautiful Miss Merriot?' he demanded.

'The rogue's gone off to sit with his lady love,' answered Prudence.

He looked incredulous. 'You tell me he entrusts his secret to a woman? No, no, do not say so, my daughter! Robin is my son, and he has sense—a little.'

'I don't say it, sir. The lady knows naught. Robin— heigh ho, he must needs fall for a pair of brown eyes!' She told him of the encounter with Miss Letty and Mr Markham on the road to Gretna Green.

He was pleased to approve. 'I embrace you, my child. The hilt to the chin! Myself or Robin taught you that trick, You do me credit, *enfin!* I permit myself to take pride in you. Who is the lady? Eh, but the little Robin inherits something of my disposition!'

'It's a Miss Grayson, sir, and an heiress as I believe. A pretty brown-eyed chit.'

The old gentleman's eyes became intent. 'Grayson?' he repeated. 'Grayson, my daughter?'

'Do you know the name, sir?'

He put the tips of his fingers together and gazed abstractedly before him. There was no reading what lay in his mind. 'Grayson!' he said softly.

'You know something of Sir Humphrey, sir?'

His remarkable eyes travelled to her face. 'My child, there are few people of whom I do not know something,' he announced, and took his stately leave of them.

Prudence saw no necessity to mention the matter to her brother, but to John, whom she found arranging pots of powder and paint in Robin's chamber, she said: 'The old gentleman's mysterious over Miss Grayson, John. Is Sir Humphrey a friend of his boyhood?'

John could not take it upon himself to answer.

'Ay, you know more than you'll admit, don't you?' said Prudence.

John set down one of the pots with a snap. 'I'll say this, Miss Prue: I don't understand the game he's playing now!'

'Why, when have any of us understood him?'

The man compressed his lips, and seemed to regret his outburst. He could vouchsafe no more.

Robin came in a while later, a vision in cherry stripes, and a lace fichu. 'The Markham hangs about Letty still,' he said abruptly. 'She meets him at houses here and there. I'm to gather he tries to ingratiate himself once more.'

Prudence raised her brows. 'She's ill-watched then,' she said.

'As to that, the aunt plays euchre, and it's supposed none but the most reputable have admission to these private parties. He's all conciliation from what she says.'

'Lord, has she a mind to play the fool again?'

Robin looked scornful. 'Oh, is it a jest?'

'One of your own, child. I take a leaf from your book.' She laughed. 'Or does she dream of the black domino?'

'God knows. The Markham has no hope of her now.'

'A persistent gentleman, faith.'

'I take it the man goes in danger of a debtor's prison. He's deeply involved, as I hear, but was used to hang upon Rensley. Now, if the old gentleman ousts Rensley, he'll have need of a fresh patron, or a rich bride. It's a dangerous dog.'

He had set his finger on the very marrow of it. Mr Markham saw himself in some need of relief. The turf played him false, and the cards went badly. It seemed to him that his noble friend's sun was setting fast: Mr Rensley had that day been informed by a grave man of law that no fault could be found with my Lord Barham's papers. If it could not be proved that my lord had stolen them from the real owner he must stand acknowledged Tremaine of Barham. There was, then, an end to a profitable friendship. Mr Markham had small hope of a happy issue. Mr Rensley, in a moment of impetuosity, had named the sum he would be glad to give the man who should prove my lord an impostor, but although Mr Markham would be willing to perform that office for him he could not at present see the means of doing it.

His recollection of the gaming-house at Munich had led nowhere. Mr Rensley had had some biting words to say of it. Mr Rensley was in a very bad temper over the whole affair, and his manner to his friend was such that Mr Markham began to conceive a positive dislike for him.

CHAPTER FIFTEEN

Challenge to Mr Merriot

THERE WAS NO means of telling what John, that stolid creature, made of the situation. His young master and mistress suspected him of being deeper in the old gentleman's secrets than they were, but he had never a word to say on the matter. When my lord had made his first startling appearance they came home and told him of it, and awaited some show of surprise. It was not forthcoming. John gave a grunt and said that he had doubted but that the old gentleman would arrive soon. As to the manner of his arrival, John seemed to think it natural enough, and he never failed thereafter to give my lord his title. The old gentleman had greeted him with an affectionate smile, and a hand carelessly outflung. John had looked beneath his brows and said gruffly that the affair of Master Robin must be seen to. He further volunteered the opinion that Robin's present guise was unseemly. As for Miss Prue, the sooner she was got out of this coil the better. John had a grim way with him, but they had none of them the need ever to stand in doubt of his devotion.

Nothing could abate the supreme belief in himself that my lord held, but certainly he used fewer extravagancies with his servant than with his children, and would condescend to listen to John's disapproving words. But not even John could hope to make much impression on that magnificent mind. My lord waved a hand, and promised ultimate success.

'You're playing a game I don't understand, my lord,' John said severely. 'It's more of your play-acting, for sure, but why you should do it, sir, I can't see.'

'I plan a great *coup*,' my lord assured him. 'There must never be aught crude in my actions, John. There has never been. I go warily, and I contrive. Oh, but I contrive a *tour de force!* Continue to watch over my children!'

'It's well there's someone to do it, my lord,' said John. 'For it's little care of them you'd be taking. Masquerades and the like!'

'My John, you are foolish. You lack understanding. My wing is spread over the children, as ever.'

'There's this Miss Grayson,' John continued, entirely ignoring his lordship. 'Master Robin must needs set his fancy on her. I'd a word or two with Sir Humphrey's man, and it's little hope there is that he'd countenance such a marriage.'

The old gentleman half closed his eyes. 'He shall countenance it, John. If I were to fail in my claim, which is not possible, he should countenance it. You shall all of you dance to my piping.' He smiled with delight at the thought. In some things he had the mind of a child.

'There's one that won't dance to your piping, my lord,' was John's parting shot. 'And that's Miss Prue's sleepy gentleman!'

My lord wasted as much as three minutes on the consideration of this announcement, but arrived at the conclusion that there could be no truth in it. He could never be got to doubt his own powers.

It was understood in polite circles that Mr Rensley had had disturbing news from his lawyers regarding the claim. It was soon bruited abroad that these men thought some inquiry should be made into his lordship's past before he should be positively declared Tremaine of Barham. My lord seemed to be quite content with this decision. He smiled, and put his finger-tips together as his habit was, and begged the lawyers to make what enquiries they would. Meanwhile he continued to parade the town.

Mr Rensley was soon infuriated to find that his supposed cousin's past was hidden in an obscurity there seemed to be no hope of piercing. Inquiries led precisely nowhere. It was true that a Mr Challoner had once kept a gaming-house in Munich, and it was believed he had gone thence to Rome. But there could be found no trace of him in that ancient city. Indeed, how should there be? Had these seekers after truth mentioned the name of a German baron who had stayed in Rome some years ago they might have learned something of considerable interest from those who remembered that remarkable gentleman. But the seekers, unfortunately, had never heard of the baron, and they were forced to abandon the search for truth.

My lord was understood now to have two children. He spoke of them enthusiastically upon all occasions. Sir Anthony, hearing him, said humorously: 'It seems you are to be congratulated, sir.'

'You have said it!' His lordship turned his compelling gaze upon the immovable large gentleman. 'My daughter—my Prudence! A Venus!' He looked soulful. 'I say it who should not. She favours her mother, my poor Maria. A statue carved in ivory and rose! A goddess, with a voice of gold! Soon you shall see her,' he promised.

'Egad, we're agog to, sir!' said Mr Molyneux, smothering a grin. 'And is your son thus godlike too?'

'My little Robin!' sighed his lordship. 'He has not the height for it, alack! But he is well enough. To see him in the duello is to say he is incomparable. I pine to clasp them to me once more.'

'And—if one is permitted to ask,' said Sir Anthony, observing a speck of dust on his great cuff through a levelling quizzing-glass. 'Where are these two paragons?'

'It is permitted. They stay with a friend in France. I send for them when this business is at an end.'

'Did you ever see or hear the like?' demanded Sir Raymond Orton when the old gentleman had gone.

'A most remarkable man,' said Sir Anthony, and yawned behind his scented handkerchief.

Prudence herself, encountering my lord at Lady Elton's rout one evening, was informed that she too should have the felicity of meeting his daughter. She bowed politely, and professed herself to be enchanted by the prospect.

A new piece of information was very soon passed from mouth to mouth. It appeared that no one could discover whence my lord had sprung when he came to make his claim. It had been supposed that he came from France, but no trace of him could be found either at Calais or on the packet boat. He seemed to have sprung up out of the earth in a manner most mysterious, and he could not be identified with any traveller from France for weeks past.

It was Mr Devereux who conceived the brilliant notion that my lord had not been in France at all, but even this flash of insight failed to lead anywhere.

Prudence, remembering past traffickings, guessed that my lord had been a passenger on one of those crafts that carefully avoid all ports and King's ships, but put into land in odd out-of-the-way coves under cover of night. But this she kept to herself.

Mr Devereux begged her to say whether or no she credited my lord's claim. She laughed, and tapped her riding whip against her boot. 'Why, sir, it's not for me to hazard an opinion. But it seems to me that his lordship was born to the part.'

'True, very true,' nodded Mr Devereux. 'Charles was saying only this moment he has more the manner of it than our friend Rensley.'

'He could scarcely have less,' said Prudence dryly.

There was a heavy footstep behind her. By an evil chance Mr Rensley had entered the room at that instant, and was bearing down upon the group by the fire. He came fresh from a gloomy interview with his lawyer; he was conscious that everywhere his chances were being discussed. And now he entered White's to hear a young upstart from the country pass disparaging remarks upon himself. He strode therefore straight up to Prudence, and with a look in his eyes not at all pleasant, rapped out: 'Who could not have less of what, my fine sir?'

It was evident that Rensley had heard all. Mr Devereux coughed and gazed at the ceiling, reflecting that it was like Rensley to choose a suckling for his prey.

Prudence turned a little to face Mr Rensley. There was danger confronting her, as well she knew. She said quietly: 'I spoke to Mr Devereux, sir, I believe.'

'Your words were not meant for my ears I make no doubt,' said Rensley evilly.

Prudence bowed. 'You apprehend the matter correctly, sir.'

There was a certain air of tense expectation in the

room. Prudence felt that she was on her trial. God
knew how it would end!

Mr Rensley might well let be now. He looked sullenly at Prudence, and thought that he heard a whisper
in the group behind her. There had been too much
whispering of late; very badly did Mr Rensley want to
avenge himself on someone. He was not ill pleased to
take Prudence for a scapegoat. This young ruffler gave
himself insufferable airs: it was time he was taught a
lesson. Mr Rensley spoke more offensively still. 'I see,
Mr Merriot, that you don't care to repeat your words.'

There fell a sudden stillness. 'I do not, Mr Rensley.'

'On what grounds, Mr Merriot, I wonder?'

'On the grounds, Mr Rensley, of good manners.'

Rensley flushed. 'In which you think me lacking,
eh?'

'I have not told you so, sir.'

'And you don't think it?'

There was a slight pause. Prudence realised, dis-
mayed, that the group behind her was awaiting curiously her challenge. Too conciliate this angry, red-
faced man, meant the loss of every man's good
opinion; in a word, it meant social ostracism. A challenge was offered, and it seemed it must be accepted.
Pride could not be swallowed. She spoke deliberately.
'That question, Mr Rensley, I prefer to leave unan-
swered.'

'Afraid, eh?'

Egad, was she afraid? She thought she was too

much her father's daughter. A cold anger took her in
its hold; she looked Rensley full between the eyes.
'You become insulting, sir. I take leave to tell you,
since you will have it, that your manners belong to
the taproom.'

It was out, and did she regret it? She became aware
of Mr Belfort at her elbow, and was conscious of the
approval of him and of the others in the circle. No,
come what might, the thing had to be, and she regretted nothing.

Mr Rensley flushed darker still. Sure, the man
would have an apoplexy one of these days. 'I shall
send my friends to wait upon yours, Mr Merriot.'

'Certainly, sir.' She looked towards Mr Belfort, who
nodded encouragingly. Mr Devereux smiled wearily,
and stepped forward a pace, 'Mr Belfort will act for
me, and Mr Devereux,' she smiled, and turned to re-
sume her conversation with them.

Mr Rensley bowed stiffly and went out. Belfort
clapped Prudence on the shoulder. 'Well said, my
boy!' he declared. 'I knew you'd never swallow that!
Gad, it's a good six months since I've acted for anyone. We'll see some sport now!'

Prudence, her anger evaporating fast, could have
found another name for it. 'I don't desire this to come
to my sister's ears, Charles,' she said. 'I needn't warn
you, I suppose.'

'Oh, not a word, my dear Merriot, trust me!' promised Mr Belfort. 'He'll name Markham and Jessup his

seconds, I dare swear. You'll choose swords, I take it?
We'll have the whole affair fixed up as snug and quiet
as you please.'

Mr Molyneux spoke disapproval. 'Rensley must
have taken leave of his senses,' he said in an undertone
to Sir Raymond Orton. 'A man of his years to challenge a boy to fight! It's child murder!'

'Oh, it won't come to that, Molyneux,' was Sir Raymond's comfortable belief. 'He'll pink him easily
enough, and Merriot will lie up for a week or so. Rensley knows better than to make it a killing matter.
People are getting damned strict over these duels, you
know.'

It was Prudence's own belief as she walked back to
Arlington Street: she had not much fear of death, but
the thing as it stood was bad enough. It was true she
had considerable knowledge of sword-play, but she
knew very well that it was one thing to play with foils
and quite another to fight in good earnest a man who
was one's declared enemy.

He was a strong man too, by the looks of him.
Maybe she might have something of an advantage in
the matter of quickness; sure, she had been taught a
trick or two not many knew. The affair was not hopeless, she believed, but she admitted she had small relish for it.

One might tell Robin, of course. Ay, and be swept
off to France, or see him throw off his disguise and
take her place in the encounter. He was quite equal to

it; he lacked her cautiousness. Against flight she resolutely set her face. One would leave a sullied name behind; the large gentleman—well, what of him? She considered the point, and found herself blushing. Oh, she must needs stand well with him? The more fool she!

There was the old gentleman, to be sure, but she could not see how he might be expected to help in this. He could whisk her off, doubtless, as Robin would, and then what lay before? She saw a dark road that way, and turned from it. There was little enough to hope for in staying here in England, when one came to think of it, but—Lord, what ailed her that she must still cling to this masquerade?

She reflected that she had steered her craft into a whirlpool; and discovered an ambition in herself to steer it out again, without assistance. To take Robin into her confidence was to overset all their plans: it was to become, in fact, a nuisance.

It was possible she might be unmasked in this encounter: that had to be considered. A wound, the apothecary—lord, what a pretty scandal! If the worst came to the worst, and her wits failed her, she believed Mr Belfort might be taken into her confidence. She had a feeling she could trust him. He could arrange matters so as to preserve her secret. She might appeal to his love of adventure. It was not what she liked, but if no better scheme presented itself it might serve. And one must not forget that there was always the possibility of vanquishing Mr Rensley.

She came home in mood somewhat silent, and Robin railed gaily at her for dreaming of her mountain.

CHAPTER SIXTEEN

Unaccountable behaviour of Sir Anthony Fanshawe

SIR ANTHONY was partaking of a solitary breakfast when Mr Belfort was announced. He looked up genially from a red sirloin as the Honourable Charles came in, and offered him a share of the meal.

'Breakfasted an hour since,' said Mr Belfort briskly 'But I don't mind taking some of that ale.'

Sir Anthony pushed it towards him. 'You're very energetic, Charles,' he remarked. 'Why this ungodly hour for a visit?'

'Well, I've had business to attend to, y'see,' said Mr Belfort, nodding mysteriously. 'But that's not what I'm come upon. It's about that grey mare, Tony.'

'My dear Charles, I really cannot talk horse flesh so early in the morning.'

'Oh, come now!' protested Mr Belfort. 'It's past nine, man! The fact of the matter is, Orton offers me a hundred guineas for her, but I told him she was more than half promised to you. But if you think she's not up to your weight—'

'I have a fancy for her,' said Sir Anthony. 'I'll give you Orton's price.'

'Good God, man, no! If you want the mare she's yours at the figure we named!' cried Mr Belfort, horrified. 'Burn it, I'm not a demned merchant, Anthony!'

They embarked straightway on a friendly wrangle. A compromise was reached at last, and Mr Belfort disappeared into his tankard. When he emerged a thought seemed to strike him. 'I say, Tony, there is no doubt as to young Merriot's courage, is there?' he inquired.

'None that I know of. Why do you ask?' Sir Anthony was watching a fly hover over the sirloin.

'Oh, no reason!' Mr Belfort answered, might offhand.

Sir Anthony regarded him thoughtfully. 'He gives you some cause for doubting his courage?' he said, with just enough show of interest to demand an answer.

'My dear fellow, not in the least! It was only that I thought— But the thing's a secret. Mum's the word, y'know!'

'Really?' Sir Anthony returned to the contemplation of the fly. 'Some weighty matter, I must suppose.'

'Why, as to that, it's kept close only for fear of Miss Merriot's getting to hear of it. Never do at all!'

Sir Anthony's fingers played with the riband that held his eyeglass. 'Do you mean,' he said slowly, 'that someone has called Merriot out?'

'As a matter of fact, Tony, that's it,' said Mr Belfort confidentially.

There was a short silence. 'Who is the warlike challenger?' Sir Anthony asked.

'Rensley. Molyneux thinks it's a scandal, and so 'tis if you consider it. However, he was all for a fight, so what was there to be done?'

'Rensley! Dear me!' Sir Anthony's eyes showed nothing but a mild surprise. 'And Merriot refused the challenge, did you say?'

'No, no!' Mr Belfort was shocked. 'Nothing of the sort! Good God, man, no! Though I will say that for a moment I'd a notion he was going to rat. But I was quite wrong, Tony: he took up Rensley's challenge mighty coolly.'

Sir Anthony rose, and walked to the mirror that hung above the fireplace and became busy with the rearrangement of his neckcloth. 'Then what, Charles, gave you the reason to doubt his mettle?' he asked.

'Oh, nothing in the world, I give you my word! Only that I'd an idea this morning that he didn't relish the affair overmuch. I have the whole thing arranged: I'm acting for him, y'see, and saw Jessup at my rooms a couple of hours since. Between the two of us we had it all fixed as snug as you please for to-morrow, out at Grey's Inn Fields, and I was off at once to let young Merriot know.'

'And he didn't seem to be so delighted with the arrangements as you'd expected?'

'Well, he was precious quiet over it—but there's nothing in the world against him, Tony. Lord, he's like you, I dare swear, and takes no pleasure in aught until he's breakfasted.'

'Very possibly,' agreed Sir Anthony, and came away from the mirror.

The Honourable Charles took his gay leave of him, and went off to inform Sir Raymond Orton that the grey mare was bespoken.

For some time after he had gone Sir Anthony remained standing in the middle of the room, staring with supreme vacancy at the opposite wall, and the portrait of his grandfather which hung there. Then he went across to his writing table, and sat down to it, and with great deliberation drew a sheet of paper towards him. He dipped a quill in the inkpot, and inscribed some half a dozen lines on it, signing his name at the end with a bold flourish. He read over what he had written and dusted the paper with sand. It was sealed up with a wafer, and a big blot of red wax, and placed in one of the drawers of the desk. Sir Anthony rose, called for his hat and his cane, and sallied forth into the street.

He went leisurely to White's, and found there a sprinkling of people, early in the day though it was. He sat down with a journal by the empty fireplace. Various people came and went, amongst them Mr Merriot, with whom Sir Anthony exchanged a pleasant word or two. He said nothing about the prospective duel, but hoped Mr Merriot would dine with him on the following evening. Prudence accepted, placid enough to all outward appearances, but she bore a sinking heart in her breast. The night had brought no good counsel, and with the morning had come the Honourable Charles, who seemed to her of a sudden, a cheerful young brute. She had small hope of keeping her appointment with Sir Anthony, but it would not do to let the large gentleman suspect that. She showed a faint desire to escape from him, and went out presently with Mr Devereux, who desired her advice in the choosing of a flowered waistcoat.

Sir Anthony returned to his paper, and did not look up again until a laughing voice said: 'Oh, he's gone off to take a lesson from Galliano! Belfort held out for swords, and of course Rensley wanted pistols.'

The heavy eyes lifted. It was Sir Raymond Orton who had spoken. He made one of a small group standing at the other side of the fireplace. Mr Molyneux was there, and Mr Troubridge, and young Lord Kestrel.

Mr Troubridge took snuff. 'It is not one's business,' he remarked, 'but one wonders that Rensley could find no one nearer his own age.'

My lord looked perplexed. 'What's that? Merriot said something about Rensley's manners, you know.'

'You are perfectly right, Troubridge,' said Mr Molyneux, preserving his air of disapproval. 'Rensley's sore—small blame to him—over all this pother of the claim, and he was out to pick a quarrel with someone by way of venting his spleen. Well, I'm glad young Merriot stood for the small sword: Rensley's killed his man with the pistols.'

Sir Anthony put away his journal, and went to join the group. 'He would not appear to have too great a faith in his skill with the small sword,' he remarked.

Orton looked scornful. 'He's skilled enough to account for young Merriot, I should have supposed. Only Devereux spread it about that Merriot was deadly with the weapon, and has some Italian tricks up his sleeve. So off goes our friend for an hour's practice with Galliano.'

'It smacks to me of some qualms,' said Lord Kestrel, with a look of distaste. 'Now Merriot's gone off to look at waistcoats, as cool as you please.'

'Rensley will be in a devilish rage when he finds the secret's out, and the whole world knows he went off to get Galliano to show him a cunning pass or two!' grinned Orton. He nodded to Sir Anthony. 'Farraday went to wait upon him, and his man let it out. He deserves to be well roasted for playing such a shabby trick.'

'Well'—Sir Anthony smiled pleasantly on the group—'I'm bound for Galliano's myself to arrange for some practice. I may stumble upon the gentleman. Give me your company, Molyneux.'

'What, are you purposing to fight a duel?' said Troubridge, laughing.

'No, my dear Troubridge, no, but I like to keep my wrist in practice. Come and have a bout with me.'

There was some raillery, for Sir Anthony was known to be a peaceable man. In high good humour, and in the expectation of entertainment to be gained from confronting Rensley at the fencing master's, not only the two invited, but Orton also, and my Lord Kestrel decided to accompany Sir Anthony. They would bait Mr Rensley a little, and take a turn with the foils. It would be an agreeable way of spending the morning.

The little Italian had a room over the shop owned by a purveyor of rappee, in the Haymarket. The small party was soon arrived there, and climbed the stairs to the first floor. There was some laughter and a deal of light talk. Signor Galliano's servant came to the head of the stairs, drawn by the sudden noise, and requested the gentlemen to have the goodness to wait only a moment in the chamber behind the fencing-room. There was a gentleman with the good signor.

'Oh, we know all about that, Tino!' said my Lord Kestrel jovially, and pushed by to the door of the front room.

Tino expostulated feebly, but it seemed there was no gainsaying these merry gentlemen.

My lord opened the door, and affected a start of surprise. 'Good gad, Rensley! You here?'

Mr Rensley was putting on his coat, and looked up with a very genuine start. In the middle of the floor the little Italian instructor stood leaning on his foil, and beaming with pleasure upon these new visitors. He descried the large form of Sir Anthony Fanshawe, and flourished the foil joyously. 'Aha, saire! Aha! You come to me to learn the newest passes, eh? I have one for you, and you may call it *Le Baiser de la Morte*. I teach it to you, for you have very nearly the soul to appreciate it.' His foil darted out to touch my Lord Kestrel lightly over the heart. 'For you, milor, no! Ah, no! It is for ze vey few—you may say for zose initiate in ze art of ze duello. You I teach a better management of ze feet.' He frowned fiercely upon Sir Raymond, but his little eyes twinkled. 'I instruct zis bad Saire Raymond not to be ze bull at ze gate, hein?'

'Oh, come now, Gally, it's not so bad as that, surely!' protested Orton blinking.

'It is worse, my frien'. It is of a vileness! For Mistaire Troubridge, I take him sedately, aha? Mr Molyneux not come to play wiz Galliano. He favours ze English school, which is just nozing at all. Mistaire Rensley he wastes my time too. *Sapristi*, but it is again ze bull at ze gate! I kill him a sousand times. Ten sousand times!'

Galliano was a privileged person, and his strictures and familiarities were received with mirth, and mock contrition. My Lord Kestrel went over to the window seat, and flung himself down upon it, demanding to be shown the *Baiser de la Morte*. Sir Anthony looked with great interest through his glass at Mr Rensley.

'Well, well!' he said. 'And have you been acquiring the Kiss, Rensley?'

'Bacchus! You accuse me of a sacrilege ze mos' infamous!' cried Galliano. 'I teach him only to keep ze head cool on ze shoulders. I sink he go to fight a duello. I sank ze gods I have not to see it. It would wring ze heart! Me, I am an artis'.'

My lord said with a wicked look in his eye: 'I'd no notion you were taking lessons of old Galliano, Rensley.'

'I have now and then an hour with him,' Rensley answered, and seemed in some anxiety to be gone.

But Sir Raymond Orton leaned casually against the door. 'Now and then being when there's a fight brewing, eh, Rensley my buck?'

'Really, Orton! Is it a jest belike?'

'The most famous one, Rensley, and spreading all over the town.'

Sir Anthony spoke to Galliano. 'We'd a mind to have the foils out, Gally, but I suppose you have Mr Merriot coming to you?'

'I do not know any Mistaire Merriot,' said Galliano positively. 'I am at Saire Anthony's disposal. Why should I have an appointment wiz a Mistaire I don' know?'

'Oh, I thought 'twas a new fashion to take a lesson before a meeting!' said Sir Anthony idly twirling his eye-glass. 'Now I see it is only Mr Rensley's fashion. But what a disappointment for him to have this new pass withheld! Can't you teach him your *Baiser,* Gally?'

The Italian looked quickly from one face to the other. Some mischief he could smell in the air, and all his sharp little brain was on the alert. 'I do not try to teach him *Baiser.* You—yes, I will show. But I do not show Mr Rensley, nor you, milor, nor Saire Raymond eizer.'

'You've no heart, Gally; positively you've none,' Sir Anthony told him. 'Have a little pity on poor Rensley!'

Mr Rensley stood still beside Sir Raymond. He had shut his mouth hard, but his eyes smouldered. Mr Molyneux was looking curiously at Fanshawe, but my lord, by the window, watched Rensley and chuckled. It was a jest he could appreciate.

'You don't apprehend the matter,' Sir Anthony went on persuasively, still twirling his glass. 'Here's Rensley feels he must let some blood—not his own, of course—and hits on the very man. That's to say, it seemed so—one of your youthful sprigs from the country. Ideal, you perceive. But the devil was in it that the sprig was held to have some cunning tricks of fence—possibly your *Baiser,* Gally; who knows? Naturally poor Rensley's monstrous put out over it, and what else should he do but fly to our friend Galliano? And you fail him, Gally! It's unkind in you, upon my word it is. Poor Rensley will be forced to withdraw from the engagement, I fear me.'

The chuckle died on my Lord Kestrel's lips; Sir Raymond looked round quickly. Mr Rensley took two steps towards Sir Anthony, and spoke in a voice barely controlled. 'Will you be good enough to explain these remarks, Sir Anthony?' he demanded.

Sir Anthony turned slowly to face him. Mr Rensley was by no means a small man, but the lazy eyes looked down at him. Sir Anthony stopped twirling his glass, and though he smiled still it was not his usual genial expression, but on the contrary a smile rather disdainful, and with the hint of sternness behind it. 'Certainly, Mr Rensley. But I should have thought my meaning was plain enough. No doubt you have your reasons for not wishing to comprehend it.'

Rensley reddened. 'This is not the first time you've sneered at me, Sir Anthony!'

'Nor the last, Rensley, unless the colour of your coat should change.'

'You make your meaning quite plain, I thank you, sir! You choose to think me a coward because I chance to take an hour's practice here to-day.'

'You have it quite wrong, my good Rensley,' said Sir Anthony imperturbably. 'I choose to think you a coward because you forced a quarrel on a man well nigh young enough to be your son.'

Under his breath Sir Raymond gave the dueller's 'Sa-sa!' The jest had of a sudden taken an ugly turn, and what in the fiend's name ailed Fanshawe to be picking a quarrel in this fashion?

Rensley spoke between shut teeth. 'May I ask what concern it is of yours, sir?'

Sir Anthony's eyes were hard and scornful. 'Make no doubt, sir, I can readily understand your anxiety for me not to make it my concern.'

Troubridge laid his hand on Sir Anthony's arm. 'Tony—' he began, expostulating.

His hand was removed. 'In a moment, Troubridge.'

Mr Rensley's fingers sought the hilt of his sword. 'I know how to take that, Sir Anthony. You shall have all the taste of my mettle you require, and maybe some more beside. Be pleased to name your seconds.'

Sir Anthony looked round the room. 'Why, here are enough for us both,' he said. 'I will take Mr Molyneux and Mr Troubridge for mine. I make no doubt my Lord Kestrel, and Orton there will be charmed to serve you.'

Mr Molyneux jumped. 'Good Gad, Fanshawe, what's this?'

'I'll choose my own friends, I thank you, sir! You shall hear from them.' Mr Rensley strode to the door but was checked by Sir Anthony's voice.

'Not so fast, not so fast! It is for me to name the time and the place. What place could be better than this, and what time half so suitable as the present?'

Kestrel's eyes danced. Fanshawe had undoubtedly taken leave of his senses, but this promised to be a rare morning's work. 'You can count on me, Rensley,' he struck in.

'Nothing, to be sure, would please me more, Sir

Anthony,' Rensley answered, 'but I have a meeting with your *protégé* to-morrow and your quarrel must wait on his.'

'Really, Tony, you must—'

'Give me leave, Molyneux.' A hand was raised to enjoin silence. 'I don't wait on young Merriot's pleasure, Rensley.'

'In this instance, sir, you will find you must.'

Sir Anthony smiled. 'You must think me a much bigger fool than I am, Mr Rensley.'

'I doubt it, sir!' There was a bite to the words.

'Oh, but you do, my good Rensley, if you suppose that I do not perfectly understand the meaning of this refusal of yours to meet me now.'

'And what is the meaning, sir?'

Sir Anthony pointed his long cane at Rensley, and answered in a voice of indulgent scorn. 'Oh, you will prove your mettle on young Merriot to the satisfaction of the world, and I shall hear next that you sustained some slight hurt in that encounter for which the surgeon prescribes a foreign clime.' He shrugged his broad shoulders. 'No, no, Rensley, it won't serve!'

Mr Rensley's hand shook on his sword hilt, but it was not from fright. 'To hell with your insinuations!' he cried. 'You'd say I fear to meet you, eh?'

'I say, Mr Rensley, that you dare not meet me now or at any time,' Sir Anthony replied, to the astonishment of his friends. His hand came up, and he struck

Mr Rensley lightly across the mouth with the glove he held.

There was a choked oath, and the rasp of steel scraping against the scabbard. Mr Rensley's sword was out.

Galliano leaped in with his foil raised. 'Ah, ah! Put up ze sword! Put up, I say! You go to make a scandal of me, ze pair of you!' he cried.

'I will fight you here and now, Sir Anthony!' thundered Mr Rensley, and flung his hat and cane aside.

There came a gleam into the grey eyes. 'Give us houseroom, Gally,' said Sir Anthony. 'What a pity neither of us had time to acquire the Kiss!'

'Anthony, you're surely mad!' Mr Molyneux's voice was urgent in his ear.

'I was never more sane, believe me,' Sir Anthony assured him, coming out of his coat. 'Lock the door, Gally.' He tucked up his ruffles. 'There's a letter in my desk, Molyneux, in case— You'll find it.'

'Fanshawe, I do beseech you—'

'Pray don't, my dear fellow; it's quite useless. Gally, my friend, help me to pull off these boots, of your compassion.'

The Italian pulled them off for him, but he looked up with a worried face. 'What comes to me over zis, hein? You make me a scandal, Saire Anthony!'

'Have no fear, Gally; there will be no scandal.'

Sir Raymond Orton came punctiliously forward to meet Mr Molyneux, and swords were measured. Mr

Molyneux said, over the business:—'It should be stopped, Orton. Fanshawe's mad.'

'Stark mad!' agreed Orton cheerfully. 'But it's famous sport, after all, and there's no stopping them now. My man's itching to be at it. Are we ready?'

There was a formal salute, and the blades came together. In a moment there was no sound in the room save the clash and scrape of steel, and the pad-pad of stockinged feet on the wood floor. The seconds stood with drawn swords in their places; little Galliano, still holding his buttoned foil, sat in the window seat and watched with quick eager eyes. Several times he frowned; once he nodded in swift approbation.

It was hard fighting, for one man had unbearable insults to avenge, and the other's whole mind and will were bent on disabling his adversary. Very soon it was clear to see which was the better man. Rensley's thrusts were savage indeed, and his attack full of fire, but his passes went wide, and more than once it seemed to the onlookers that Sir Anthony held him at his mercy. The big man, who was yet so curiously light on his feet, was playing with Rensley, and slowly the men standing by realised that he was making for just one spot, and would be satisfied with no other.

The end came quickly. Rensley saw an opening, and lunged forward. There was a scurry of blades, a lightning thrust, and Rensley went staggering back, with a hand caught to his right arm.

The seconds sprang in; Galliano clapped delighted

hands; Sir Anthony stood back, and wiped his wet sword. A red stain was spreading over Mr Rensley's shirt, and his right arm hung useless.

Galliano skipped into the middle of the room. 'Bravo, bravo!' he exclaimed. 'I taught you zat pass! I, Girolamo Galliano!'

'Curb your enthusiasm, my friend,' Sir Anthony advised him.

Galliano tossed up his arms. 'Ensusiasm! Bah, it was bad, bad—all of it! You English you do not understand ze art! But just once or twice was a pass I might myself have make! Do not flatter yourself! You cannot fence: not even you, Saire Anthony!'

CHAPTER SEVENTEEN

Sad falling out of friends

BY THE AFTERNOON the news was all over town that
Fanshawe had wounded Rensley in a duel that had
taken place that morning in Galliano's rooms, of all
places in the world. Every sort of tale was told. Fanshawe had taken leave of his senses and struck Rensley across the face with his glove: no, it was Rensley
struck Fanshawe; faith, it must have been that way,
for everyone knew that it was not like Fanshawe to
pick a quarrel. The affair had sprung up out of a clear
sky: there had been some raillery which Rensley took
exception to, and Fanshawe had carried it too far.

Mr Belfort heard it from my Lord Kestrel, and was
thunderstruck. My lord told it him between chuckles
and with many embellishments, and described, with
gesture, the thrust that had put Rensley out of action
for many weeks to come. Mr Belfort went hurrying
off to confer with Mr Devereux, whom he found writing execrable verse to a lady of uncertain morals, and
bore him off straight to Arlington Street.

My lady laughed when the message was brought to

Prudence, but Robin looked queerly, and showed a desire to inquire further into the need for a private conference. Prudence said lightly that it was some matter concerning a horse, and escaped before Robin could read the trouble in her face. He had the uncanny knack of it.

She found Mr Belfort looking portentous, and Mr Devereux melancholy. 'Why, Charles, what ails you?' she asked. It seemed to her that there was no one but herself had the right to look solemn.

'My dear fellow, it's the devil of a business,' Belfort said severely. 'A most disgraceful affair, 'pon my soul!'

Mr Devereux shook his head. 'Very, very disgraceful,' he echoed.

'Lud, sir, you horrify me! What's toward?'

'Rensley,' said Belfort, 'has committed a—damme, a cursed breach of etiquette! You can't meet the man, Peter. Can he, Dev?'

Mr Devereux was of the opinion that it would be impossible.

A flush sprang up in Prudence's cheeks. It was of sudden, overwhelming relief, but Mr Belfort took it to betoken anger. 'Ay, Peter my boy, I knew you'd take it hard, but positively you can't meet the man after such a slight.'

'Very shocking business,' Mr Devereux said mournfully. 'Can't understand it at all.'

Prudence had command of herself again. If she must

not fight it seemed safe enough to protest a little, as was proper. 'But pray let me hear what it is!' she said. 'I don't draw back from an encounter, Charles, be sure.'

'It's Rensley has drawn back,' Mr Belfort said, still with awful solemnity.

'Not drawn back, Bel. You couldn't say he had drawn back,' protested Mr Devereux.

'It's the same thing, Dev. He can't meet Peter tomorrow, and I say it's a cursed insult. I shall tell Jessup our man won't fight.'

'Has Rensley fled the country?' demanded Prudence.

'Worse, my dear boy!'

'Not worse, Bel! Hardly worse! Plaguey unfortunate happening.'

Mr Belfort laid an impressive finger on Prudence's shoulder. 'He's offered us a damned slight, Peter. It can't be swallowed. Take my word for it, there can be no meeting.'

'Why, Charles, you mystify me! Let me know what this slight is I beg of you.'

'He has fought another man this morning,' said Mr Belfort, and stood back to observe the effect of this terrific pronouncement.

Prudence was all honest incredulity. 'You tell me he has met some one else in a duel?' she cried. It seemed to be a positive dispensation of a kindly Providence, but it would not do to let the gentleman suspect she felt this. She affected anger. 'He sets me aside, you would tell me! It's for some later quarrel? You call it a slight! You're moderate, Charles!'

'Devilish irregular,' said Mr Devereux. 'I was monstrous shocked when I heard of it, give you my word. They say there's a tendon cut in his sword arm that won't heal this many a day. Quite impossible to meet him.'

'But apart from that, Dev—apart from that, mind you, I would not have our man swallow such a cursed piece of rudeness,' Mr Belfort reminded him. 'Our quarrel came first, demm it!' A frown marred the cherubic look in his face. 'And what's more, Dev, Fanshawe knew it!'

'Fanshawe!' the exclamation broke from Prudence, who stood staring.

'Fanshawe himself,' nodded Belfort. 'And I saw him this morning, and somehow or other the thing slipped out, and I told him you were to meet Rensley.'

'But—you say Fanshawe is the man who fought Rensley?'

'You may well ask, Peter. Fanshawe it was. Found our man at Galliano's, and forced a quarrel on him.'

'Carslake tells me it all began as a jest, Bel,' pleaded Mr Devereux.

'Jest or no, Dev, the man had no business to meet Fanshawe till our little affair was settled. And so I shall tell Jessup.'

'But why did Sir Anthony—?'

'Ah, that's the question,' nodded Belfort. 'I don't know, but they do say he told Rensley he was a poltroon, and struck him in the face with his glove. Kestrel—he was there, y'know—will have it Tony was out for a fight from the first, but Orton thinks it all sprang up out of naught.'

An idea struck Mr Devereux. ''Pon my soul, Merriot, you might call Fanshawe out, so you might!'

Prudence laughed, and shook her head. 'Oh, hold me excused! I count Sir Anthony very much my friend, in spite of this day's work.'

Mr Belfort pondered it. 'I don't see that, Dev. No, I don't see that he can do that. But as for meeting Rensley after this, it's not to be thought of. Mind that, Peter! Not to be thought of!'

Prudence assumed an air of hesitation, and made some demur. It seemed safe. She was sternly overruled, but Mr Devereux said it did her credit. He went off with Mr Belfort to wait upon Mr Rensley's seconds.

Prudence was left to make what she might of it. On the face of it, it looked as though the large gentleman had once more scared away the wolf. But why? That gave food for serious reflection. What did he suspect, forsooth? Or had he merely a mind to interpose on behalf of a boy for whom he had some kindness? She could not think he had pierced her disguise; faith, it was too good for that, surely! She went upstairs to Robin, and gave him the full sum of it.

Robin threw her a straight look under his lashes. 'I'm to understand you had it in mind to meet Rensley with never a word to me?'

'Just, child. Don't eat me!'

'I'm more likely to beat you. You must be mad indeed!'

She perceived him to be in something of a rage, and made haste to divert him. 'I've to thank Sir Anthony, for my deliverance. What have you to say to that?'

'You're of opinion he has your secret? You must have been mighty indiscreet!'

'Not a whit. I've given not the smallest reason for him to suspect me, I swear. Unless—' She broke off, frowning. 'There was the little matter of staying with me at Wych End. No more.'

Robin shrugged that aside. 'I hold to my opinion. But if he suspects—why, it seems he's a mind to keep his counsel.'

'It's a comfortable belief, child. Give you joy of it. I dine with him to-morrow. Be sure, I step warily.'

In another part of the town there was a gentleman quite as shocked as Mr Belfort over the morning's happenings, and infinitely more enraged. Mr Markham went off to Grosvenor Square, and found his friend Rensley abed, and very sore.

Mr Markham broke out with a 'What's to do now, a' God's name?'

Rensley lay staring at the bedpost, and said only:— 'Fanshawe forced the quarrel on to me.'

'God's life, were you not pledged to Merriot?'

'Oh ay, you're might anxious to see him trounced, aren't you?'

'To hell with that!' All Mr Markham's flattering deference towards his friend was fast departing. 'Here's Belfort and Devereux mighty haughty— damme, they've reason!—and say their man won't fight. And Jessup and I have to make your excuses for you, and look a pair of fools! You make us ridiculous, Rensley, curse it!'

Mr Rensley received this in silence.

'Burn it, you must needs spoil all!' Markham said in disgust. 'What madness took you?'

'I tell you it was forced on me!' Rensley exploded.

'Forced be damned! You were pledged to meet Merriot, and Fanshawe must have known it.'

Mr Rensley raised himself on his sound elbow. 'What, you'd have me swallow a blow in the face, would you? Ay, I make no doubt you'd take it!'

'Oh, I'll leave you!' Markham said, and swung round on his heel.

'It's little enough help you've ever been to me, sure!' sneered Rensley. 'Your Munich gaming-houses!'

'It's little help you'll have from me in the future!' Mr Markham cried, and left his friend fuming.

He was let out of the house by a solemn lackey, who had spent the morning discussing his master's freak below-stairs. He walked down the steps, and became aware of a shabby gentleman, hesitating by the railings. He looked with casual interest, wondering what this individual wanted.

The shabby gentleman accosted him. 'Your pardon, sir, but does my Lord Barham live here?'

Mr Markham gave a short laugh. 'There's certainly a man within calls himself Lord Barham,' he said.

The shabby gentleman looked a little puzzled. 'It's—it's a small man, with a hook nose,' he ventured. 'That's the man I want to see, sir.'

Mr Markham paused, and his eyes took in the stranger more thoroughly. There was an air of mystery about the man, and some slight savour of nervousness. If this was one of my lord's late associates it was quite possible that something might be gathered from him of no little importance. 'I'm a friend of Lord Barham,' said Markham, in a tone meant to inspire confidence. 'Do me the favour of stepping up to my rooms with me.'

The stranger seemed to shrink into himself; hurriedly he declined the honour: he desired to see my lord, and none other.

Mr Markham's suspicions were thoroughly aroused. He took the stranger by the elbow, and abandoning the conciliatory tone, said unpleasantly:—'Ay, you're in a mighty hurry to be off, aren't you? Now what should the likes of you have to say to Lord Barham that no one else may hear?'

The stranger tried to break away. 'Nothing, sir, I

assure you! A matter for my lord's private ear! I beg you won't detain me.'

'Ay, but I've a mind to know something more of you, my friend,' said Mr Markham, retaining his hold. 'You look to me as though you have information to sell. I know something of this Barham, you see.'

The stranger disclaimed quickly, shooting a swift, scared glance up and down the road. Markham's suspicions grew, and he drew a bow at a venture. 'I believe you're some damned Jacobite, skulking in hiding,' he said.

There was the faintest start, and a fresh movement to be free. Markham's grip tightened on the arm he held, and he began to walk down the square, taking the stranger with him. The stranger protested in a high voice of alarm; his vehement oaths that he was no Jacobite left Mr Markham unmoved. Markham said:—'If you've information for sale about Lord Barham you can go free for aught I care. If not—why, we'll see what the law will get out of you!'

The protestations died away; the stranger went sullenly beside Mr Markham until the house where Markham lodged was reached. He was ushered into his host's rooms, and told to sit down. On either side of the table they sat, the stranger holding his battered hat between his hands, and stealing furtive glances towards the door.

'Now then, fellow, I'm a friend of Lord Barham's, and I'll hear what you have to say.'

'If you're a friend of his, you'd best let me see him,' the other said sulkily. 'His lordship won't desire to have me given up. I can tell too much.'

'Why, what should Barham care for aught you could say?'

'Ask him!' the man replied. 'I'm ready to sell his lordship what I hold, but if you, who say you're a friend of his, are fool enough to give me up. I'll disclose all I know, and then where will his fine lordship be?'

'You'll give up what you hold to me, my man.'

'If you're a friend of his,' the stranger insisted, 'you dare not hand me over to the law. Take me to Lord Barham.'

'You mistake, fellow,' said Markham cruelly. 'I am a friend of the other Lord Barham.'

'I don't know what you're talking of. The man I mean is a little man, with bright eyes, and a soft-spoken manner. I saw him riding in a fine coach the other day, and I was told it was Lord Barham.'

In a few words Mr Markham let him know the true state of affairs. He watched closely the effect, and saw again the furtive look around for a means of escape.

'So now, fellow, you perceive into what trap you have fallen. Faith you're a bad plotter! I make no doubt your Barham would pay well for the information you hold, because he dare not give you up. But make you no doubt that you'll get little enough from me. I've naught to fear from handing you over to the law.

You deserve to hang, but I'm kind. If your information's worth something I'll give you twenty guineas to help you out of the country. If you're stubborn—why, we'll see what the law-officers have to say to you.'

The stranger attempted to bluster and disclaim, but it was plain he had some fears. Mr Markham bore with this awhile, but arose at last with a significant word of calling to his servant. Bluster turned to a whine; there was produced at last a folded letter from an inner pocket upon which Mr Markham pounced with some eagerness.

He read some half a dozen finely inscribed lines addressed to no less a person than my Lord George Murray, concerning certain hopes of drawing in two gentlemen to the Rebellion whose names were only indicated by an initial; and came at last to the signature. The name of Colney conveyed nothing to Mr Markham, but the stranger said sulkily:—'That's the name of the man I saw out driving. He who calls himself my Lord Barham.'

'How came you by this letter?'

The stranger said evasively that it had fallen into his hands. He saw no reason to tell Mr Markham that he had stolen it along with some others of little or no importance, in the vague belief that they might be of use to him. Fortunately, Mr Markham's interest in the manner of the letter's acquisition was but fleeting, and he inquired no further, but sat frowning down at that elegant signature.

'Can you prove this Colney to be indeed the man you say he is?'

The stranger answered in some alarm that of a certainty he could prove nothing, since he could not, for obvious reasons, come into the open. Mr Markham's dissatisfaction grew. 'I don't see what use this is. I believe I'd better give you up.'

It was pointed out to him, with some haste, that an inquiry set on foot regarding the movements of Mr Colney must inevitably lead to the present claimant of the Barham title. Mr Markham sat pondering it, and began to see his way. The letter was hidden away in a pocket and twenty guineas changed hands. Mr Markham thought it would be as well for the stranger to leave the country: he preferred that no one save himself should know of this letter. There was some expostulation and some tearful pleading, but upon fresh mention of the law officers the stranger took a hurried leave of his host, and left him to his reflections.

These were weighty enough. It was Mr Markham's first impulse to go with the document to Rensley, who had said he would give as much as ten thousand pounds to the man who should expose his cousin. But Rensley was a mean dog: there could be no trusting him. Rensley had, moreover, used some very cutting expressions to his friend lately; there had been a falling out, and it would not be displeasing to Mr Markham to do his friend Rensley an ill turn.

His thoughts came round to another market for his

document. Ecod, he had naught against the pseudo-Lord Barham, and his lordship seemed to be an open-handed old gentleman. Of a surety it would not do to act precipitately in this matter, but the alternative of taking his document to Barham must be fully considered. Rensley would be bound to pay well for this precious paper, but would not my lord be bound to pay better? This led to a fresh thought: once sold to Rensley, there was an end to the business, so far as Mr Markham was concerned. But he could dimly perceive years ahead if he made Barham his man. Barham would buy the paper, true, but even that would not make Barham feel quite safe. He could surely be further bled on fear of disclosure. True there could be nothing proved without written evidence, but Mr Markham could imagine that even a verbal accusation with the paper safely destroyed would prove mighty uncomfortable for my lord. Mr Markham believed that he might easily hold my lord under his thumb for a good many years to come. He licked his lips at this thought, but decided that the thing must be earnestly weighed. He would sleep on it.

CHAPTER EIGHTEEN

The large gentleman is awake

THERE WOULD BE cards at Fanshawe's house, Prudence guessed; a fair number of young bucks might be counted on to be present; and her frustrated duel with Rensley must be sure of receiving notice.

She chose, at random, a coat of peace satin from her wardrobe, and found a fine waistcoat embroidered in silver to wear with it. Robin came to dredge powder on to her brown locks, and was busy with hot irons for a while. Coaxing a rolling curl into place, Robin said:—'Leave early, and have no private talk with Fanshawe. It's my belief it's a Quixotic gentleman with no other mind than to step between a callow youth and death. But it's as well to have a care.'

Prudence agreed to the first part of this speech, but held her peace for the rest. No use in alarming Robin, but she felt there might be more in the large gentleman's mind than her brother guessed. She waited patiently for Robin to finish tying the black riband in her neck, and rose afterwards to be helped into her coat. Her glance strayed to the mirror, and showed satisfaction. Faith, she made a neat young gentleman. Who should think more? She slipped a ring on to her finger, and her snuffbox into one of the great pockets of her coat. Her stockings seemed to her to be rolled too loosely above the knee; she bent to rectify the fault; gave a final pat to the ruffles about her throat, and sallied forth to the waiting chair.

The house in Clarges Street was strangely quiet. As she gave her hat and cloak into the servant's care she listened for sound of voices, but none came. The lackey went before her to the door of Sir Anthony's library, flung it wide, and sonorously called her name.

Sir Anthony was standing alone before the fireplace, where a small wood fire burned. There was no one else in the room. He came forward to greet Prudence, took her hand a moment, and asked a jovial question. She answered in kind, and realised with his next words that she was to be his only guest.

'I've positively no entertainment to offer you, excepting a hand at picquet after dinner,' smiled Fanshawe. 'I feel I invite you under false pretences, but you'll forgive me.'

'Why, I'm pleased to have it so, sir!' There was not much truth in that, but one must say something of the sort, she supposed. She paused. A word must be said also of his strange behaviour of yesterday, since it concerned her so nearly. There was not a tremor in her voice as she spoke: nothing but a mixture of amusement and some reproof. 'I have a quarrel with you, Sir Anthony. You must be aware of it.'

He pulled forward a chair for her, and himself stood leaning with his broad shoulders against the mantel-shelf. 'Faith, not I,' he answered. 'Have I offended you?'

One of her long fingers played with the fob of her snuff-box. She looked up tranquilly into the gentle-man's inscrutable, good-humoured countenance. 'Well, sir, Mr Devereux is of the opinion I might call you out,' she said, and the twinkle was in her grave eyes.

'God forbid, little man! What have I done to incur this wrath?'

'You must know, sir, that I had an engagement this morning to meet Mr Rensley out at Grey's Inn Fields. In this I'm baulked by Sir Anthony Fanshawe. I can't pretend to be pleased.'

She had the feeling she was being watched all the time. He smiled a little, and made a slight bow. 'Oh, I cry your pardon, Mr Fire-Eater. But your complaints were better addressed to Rensley than to me.'

Prudence said coolly:—'You may be very sure Mr Rensley will hear from me just so soon as he leaves the surgeon's care.' It seemed to her that the straight brows rose in momentary surprise. She went on. 'Charles is of the opinion I can't meet the man, but for myself I conceive that so far from considering my-self debarred from fighting him after this insult I have the more reason. If Charles won't act for me—faith, his sense of propriety in these matters is prodigious!— may I call on you, sir?' This was something of a bold move, to be sure, but by the time Mr Rensley was recovered there would be no Mr Merriot in town, she believed.

'I'm of Belfort's opinion, little man,' Sir Anthony said slowly. 'You are exempt from the obligation of meeting Rensley.'

'By your leave, sir. I think the choice rests with me.' She looked up with an assumption of displeasure. 'Next time I trust there will be nothing to hinder our meeting,' she said.

'Myself, for instance?' Sir Anthony put up his glass. 'I believe I don't repeat myself.'

She bowed and let it go at that. A servant came to announce dinner, and Sir Anthony led the way into the dining-room at the back of the house.

There were wax candles in wrought holders on the table, and silver winking in the golden light. Two chairs were set, and two places laid, with wine in cut glass decanters, shining covers, and fine white napery.

They sat down, Sir Anthony at the head of the small table, and Prudence on his left. Dishes were presented to her; she made a fair meal, and the talk ran merrily. Sir Anthony spoke of a visit to Newmarket, and begged Prudence's company. When she paused before making reply he said provocatively:—'You daren't say me nay this time, Peter. Remember my displeasure on another such occasion.'

She suspected him of teasing her and looked up smilingly. 'What, am I supposed to fear that, sir?'

Sir Anthony was busy with the carving of a chicken, but he found time to meet the challenge in the grey eyes with a look quizzical and humorous. 'Don't you, little man?'

Well, if the truth be told, one did fear it. But what was the gentleman's drift? 'I take that to be a reflection on my courage,' she said gaily. 'I believe I've no cause to fear you.'

'You never can tell,' Sir Anthony answered. 'I might lose patience with so fugitive and reserved a youth. Then have you naught to fear?'

Was this a threat, perchance? No, for the large gentleman was smiling with the same good-humour. 'Oh, am I to be called out?' she wondered.

'Acquit me of child murder. But I might refuse to scare away the wolf—a second time.'

She sipped the Burgundy in her glass, and frowned a little, 'Ah!' She set down the half empty glass, and her host filled it again. It was the second time. 'You lead me to suppose, sir, that what you did yesterday was in the nature of wolf-scaring?'

'Would you call it that?' Sir Anthony filled his own glass very leisurely. 'I had thought it more in the nature of disabling the wolf.'

'If you like. Then what I suspected was truth indeed?' She looked steadily at him, with some dignity in her glance.

'That depends, young man, on what your suspicions were.'

'I thought, sir, that you had intervened—quite incomprehensibly—on my behalf.'

'But why incomprehensibly?' inquired Sir Anthony.

This was something of a check. 'Well, sir, I believe I am not, after all, just out of the nursery, though it pleases you to think so. I'm grateful for the kindliness of the action, but—frankly, Sir Anthony. I had rather be given the chance to prove my mettle.'

There came a fleeting look of admiration into the eyes that rested so enigmatically on her face, but it was so transient an expression that she doubted she had been mistaken. 'I compliment you, boy. But prove your mettle on one nearer your own age.'

She bowed, and for form's sake sipped at her wine again. A dish of nuts was pushed towards her; she chose one and cracked it without having recourse to the silver crackers in the dish. A boy's trick, and she hoped the large gentleman noted it well.

The indolent voice continued. 'Thought to be sure I'd an idea your mettle had been proved already. You've had an engagement before this.'

She was peeling the nut, and her fingers did not falter, though she was taken by surprise. What was he at now, pray? She looked up inquiringly, but had sense enough to commit herself to nothing.

'Some duel when you sustained a wound in the shoulder,' said Sir Anthony.

She was at a momentary loss, and knew herself closely scrutinised. Recollection of the night when she was set on by Mohocks returned to her. She remembered the excuse manufactured on the spur of the moment for Belfort's edification. 'True, Sir Anthony, but that took place abroad.'

'Like so many of your experiences,' nodded Sir Anthony, and again picked up the decanter. 'But you don't drink, my dear boy.'

She thought she drank a deal too much of this heavy Burgundy, and deplored the absence of claret. Once more her glass was filled. To refuse it would give food for suspicion in these days of hard drinking. She swallowed some of the deep red wine, was aware of a lazy glance upon her, and emptied the glass recklessly. God send she kept a sober head on her shoulders! If there was to be more of it the next glass must go down her arm.

'But we drift from the point,' Sir Anthony said genially. 'We were talking of Newmarket, and, as I remember, I queried an assertion on your part, child, that you'd no fear of me.'

'Why, what should I fear in you?' Prudence asked, and chuckled, 'You tell me you won't call me out, and I'm able to breathe again.'

Sir Anthony's mouth relaxed into a smile of real

amusement. 'I do verily believe, young man, that you'd meet me with perfect sangfroid.'

'Oh, as to that, sir, I might know some serious nervous qualms. I'm to understand you're accounted something of a master of the small sword.'

'You've been misinformed. Do you ever have nervous qualms I wonder?'

Her fingers closed round the stem of her wine-glass; she was looking at the ruby liquid sparkling in it. 'Often, sir. Why should you suppose me cast in the heroic mould?'

'I'd a notion you'd a vast deal of courage, my friend,' placidly replied Fanshawe.

'Good Gad, sir, why? Because I would fight Rensley?'

'That, and some other things.' Sir Anthony drained his glass, and refilled it, glancing at the untouched wine in the glass Prudence still held.

He selected a nut from the dish, and became busy with the cracking of it. Now was her moment, while his eyes were bent on his plate. Prudence raised her glass to her lips, as though to toss off the whole; there was a quick practised turn of the wrist, over in a flash, and the contents of her glass were sent down her arm.

But quicker even than her own movement, Sir Anthony leaned forward. His hand shot out, and the hard fingers closed round her wrist. Relentlessly her arm was borne down: down till the glass she held emptied its dregs on to the floor.

She made no effort to break free; perhaps she breathed a little faster. The fingers were clamped still about her wrist; Sir Anthony was looking down at her hand, watching the wine trickle down hear arm, and drip on to the carpet.

She sat perfectly still; her eyes were calm, even meditative, resting on Fanshawe's face. She had lost some of her colour, and the lace at her bosom rose and fell rather quickly, but other signs of alarm there were not.

It seemed an age before her wrist was released. At last the merciless fingers left it, and Sir Anthony sat back in his chair. She brought her hand up, and set the glass down on the table. In a detached manner she noticed that her hand did not shake, and was vaguely pleased.

The large gentleman's voice broke in on her reflections. 'There is no Borgia blood in my veins, Peter Merriot.'

There was some sternness in the tone. Her left hand came mechanically to cover the maltreated wrist; the marks of the gentleman's fingers still lingered. 'I did not suppose it, sir.'

Sir Anthony rose, pushing back his chair. He walked to the window and back, and the grey eyes followed him. He stopped, and looked down at Prudence; there was gravity in his face, but no anger, she thought. His words gave her a slight start. 'My dear,

I wish you could find it in your heart to trust me,'
he said.

'Deed, but trust was there, in her heart, but how tell
him?

'I've had suspicions of your secret since the first
evening you dined with me here,' he went on. 'Of late
I have been as certain as a man may be of so wild a
masquerade.'

So much for Robin, and for my Lady Lowestoft,
scornful of his perspicacity. Well, she had had fears
of this. But not even she had realised how much the
sleepy gentleman saw. Egad, what must he think of
her? The colour rose at the thought. She lifted her
eyes; it did not occur to her to try evasion. 'I would
trust you willingly, Sir Anthony,' she said in a still,
calm voice. 'I have not liked the lies I have told, and
the great lie I have acted.' She put a hand up to her
neckcloth; it was tight round her throat of a sudden.
'But there is not only myself involved. If it were all
to do again, I would do it.' A look of pride came into
her face; her chin was up, but it sank after a moment.
She looked down at the ring on her finger, and wiped
the trickle of wine from her hand with a crumpled
napkin.

'Will you tell me your name?' Sir Anthony said
gently.

'It is Prudence, sir. In truth, I know no more. I have
had many surnames.' There was no hint of bitterness

in her voice, nor any shame. It was best the large gentleman should know her for the adventuress she was.

'Prudence?' Sir Anthony was frowning now. 'So that is it!' he said softly.

She looked up, searching his face.

'You are not very like your father,' said Sir Anthony.

She gave nothing away in her expression, but she knew that he had very nearly the full sum of it.

There fell a silence. 'Prudence...' Sir Anthony repeated and smiled. 'I don't think you were very well named, child.' He looked down at her, and there was a light in his eyes she had never seen there before. 'Will you marry me?' he said simply.

Now at last there came surprise into her face, on a wave of colour. She rose swiftly to her feet, and stood staring. 'Sir, I have to suppose—you jest!'

'It is no jest.'

'You ask a nameless woman, an adventuress to marry you? One who had lied to you, and tricked you! And you say it is no jest?'

'My dear, you have never tricked me,' he said, amused.

'I tried to do so.'

'I wish you would call me Tony,' he complained.

She had a tiny suspicion she was being punished. Sure, the fine gentleman would never ask her to be his wife in all seriousness. 'You have the right to your revenge, sir,' she said stiffly.

An Important Message from the Editors

Dear Reader,

*Because you've chosen to read one of our fine romance novels, we'd like to say "thank you!" And, as a **special** way to thank you, we've selected <u>two more</u> of the books you love so well **plus** an exciting Mystery Gift to send you — absolutely <u>FREE</u>!*

Please enjoy them with our compliments...

Pam Powers

Lift here

How to validate your Editor's "Thank You" FREE GIFT

1. Peel off gift seal from front cover. Place it in space provided at right. This automatically entitles you to receive 2 FREE BOOKS and a fabulous mystery gift.

2. Send back this card and you'll get 2 brand-new *Romance* novels. These books have a cover price of $5.99 or more each in the U.S. and $6.99 or more each in Canada, but they are yours to keep absolutely free.

3. There's no catch. You're under no obligation to buy anything. We charge nothing—ZERO—for your first shipment. And you don't have to make any minimum number of purchases—not even one!

4. The fact is, thousands of readers enjoy receiving their books by mail from The Reader Service. They enjoy the convenience of home delivery...they like getting the best new novels at discount prices BEFORE they're available in stores... and they love their Heart to Heart subscriber newsletter featuring author news, horoscopes, recipes, book reviews and much more!

5. We hope that after receiving your free books you'll want to remain a subscriber. But the choice is yours— to continue or cancel, any time at all! So why not take us up on our invitation, with no risk of any kind. You'll be glad you did!

GET A *Free* MYSTERY GIFT...

SURPRISE MYSTERY GIFT COULD BE YOURS ***FREE*** AS A SPECIAL "THANK YOU" FROM THE EDITORS

The Editor's "Thank You" Free Gifts Include:

- *Two BRAND-NEW Romance novels!*
- *An exciting mystery gift!*

Yes!
I have placed my Editor's "Thank You" seal in the space provided above. Please send me 2 free books and a fabulous mystery gift. I understand I am under no obligation to purchase any books, as explained on the back and on the opposite page.

PLACE
FREE GIFT
SEAL
HERE

393 MDL DVFG   193 MDL DVFF

FIRST NAME	LAST NAME

ADDRESS

APT.#	CITY

STATE/PROV.	ZIP/POSTAL CODE

(PR-R-04)

Thank You!

The Reader Service — Here's How It Works:

Accepting your 2 free books and gift places you under no obligation to buy anything. You may keep the books and gift and return the shipping statement marked "cancel." If you do not cancel, about a month later we'll send you 3 additional books and bill you just $4.74 each in the U.S., or $5.24 each in Canada, plus 25¢ shipping & handling per book and applicable taxes if any.* That's the complete price and — compared to cover prices starting from $5.99 each in the U.S. and $6.99 each in Canada — it's quite a bargain! You may cancel at any time, but if you choose to continue, every month we'll send you 3 more books, which you may either purchase at the discount price or return to us and cancel your subscription.

*Terms and prices subject to change without notice. Sales tax applicable in N.Y. Canadian residents will be charged applicable provincial taxes and GST.

If offer card is missing write to: The Reader Service, 3010 Walden Ave., P.O. Box 1867, Buffalo, NY 14240-1867

BUSINESS REPLY MAIL
FIRST-CLASS MAIL   PERMIT NO. 717-003   BUFFALO, NY

POSTAGE WILL BE PAID BY ADDRESSEE

THE READER SERVICE
3010 WALDEN AVE
PO BOX 1341
BUFFALO NY 14240-8571

NO POSTAGE
NECESSARY
IF MAILED
IN THE
UNITED STATES

He came round the corner of the table, and took one of her hands in his. She let it lie there resistless. 'Child, have you still so little faith in me?' he asked. 'I offer you all my worldly goods, and the protection of my name, and you call it a jest.'

'I've—I've to thank you, sir. I don't understand you. Why do you offer this?'

'Because I love you,' he answered. 'Must you ask that?'

She raised her eyes to his face, and knew that he had spoken the truth. She wondered that he did not take her into his arms, and with a fine intuition realised the chivalry of this man who would take no advantage of her being alone in his house, and quite defenceless. She drew her hand away, and felt a hot pricking beneath her eyelids. 'I cannot marry you, Sir Anthony. I am no fit bride for you.'

'Don't you think I might be permitted to judge of that?' he suggested.

She shook her head. 'You know nothing of me, Sir Anthony.'

'My dear, I have looked many times into your eyes,' he said. 'They tell me all I have need to know.'

'I—don't think so, sir,' she forced herself to say.

Her hand lay on the chair-back. He took it in his again, and carried it to his lips. 'You have the truest eyes in the world, Prudence,' he said. 'And the very bravest.'

'You don't know me,' she repeated. 'I have led the

life of an adventurer; I am an adventurer—a masquer-
ader! I have no knowledge even of my true name. My
father—' She paused.

'I take it your name may well prove to be a Tremaine,' he said, with a soft laugh.

'You've guessed my father, sir?'

'Why yes, it's the remarkable old gentleman who
claims to be the lost Viscount, I believe. You told me
once your father would surprise me.'

'Did I, sir? Well, that is he. I think you are one of
those who have little faith in his claim.'

'To say truth,' remarked Sir Anthony, 'I care very
little whether he proves to be Barham or not.'

'But I care, Sir Anthony. If he is Barham indeed,
and I am thus a woman of birth noble enough....' She
found it was impossible to continue.

'Then you would marry me?' Sir Anthony
prompted. 'Is that it?'

She nodded. It was not in her nature to deny she
cared for him.

'And do you know what you will do if he is not
Tremaine of Barham?' inquired Sir Anthony conversationally.

She made a gesture of fatalism. 'I shall be off on
my adventuring again, sir.'

'You may call it adventuring if you please, but I
believe I'm a staid creature. You will marry me just
the same, you see.'

She smiled a little. 'This is madness, sir. You will be glad one day that I said you nay.'

'And will you be glad, Prue?' he asked gravely.

'I shall be glad for your sake, sir.'

'My dear, I want to take you out of this masquerade of yours at once. There's danger on all sides, and—I love you.'

'Ah, do not!' she made swift outcry. 'It's not possible, sir. More depends on the masquerade than you know.'

'I believe I may guess. You've a brother took part in the late Rebellion, dressed now in woman's clothes. His name is, I think, Robin.'

She looked wonderingly up at him. 'Do you know everything, sir?'

'No,' he answered, smiling. 'Not quite. Marry me, and put both your fortunes into my hands. I can help this Robin, maybe.'

'Not even for that. I could not, sir. Grant me a little pride! You would be King Cophetua, but I've no mind to play the beggar-maid.'

He made no reply for a moment, but stood looking down at her. 'I cannot force you to marry me,' he said at last.

'Sir Anthony—I would have you marry a woman of whom you can be proud.'

'I have nothing but pride in you. In your courage, and in the quick wits of you. I have never known so wonderful a woman.'

'You can have no pride in my birth, sir. I do not know what my father is; we have never known, for he loves to be a mystery. If this claim is true—if he is indeed Tremaine of Barham—ask me once more!' Her eyes were wet, but her mouth smiled resolutely.

'I am to wait, then! You deny me the right to protect you now?'

'You have me at your feet, sir,' she said unsteadily, 'but I do deny you. I must.'

'You at my feet!' he said. 'That is a jest indeed!' He let go her hand, and took a turn about the room. She watched him wistfully, and at last he spoke again. 'Ay, you've pride,' he said. 'Did that spring of low birth? You must needs cleave your own path, and take no help even from the man who loves you. You ask me to wait. I will wait, until this father of yours has settled his affairs. But when that day comes, and whatever the issue—believe me I shall take you then, by force if need be, and carry you off to Church. Is it understood?'

She smiled mistily, and tried to shake her head. He laughed and there was no laziness either in his face or in his voice. 'Better come to me willingly then,' he said, 'for, by God, I shall have no mercy!'

CHAPTER NINETEEN

Meeting in Arlington Street

PRUDENCE showed an impassive face to John who was waiting to let her into the house, but she slipped past the door of Robin's chamber on tiptoe, and was gone into her own without the usual visit to him. She preferred to meet her sharp-eyed brother in the morning, when she might have acquired some command over herself.

Sure the world was upside down. And who would have thought it of the large gentleman? She had come to think she could no longer be surprised, but this strange proposal of his came to dispel such fancies. He meant it, too: not a doubt of that. As she prepared for bed she thought over it long, and with some agitation. The gentleman's last words lingered; they had been forcefully uttered; she believed he was not the man to promise what he would not perform.

Well, she had said him nay: that had been of instinct, because she loved him, and it was not in a lover's part to take the selfish course. But the devil was in it the gentleman refused to take her nay. There seemed to be no counter for that; she perceived that she was doomed to become Lady Fanshawe. A slow smile played around the corners of her mouth. No use pretending it was not a rôle she had an ambition to play; not much use either to pretend she would escape from Sir Anthony, and hide herself abroad. It might be a difficult matter, she reflected, but honesty forced her to admit it was not the difficulty of it deterred her. If when the time came the sleepy gentleman still claimed her she would be his for the taking: there was, faith, a limit to altruism. But he should be granted a respite; he must have time to think it over carefully. Maybe he had fallen under a spell of her unconscious weaving, and might later achieve sanity again. Egad, he had a position to maintain in the world, and an old name to consider. He would thank her perhaps for her nay. A gloomy thought to take to bed with one.

She slept but fitfully; the evening's word haunted her dreams, and in the waking moments a vision of security, and the love of a large gentleman came to tantalise her. The night hours passed in wakeful contemplation; she fell asleep with the grey dawn, and was sleeping still when Robin peeped in on her in broad daylight.

Robin forebore to wake her. Something had gone amiss; that was sure. He had awaited her homecoming last night, and he had heard her creep past his door to her own. That told its own tale. Robin declined to drive out to visit friends with my Lady Lowestoft, and sat him down to await his sister's pleasure.

There came soon a knock on the door into the street, and a few minutes later Sir Anthony Fanshawe was ushered into the room.

Robin made his curtsey, and was startled to see no gallant bow in response. 'Sir?' said he, in a voice of some dignity.

Sir Anthony laid down his hat and gloves. 'I've to suppose you've not yet seen your sister,' he remarked.

This came as something of a shock to Robin, but long training stood him in good stead. He showed no signs of shock, but looked watchfully under his long lashes, and softly said: 'Pray how am I to take that, sir?'

'Honestly, I beg of you.'

The time for dissimulation was obviously past. Robin felt some annoyance at being found in all this woman's gear, but no shadow of alarm crossed his face. 'So! I'm to understand Prue takes you into her confidence?'

'Say, more truly, that I forced her confidence.'

Robin's dazzling smile came. 'I have to offer you my apologies, sir. I under-rated your intelligence. What now?'

Sir Anthony replied placidly: 'I've a very lively desire to marry your sister, Master Robin.'

'You cannot suppose me astonished to hear that,'

said Robin. But he felt some astonishment neverthe-
less. 'Do you come to ask my consent?'

'It was not exactly my object,' Sir Anthony said. 'I
take it I had best apply to my Lord Barham for that.'

Egad, Prue was in the right of it all along when she
said there was little escaped those sleepy eyes. It
would not do to appear confounded. 'When you are
better acquainted with the family, sir, you will realise
your error.'

'My dear boy,' said Sir Anthony lazily, 'from the
little I have seen of your remarkable parent I should
imagine he pulls all the strings to set you both dancing.'

Robin laughed. 'There's some truth in that, sir. But
if you don't want my consent, what do you want of
me?'

'You've not had speech with your sister?'

'Devil a word.'

Sir Anthony sat down on the couch. 'I see. Well,
Master Robin, I have asked her to marry me, and she
refuses.'

If that was so then Prue must be mad. 'You don't
say so, sir! Well, well, she was ever a fastidious piece.
Am I to force her into your arms?'

'Do you think you could do it?' There was an
amused smile went with the words.

'I don't, sir. I am fairly certain that I should not
make the attempt. Prue has a knack of managing her
own affairs.'

'So I apprehend. She will marry me, she says, if your father proves his claim to be just. Failing that, she would have me know I stand no chance with her.'

A quick frown flitted across the smoothness of Robin's brow. He spoke the thought in his mind. 'Lord, what ails her? That's a nonsensical piece of miss-ishness.'

'Don't let it perturb you. Allow me some say in the matter. She'll marry me whatever be the issue, and she knows it. I've said I'll wait upon Barham's claim; it's to solace pride, I take it. But I want her out of this masquerade with all speed. That's why I'm here.'

'As a family, sir, we stand by each other. It's for Prue to decide, and for me to support her decision. To say truth, I am a little of her mind. I believe the old gentleman may settle his affairs. Well, we're bound to him; we've played too many of these games to turn our backs now.'

'I don't ask it of you. I ask only that I too may be permitted a share. You stand in some danger, as I understand. I've influence in certain circles; I think I can serve you. If I could get a pardon for you, the Merriots may disappear, and await the issue of the Barham claim in a safe seclusion.'

The door was opened again. 'My Lord Barham!' announced a lackey, and my lord came in, all scented, and powdered, and patched.

He stopped just inside the room, and seemed to be enraptured at the sight of Sir Anthony. 'My friend

Fanshawe!' he exclaimed. 'And the beautiful Miss Merriot!'

'It won't serve, sir,' Robin broke in. 'Your friend Fanshawe is more intimate with you than you know. You may say that we all lie in his power.'

My lord evinced not the smallest discomfiture. 'My son, if you think I lie in any man's power you do not know me. As for you to be in danger when my wing is spread over you is not possible.' He spoke with a tinge of severity in his voice.

Sir Anthony had risen at his entrance, and bowed now. 'You stand in no danger from me, sir.'

My lord surveyed him haughtily. 'I stand in no danger from anyone, my dear Sir Anthony. You have no knowledge of me. You are to be pitied.'

'Envied more like,' said his undutiful son.

Sir Anthony's mouth twitched, but he suppressed the smile. 'Let us hope, sir, that I'm not to be long in dismal ignorance. I aspire to the hand of your daughter.'

The severity left my lord; he beamed, and spread open his arms. 'I am to embrace a second son, *enfin!* You aspire—it is well said! Tremaine of Barham's daughter may look to the highest quarters for a mate.'

'You're abashed,' Robin told Sir Anthony.

He seemed to be struggling more with amusement, however. 'Why, sir, I hope you'll look kindly on my suit.'

'I will give my consideration,' my lord promised. 'We must speak more of this.'

'By all means, sir. But I think it only fair to tell you I have the fixed intention of wedding Prudence whatever your decision may be.'

My lord eyed him a moment in silence, but displayed no anger. On the contrary, his smile grew. 'I perceive you to be a man after my own heart!' he announced.

'It's a compliment,' Robin said, on a note of information, and folded his hands in his lap.

'Certainly it is a compliment. You see clearly, my son. But we must think on this; it is a matter of some weight.'

'There's another matter of some weight also, sir. I desire to serve your son here. I've some influence, as I tell him, and I will use it on his behalf with your consent.'

My lord became all blank bewilderment. 'I don't take you, sir. What is it you have a mind to do for my son?'

'Well, sir, I've some notion of getting a pardon for him. I believe it may be done.'

My lord struck an attitude. 'A pardon, sir? For what, pray?'

'For his share in the late Rebellion, sir. Does he want one for something else beside?'

'That!' My lord brushed it aside. 'I have forgotten

all that. It is nothing; it lies in the dead past. Oblige me by forgetting it likewise.'

'Oh, with all my heart, sir, but there are perhaps some whose memories are not so short. A pardon is necessary if Robin wants to remain in England, and come out of those clothes.'

My lord put up an admonishing finger. 'Sir Anthony, I acquit you of a desire to insult me. Don't cry pardon. I have said that I acquit you. But you do not know me; you even doubt my powers. It is laughable! Believe me, there is greatness in me. It would astonish you.'

'Not at all,' said Sir Anthony politely.

'But yes! I doubt now that you, even you whom I would embrace as a son, have not the soul to appreciate me. You make it plain. I pity you, sir!'

'At least I have the soul to appreciate your daughter,' mildly remarked Sir Anthony.

'That I expect,' said his lordship loftily. 'To see my daughter is to become her slave. I exact such homage on her behalf. She is incomparably lovely. But I—I am different. My children are very well. They have beauty, and wit—a little. But in me there is a subtlety such as you don't dream of, sir.' He pondered it sadly. 'I have never met the man who had vision large enough to appreciate my genius,' he said simply. 'Perhaps it was not to be expected.'

'I shall hope to have my vision enlarged as I become better acquainted with you, sir,' Sir Anthony replied, with admirable gravity.

My lord shook his head. He could not believe in so large a comprehension. 'I shall stand alone to the end,' he said. 'It is undoubtedly my fate.'

Sir Anthony gave the conversation a dexterous turn: the old gentleman seemed to be in danger of slipping into mournful contemplation of his own unappreciated greatness. 'Just as you please, sir, but I want to put an end to a notion Prudence has of emulating your noble solitude. I wish to take her out of this masquerade, and have her safe under the protection of my name.'

My lord's piercing eyes flashed at that. 'I make allowance for a lover's feelings!' he cried. 'But while I live she stands in no need of another's protection. I am the person to guard her, Sir Anthony.'

'You are, sir, certainly,' Fanshawe said. There was an edge to his words which did not escape my lord.

'I admire my forebearance. Concede me a great patience. You may call it toleration. I do not call you out. I curb myself!'

'I could not possibly meet my future father-in-law, so pray continue to curb yourself, sir.'

'You need have no fear. But were I to meet you, sir, you would lie dead at my feet within the space of five minutes. Possibly less. I do not know.' He appeared to give the matter his consideration.

'That,' said Robin reluctantly, 'is really true.'

Sir Anthony preserved his calm. 'I don't think it. But I trust his lordship will spare me.'

His lordship signified with a gracious wave of his hand that he would spare Sir Anthony. 'But do not try me too far!' he warned. 'Like all men of great brain, I am choleric when pressed. You give me to understand that you do not consider that I—I, Tremaine of Barham!—can take care of my daughter!'

'Not in the least, sir. I make no doubt you can. But when you permit her to engage on so dangerous a masquerade—'

'Permit?' cried my lord. 'You conceive that my children thought of this for themselves? Your partiality makes you blind. Mine was the brain that evolved this plot; mine was the inspiration. I do not permit: I ordain.'

Robin ranged himself on the side of his father. 'We spin our own web, sir. Give us credit for some little resource.'

Fanshawe turned to look at him. 'I suppose I am far from appreciating any of you,' he said humorously. 'But did you never think what might be the issue if Prudence were discovered?'

'I could not imagine such a possibility, sir, to be frank with you. But then it was not our intention to cut such conspicuous figures in town. I will pay you the compliment to say that I think no other man would have discovered the imposture. I should like to know what made you suspect.'

'I should find it hard to tell you, Robin. Some little things and the affection for her I discovered in myself. I wondered when I saw her tip wine down her arm at my card-party, I confess.'

My lord frowned. 'Do you tell me my daughter was clumsy?'

'By no means, sir. But I was watching her closer than she knew.'

My lord still seemed dissatisfied. After a moment Sir Anthony went on. 'And I want now, sir, to spirit her off. She tells me she must needs wait upon your claim.'

'Certainly,' said my lord. 'She shows a proper feeling. She has faith in me, *enfin.*'

'That's as maybe, sir, but I rather see her in safety now.'

'I applaud her decision,' said my lord. 'She will await my re-instalment; and you may then pay your addresses to her with all propriety. As for Robin, he is my son, and I want no pardons for him. I arrange all in a manner sublime beyond your comprehension. You may place your trust in me.'

A deep, calm voice spoke from the doorway. 'In fact, sir, we are all of us wandering in a maze, and there is only one of our number knows the path out of it.'

Sir Anthony turned quickly; my lord bowed ineffably in acknowledgement of a compliment he had no hesitation in taking to himself. Prudence stood on the

threshold, neat in brown velvet, with brown hair unpowdered. She met Sir Anthony's gaze, and there was
a little smile playing at the corners of her mouth. 'I've
this much faith in my father, sir, that I believe we may
ruin all by a step taken without his knowledge.'

'My Prue!' His lordship stretched a hand towards
her. 'I said you had intuition.'

'It seems to me,' said Sir Anthony whimsically,
'that I, too, am being drawn into this maze.'

'Inevitably,' nodded his lordship. 'You, too, are in
my toils.'

'I'm a respectable creature, sir, I believe.'

'If I did not think it, sir, I should deny you the right
to aspire to my daughter's hand.'

Sir Anthony bowed, but Prudence was not pleased.
'Let's have done with that, sir. Sir Anthony honours
me beyond my deserts. I don't desire to see him in the
maze.' She came forward and put her hand on Fanshawe's sleeve. She looked up at him seriously. 'Stand
back from us, sir. I ask it of you.'

He covered her hand with one of his. 'Faith, you
ask more than I can perform. I don't meddle, but I
reserve to myself the right to watch over you.'

My lord smiled indulgently, and helped himself to
a pinch of snuff. Prudence said earnestly: 'Believe me,
we were born to this game of hazardous chances. But
you are not. Stand back from us.'

'My child, you need have no qualms,' my lord assured her. 'My plans are not overset even by Sir Anthony's entering into them.'

'That was not what was in my mind, sir,' said Prudence dryly.

Sir Anthony smiled down at her. 'My dear, I know, but I may take care of myself. Don't worry over my safety. I am to wait: you'll none of my help. Well, I said that it should be so, and I abide by my word. But things must be the same between us, if only to avert suspicion. You will visit me as frequently as ever. My Lord Barham can trust me.'

My lord waved his hand. 'Implicitly, my dear Fanshawe! Are you not to be a second son to me? I can even applaud your forethought. Certainly my daughter visits you the same as ever.'

Observing a troubled crease between Prudence's brows, Sir Anthony said softly: 'And Prudence herself has naught to fear from me, neither exposure nor importunities. I remain her friend Tony.'

'Admirable,' nodded my lord. 'You are all delicacy, sir.'

Prudence looked up into the square face, and smiled mistily. 'Indeed, Tony, I think so,' she said.

CHAPTER TWENTY

Ingenuity of My Lord Barham

ROBIN HAD, perforce to wish his sister joy of her conquest. He perceived her to be troubled, an unusual state of mind with her, and abandoned the teasing note. 'To be honest, my dear, I was wrong in underrating the mountain. What happened last night?'

She told him, choosing her words carefully, he thought. 'He caught my wrist,' she ended, 'and bore it downwards. I knew then, of course. There was no more to say. I know when it is time to have done with lies.' She pushed back the ruffles from her hand, and inspected the wrist closely.

'What, do the marks still linger?' Robin was inclined to be indignant.

'No. I thought they did,' she said inconsequently. 'He asked my name; I told him. He guessed that I was the old gentleman's child. The rest is nothing.'

Robin let that pass He fell to playing with his rings. 'I'm of the opinion he'll have you, Prue.'

She smiled at that, but the smile died. 'I don't like it, Robin. It was very well to play this part when none knew the truth, but now—*he* knows, and—do you understand at all?'

'Certainly, child. You might leave your part. He offers you a change.'

She turned her head. 'Oh, and you thought that I would take it, did you not?'

'No, my Prue. I thought you would not,' Robin grinned. 'For myself I don't mind the large gentleman. For all his respectability there's some humour in the man. I've a notion he doesn't approve of your little brother. We shall see.'

The Honourable Charles, appearing then to claim Mr Merriot, there was an end to further discussion. Prudence went off with Mr Belfort. Later in the day she me Sir Anthony at White's Club. She knew a momentary embarrassment, but something in Fanshawe's demeanour banished it. He walked home with her, and if she had dreaded some love-making, that fear was quickly dispelled. He was as he had said he would be, her very good friend. It was only when she had parted from him that she realised how possessive was the gentleman's attitude. He seemed to consider that she belonged to him already. She pondered the question thoughtfully, and arrived at the conclusion that perhaps he had reason.

My Lord Barham, when he left Arlington Street, sauntered back to his lodgings in great good-humour. He had no objection to Sir Anthony having complete knowledge of the masquerade; so slight a deviation from the original plan was not enough to perturb his lordship. That quick brain was busy with the fitting of Sir Anthony into my lord's machinations. He reflected with a pleased smile that John, the unbelieving, should see how even a big man with sleepy eyes should dance to his piping.

My lord came to his rooms in Half Moon Street to find that a visitor awaited him. My lord's valet took his hat and cane, and murmured the name of Markham. My lord listened with a head gently inclined in interest, and went into his dining-room, smoothing a wrinkle from a satin sleeve.

Mr Markham arose at his entry, and bowed slightly. My lord smiled with the utmost affability, and put up his quizzing-glass. 'My friend of Munich days!' he said softly. 'How I am honoured!' His eyes dwelt lovingly on Mr Markham; there was no reading in them the smallest hint of what thoughts were passing swiftly across that subtle mind. 'But sit down, my dear Mr Markham! Pray sit down!'

Mr Markham obeyed this injunction, and was silent while the valet set wine and glasses on the table. My lord's white hand hovered over the Burgundy decanter; my lord looked inquiring.

'I won't drink, I thank you,' said Mr Markham.

'But positively I insist!' My lord was pained. 'You will permit me to give you some claret.'

Mr Markham watched the valet go out of the room.

'You must guess I've come upon business,' he said curtly.

'No; but no, my dear Markham. I thought you had come to recall old days,' said his lordship. 'I never occupy myself with business. You cannot interest me in such a subject. Shall it be claret or Burgundy?'

'Oh, claret, then!' Mr Markham said impatiently.

'I am quite of your opinion,' nodded my lord. 'Burgundy is the very King of Wines, but it was not meant to be taken in the morning.' He handed his guest a brimming glass, and poured another for himself. 'To your very good health, my dear sir!'

Mr Markham made no answer to his toast. He drank some of the wine, and pushed the glass from him. 'I venture to think, my Lord Barham, that the business I am come upon will interest you vastly,' he said.

My lord re-filled his glass. 'I am sure if anyone could interest me in such a subject, it must be you, dear Markham,' he said warmly.

Against such smooth-spoken politeness Mr Markham found it difficult to proceed. He felt somewhat at a disadvantage, but comforted himself with the thought that it was my lord who should feel at a disadvantage in a very few moments. He plunged abruptly into the subject of his errand. 'As to this claim of yours, sir, that you are Tremaine of Barham, I don't believe in it, but I am taking no interest in it now.'

'That is very wise of you,' my lord approved. 'You must allow me to compliment you.'

Mr Markham ignored this. 'For all I care, you may ape the part of Barham to your heart's content. It's nothing to me.'

'Positively you overwhelm me!' my lord said. 'You oppress me with kindness, sir. And you come, in fact, to set my mind at rest! Believe me all gratitude.'

'I don't come for that purpose at all,' said Mr Markham, annoyed. 'I come for a purpose, for which you may not be so damned grateful.'

'Impossible!' My lord shook his head. 'The mere felicity of seeing you here in my rooms must fill me with gratitude.'

Mr Markham broke in on this without ceremony. 'Barham you may be, but there is one thing you have been which is certain!' He paused to let this sink in.

My lord did not seem to be greatly impressed. 'Oh, a number of things!' he assured his guest. 'Of course, there are a number of things I have not been, too. They have never fallen in my way, which is the reason, you see. But continue! Pray continue!'

'I will, my lord. You may not find it so palatable as you imagine. You have been—you may be still, for aught I know—a cursed Jacobite!'

My lord's expression of polite interest underwent no change. 'But you should tell this to my cousin Rensley,' he pointed out.

'You may be thankful I don't, sir. It's nothing to

me: my information goes to the highest bidder. If you haggle, my lord, Rensley shall have it. But I don't think you will haggle.'

'I'm sure I shan't,' my lord answered. 'I am not a tradesman.'

'You're a damned Jack-of-all-trades, in my opinion!' said Markham frankly. 'You assume a mighty lofty tone, to be sure—'

'No, no, it comes quite naturally,' my lord interpolated sweetly. 'I assume nothing; I am a positive child of nature, my dear sir. But you were saying?'

'At, it doesn't interest you at all, does it?' Mr Markham achieved a sneer.

My lord was apologetic. 'Well, not just at the moment, my dear friend of old days. But presently I feel you will arrive at a climax which will astound me. I am all expectation.'

'It may well appal you, my lord. I have here'—he laid his hand on the breast of his coat significantly—'something that spells ruin for you.'

'What, in your heart?' My lord was puzzled.

'No, sir! In my pocket!' snapped Markham.

'Oh, I see! An inner pocket! A very cunning contrivance, sir: I must have one made for myself. What did you tell me you had in it?'

'I have a certain paper, sir—a letter writ to my Lord George Murray: writ by a man who called himself—Colney!'

'Good Gad, sir!' said my lord placidly. 'But you

don't drink! You find my claret insipid, I fear. Let me send for some canary. Or do you prefer ale in the morning? My man shall procure you some on the instant. You have but to say the word.'

'You, sir, are that man!' declared Mr Markham in a ringing voice.

My lord jumped and blinked. 'I am anything in the world you please,' he assured Mr Markham. 'But don't. I implore you, give me another such start!'

Mr Markham put a hand to his pocket, and pulled out a folded sheet of paper. This he spread before my lord's eyes, keeping it well out of reach.

My lord looked at it and nodded. 'Very interesting,' he said.

'Very dangerous, my Lord of Barham!'

'Then I should take care of it,' advised my lord. 'I do wish you would drink. I feel you detect something amiss with the claret which has escaped my palate.'

'To hell with the claret! What will you give for this document, my lord? What's it worth, eh? A man's life?'

My lord shook his head decidedly. 'If you want that for it, take it elsewhere, my dear Markham.'

Markham stowed it safely away. 'With your leave, sir, we'll ha' done with this foolery. I know you for Colney. I hold a paper that would send you to the gallows-tree. Come out into the open, sir, and be plain with me. I've no animosity towards you; I wish you no harm. But you'll pay well for the letter.'

My lord rose, and made a fine gesture. 'I perceive that you would be a friend indeed. I embrace you! We understand one another.'

'As to that,' said Markham, rather bewildered by this sudden effusion, 'I am neither your friend nor your foe. But I hold you in the hollow of my hand.'

'You do, my dear Markham, you do! And if I were given the choice of a hand to be held in, I should choose yours. My word for it, sir, my solemn oath!'

'I might have taken this paper to Rensley,' Markham went on, disregarding. 'I thought of it; I weighed it well. I decided it was more vital to you to get the paper than Rensley. And I came as you see.'

'A master-mind!' said my lord. 'I drink to it.' He did so, with considerable flourish. 'You must accept my homage, Mr Markham. I descry in you a shrewd brain. I venerate it; we were made for each other. Rensley could never have given you what I can give you. My dear friend, I have something which might have been designed expressly for you. But still you don't drink.'

Mr Markham tossed off the wine, and set his glass down again. 'You're mighty pleased over it,' he remarked.

'I am, sir. You have divined me correctly. I could embrace you.'

'It is not your embraces I want, my lord.'

My lord smiled wickedly. 'But do I not know it! It

is Letitia Grayson's embraces you crave, my dear Markham.'

Mr Markham choked and swore. 'Curse it, what do you know of Letty Grayson?'

'Very little, sir, but I shall hope to know more when she is Mrs Markham. I drink to that happy day.'

A gloomy look came into Mr Markham's face. 'You may spare your pains: it's far off.'

'No, no, my friend, it is close at hand!' said my lord radiantly.

Mr Markham looked suspicious. 'What do you know of it? You are off at a tangent. I've come to sell you your own treasonable letter, not to talk of Letty Grayson.'

My lord sat down again. 'My friend, I will show you a sure road to Miss Letty,' he promised.

'I wish there was such a road,' Markham said. The truth was Miss Grayson's dimpled loveliness haunted him almost as much as did Miss Grayson's golden fortune.

'There is,' said my lord. 'But it is known only to me. Let us be plain—you did wish me to be plain with you, did you not? Well, my dear Markham, at first I thought, no: I will not show my Munich friend the road. But then, sir, then I fell in love with your wit. You remember that I was impelled to compliment you. You seem to realise that I might not be quite all I pretend to be. I admire that perspicacity. Then you assured me that you had no animosity towards me. I was struck by this, sir: I was amazed. I saw in you a friend: I changed my mind. I will put into your hands a certain means of winning Letitia Grayson. You might be away to Gretna in a week, if you chose.'

'H'm!' said Mr Markham sceptically. 'That's to play the same game twice. With Fanshawe on my heels, as he was before. No, I thank you.'

'I myself will keep Fanshawe away,' announced my lord. 'You will stop only to change horses; you arrive at Gretna—'

'And Letty refuses to marry me. Very pretty.'

'You have it quite wrong, 'said my lord. 'She goes willingly. You are married; she becomes mistress of her mother's fortune on that day. You are at once rich, and a happy bridegroom.'

Mr Markham's eyes glistened. It was an attractive picture, and he could not resist dwelling on it for a space. 'You seem to know a devilish lot about the Graysons,' he remarked.

'I do, my friend, as you shall see. I know she becomes mistress of a charming fortune on the day she marries, with or without Sir Humphrey's consent. You must be master of it. I am determined on it.'

'But how?' demanded Mr Markham.

My lord arose, and went to where a locked desk stood. Mr Markham watched him open it, and saw him take a bundle of papers from a hidden drawer, and select one from the bundle. My lord came back with it in his hand, and spread it for his visitor to read. A smile of simple triumph illumined his countenance.

Mr Markham read with knit brows. It was a letter from Sir Humphrey to a man Markham did not know. It was vague in tenour, but there were references to the 'Prince,' and a half promise to render assistance in the 'venture to be attempted,' if the Prince would come without foreign aid into England. Mr Markham sniffed. 'The old dog!' he said. 'That wouldn't send him to Tyburn. He's a friend of Bute's. He never lifted a finger in the Rising, and they'd never touch him.'

'But would the little Letty see that with the same quickness, my friend? Your brain leaps to it, true, but do you rate her intelligence as high as yours? I cannot allow it to be so.'

A dim scheme began to form itself in Mr Markham's brain. 'I'll take it,' he said suddenly.

'You shall, dear sir. And I will take that letter you keep in your cunning pocket. It's all so delightfully simple.'

'That won't quite do, I'm afraid,' said Mr Markham. 'I want more for it than that. I'll see the colour of your money, my lord.'

My lord folded the paper. He was still smiling. 'It would disappoint you, my friend. It is just the same colour as everyone else's. And you never will see it.'

'I shan't, eh? You prefer me to take my letter to Rensley?'

'Infinitely,' said my lord. 'You won't see the colour

of his money either. You must look ahead, my friend; you must look far, and consider the situation well. You have not thought on it deeply enough. I am not Lord Barham yet. You have your doubts of me; you are a very clever man, Mr Markham; I felicitate you. I am not going to tell you whether my claim is true or not. There is not, perhaps, the need. You seem to understand me so well, my dear sir. Now, you want a large sum for your letter. You realise, of course, that unless my claim is just, I can have nothing approaching it. All I have lies in the letter I hold, and I offer it to you. I can give no more.'

This speech of my lord's had an uncomfortable effect on Mr Markham. My lord appeared to admit an imposture, which was not now at all what Mr Markham wanted to have proved. He looked warily, but decided to ignore the hint. 'You can give me a written promise, my lord. You haven't thought of that, have you?'

'I have not. You always contrive to understand me. It is a delight to me, for so few people do! I have a great objection to parting with my money; I do positively abhor the very thought of it. Rather than contemplate it I would relinquish my claim, and vanish!'

Mr Markham's expression changed. 'What?'

'Yes, my friend, yes. You understand me yet again. Refuse my offer; take your letter to Rensley—What happens?'

Mr Markham was looking at him with a fascinated
eye. 'Well, what does happen?' he asked.

'Why, only that I am as though I had never been.
There will no longer be a rival claimant to the estates.
I shall have gone, and Rensley will be Viscount Barham without need of letters, or of any assistance whatsoever. You see, you must think ahead, Mr Markham;
you must visualise possibilities.'

It was quite evident that Mr Markham was visual-
ising this particular possibility. 'You wouldn't do it,'
he said.

'But of course I should! I am not a fool, my dear
Markham. I do not say that I have your brain, but still
I am not a fool. If you walk out of this room with the
paper still in that pocket of yours—you must show me
how that is contrived—what can I do but fly the country? I am in the hollow of your hand, as you so aptly
phrased it.'

Mr Markham began to entertain doubts of the truth
of this. It had certainly seemed true enough at the outset, but things were taking an unfortunate turn. 'I know
very well you don't mean to give up your claim.
You'll pay, safe enough!'

'Still you follow me,' admired my lord. 'I have an
ardent wish to pursue my claim, and certainly I will
pay. But within reason, my dear Markham, within reason! I give you my paper, and—unless you are a man
of very clumsy address, which I will not, nay, cannot
believe—you are bound to prevail with Miss Letty.

You become thus the master of the fortune you require, and I am rid of a menace. That talk of written promises—no, no, my dear sir, it's not worthy of you! I, who am not even sure yet of the success of my claim, am to purchase your paper from you at the cost of fresh documentary evidence? You cannot, I beg you *will* not believe me to be so big a fool! Credit me with a preference for a free gamester's life to a bound Viscount's.' He ended on a little laugh. His arresting eyes were glowing with a light of triumph.

There fell a silence. Bit by bit the force of my lord's argument sank deep into Markham's brain. He cursed himself for not having taken his paper to Rensley, and made sure of a snug ten thousand pounds. He began to see that he had snatched at a shadow. His glance fell on the paper that my lord held between his thin fingers. Involuntarily he started to form plans for its use. Certainly it had some value. Miss Letty would not be hard to terrify with threats; he could find the opportunity. She was worth more than ten thousand pounds, to be sure, if the scheme worked.

He pondered moodily, and realised that the letter and the chance it held was all that he could now hope to gain out of the affair. He began to arrive at the discovery that somehow or other it was he who seemed to be in the hollow of my lord's hand. 'You're a damned trickster!' he said.

'You pain me,' my lord said reproachfully.

Mr Markham relapsed into silence. If he did snare

Letty—Gad, she was a dainty piece!—there might still be something to be got out of my lord. Even a verbal accusation could be unpleasant and might lead to disaster. He reflected that if he had Letty he would no longer be in need of large monetary assistance. Still, it would be useful to hold that weapon; to feel it to be within his power to squeeze my Lord Barham—if this smiling man were indeed Tremaine, though it now seemed doubtful. He perceived that his lordship had omitted to follow his own advice of looking far ahead, and smiled inwardly. He would take that letter in exchange for the one he held, and if he got Letty—well, he would be fairly satisfied, for after all, he wanted her, had always wanted her, even apart from her fortune. If he failed, if she would not be frightened by a threat to expose her father, then my lord would find he had not bought his dear friend's tongue, though he might have bought his letter. 'I'll take it!' he announced.

'You are always so wise,' said my lord. 'It is a pleasure to have to do with you, sir.'

The exchange was effected. Mr Markham refused an offer of more claret brusquely, and strode off in the wake of my lord's man.

My lord remained standing by the table, one hand resting lightly upon it, and the smile curling his lips. He heard the front door shut behind Mr Markham, and he listened to the heavy footsteps growing fainter and fainter in this distance. He raised his head then, and laughed softly to himself, in exquisite enjoyment. His man, returning to clear away the wine and the glasses, looked at him in some surprise.

'Henry,' said my lord. 'You are fortunate. You serve a master of infinite resource.'

'Yes, sir,' said Henry stolidly.

My lord looked at him, but it is doubtful whether he saw him. His gaze seemed to go beyond. 'I am a great man,' he said. 'Oh, but I am a very great man!'

'Yes, my lord,' said Henry.

CHAPTER TWENTY-ONE

Proceedings of Mr Markham

THE ELEMENT of uncertainty made the prize not quite all Mr Markham had hoped for, but since it was all he had been able to get, he determined to make the most of it. An evening spent in plan-making restored him to satisfaction and good humour. He thought he saw his way clear. No thought of the light in which his conduct might possibly be regarded crossed his mind. Probably he held to the maxim that all was fair in love and war. Certainly no reflection of Miss Grayson's feelings in the matter troubled his head, or abated one jot of his new cheerfulness. If he thought about the affair from her side at all, he considered that she would very soon settle down to the married state, especially since she had, not so long ago, fancied herself in love with him. This time there would be no Merriots to interfere in what was no concern of theirs; he would not even take the risk of alighting for so much as a bite of supper, until well out of reach of London, but speed on towards Scotland with no more stops than the changes of horses would necessitate.

Had Mr Markham heard my Lord Barham's laugh,
he might not have felt quite so sanguine; and had he
heard my lord giving sundry instructions to a respectable middle-aged servant he might have entertained
serious doubts as to my lord's good faith. My lord said
quite a lot to this man on the subject of coaching
stages, and at the close of that interview the unre-
sponsive servant had orders to keep an eye not only
on the movements of Miss Grayson, but also to discover what horses were ordered at the first stage on
the North Road, for what date, and by what gentlemen.
The servant received these instructions impassively,
and seemed to foresee no difficulties ahead of him.
The truth was that he had performed far harder tasks
for my Lord Barham. It would not have appeared from
his demeanour that he either understood or approved
his orders, but he had nothing to say beyond a re-
signed: 'This is more of your devilry I suppose, my
lord.'

Far from resenting this familiar form of address, my
lord was flattered, and admitted the impeachment, adding a rider to the effect that it was a positive master-
piece of subtlety, whereupon the servant grunted, and
went off.

But Mr Markham had no knowledge of this trans-
action, and he had no suspicion of foul play. All the
foul play in the business was to be performed by himself, though it is doubtful whether he phrased it quite
so candidly.

He foresaw few obstacles: this time there should be no hitch. The only difficulty, and that a small one, was to gain a hearing with Miss Grayson, and a little careful espionage soon disclosed an opportunity. Miss Grayson was to be present at a ball in town for which Mr Markham might quite easily procure an invitation. With the help of a friend this was contrived, and midway through the evening, Mr Markham was presented to Miss Grayson by a kindly hostess.

There was no aunt to play dragon, for the elder Miss Grayson had joined the rest of the dowagers in the cardroom. Even Miss Merriot was away at the other end of the long room, flirting outrageously with Sir Anthony Fanshawe. Letitia, unskilled in the dealing of snubs, blushed fiery red, hesitated, stammering over a refusal to dance, and found that the kindly hostess had gone away to supply other young ladies with eligible partners. Very cross, Letty blurted out: 'I do not want to dance with you, sir!'

It seemed that Mr Markham had no desire to dance either. He wanted to talk to Letitia.

'You know very well I don't want to have anything to do with you,' said Letty, still very red.

'Don't be so unforgiving,' Mr Markham said. 'I have something of very great importance to say to you. It can't be said here. It is a secret and a dangerous matter.'

That sounded prodigiously exciting to be sure, but

Letty was still suspicious. 'You will lure me out and abduct me,' she said.

'All I ask of you is that you should come into the little ante-room, across the passage, with me. How could I abduct you here? If you don't come you will regret it all your life. You do not know how weighty a matter it is I have to disclose.'

Letty reflected that Mr Markham would indeed find it hard to carry her off from a crowded ball against her will, and rose undecidedly to her feet. Anything in the nature of a mystery intrigued her at once. She intimated graciously that she would hear what Mr Markham had to say. Unobserved of the Merriots or of Sir Anthony Fanshawe, she went out with Mr Markham.

She had leisure to repent her action when Mr Markham made his startling disclosure. He allowed her but a glimpse of her father's incriminating letter, and sat back in his chair watching her with a satisfied smile.

Her big eyes grew round in horrified wonder. 'B—but my papa is not a Jacobite!' she exclaimed.

'Do you suppose anyone will believe that if I show this letter?' Mr Markham inquired.

'But you won't, sir! You won't, will you?'

Mr Markham leaned forward. 'Not if you will marry me, Letty,' he said softly.

She recoiled instinctively. 'No, no!'

'What, you had rather see your father's head adorning London Bridge?'

Letty's cheeks grew pale at that, and she shuddered.

It was impossible not to feel sick horror at the thought. All who lived in London had seen those ghastly sights in the past months. The pictured conjured up was terribly real to her. 'You would not! You would not do such a cruel, wicked thing!'

'I would do anything to win you, Letty!' Mr Markham said, with fine lover-like ardour.

'Papa will never let me marry you!' cried Letty, cowering away.

'But could you not fly with me again? We set out once, did we not, my little Letty? It can be done again—this time with a difference.'

'No, no, I won't!'

'Not even to save your father?' persuaded Mr Markham.

Miss Letty's bosom rose and fell quickly. 'If you forced me—if you did such a wicked thing, sir—I should hate you all the rest of my life! Do you want a wife who loathes you?'

Mr Markham laughed indulgently. 'You'll soon get over that when we are married, my dear. Won't you care for me a little when I give you this letter to burn?'

She stretched out her hand. 'Give it to me now, sir, and indeed, indeed, I shall never think hardly of you again!'

'On our wedding day,' said Markham. 'Not before, but just as soon as my ring is on your finger.'

'It will never, never be there,' she declared, bursting into tears.

It took Mr Markham twenty minutes to convince her that she was sending her papa to the gallows-tree by such unreasonable behaviour. She struggled and wept; she cried that she would tell papa all about it, and he would talk to my Lord Bute, and all would be well. Mr Markham said that it would not be in my Lord Bute's power to assist Sir Humphrey, even if he wanted to, which was hardly possible. Sir Humphrey had written treasonable matter in this letter. Surely Letty knew what that meant?

She did; the very thought of it drove the blood from her face. Desperately she cast around in her mind for some source of help.

Mr Markham thought it well, since she struggled so, to extemporise a little. 'When I leave this ball to-night,' he said, 'this letter goes into a friend's keeping. If anything were to happen to me it would be published at once, and if, in a week from now you and I are not on the road to Scotland I myself shall take it to the proper quarters. You will be sorry then that you would not lift a finger to save your father!'

It seemed she was a monster of selfishness. Where, oh where was the Unknown in the Black Domino, who had said that he would come again in her hour of need? Nothing but a dream. Here was herself only, and Gregory Markham, who had become hateful to her. She could see no road out of the trouble, saving the one he pointed out to her. Almost she went down on her knees to him, imploring his mercy. He used some endearing terms in his reply, but she could see that behind all his soft address he was quite adamant.

She declared she would tell papa; Mr Markham pointed out the immediate and evil consequences of such an action. She saw them; she was induced to believe that to tell anyone would bring disaster upon the house of Grayson. She capitulated, and while he outlined a plan of flight to her, she sat wondering whether she would have strength enough, and courage, to stab him on the road to Scotland. She thought if there were pistols in the coach she could brave the dreadful explosion and shoot her lover, and steal the letter from his person. What would happen to her after that she had no notion, but she expected it would be all very awful.

Something of these murderous designs Mr Markham read in her face: he saw enough in those brown eyes, ordinarily so soft, to make him decide to have no pistols placed anywhere within his bride's reach on the journey to Scotland.

Letty was taken back into the ballroom, and claimed by a young man of fashion. It struck this not very observant youth that she was out of spirits, and he ventured to inquire the cause. Letty confessed to a headache, and began to chatter and laugh at once, as though to refute her own statement. The laughter might be forced, even hysterical, and the chatter somewhat irrelevant, but the young buck was quite satisfied.

Letty found Miss Merriot and Fanshawe quite close

to her in the set, and redoubled her efforts to appear gay and unconcerned. As the dance closed she saw Miss Merriot looking rather closely at her, and was inspired to whisper: 'Oh Kate, I have a monstrous bad headache! It makes me feel sick.'

'My dear,' Miss Merriot said instantly, 'you should be at home and in bed. Will you have me go and find your aunt?'

'I hate to go away early from a ball,' Letty said, 'but my head is dreadfully bad.'

She was promptly swept off under the wing of Miss Merriot to find her aunt. Sir Anthony was left to await the return of his partner, and strolled away to where my Lord Barham stood by the wall.

'No, Clevedale, my dancing days are done,' my lord was saying. 'I am now a spectator only.... Well, my dear Fanshawe? But what have you done with your lovely partner? Surely I saw you with the beautiful Miss Merriot but a moment since?'

'She has deserted me, sir,' Sir Anthony replied. 'Miss Grayson has the migraine, and Miss Merriot has taken her off to find her aunt.'

'Indeed?' said my lord, and proffered his snuff-box. Mr Markham's late exit with Miss Letty had not escaped that eagle eye.

A gentle touch on his sleeve made Sir Anthony turn round. Prudence stood at his elbow, and smiled shyly as he looked down at her. 'Have you lost my sister, sir? I saw you a while back flirting prodigiously with her. It's a sad piece, I believe.'

Sir Anthony walked apart with her. 'It is,' he agreed. 'How came you by so impertinent a brother, my dear?'

Prudence chuckled. 'You've met the old gentleman, Tony. Don't you perceive the resemblance? Robin is a rogue.'

'I'm of the opinion he's a young hothead. I asked him to-night, as the thought occurred to me, whether he knew anything of a Black Domino, calling himself *L'Inconnu*.'

'And does he?' asked Prudence innocently.

'It's in my mind,' said Sir Anthony slowly, 'that you're a fitting pair. Is there nothing of the rogue in Peter Merriot?'

'Oh, sir, it's a most sober youth.'

Came the rustle of silks; Robin swirled down upon them, gracefully fanning himself. 'What, my Peter! You'll make a third, will you? I vow, 'tis unkind in you!'

'I must have a care for your reputation, child. You conduct yourself monstrously when I'm not by.'

Robin cast a languishing glance up at Fanshawe. 'Sir, my Peter must think you a sad rake. And here was I thinking you meant marriage!'

'I think,' said Sir Anthony, 'that you stand in need of birching, young Hop o' my Thumb.'

Robin feigned alarm. 'Oh Prue, have a care! That

is the second time you have heard the mountain talk of offering violence to a poor female.'

'What did you call me?' demanded Sir Anthony, pricking up his ears.

'My tongue—oh, my luckless tongue!' Robin hid behind his fan. 'Only a mountain, dear sir. Would you have me call you a mole-hill?' A laughing pair of eyes showed above the fan. To any who might chance to be watching it seemed as though Miss Merriot was still flirting disgracefully with Sir Anthony Fanshawe. ''Tis a term of endearment I have for you: no more, believe me.'

Sir Anthony's eyes were twinkling. 'My dear,' he said to Prudence, 'if it weren't for you I would expose this shameless boy. You'll permit me to take him in hand when he comes out of this masquerade.'

She shook her head. 'I must protect my little brother, Tony. You see what a pert madcap he is. Give you my word, he would be lost without his big sister. You had better abandon us, you know.'

'Oh no!' Robin besought. 'What amusement should I have left to solace me if I no longer saw the respectable Fanshawe caught in the toils of a set of adventurers? Does it not go against the grain, my dear sir?'

'No, midget, it tickles my sense of the ridiculous. All that goes against the grain with me is to see Prue in a dangerous position, and to watch you courting Letty Grayson. What do you hope for there?'

'The old gentleman assures me that I am also Tremaine of Barham,' Robin answered lightly. 'What do you make of that, O mountain?'

'Very little,' said Sir Anthony. 'As for the filial respect you do *not* show to your father—'

'Prue, did I not say it was all propriety? My very dear sir, I reserve all my respect for my so eminently respectable brother-in-law. The old gentleman is not in the least respectable. If you had had the doubtful pleasure of knowing him for as long as I have, you would realise that.'

'I might, of course,' Sir Anthony conceded. 'But so far, the more I see of him the more I feel that he is a person to be treated with considerable respect, and—er—circumspection.'

CHAPTER TWENTY-TWO

Tortuous methods of My Lord Barham

ROBIN PRESERVED the light manner, but he had begun to chafe at his petticoats. Faith, the old gentleman seemed to do nothing and there were rumours current now that Rensley, as soon as he was able to leave his room, meant to bring a case against his would-be cousin. Robin had small mind to go on playing the lady indefinitely. He believed the Black Domino remained in Letty's memory, but he had little chance of seeing her as the days passed. She was out driving, or she was visiting, or even she was indisposed. When he did meet her she was abstracted, and volunteered no confidences. There were shadows under her eyes: her aunt said it was no wonder, since nowadays she was seldom in bed before midnight; Robin dared to hope a Black Domino had induced this wistfulness.

Prudence thought nothing at all of it; she was rather preoccupied with her own affairs, and showed but slight interest even when Robin spoke of John's new behaviour. Robin became aware of the frequent absences of his faithful henchman, and receiving only evasive replies to a sharp question or two, immediately suspected activity on the part of my Lord Barham. Prudence said placidly that it was very possible she thought they were like to know all soon enough.

She was right: in a short while my lord came to pay a morning visit in Arlington Street, and having rapturously kissed my Lady Lowestoft's hands, requested the favour of some private talk with his son.

My lady opined mischief to be brewing, shook a playful finger, and went off most obligingly.

Robin turned one of the bracelets on his arm, and shot a quick look at his father. 'Well, sir?'

My lord dusted his sleeve with a lace handkerchief. 'I come, my Robin, at last. There is work on hand for you, my son.'

'God be praised for that! Do I come out of these petticoats, sir?'

'For a little, son, for a little only! Patience! I unfold a miracle.'

'I'm all attention, sir. Let me hear it.'

My lord sat down by the window. There was a gleam in his eyes Robin knew full well, and the smile curling his lips was one of reflective pleasure. By the signs my lady was right, and there was mischief brewing indeed. 'My son, I see the end of the road. It becomes plain at last. I arrange all with wonderful subtlety. You may say that I pull a string here, and a string there, and the puppets move.'

'Lord, sir! Am I one of your puppets?'

'But, of course, my Robin!' said his lordship affectionately. 'I set the stage for you to play the hero. You shall thank me.'

'Shall I, sir? It's a part I'm not in the habit of playing, that of hero.'

'I assign to you a rôle the most romantic,' announced my lord. 'Certainly you shall thank me.'

'Well, let me hear it, sir. You become interesting.'

'I become dangerous, Robin—dangerous as only I can be. I am Nemesis, no less! And you—you are the instrument to my hand. You shall rescue a lady, and kill the villain.'

'Out, sword!' said Robin flippantly. 'You hold me entranced, sir. Who is the lady?'

My lord looked surprised. 'Who but the lady of your heart, my son? Do I arrange so clumsily?'

Robin stiffened. The flippancy left him, and he spoke crisply. 'What's this?'

'I kiss my fingers to her!' My lord made a gesture very French. 'She is ravishing!'

'Who?'

My lord's eyes widened reproachfully. 'Why, Letitia, of course; I should not arrange for you to rescue another. Did you—it is really possibly that you thought I did not know? My son, my son, you grieve me, positively you grieve me!'

'Accept my apologies, sir. I suppose you know everything. But what's this talk of rescues, and who's your villain?'

'Gently, my hothead, gently! You shall know all. You will rescue her to-morrow night; the villain is my poor blundering friend of Munich days.'

'What! Markham again! You're mad, sir; he would never dare a second time, nor she consent.'

'You discount my influence, Robin. Remember that she and Markham too are my puppets.'

Robin got up rather quickly. 'What devilry's this? Be plain with me, if you please, sir!'

My lord put the tips of his fingers together. 'She elopes with my Munich friend to-morrow evening, from Vauxhall Gardens, whither she is bound.'

'She elopes!' Robin was thunderstruck. 'And you tell me you arrange it!'

'Certainly,' said my lord. 'It is entirely my doing. I am to be congratulated.'

'Not by me, sir,' said Robin, and there was an edge to the words.

'Even by you, child. You shall at last appreciate me. Sit down and all shall be told you.'

Robin sank back into his seat. 'Go on, sir. I suppose one of us must be mad. Why have you arranged—if indeed you have—a thing so criminal?'

My lord reflected. 'It seemed the most poetic justice,' he explained. 'It is really exquisitely thought of.' He swung one foot, and smiled sweetly down at the silver buckle. 'Nemesis!' he sighed. 'My Munich friend thought me of so small account: I don't forgive that. He conceived that he could bend me—me, Tremaine of Barham!—to his paltry will! He dared—you shudder at such temerity—he dared to use threats to me! He sees me as a cat's-paw. Almost I can find it in my heart to pity him. But it was an impertinence.' He shook his head severely.

'Markham knows something of you?' Robin was frowning. 'That letter?'

My lord raised his eyes. 'My son, you have a little of my swiftness of apprehension. He had that letter of which I told you. How he came by it I do not know. I admit it freely: I do not know. It is entirely unimportant, or I should have found out. He brought it to my rooms. He demanded money.' His lordship laughed at the thought. 'He was very clever, no doubt, but he did not know that he had chosen a man of supernatural parts for adversary. He showed me my own letter; he told me he knew me for Colney, and I am sure he expected to see me in a palsy of fear.'

A smile flitted across Robin's face. There was a light in his eyes which made his resemblance to his father very strong. 'I dare swear he was disappointed, sir.'

'I fear so, I fear so, my Robin. And was I afraid? Was there fear beneath my *sangfroid?* No, my son! There was a relief quite enormous. At last I knew where my letter was to be found. I do not fear the danger I can see. My Munich friend—his manners appal me; I am aghast at such a lack of polish!—had delivered himself into my hands.'

'Lord, the man's a fool!' said Robin. 'But, troth, he doesn't know you, sir!'

'No one knows me,' said my lord austerely. 'But might he not have descried that in my bearing which speaks greatness? No, he was absorbed in the admiration of his own poor wits. I descended to crush one infinitely inferior to me, and he could not even appreciate the manner in which it was done. I could wish him worthier of my enmity. Observe, my son, the deficiencies in his intelligence! He thought to obtain a promise in writing from me to pay him untold gold on the day when I am acknowledged to be Tremaine of Barham!'

'H'm!' said Robin. 'An optimistic gentleman. And you said?'

'I had to open his eyes. I dispelled the illusion. A plan so subtle that almost it took my breath away formed itself in my brain. You remember, my son, those papers I told you I held?'

'Good God!' said Robin. His father began seriously to alarm him. 'I remember.'

'There was one written by—you would never guess—that foolish Humphrey Grayson. A trifle: half promises which he never fulfilled. But enough for my purpose.'

'Thunder an' turf! Was Grayson in the Rebellion?' cried Robin.

'You may say he once toyed with the notion. It came to naught. He is one of those who waits to see which way the weather-vane points. That silly letter I gave to Mr Markham in exchange for my own, which I have since burned. Do you begin to appreciate the subtlety of my plan, Robin?'

'I'm very far from appreciating it, sir. Be a little plainer! Am I to understand that you gave Markham this paper so he might force Letty into marrying him?'

My lord nodded. 'You have it pat, my son.'

Robin's brow was black. 'Do you ask my appreciation of this, sir? You think I shall admire so dastardly a plot? Good God, was there no other way of getting your letter back?'

'Oh, at least a dozen!' answered his lordship airily. 'I rejected them all; they were too clumsy. And I want Markham out of the way, besides. He were far better dead. You will attend to that. Consider also that this way I present you to your lady in the guise of a hero. It is a *tour-de-force,* and as such—irresistible to me!' He smiled benignantly. 'Until now you are a woman in her eyes; she has no chance to fall in love with you. When you are disclosed a man she might even feel anger. But I arrange that you shall be her deliverer. In a word, I provide for your romance at the very moment of removing the last boulder from my own path. When I think on it, my son, I begin, faintly, to realise the extent of my greatness.'

For the life of him Robin could not help laughing. Faith, how like the old gentleman to choose a way so tortuous and intricate. But to place Letty in such a position—to work so on her fears—that was unpardonable. 'I believe you mean well, sir, but I must censure your methods. I could have got that paper from Markham without drawing Letty in.'

'But how crude! how unworthy a scheme when placed beside mine!' protested my lord. 'And you forget that I arrange this way the death of Markham. A person of such boorish manners is not fit to remain in the same world with me. You must perceive the truth of that.'

Whether Robin saw the matter in quite that light is doubtful. He was dwelling on Letty's share of the plot, and he waxed more indignant still. 'Markham held that letter over her poor little head? He was cur enough to work on her fears for her father? He forced her to agree to a fresh elopement? My God, sir, you need not be afraid that he will live many days longer!' He rose, and fell to pacing the room. His skirts rustled, and the big hoop swayed to a stride no woman would take. 'Oh, I see my way! Without this I might well have hesitated to meet even an enemy of yours with the notion of killing him, sir! But this changes things; I grant you some subtlety, sir, but don't ask me to approve a plan that involves my Letitia so damnably. When do they fly?'

'To-morrow. That I have from our inestimable John. Change of horses has been ordered at Barnet. The strangeness of the hour made the discovery of the rest simple. Letitia goes in a party to Vauxhall Gardens.

What easier to be lost in the crowd there? It will be some time before her absence is even noticed. It is really quite clever of my Munich friend to think of Vauxhall. You, my Robin, may stop them with little inconvenience to yourself on Finchley Common. You will, of course, be masked. I leave the details to you. I make no doubt you will arrange all to my satisfaction.'

Robin paused in his pacing. 'I shall.' His eyes were alight. Concern for Letty had faded a little before the sheer joy of battle. He stretched his arms exultantly. 'Ah, to feel a sword in my hand again!' he said, and made an imaginary pass in the air. 'Not pistols—no, no, that would be clumsy. Am I not your son?'

My lord became enthusiastic. 'You are, my Robin! I perceive some shadow of myself in you. Remove my Munich friend! Do not unmask: you shall remain a mystery to your Letitia for a little while yet, but not for long! Remove me this Markham from the path, and you shall see me go swiftly forward to the promised goal. I am Tremaine of Barham!'

Robin looked sceptical. 'Are you, sir! I wonder!'

'So too did Markham,' said my lord. 'So do you all, and there is only one who knows the truth concerning me. It affords me infinite amusement. I say nothing: all shall soon be disclosed.' He picked up his hat. 'I leave you to your plans, my Robin. See you do not bungle them. There must be no suspicion of your identity. Play the highwayman, and take John along with you. But I don't interest myself in the petty details; you will think on them at your leisure. By my reckoning, and you will hardly question it, they should leave Vauxhall at nine in the evening, maybe later. It does not signify. *Au revoir,* my son! I wish you, though there is not the need, all success!' He waved his hand and was gone next instant, through the doorway into the hall beyond. There he came upon his daughter returned from a morning's ride with Charles Belfort. He tapped her cheek with one indulgent finger, and said gaily: 'My Prudence! You come too late to hear the tale of my achievement. You will find your brother in amaze.'

'Lord, sir!' said Prudence placidly, and watched him go out. She was chuckling a little: he had always the effect of making her laugh. She went into the room he had left, and found Robin biting his fingers in meditation. 'What's the old gentleman so pleased about now, Robin?' she asked. 'Is there work for us afoot?'

He looked up, appraising her. 'Have you a mind to it? It's to be rescue, and slaughter, child!'

'You shock me,' said Prudence, sitting down upon the table's edge. 'Count on me; you will need me belike. What's toward?'

CHAPTER TWENTY-THREE

The fight by moonlight

SUCH A ROMANTIC VENTURE as an elopement from Vauxhall Gardens should have delighted Miss Letty, in love with excitement, but alack! she performed her part sadly, in a spirit very different from that in which she had run away with this same gentleman so short a while back. Then it had been done with dare-devilry, and in expectation of romance; now it was done with a heavy heart dwelling on a Black Domino with an elusive, tantalising smile.

Miss Letty had to admit she was reaping the reward of past folly. Ruefully she reflected that if she had never allowed herself to become dazzled in the first place by Mr Markham's wiles and compliments she would not now have been in a situation so gloomy and hopeless.

She had not been able to think of a way out of the difficulty. Her ideas of law and treason were very vague; she thought that incriminating letter of her father's so fraught with danger that she dared do nothing but what Mr Markham told her, for fear of what awful things might happen. Before she could take any measures against him she must have the letter safe. She thought she might perhaps be able to steal it from him while he slept, for in spite of his talk of heading straight for Scotland she knew very well that he must break the journey sooner or later. It was a forlorn hope, and failing it she could shoot him, she supposed, if only there were a pistol to her hand.

She had never visited Vauxhall with so little pleasure before; it was as though the brilliantly-lit gardens, all a-hum with festivity, were a place of execution. It was easy—wretchedly easy, she thought—to slip away from the rest of her party. She drew her cloak around her, and hurried away down a walk lit by lanterns to the appointed meeting place. Mr Markham was there, and he showed relief at seeing her, and took her hand. It was withdrawn. 'I may be forced to marry you,' said Letty acidly, 'but at least you shan't touch me till then.'

It was no part of Mr Markham's plan to goad her to rebellion. He begged her pardon, and led her swiftly away down the winding walks till they came to an entrance to the gardens. He told her then to pull the hood over her head. She obeyed listlessly, and in a very short time found herself seated in a post-chaise beside her hated lover.

She drew far into her own corner. 'You might at least ride beside the coach!' she said. 'Can you not see how much I detest you?'

He had her safe at last; he cared nothing for her whims; he could even afford to be generous. 'Bear with me, my dear. I won't plague you with talk.'

'You had much better not,' said Letty, 'for I should certainly not answer.'

This was not a very promising beginning, Mr Markham thought. When a haughty shoulder was resolutely turned on him he decided that Miss Letitia needed a lesson. His fingers itched to slap her, but he controlled the desire, remembering that there was a lifetime ahead in which to tame a refractory wife. Frightened for her father's safety as she undoubtedly was she was yet quite capable of raising a disturbance if he tried her too far. So he sat back in his own corner and meditated with some satisfaction on the excellence of his plans, and the delightful time to come.

Letty's thoughts were not so pleasant. The only food for comfort she could find lay in the pistol holster beside her. There was a weapon in it, large and clumsy for her little hands, but still a weapon.

Mr Markham observed the direction of her glance and smiled grimly. 'Ay, you're a violent piece, aren't you? You'd shoot me if you had the chance, I'll lay my life. The pistol's not loaded. Yes, there's another my side, but it's in the same state. The only loaded pistol, my dear, lies snug in my pocket and there it will stay.'

Letty vouchsafed no answer. She gave herself up to the concoction of a plan to get that gun away from her bridegroom. She could evolve nothing but the haziest of schemes, and involuntarily her thoughts drifted on to the contemplation of the impossible. This time there was no large Tony to come after her. She had left no note of farewell, and it would be hours perhaps before her father knew of her flight. Even then he could have no means of knowing whither she had gone. There were no quick-witted Merriots either, and, worst of all, no stranger in a Black Domino.

Well, she was a great fool to think of the Unknown, who was in all probability nothing but a young buck bent on amusing himself at the expense of a silly chit. Once tied up to this monster at her side she had best banish the Unknown entirely from her thoughts: he could no longer be of avail.

She looked miserably out of the window at the tall houses slipping by. There were flambeaux at a few of the doors, but a bright moon cast a silver light over all, and made lamps superfluous. They were travelling at a prodigious speed; to be sure, Mr Markham meant to lose no time in putting London well behind him. In a very short while, so it seemed to poor Letty, the houses grew further and further apart, and at length stopped altogether. She had very little idea of where they were: on that other journey north she had noticed nothing. She saw a heath soon, dotted over with clumps of bushes, casting long black shadows in the moonlight and some tall larch trees stretching up to a sapphire sky. There was nothing else to be seen, and

Letty had never felt less in the mood for admiring the beauties of Nature. She pulled her cloak closer about her still, and looked down at her hands, clasped tightly in her lap. She would not cry, however hard a fight it might be to keep the tears back. The monster beside her should not have that satisfaction.

On went the coach, bumping and jolting over the bad road. The pace had slackened somewhat: one could not drive hell-for-leather along the highways of England; they were not in a state for such usage.

They had been passing through this desolate heath some way when she thought she caught the sound of horses galloping: horses other than the ones that were drawing her to her doom. Scarcely had her ears been made aware of this sound than there came a thunder of hoofs, a shout, a lurch, and a medley of confused noises as the coach was pulled quickly to a standstill. A pistol shot sounded; there was a yell of terror from the box, and at the same moment the glass in the window by Mr Markham was shattered by a blow with something made of metal, and a small goldmounted pistol held by a slim white hand pointed straight at Mr Markham's heart.

It had all happened so quickly that Markham, no less than Letitia, was taken quite by surprise. From the moment of the horses being pulled up to the moment of the breaking glass there had been no more time than sufficed to sit up exclaiming: 'What's toward?' Before Markham could pull the pistol from his pocket he was covered, and had perforce to sit perfectly still, glaring at that deadly barrel.

Letty's heart beat fast. It was a highwayman, beyond all doubt, but she was not in the least afraid. Nothing could be worse than her elopement, and she was inclined to think that it would be better to be killed by a highwayman than to be married to Mr Markham. If fortune smiled Mr Markham might be killed, which would be an excellent thing. She sat up all agog with excitement, and stared through the broken glass at the man who held that pistol.

He was speaking. 'Put up your hands!'

The voice made Letty jump, so oddly familiar was it. She leaned forward, trying to see the horseman's face. There was a black mask over his eyes, and a tricorne was pulled low over his brow. He was a slight man, as far as she could see for the many-caped greatcoat that enveloped him. A wild hope sprang up in her breast: she peered at the stranger's right hand, holding the pistol just inside the window. There was a glint of gold on the little finger. The hand moved a fraction, and the moonlight caught a ring, cunningly wrought.

'The Unknown!' Letty gasped, and began to tremble with excitement, relief, and a queer glad sensation she had never known till now.

'Hands up!' The voice was sharp and compelling. There was nothing for Markham to do but to raise his arms above his head. Inwardly he was cursing: this meant not only delay, but loss of all the money he had brought with him.

'Madam,'—the Unknown was speaking to Letty, but he did not take his eyes from Markham's face— 'oblige me by searching this gentleman's pockets for a pistol.'

Letty pulled herself together. He spoke as to a stranger: she was not to know him then. Oh, here was romance indeed! Romance, and a rescue such as she had not dreamed to be possible. She pushed back her cloak, and with hands that shook, but with a business-like determination in her small face, dived into the pocket nearest her. There was nothing there. She stretched an arm across Mr Markham, taking care not to obtrude herself between his person and the Un-known's pistol, and felt in the righthand pocket. As her fingers closed round the butt of a pistol she felt Mr Markham's hard breathing, and guessed his im-potent fury. With a little laugh caught in her throat she pulled out the weapon. 'I have it, sir! I'll take care of it!'

She saw the flash of white teeth. 'Bravo, madam! Hold fast to it. Sir, be pleased to come down!'

The chafing, fidgeting horse was pulled back; the Unknown bent gracefully in the saddle, and his hand left the bridle to swing open the coach door. Letty sat grasping the pistol, and pointing it at Mr Markham. Her eyes were bright, and her pretty mouth was set tightly. Mr Markham took one look, with a vague notion of wresting the pistol from her, but decided that the further he got from a weapon held in such determined but inexpert hands the better. He jumped down on to the road, just as the Unknown sprang lightly from the saddle.

'You damned footpad!' Mr Markham exploded. 'By God, I'll have you hunted down for this! You cowardly fools there, why didn't you fire?' He had flung round angrily to look at the men on the box, and saw soon enough the reason for their inanition. In spite of that first shot no one seemed to be hurt, but the two men on the box sat huddled together, staring with popping eyes at the long barrel of a pistol held by a second horseman, who had them covered. The man on one of the leaders sat as still as the fretting horse would let him, and his gaze was as fixed and as fearful as his companion's. On the road lay a heavy blunderbuss: there had evidently been no time to fire the cumbersome weapon, and it had been surrendered immediately. This second horseman was masked as well and greatcoated. Letty peeping out, could see only the line of a square jaw, and a stocky silhouette. He did not appear to be much interested in what his companion was about, but kept his head and his pistol turned towards the box of the coach.

The Unknown had flung off his greatcoat. 'Oh, what an unkind spirit!' he mocked in answer to Mr Markham. 'But I'm generous: I offer you a fight, a fair fight, when I might shoot you like the dog you are. Come, where's your sword, sir? Here's the gracious moon to light us, and witnesses enough to see fair play!'

'Fight a damned cut-throat robber?' cried Markham. 'If I'd a cane you should taste of it!'

The Unknown laughed merrily. 'Should I, sir? Should I indeed! Keep him covered, madam!'

'I am!' avowed Letty, grasping her pistol tighter than ever.

The Unknown's weapon was laid aside with his cloak. The plain buff coat he wore followed it, and the scabbard of his sword. 'Come, sir, come! Will you not fight for the privilege of keeping the lady and the riches? Or shall I fleece you of all? What, must I call you coward?' Off came the heavy riding boots, and the elegant flowered waistcoat. He stood straight in the moonlight, a lithe figure in a white shirt, with fair hair caught in the nape of his neck, and a strip of black velvet hiding the upper part of his face. A naked sword was in his hand; he shook it in the air, and the steel flashed in the moonlight. 'A fair duel, sir, and you are the larger man! Faint heart!' Again he laughed 'If I kill you the lady goes free but if you kill me you win all! Shall I rob you as you stand, or will you cross swords with me? Yours is the choice.'

'You kill me, you miserable little dwarf?' Markham cried. 'You'll fight, will you? You're tired of life! Hand down my sword, girl, this instant! By God, I'll teach you a lesson, you impudent dog!' He began to strip off his coat as he spoke, and kicked the buckled shoes from his feet.

The Unknown came to the coach door, and reached up a hand for the sword, and spread his fingers a moment for Letty to see the ring.

'I know! Oh, I know!' she whispered, looking down into the face that had haunted her dreams for so many nights past. 'Kill him, oh, please kill him!'

'I will,' he promised, and took the sword from her trembling hold.

Mr Markham stood ready now and snatched his rapier from the Unknown's hand. 'You asked for this!' he snarled. 'You'll regret it too late. I'm not a novice with the small sword! On guard!'

There was the briefest of salutes, and the blades rang together. Markham lunged in quarte; Letty had a moment's sick apprehension and shut her eyes. They flew open the next instant, to see the Unknown disengaging adroitly.

There was no sound on all this deserted heath but the scrape of steel; no movement save of those two figures on the grass, fighting sternly, desperately, with lives at stake.

The silver moonlight flooded the scene, and tinted it with an unreal ghostliness, glinting along the blue-grey blades, and touching the fair head of the Unknown, and the dark head of Markham.

To Letty, standing in the doorway of the coach, it was as a dream. Her wide eyes never left the graceful

figure of the masked man; they followed every lightning thrust, and every dexterous parry. He was slight
and small indeed, but he seemed to be made of wires,
so agile were his movements, so unerring and untiring
his arm. To see both men one must feel him to be
hopelessly overweighted. Markham had the advantage
in height, in reach, and in strength; he was a good
swordsman besides, with a quick eye and a steady
wrist. He had once killed a man in a duel, Letty knew.

But even to her, ignorant of sword play, it was plain
that the smaller and the lighter man had a wizard's
cunning with the rapier. His style was quite different
from Markham's; he was a miracle of swift grace and
neat footwork, with a wrist like flexible steel, and eyes
like a hawk's to descry an opening. Fascinated, Letty
followed the quick thrust and parry, and she saw the
smile still on the Unknown's lips.

There was a scuffle of blades; Letty's hands flew to
her mouth to press back an involuntary cry; Markham
had lunged forward savagely, and for an awful moment Letty thought that his point must go home. But
there was a swift parry, and barely had Markham recovered than the Unknown's sword flashed forward.
Forte touched foible, and Letty saw Markham disen-
gage quickly.

She threw a glance round at the second masked
man, and saw him intent too on the strange duel. And
the pistol in his hand was pointing no longer at the
men on the box: it covered Mr Markham. John would

have no compunction in shooting if aught befell his young master.

His lesser height and strength did not seem to discompose the Unknown; he showed no signs of tiring; he was fighting still with the same force and cunning; he even seemed to be pressing his opponent. There was a parry, and, it seemed to Letty, two simultaneous lunges. Mr Markham thought he had found an opening, but as he lunged the Unknown's sword shot out in a time-thrust quicker than the eye could follow, took Markham's foible in a flickering parry, and passed on without a check to the heart. It was all over in the flash of an eyelid; dimly Letty realised that she had seen a marvellous piece of sword play. The Unknown sprang back, gasping for breath; Markham seemed to crumple where he stood, and fell heavily to the ground.

Letty's eyes rested on him, full of horror and amazement. Only an instant back he seemed on the point of killing his opponent, and now there he lay, a dark heap on the ground.

The Unknown was on his knee beside him, shutting him from Letty's view; she stood still, clinging now to the frame of the door. After a minute the Unknown rose, and came to the coach. He was no longer smiling, and Letty saw the sweat glistening on his brow. She held out her hands to be helped from the coach. He put up his, and she sprang lightly down.

'It's over,' he said. 'He was a villain, but he fought

well.' He turned, and bent to pick up Markham's coat. In a moment he had a paper in his hands, and bent his head to inspect it. He turned, and gave it to Letty. 'Destroy that, Letitia. You know what it is.'

She hid it in the bosom of her gown. 'Oh, thank you! thank you!' she whispered.

He held out his hand. 'Remember that I am a high-wayman!' he said. 'Give me the pearls you wear. I will return them to you very soon now. Can you trust me?'

She unclasped the string. 'Trust you! Oh, must you ask?'

He shook his head, smiling faintly, and held out his hand again. She put hers into it, and he bent to kiss it. 'I shall come again,' he promised. 'And next time you know what I shall demand.'

She nodded; her eyes were shining; she knew neither hesitation nor bashfulness. He would come to claim her; if he chose he might ride off with her over his saddle now.

He had pulled on his boots, and was struggling into his coat. In another few minutes he had leaped into the saddle again, and was bowing low over the horse's withers. The fair hair was touched to silver by the moonlight; a jewel at his throat winked; and behind the mask Letty thought she saw his eyes gleaming blue. *Au revoir, ma belle!* he said, and straightened n the saddle. 'Drive the lady back to town!' he said curtly to the coachman. There was a quick word in a strange tongue for the man with the pistol; the restless horse was wheeled about, the three-cornered hat was waved once to Letty. Then the horse bounded forward, across the heath; the pace quickened to a gallop, and in a few moments both riders had disappeared over the brow of a little hill.

Miss Letty rubbed her eyes; it was so like a dream, so unreal, that she began to doubt her senses. But the pearls were gone from her neck, and a few paces distant a dark figure lay on the ground—a figure that had once been Gregory Markham.

CHAPTER TWENTY-FOUR

Return of Miss Grayson

OVER THE HILL, some few yards from the road, which turned sharply that way, Prudence waited beside a light chaise. She was in riding clothes, with her bridle over her arm. The horses had been taken from the chaise; Prudence herself had dismounted, and she was standing in the shadow of a tree, a big coat covering her, and her hat drawn over her eyes. There was a worried look in her face; the fine mouth was close shut, and the grey eyes troubled and anxious. She could never be at ease when Robin danced abroad in this fashion, but long training had taught her to assume a calm she was far from feeling. She would scorn to importune her brother with her fears, but there could be no peace for her until he was come safe back again.

She had not long to wait now before the sound of horses came to her listening ears. In another moment or two Robin had pulled up beside her.

She stepped forward, with eager hands stretched out to touch him, as though she must make sure that way of his safety. He bent in the saddle to grip her shoulder a minute. 'Madam Anxiety!'

'All well, child?'

'You see me safe and sound.' Robin swung himself down from the saddle.

'Markham?'

'Just as the old gentleman planned. A good fight.'

'You killed him?'

'Certainly, child.' Robin gave his bridle into John's hands, and took off his coat. 'Well, I must get me into my petticoats, I suppose. Hey-day!'

'I can find it in me to be sorry for the Markham,' Prudence remarked. 'I tell the old gentleman it's a polite murder.'

'Oh, I did not have it quite all my own way, be sure. He had some knowledge of the duello. I might pity him but for his treatment of Letty. That puts him beyond pity. Well, I'll away to my dressing-room. Put the horses to, John.' He went with a quick stride to a clump of bushes, and disappeared behind it.

Prudence went to help John with the horses. Busy with a cheek-strap, she said: 'Did he fight well, John?'

'You know his way, Miss Prue! Ay, he was like a demon. But the other man had some skill, as he said.' John smiled grimly. 'I'd my barker ready.'

Prudence chuckled. 'John, John, you're a rogue! Foul play, and would he ever have forgiven it?'

'Or you forgive me for letting harm come to him, mistress?' John backed his horse into the shafts. 'His lordship will have it he's the world's greatest swordsman, but to my mind Master Robin's his master. Ay, 'twas a good fight.'

'How came the end?'

'He made a time-thrust, Miss Prue. It would have done his lordship's heart good to have seen it. Dangerous work, but there was never a head like Master Robin's in a fight.'

Robin came out presently from his sylvan dressing-room. 'I doubt I look a hag,' he remarked, stowing a bundle of clothes away under the seat of the chaise. 'No mirror, nor any lights. How is it, my Prue?'

She inspected him critically, and rearranged the loose curls as best she might. 'It will serve. Do we come up with your lady?'

Robin frowned. 'There's a risk, of course, but I don't care to leave her to travel with Markham's body. I suppose they will take him up.' He glanced at her. 'I had rather keep you out of this, child.'

'Fiddle!' said Prudence. 'We've been to visit friends. Who's to suspect? We must escort Miss Letty home. Lord, what a mad piece it is!'

Robin slipped the gold ring from his finger and tossed it to Prudence. 'Pocket that: she's not to know. Egad, if this comes to your mountain's ears I'm like to be sped.'

'I'll protect you,' promised his sister. 'I daresay he might guess the truth.'

Robin watched John climb on to the box and gather

up the reins. 'It's a most suspicious mind, alack. Well, *en avant*!' He jumped up into the coach, and Prudence swung herself into the saddle again.

Proceeding at a fair pace they came very soon upon the scene of the late duel. Contrary to Robin's expectations the coach still stood in the road, though it had been turned to face towards London. Obviously much time had been wasted in discussion and argument. Miss Letty stood by the door; two of the men were carrying Markham's body, covered by a cloak, to the coach.

Prudence spurred forward, and came up to the group. 'Good gad, what's toward?' she cried. 'Upon my soul—Miss Grayson!'

'Mr Merriot!' Letty's voice held a sob of relief. 'Oh, Mr Merriot, please help me!' She ran forward to Prudence's knee.

Prudence was all wonder. 'But what a' God's name has happened? How do you come to be here at this hour o' night? Who is with you? And what the plague have you there?' Her riding whip pointed to the two men's burden.

'I can't tell you; I can't tell you; it's all so dreadful!' Letty shuddered. 'Gregory Markham's dead, and oh dear! I can't travel all the way back with him beside me. I can't!'

The light chaise pulled up with them; Miss Merriot's face appeared at the window. 'What's this, my

Peter? *'Pon rep*, not you, Letty? Why, child, how comes this? Where's your aunt?'

'Kate!' Miss Letty ran forward. 'Oh, take me in with you! Mr Markham has been killed by highwaymen, and I don't know what to do!'

'Good God, child!' Miss Merriot was aghast. 'Markham? Highwaymen? But what have you to do with all this?'

'I cannot tell you,' Letty said hopelessly. 'Please do not ask me!'

Prudence gave a sharp order. One of Mr Markham's men came to let down the steps of Robin's coach. Letty was up to them in a twinkling, and had cast herself into the arms of Miss Merriot.

Prudence began to ask questions, and received a multitude of answers. One man swore to two enormous ruffians; another described one small villain, and one huge one and the third man had no very clear idea of anything save that Miss Grayson's pearls had been torn from her neck by a fellow who held a pistol to her head. There was some argument over this: not one of the braves could agree with another's version. Prudence let them run on awhile, but silence all soon with a curt word. 'And not one of you to lift a finger? I make you my compliments. Put the body into the coach and drive back to town. You will be required to answer for this.'

Then it seemed that no one could decide where to take Mr Markham's body: that was the reason of all this delay. Prudence settled it out of hand, and gave orders for its conveyance to Mr Markham's lodgings. With cool foresight she recommended that the officers of the law should be instantly apprised of this terrible happening. Having seen the post-chaise drawn to one side of the road, she nodded to John, and Miss Merriot's carriage drove past.

Inside the light town coach Miss Letty clasped Robin's hand and shivered. Robin had much ado to keep from catching her in his arms. She was shaken and frightened; she had seen death—and violent death at that—for the first time; and she had undergone an eleventh-hour rescue. Robin soothed gently, and when she grew calmer ventured a question or two. 'Did you say it was highwaymen, child?' he asked in a puzzled voice.

Miss Letty nodded vigorously. 'Yes, two of them. They stole my pearls.'

Robin affected surprise. 'But, my dear, highwaymen don't offer to fight duels,' he pointed out.

'I don't know anything about that,' said Miss Letty, 'but these men were certainly robbers.'

Robin smiled in the darkness, well-pleased. His flighty lady-love could keep a discreet tongue in her head, it seemed. 'What was the man who fought Markham like to look at?' he inquired.

There was the tiniest pause. 'I don't know,' said Letty. 'Just like anybody.'

'Short or tall?' Robin pressed.

'Oh, of medium height—rather tall! said Letty, blandly disregarding the truth. 'And he had brown hair—and—and he was not at all out of the common way.'

There was nothing more to be got out of her. Her unknown hero had imposed silence, and silent she would be. Questioned, she had not the smallest hesitation in lying. If there was to be a hue and cry after the Unknown she would do all that lay in her power to throw dust in the eyes of his pursuers.

It was close on midnight when the chaise drew up at Sir Humphrey Grayson's door, and no sooner had the steps been let down than both Sir Humphrey and Miss Grayson came hurrying out. There was at once a babel of exclamation.

'Letitia!'

'Thank God!'

'Oh, my child, where have you been?'

'Once more your good friends to the rescue!'

Robin leaned out to speak to Sir Humphrey. 'I bring her back to you again, sir. I daresay she will tell you more than I am permitted to know. I don't need to ask you to be kind to her.'

Sir Humphrey sighed. 'Another scrape! I have to thank you once more ma'am.'

'There is not the necessity, sir. We happened to chance that way; we had been visiting at Barnet. Take her in, sir: she's worn out, and, I believe, has suffered much. Drive on John.'

'You will not enter? A glass of wine—?'

'I thank you, sir, but it grows late, and we must hurry back to my Lady Lowestoft's. You're ready, my Peter?'

Letty, clinging to her father's arm, watched the chaise roll away down the street, with the neat figure of Mr Merriot riding behind it. She heaved a deep sigh, and whispered urgently: 'Papa, Papa, I must speak with you alone! Send Aunt to bed!'

Miss Grayson the elder was in a severe bustle. 'Letitia, you pass all bounds! Come within doors, for heaven's sake, brother. You will explain yourself, Letitia, if you please. How came you to be lost in the gardens, and where, pray, have you been?'

They stood now in the lit hall of the house. Letty shook her head wearily, and cast an appealing, urgent glance up into her father's face. His mood was of annoyance at this fresh escapade, but he read such lingering horror in his daughter's brown eyes that he silenced his sister. 'I will have a talk with Letitia myself, sister, with your leave. Come into the library, child: you will be the better for a glass of Madeira.'

Miss Grayson was affronted. 'As Letitia's chaperon, brother, I feel I have the right to know more of this!' she declared.

'So you shall, Cordelia, but later. Do not let us forget that I am Letty's father.'

Hearing that note in her brother's voice Miss Grayson thought it as well to retire. She sniffed loudly, and saying that she hoped Sir Humphrey would read his erring child a sharp lesson, flounced off up the stairs to her own apartment.

Sir Humphrey took Letty into the library, where a fire burned still. With austere kindliness he forbade all attempt at explanation until she should have swallowed some wine. This was soon brought by a curious servant. Letty was obliged to drink, and her father had the satisfaction of seeing some of the colour return to her pale cheeks.

She put back her cloak, and with quivering fingers pulled the letter from the bosom of her gown. 'Take it, Papa! Take it, and burn it!' she said in a voice of strong agitation.

Surprised he received the paper, and unfolded it. An exclamation broke from him; he stood with the letter in his hand, staring down at his daughter. 'How came you by this?'

Her tired eyelids fluttered upwards. 'Mr Markham had it.'

'That scoundrel! He gave it to you?' Sir Humphrey's voice was sharp with anxiety. 'Good God, child, don't tell me—' He broke off, afraid to put his dread into words.

'He said—he said he would expose you unless I would elope with him again. I could not think of a way out.' She clasped her hands nervously in her lap. 'He said if I told you he would publish the letter. There seemed to be nothing I could do. I was to fly

with him to-night: I did not want to, Papa! I have been
so miserable! We reached as far as to Finchley Common, and then—' She stopped, and after a moment's
hesitation leaned forward in her chair. 'Papa, if I tell
you the truth, will you promise to keep it secret? I am
bound to divulge nothing, but I must tell you. He could
not have meant me not to tell you. If I don't you could
never understand. But you must keep it secret, Papa,
or I may not tell you!'

He put the letter into the fire, and watched it shrivel,
and burn. 'Hush, child! My poor girl, you suffer for
my folly, but that villain imposed on you. There was
not enough in that paper to send me to the gallows.'

'Was there not?' she had but a faint interest in it
now. 'I did not know. But you do not promise, Papa!
you do not promise!'

He sat down beside her and took her hand. 'What
is this secret? You won't tell without my promise?
Why then, I must give it you. Don't keep aught back
from me, Letty!'

'I must go back so far,' she said hurriedly. 'As far
as to the masked ball my Lady Dorling gave. You
remember?' The whole story came tumbling out, and
ended with the Unknown's reappearance this evening.

Sir Humphrey was thunderstruck. A gasp escaped
him at the tale of the duel; he put a quick question or
two, and seemed to be almost incredulous. When his
daughter came to the end he rose up from his chair,
and took a turn about the room, his hands linked be-

hind his back. 'Markham dead!' he ejaculated several times. 'Good God, the scandal!'

'I know, I know, but I could not help it, Papa!'

'No, it has been my fault,' he said sadly. 'And but for this strange masked man you would be in a bad case now. We must brave it out. But have you no notion who your preserver may be? If he knows you, you must surely know him!'

'I do not, Papa. He is not like any man of our acquaintance.' A blush flooded her cheeks. 'Papa...'

He observed her heightened colour. 'Well, child?'

She looked frankly up at him. 'I do not know his name, papa, nor anything about him, but I am going to marry him. He said—he said that next time he came it would be for me.'

Sir Humphrey did not know what reply to make. At last he said: 'That is for the to-morrow, Letitia. We must know something more of him. But certainly, provided his birth be respectable, he deserves to win you. I look forward to the day when I may have the honour of taking his hand.'

Whereupon Miss Letty promptly cast herself into his arms, and burst into tears.

CHAPTER TWENTY-FIVE

Mystery of the masked man

THERE COULD BE NO evading a lively scandal; Sir
Humphrey had foreseen it; Robin had a dread of it.
By noon next day Society spoke of nothing but the
sudden and horrid death of Gregory Markham, and the
frustrated elopement of the pretty heiress. The news
was all over the town; the Merriots' share in the
night's work was known with the rest, for Mr Markham's coachman naturally told it all to Mr Markham's
valet, who, in his turn, repeated it to Mr Devereux's
man. The ball once started rolled swiftly through London, and at length reached the ears of Sir Anthony
Fanshawe. He had it from Mr Belfort at White's club,
and Mr Belfort was able to give him better information
than most, for he had made a point of calling in Arlington Street as soon as he heard the strange story.
Mr Belfort, never having been at all in sympathy with
Markham, saw the happenings as a rollicking adventure, and was about to make a ribald comment on Miss
Letty's share in it, when he remembered Sir Anthony's
close friendship with the Graysons. He coughed,

glared at Devereux, standing by, and relapsed into solemn silence.

'Very queer affair,' said Devereux, shaking his head. 'Oh monstrous, Fanshawe! I did hear that there's some doubt of the masked man being a highwayman. What do you say to a rival, hey?' He looked very knowing, and gave a prim smile. 'Oh, quite shocking, my dear Fanshawe.'

Sir Anthony took snuff with a meditative air. 'Who says they were not highwaymen?' he asked.

''Pon my soul, I cannot quite recollect where I heard it first,' said Mr Devereux. 'It might have been from Kestrel that I had it.'

'As to that,' Mr Belfort interposed, 'I've seen Peter Merriot to-day, and he says Miss Grayson swore they were highwaymen. Her pearls were taken, y'know.'

'All the same, Bel, you must remember the duel! You must remember that. I never heard of a common robber offering to fight.'

Mr Belfort looked portentous. 'Now I've a notion of my own as to it,' he confided. 'What do you say to its being one of these escaped Jacobites, taken to the High Toby?'

Mr Devereux seemed greatly struck by this. 'Ay, there might well be something in that, Bel. That's an idea, you know. 'Pon my soul, that's a devilish clever notion! What do you say to it, Tony?'

Sir Anthony would not volunteer an opinion. There might or there might not be some truth in it. He strolled away in a few minutes, and was very soon on his way to Arlington Street. Sir Anthony had a notion in his own head, but it was not for Mr Belfort's delectation.

The lackey who admitted him into the house believed that my lady had gone out. Sir Anthony asked for Mr Merriot, and was conducted to the smaller withdrawing room.

Miss Merriot was seated in the window, supporting her fair head on one delicate hand. An enchanting profile was presented to the room. There was the straight nose, the beautifully curved lips, and the drooping eyelid. The light curls were unpowdered, and caught up carelessly in a riband of Robin's favourite blue; there was a locket round the white throat, and a fan held in one hand. A gown of blue silk billowed about the lovely lady; the sleeves ended at the elbow in a fall of heavy lace. She did not look as though she could kill a man in a duel.

Mr Merriot stood in a truly masculine attitude, with a foot on the window seat, and an elbow resting on that bent knee. It seemed he had been riding, as was his wont each morning, for he wore shining topboots, and buff smallclothes. A coat of claret-coloured cloth set off his trim figure; his hand played negligently with the lash of his long whip.

Sir Anthony, pausing in the doorway, had a moment's opportunity to admire a pretty picture. Then

Robin looked round, and pulled a face. 'Lord, Prue! The mountain.'

Prudence turned, and brought her foot down to the floor. 'Give you good-day, sir,' she said.

Robin became impish. 'Faith, the world's full of curiosity!' he remarked. 'Even the phlegmatic mammoth must needs come to visit us to-day.'

Prudence held up a finger. 'Treat the gentleman with respect, child. I perceive he frowns on you.'

Robin sighed. 'Alack, I could never succeed in captivating the mammoth,' he mourned. 'I doubt I'm too flighty for a sober man's taste.'

Sir Anthony put down his hat, and smiled placidly. 'Quite right, Robin.' He looked keenly under heavy eyelids. 'So you chanced to come upon Letty in this fresh trouble last night?'

'A most fortunate occurrence,' nodded Robin. 'We were on our way back from Barnet.'

'Were you so?' Sir Anthony was all polite interest. 'Fortunate, indeed!' He looked across the room at Prudence, tranquilly regarding him. 'Do you credit me with any wits or bone?' he asked.

Prudence smiled. 'Now how am I to answer that?'

'I beg you won't flatter me,' said Sir Anthony sardonically.

'Impossible!' murmured Robin. 'Prue, we distress the large gentleman.'

'You do. You may say that you annoy me.' Sir Anthony turned to face him. 'You drag your sister from scrape to scrape.'

Robin bowed. 'And out of them, sir. Do me that much justice.'

'Why, what's this?' Prudence came to lay a hand on Sir Anthony's arm. 'You don't know me, Tony, if you think I am dragged anywhere.'

He looked down at her with no smile in his eyes. 'Ay, I'll believe you went on that mad errand of your own free will.'

Robin's brows went up; the laugh died on his lips. The gentleman was seriously annoyed, it seemed. Prudence met the hard look squarely. 'You're angry with me, Tony? Why?'

'You can't guess? It did not occur to you that I might wish to be told of this escapade?'

'Yes, it occurred to me. But I have told you, Tony, that I do not desire to see you tread our maze.'

'I've the right, I think, to choose for myself. You must still exclude me?'

'You said that you would hold back from us,' she said.

'You mistake, my dear. I said that I would wait to claim you. No more. Mr and Miss Merriot desire no interference or aid in their schemes. Accept my thanks for the compliment.'

'Tare an' 'ouns, I believe you're disappointed you'd no share in it!' Robin exclaimed.

'Well, why not?' said Sir Anthony coolly.

'My dear sir, you're not an adventurer. But egad, if I'd guessed this I'd have taken you along. Oh, but conceive Sir Anthony Fanshawe masked upon the high road!'

The stern look abated somewhat. 'My good boy, must you always harp upon my respectability? I confess I'm hurt. I was always accounted a useful man in a fight.' He took Prudence's hand. 'I wish I could make you understand that I desire nothing better than to walk the maze at your side. You can't credit it?'

'Yes, sir, but can you not understand that I would do my uttermost to keep you free of the dangers that surround us? You shall not be angry with me for that.'

'Give me your word that this shall be the last scrape you enter into without my knowledge.'

There was a serious look for this. Robin spoke from the window. 'He has the right, I believe, Prue. If he aspires to wed you he must needs share your fortunes.'

'That,' said Sir Anthony, 'is the only sensible thing I have heard you say so far, young man. Come Prue!'

'If I must, sir,' she said reluctantly. But—' she paused. 'Oh, it's a man's reasoning, and I must still play the man. I promise, Tony.'

'The storm blows over,' said Robin. 'So you guessed the whole affair, O mountain?'

'It was not very difficult,' Sir Anthony pointed out.

'Egad, I hope there are no more of that opinion!'

'You have to remember that I know something of you. But I'm in the dark. What possessed Letty to elope a second time? I could have sworn she had not a jot of tenderness left for Markham.'

Robin frowned. 'There's more to it than that,' he said.

It was at this moment that my Lord Barham swept into the room. My lord waved a hand in recognition of Sir Anthony, but swooped upon his son. 'My Robin!' he cried. 'Superb! A time-thrust worthy of myself! I have the whole from John. I knew I might rely on you!'

Sir Anthony cast up his eyes, and retired to the fire-place. 'I might have known!' he said. 'Of course I should have known!'

My lord's eagle eye was upon him. 'I assume this gentleman to be in your confidence, my children. I admit him into mine. Sir Anthony, you behold in my son a master-swordsman. I permit myself to take pride in him. A time-thrust—the most dangerous, difficult thrust of all! I kiss your hands, my Robin! I remember that I taught you that pass.'

'The honours would appear to be divided,' murmured Sir Anthony, unable to repress a twinkle. 'Sir, I am wholly at a loss. I wish some one would enlighten me. Do I understand that you planned this affair, my lord?'

My lord was surprised. 'But can you ask?' he said.

'I suppose there is not the need. But I should like to know how you had wind of the elopement.'

My lord gazed at him. 'Wind of it? I planned it!' he said magnificently.

The smiled died on Sir Anthony's lips; he stopped twirling his quizzing glass. He opened his mouth to speak, and shut it again, as though he could find no words.

'You amaze the large gentleman, sir,' said Robin dryly. 'I am not altogether surprised.'

Sir Anthony swung round. 'Were you in this?' he asked, and there was that in his voice which made Prudence grimace oddly. 'Am I to believe you were party to such a scheme?'

'Acquit me, kind sir. My indignation almost equalled yours.'

Sir Anthony looked at him a moment, and appeared to be satisfied. He turned back to my lord, who was still dwelling fondly on his son's prowess. 'You must explain a little further, sir, if you please. I suppose you had some reason for this.'

The compelling gaze rested on him. 'Certainly!' said my lord. 'Be very sure of it. I regard the whole affair as one of my *chef's d'oeuvres.*'

'Do you indeed?' Sir Anthony was again sardonic. 'Make it plain to me, sir. I beg of you! I am unable to appreciate it at present.'

Prudence interposed. 'You had best be frank with Tony, sir. He knows us for escaped Jacobites.'

My lord appeared to censure the term. 'My child, I live in the present, not in the past. Not even I could save the Prince's affairs from being bungled: I reject his whole cause. It was a venture not worthy of me. Do not call me a Jacobite.'

'I beg your pardon, sir,' Prudence bowed. 'Say then only that Sir Anthony knows the truth concerning us.'

'I deplore the indiscretion,' said my lord. He became reproachful. 'Never divulge more than is necessary, my Prudence. Surely I taught you that lesson many years ago!'

'To be frank, sir, the gentleman had already guessed it.'

Robin arose from his seat by the window. 'No matter. The whole scheme was complicated beyond your imagination, Sir Anthony.'

'Subtle,' amended his lordship.

'Tortuous, sir. You're to know, Fanshawe, that my father was unwise enough to set his name to a certain treasonable letter.'

'An indiscretion,' said my lord. 'I admit it. But it was not my own name, Robin. Do not forget that.'

Sir Anthony was surprised. 'I had not thought that of you, my lord. It seems unlike you.'

My lord was at once benevolent. 'You are blessed with a good understanding, my dear sir. I have admitted an indiscretion. One is sometimes carried away by one's enthusiasms. You see that even I can make mistakes. A lesson may be learned from that.'

'Give me leave, sir,' interrupted Robin. 'This letter, Sir Anthony, came into the hands of the late Mr Markham, who thought to sell it to my father at a fabulous price. You take?'

Sir Anthony nodded. 'There's a ray of daylight,' he said.

'There shall be more. My father held in his possession a letter writ by Sir Humphrey Grayson, containing half-promises to help the Prince's cause. It does not surprise you?'

'Only that your father should have the letter. The rest I knew.'

'Then there is nothing in the world to surprise you. When you know my father better you will know that he would of course hold the letter.'

'Don't cry God forfend, sir!' Prudence said on a chuckle. 'Spare our filial feelings!'

My lord held up his hand. 'My daughter, Sir Anthony must surely realise that it is a privilege to know me.'

Sir Anthony's mouth twitched at the corners. 'I wonder if Markham thought so?' he said. 'Proceed, Robin. I begin to understand.'

'My father, sir, exchanged letters, and that is all there is to it. He assures me that there were at least a dozen other ways of getting Markham's paper from him, but this one appeared to him to be the neatest.'

'Of course,' said his lordship. 'It needs no explanation. I was able thus to rid myself for ever of my Munich friend, and to present my son to Miss Grayson in the rôle of a hero. I surpassed myself.' He became aware of Sir Anthony's wondering gaze upon him, and waved his handkerchief gracefully. 'You are spellbound. I expected it. You can never before have seen my like.'

'Never, upon my honour!' said Sir Anthony emphatically.

'And you never will again, my son,' said his lordship with a touch of vicarious regret.

'Thank God fasting,' advised Robin.

Sir Anthony laughed suddenly. 'No, it *is* a privilege,' he said. 'I would not forego your acquaintance, sir, for the worlds. My horizon broadens every hour.'

My lord smiled graciously. 'That was inevitable,' he said. 'It could not be otherwise.'

Sir Anthony walked to the window and back again, struggling with varied emotions. At last he turned, and made a gesture of despair. 'Sir, you demoralize me. Until the privilege of knowing you was conferred upon me I protest I led a sober life, and my opinions were all respectable. I find myself walking now in your train, sir, caught up in I know not what lawless schemes, and I perceive with horror that the day approaches when I shall be lost to all sense of propriety and order.'

My lord acknowledged a compliment. 'I had once some acquaintance with a Jesuit father,' he said reminiscently. 'That was in the days of my youth. I profited by it. Yes, I learned some few things.'

'More than the Jesuit father taught you, I'll lay my life,' said Robin.

'Yes,' admitted his lordship. 'But then, my son, his brain had its limits.'

'Have you limitations my lord?' asked Sir Anthony.

My lord looked at him seriously. 'I do not know,' he said, with a revealing simplicity. 'I have never yet discovered them.'

Came my Lady Lowestoft into the room in a fine bustle. Her sharp eyes darted from one guest to the other. *'Tiens!* Such a party!' She untied the strings of her mantle, and cast it from her. 'Robert, I know very well you have done some wickedness! Your children of a certainty did not visit friends at Barnet last night.' She pointed an accusing finger. 'It is my belief Robin killed the Markham—by your orders, Robert! It is a scandal! a madness! I gasp at it!'

'A time-thrust,' nodded my lord. 'Superb!'

'What's that? What is it, a time-thrust?' cried my lady.

'You would not understand, my dear Thérèse. It is to lunge as your opponent lunges—you may judge how ticklish!—to parry his blade as you come through, and to pass on with not the smallest check to—the heart, was it not, my son?'

'Then it is true!' said my lady. She seemed to have no interest in the brilliance of Robin's sword play, unlike Sir Anthony, who was looking at Robin with an appraising, marvelling eye. 'Good God, Robert, what shall come of this?' She pounced on Sir Anthony. 'And you! Do not tell me you had a hand in this too!'

'Alack, ma'am, no.'

My lady put her hands to her temples. 'The head turns on my shoulders. Of a certainty we are all mad!' She sat down weakly. 'You want to end at Tyburn, all three?' she demanded.

'I'm inclined to think the honour of being executed on Tower Hill must be conferred upon the old gentleman at least,' said Prudence. 'Tyburn might do for us, I suppose.'

'You are ridiculous, Thérèse.' My lord was severe. 'What have the Merriots to do with duels and masked men?'

'I may be ridiculous,' said my lady, 'but this I say! the sooner you end this masquerade the better now. Mark me well! We will retire to Richmond, my children. Then if the wind of suspicion should blow your way—eh, but Robert shall send word, and you vanish!'

'I will go further than that,' interposed Sir Anthony. 'I've to visit my sister, Lady Enderby, in Hampshire next week. I desire to take Mr Merriot along with me.'

Prudence shook her head. My lord arose, and picked up his hat. 'Do not meddle in my plans,' he advised them all. 'Go to Richmond if you will, but await there my orders. It is not possible that suspicion should fall upon my son.'

He was right thus far, but he had reckoned without Miss Grayson. Prudence, summoned to make a deposition, could tell the gentlemen of the Law very little. Her evidence was admirably given; nothing could exceed the tranquillity of her bearing, nor the frankness of her replies. She was complimented on her share of the night's work, disclaimed gracefully, and departed.

Miss Grayson's evidence was of another colour. She had a worried father in support, but her self-possession was, under the circumstances, almost as creditable as Mr Merriot's. She listened acutely to the conflicting stories of the coachman and the postilion, and adapted her own as best she might to theirs. The tale as told by these lackeys would perhaps have surprised Robin and John. The postilion was inclined to grant Robin a height he lacked; the coachman, more cautious on this point, waxed impassioned on the subject of the unparalleled ferocity displayed by both men. The third man was the most cautious of all. He said that one man had fired at him before he could raise his blunderbuss, but although he had been forced to surrender it he had not thought the masked men ferocious. Pressed further, he deposed that the smaller man had told the lady to keep Mr Markham covered with his own pistol, which she had done.

This produced quite a sensation. Miss Letty said with spirit:—'I did not care whether I fell into a highwayman's hands so long as I was rid of that odious Abductor.'

It was felt that there was some sound sense displayed in this, but still it was unusual for a lady to be so completely at ease with a couple of highwaymen.

Miss Letty thought it best to adhere as closely as possible to the third man's tale. She avowed unblushingly that the highwayman who had fought the duel was of medium height, had brown hair, and was nothing out of the ordinary in appearance. When asked if he was not, as the coachman said, a man of polished address, she seemed uncertain. She would hardly say he had polish, but she admitted he had something of the air of a gentleman. Yes, he had kissed her hand, certainly, but to her mind that was little better than an insult considering he had previously filched her pearls from her. 'Whoever it was,' she announced, 'he rescued me from a monster, and I am very grateful to him.'

Faced with the question of abduction, the questioners shook dubious heads. That was a criminal offence, but murder on the King's Highway—

Miss Letty broke in hotly with a flat disclaimer. She turned to the coachman and demanded whether it was not a fair duel. Perceiving that his late master was in danger of being convicted—if you could convict a dead man, of which ticklish point he was not certain—of abduction, the coachman bestowed some of his support on the other side. Decidedly it had been a fair fight, so far as he was able to judge.

The affair was, in fact, a strange mystery, but the officers of the Law hoped to unravel it.

Sir Humphrey shook his head gravely when he found himself alone with his daughter, and said only that they were not likely to hear the end of this for many a long day.

CHAPTER TWENTY-SIX

Arrest of Mr Merriot

MY LADY LOWESTOFT was true to her word: she bore her guests off to the Richmond house, and gave there, lest any should think the retirement suspicious, a large ball. All London came, including my Lord Barham, who was overpoweringly resplendent in silver brocade, and wonderfully benign. Sir Anthony Fanshawe was also there. He danced several times with Miss Merriot, and Mr Molyneux was inclined to think that there was a match in that direction. Quite a number of people were of his opinion: Prudence told Robin she was growing jealous.

She had a little tussle of wills with the large gentleman that evening: he was pledged to visit his sister, and he wanted to take Prudence with him. She would have none of it; she, too, had some strength of purpose and her nay could be very steadfast.

She had, in fact, small desire to be presented to my Lady Enderby in her present guise. Sir Anthony guessed something of this, and drew a reassuring picture of his sister. She was, he said, a comfortable soul, with no respect for conventions. Still Prudence held to her refusal. To go down to Hampshire with Sir Anthony meant that she must marry him forthwith; she wanted to see first the issue of the old gentleman's claim. Sir Anthony must be guarded against himself.

It cost her something to stand out so resolutely against him; for all her calm she was troubled, and looked wistfully when Sir Anthony ceased to press her. She had seen that expression in his face once or twice before; she remembered how at the very outset she had remarked to Robin that she would not choose to cross him. Well, it was true, and he was an ill man to withstand. But one had one's pride after all. Egad, it was a poor love that could wish to see the gentleman pulled down to marry an adventuress. That sister of his had probably some views other than he knew of on the subject of his marriage. My Lord Barham's daughter would be well enough; an impostor's daughter very ill indeed.

She stood still before him, a slim figure in dove grey velvet, one hand fingering the black riband that held her quizzing-glass, and her tranquil eyes resting on his face. Even though he was angry with her for her obstinacy he could find it in him to admire the firm set of her mouth, and the clean-cut determination of her chin. She had spirit, this girl, in the man's clothes, and with the man's brain. Ay, and she had courage too, and a calmness of demeanour that pleased. No hysterics there; no sentimentalism; no wavering that one could see. Bravery! He warmed to the thought of it. She made nothing of this masquerade; she had faith in herself, and for all the restfulness that characterised her, that slow speech, and the slow smile she had, the wits of her were quick, and marvellously resourceful. She would fleece the wolf at cards, flash a sword out on a party of Mohocks, and stand by with a cool head while her brother fought a grim duel. She could even contemplate a duel on her own account without outward flinching.

Involuntarily Sir Anthony's face softened. 'My dear, I hate to leave you here,' he said.

The smile crept back into the grey eyes. 'I was afraid you were angry with me, Tony.'

'I was,' he answered. 'But you disarm anger. Will you not come with me?'

He was not to know how that shook her resolve. She shook her head. 'Don't ask me. I must stand by my word. If my father's claim succeeds—'

There was a momentary tightening of the mouth. 'If that tiresome old gentleman were not your father, Prue—'

Came the deep twinkle. 'Oh, I know, sir! You would say to the devil with him. We often do.'

He laughed. 'You're a disrespectful couple. I believe I'll postpone my visit to Hampshire.'

'If you would please me, Tony, you will go as you planned.'

'So that you may disappear while I am away?'

'Can you trust my word?' He nodded. 'I won't disappear. But I would rather that you went.'

'For a week I will, since you ask it of me. I wonder why you wish it?'

She had few feminine evasions at her command, few subtleties. 'To say truth, sir, you shake my resolution.'

There was an eager look, dispelling sleepiness. 'Give me back my promise!'

She shook her head, and smiled a little. 'I hold you to it.'

There was no more to be said. He bowed. 'I obey you—now. Take a lesson from me.'

She felt herself weakening. Lord, she desired nothing better than to do his bidding. It would not be wise to let him see that. She said lightly: 'Oh, if you marry me in the end, sir, I promise you a dutiful wife.' Her eyes fell before the look in his. 'As for your fears for me, you need have none, Tony. I'm not like to come to any harm.'

She did not know how exactly Miss Letty, all unconsciously, had described her to the gentlemen of the law.

Nor did she suspect the hand of an enemy to be turned against her. She had forgotten Mr Rensley, newly arisen from his bed of sickness.

Mr Rensley, permitted to sit up in his room, heard the news of Markham's death rather late in the day from his chatty surgeon. He was quite shocked, even

a little put out. There had been a sudden coolness between himself and Markham, but this news was up-
setting. He evinced a lively interest; the surgeon liked
to talk; Mr Rensley soon had all the circumstances
from him. He was particularly anxious to know how
the Merriots came to chance along the road at such a
late and opportune hour. To one who knew of enmity
existing between Mr Merriot and Markham, the thing
had a significance. When the surgeon had departed
Rensley spent some time in earnest thought. Young
Merriot had hung about the heiress quite noticeably;
it was possible, nay, probably, that the original quarrel
had sprung up out of some rivalry.

At the end of an hour's cogitation Mr Rensley told
his aghast servant to order a chair, for he intended to
go out.

The servant tried to dissuade him, but in vain. Mr
Rensley rather pale, and uncertain yet on his legs, sallied forth and was gone all the afternoon. When he
returned he was certainly very tired, but his man had
to admit the exertion seemed rather to have improved
his condition than to have set him back. Indeed, Mr
Rensley came home with a pleasant feeling of having
done his duty, and paid off a rankling debt.

What he had to say to the representatives of the Law
was interesting to them, but created not much surprise.
Suspicion had fallen on Mr Merriot before Rensley
spoke: his disclosures only served to strengthen suspicion. The Law went carefully to work. Miss Letty

was questioned again, and stood fast to her description of a brown-haired man of medium height, with the air of a gentleman. Mr Merriot now appeared in the light of a secret lover, and circumstances certainly rather damning were pieced together. The Authorities put wise heads together, and considered it time to act.

On Tuesday of next week two coaches set out on the road to Richmond. One was a smart chaise with arms on the doors, carrying Sir Anthony Fanshawe's baggage down to Hampshire; the other was a sober vehicle, containing two sober gentlemen who held a warrant for the arrest of Mr Merriot. This equipage set off shortly before four in the afternoon; Sir Anthony's chaise started rather later, for my lady, soft-hearted towards a lover, had begged Sir Anthony to make Richmond his first day's halt, and to rest at her house that night. Sir Anthony had accepted this invitation, though Richmond was not precisely on the direct route. That seemed to be immaterial. His chaise set forward in good time; Sir Anthony, not a man of sedentary habits, followed later on horseback.

At White's in St James's my Lord Barham played at faro, and informed my Lord March genially that he hoped to give the pettifogging lawyers all the proofs they needed of his identity at the end of the week.

In the big house in Grosvenor Square Mr Rensley nursed his wound and speculated on the results of the meeting to be held in this very room, a few days hence.

At Richmond Robin drove out with my lady to drink a dish of Bohea, which he detested, that Prudence might be alone to receive Sir Anthony Fanshawe when he arrived.

She sat in the library, overlooking the river, and tried to interest herself with a book. But the book could not hold her attention; she must ever be harkening for the sound of coach wheels.

It came at last. She was woman enough to cast a glance at the big mirror hanging over the fireplace. The mirror showed a handsome young gentleman in a powdered wig. A slightly disordered neckcloth had to be adjusted; Prudence bent her eyes once more on the book.

A lackey opened the door; she looked up and saw a scared expression on his face, not unmixed with curiosity. She kept her finger in the book; she was at once on the alert, completely mistress of herself.

'Sir—two men!...' The lackey did not seem to know what next to day.

Prudence's eyes went past him, and rested inquiringly on the two soberly clad individuals who had entered the room. Leisurely she crossed one booted leg over the other; inwardly she was thinking fast, but no signs of it appeared in her face.

She knew what these visitors had come for; it did not need for them to show her the warrant they held. She looked at it with raised brows, and then at the two men. She seemed to be faintly amused, and slightly at a loss. 'What a'God's name is all this?' she asked.

'Warrant for arrest,' said one of the men succinctly. 'Alleged murder of Gregory Markham, Esquire, of Poynter Street, Number Five.'

The grey eyes widened in surprise, and travelled on to the second man, who seemed apologetic. 'Dooty!' he said, and stared at the ceiling, and coughed.

Prudence wondered where John was. Obviously she was to be taken to town under arrest, and something must be done to liberate her, and that speedily. Egad, who would have thought it? This bade fair to mean her unmasking, and then what? Lord, but the old gentleman had bungled this! Or had he? To be honest, her presence at the duel had not been a part of his plan. Nor, if one thought of it had he planned the bringing of Miss Letty back to town. Well, this was what came of deviating from his orders by so much as a hair's breadth. And what to do now? If John had seen these harbingers of disaster, he would be off to my lord at once, and—faith, one had trust in the old gentleman!

'Am I to understand I'm supposed to have killed Mr Markham?' she inquired.

The leader of the two pointed silently to the warrant. It was not for him to elucidate these mysteries.

'Good God!' said Prudence. 'Well, what do we do now, gentlemen?'

'If you'll send for your hat and coat, sir, we'll be off to London,' said the spokesman.

'Must do our dooty!' said his fellow hoarsely. '*How*ever unpleasant!'

'Certainly gentlemen,' agreed Prudence. She turned to the waiting lackey. 'Fetch my hat and coat, Stephen. And apprise my lady and Miss Merriot upon their return of this ridiculous mistake. You will tell Miss Merriot to be in no anxiety on my account. I shall be back again almost at once, of course.'

The lackey went out; the apologetic gentleman whispered diffidently the word 'Sword!' The spokesman nodded. 'Not wishing to offend, your honour, but it won't do to wear a sword.'

'I am not wearing it, gentlemen.'

They perceived that this was so. 'Thank you, sir. And of course, pistols....'

Prudence got up. 'Pray search me. It's not my habit to carry pistols on my person.'

She was assured again that no offence was intended; a perfunctory hand felt her pockets; the gentlemen professed themselves satisfied, and the hoarse member begged pardon, and resumed his study of the ceiling.

Prudence remained standing by her chair, awaiting her hat and cloak. The officers of the Law stayed by the door, sentinel fashion. Prudence looked meditatively out of the window that gave on to the garden and the river.

Her eyes were indifferent, and returned to the contemplation of her captors. But there was hope in her breast, for she had seen John.

The lackey came back with her hat and cloak, and beribboned cane. Out of the corner of her eye Prudence saw that John had disappeared. Unhurriedly she repeated her message to Robin, and laid the coat over her arm. She shook out her ruffles, put on her pointedged tricorne, and professed herself in readiness to start. She was conducted into the hall, past peeping servants, and out to the waiting coach. She entered it, and seated herself in the far corner, perfectly at ease. The two officers got in after her, and sat down, one beside her, and one opposite. The two steps were drawn up, the door shut. The coach moved ponderously forward. God send Robin did nothing foolhardily.

In my lady's stables, in desperate haste, John was buckling the saddle-girths of a fine chestnut mare. She was saddled and bridled in a space of time that would have made my lady's coachmen gasp, and led out into the yard. A groom coming out of the harness-room, with a straw between his teeth, stared, and wondered where John might be off to. John said curtly he had a message to deliver, and was off before the groom could utter another word. That stolid person was left gaping. One moment John was there, in the yard, with a mettlesome mare under him; the next, he simply was not. He had vanished out of the gate before one was aware of him moving at all. The groom thought that he must be in a hurry, and continued to chew, ruminatively, his straw.

CHAPTER TWENTY-SEVEN

Violence on the king's high road

HAVING CAUGHT A GLIMPSE of the sober coach's equally sober pace, John had little doubt of reaching London far ahead of it. The mare was fresh; she desired nothing better than a good gallop. John left the road for the fields, and gave her her head.

It was a short cut. He would pass the coach without the men on it seeing him, and could join the road again further on. Then for my Lord Barham, with all possible speed, and back again to hold Master Robin in check.

John could see no way out of the present dilemma, but he never saw the way in any crisis: he could only obey instructions. He had not the smallest doubt that my lord would at once perceive a way. The greatest anxiety, once my lord was informed, must be Master Robin's behaviour, John knew quite enough of this young gentleman to picture all manner of foolhardy deeds. Certain, he must hasten back to Richmond with all speed.

The mare was covering the ground in a long, easy

gallop. John came on to a cart-track he had been making for, and turned down it. In a little while the cart-track joined the road; John reined the mare into a canter, easing her for a space. A strip of close turf bordered the road; he pressed on to it, and the mare, nothing loth, quickened to the gallop again.

John began to consider the time. Judging by the long shadows it was nearly dusk, and Mistress Prue must not be left to spend the night in captivity. And where should he find my lord at this hour? There came a worried look into the square face: John foresaw much waste of time spent in search of his master. Unconsciously he pressed his knees closer to the mare's flanks. He was well ahead of the coach, but there was not a moment to be lost.

The road turned a corner; there was a horseman in sight, trotting along the strip of turf towards John. John pulled the mare in a little, anxious to attract no attention, and she slackened to a canter.

He would have passed this other rider without a glance, but of a sudden the big roan horse was pulled across his path, barring the way, and he heard the voice of Sir Anthony Fanshawe.

'Well, my man? Well? Whither away so fast?'

The mare had been brought perforce to a standstill. John looked into that handsome, lazy face, and spoke urgently. 'Let me pass, sir. I must get to his lordship.'

The eyes were keen and searching. 'Yes?' said Sir Anthony. 'And wherefor?'

'It's Miss Prue!' John said in an agony of impatience. 'She's taken by the Law for the killing of Mr Markham! Now will you let me pass, sir?'

The large hand on the bridge had tightened; the indolent air was gone. 'Less than ever, my man. When was she taken? Come, let me have the whole story, and quickly!'

'She's on the road now, sir, behind me! I must get to my lord.'

'We won't trouble his lordship,' said Sir Anthony. 'This is my affair.'

John looked doubtful. The large gentleman had a masterful way with him, but John was inclined to trust to no one but my lord. He waited.

Sir Anthony passed his riding whip absently down the neck of his horse. His eyes looked straight ahead, and they were frowning. After a moment he turned his head, and spoke. 'Yes, I think we might compass it, John,' he said placidly. 'Have you a mind to a fight?'

John smiled grimly. 'Try me, sir! You'll stop the coach?'

Sir Anthony nodded. 'I hope so. How many men?'

'Two inside—naught to fear from them. There's the coachman on the box, and a man with him.'

'Four.' Sir Anthony was unperturbed. 'Possibly a pistol in the coach.'

'There'd be one in the holster, maybe. But Miss Prue's inside and she has all her wits, sir.' John looked at the large gentleman in some awe. From the first he had felt respect for Sir Anthony, but he had not thought that he would undertake such a lawless venture as this quite so calmly. John was of the opinion that he might well be a good man in a fight, provided his size did not make him slow.

Sir Anthony came down out of the saddle, and produced his handkerchief. 'Have you a muffler, my man? Cover your face to the eyes, and pull your hat well over your nose.'

John loosened the cloth at his neck. 'There's enough of it for two, sir. You'd best wear your greatcoat.' His glance rested expressively on Sir Anthony's fine cloth coat.

Sir Anthony was unstrapping it from the saddle. He was handed a half of John's generous neckcloth, and proceeded to arrange it to cover the lower half of his face. The greatcoat was buttoned up, and the swordhilt pulled through the placket. 'I've pistols,' Sir Anthony said, 'but I don't want to make this a killing matter. Break yourself a thick stick: it should suffice.'

'Give me one of your barkers, sir. I'll do as I did when we held up Mr Markham—fire over the coachmen's heads. It frightens them so they think they're killed.'

'My dear good man, do you want every cottager running from miles round to see what the noise means? Threaten a shot if you like, but on no account fire. It is understood?'

'Ay, sir,' said John, abashed. He went off to find a

likely cudgel in the little spinney close at hand. Returning presently with a rough stick of ash, he ventured a piece of information. 'Miss Prue has her sword-stick, sir. I saw to that. They don't know it, but she does, and she knows how to use it, too.'

Sir Anthony smiled a little. Ay, she would know, that cool, daring bride of his. He mounted again, and pushed forward to the spinney. 'We'll lie in wait here. It's as lonely a stretch of road as there is. Now attend to me a moment, John. You can do as you're told?'

John, reining in under the trees beside the large gentleman, nodded assent. It was in his mind that there were few who would care to refuse to do Sir Anthony's bidding.

'I am going to take your mistress down to my sister in Hampshire. I shall want the mare for her, but I'll throw her up before me on the roan until we're out of sight. We stop as soon as possible to mount her, and I fear me, John, you will have to walk back to Richmond. You'll tell Mr Robin what I've done, and get him out of the place as soon as maybe. Let him know I have his sister safe, and be urgent with him to fly.' He paused; John nodded. 'As to my chaise:—You'll send it on to my Lady Enderby's. I'd best give you a note for my man.' Out came tablets: Sir Anthony scrawled a few lines, and gave them to John. 'You are to be understood to have carried a message to me. Naturally I don't stay with my Lady Lowestoft when Mr Merriot is not there to play host. I've told my man

that I may break my journey at the house of a friend,
a little out of the way, so there will be naught to wonder at when I don't join my chaise at the stage to-
night. It's clear?'

'Ay, sir.' John bestowed grudging praise. 'You've
a fine head on your shoulders, sir.'

'I don't aspire to my Lord Barham's genius, but I
believe I have my wits. As for your mistress—why,
you may trust her to me. If she has woman's clothes
with her bring them to Dartrey in Hampshire as soon
as may be. She's done with this masquerade.'

'H'm!' said John. 'Mistress Prue has a will of her
own, sir, I'd make bold to tell you.'

'I know it full well, my man. But I too have a will.'

John did not doubt this: the large gentleman looked
as though he would carry all before him. Well, it was
a man worthy of Miss Prudence, and certain, she
would come to no harm while she was in his charge.
John said no more, but sat still under the trees, awaiting the coming of the coach.

There was not long to wait. The clip-clop of the
horses plodding stolidly along was heard, and the
creak and rumble of the coach. Came a scrape of steel
beside John: Sir Anthony's sword was out, and Sir
Anthony's hand was tight on the bridle. John took a
good grip on his cudgel, and awaited the word of command.

'Take them in a charge,' Sir Anthony said, and
pulled the muffler up over his mouth.

The coach rounded the bend in the road; Sir Anthony drove in his heels hard, and the big roan bounded forward, snorting indignantly. The mare, fidgeting all this time, needed no spur to follow suit; together the two horsemen came thundering down upon the staid equipage journeying so placidly along.

John followed the large gentleman's lead as best he might, but he had to admit he lacked that consummate horsemanship. Ahead of the chestnut mare a few paces Sir Anthony came down the centre of the road in a cloud of dust. It seemed as though he must crash full into the horses drawing the coach. So at least the coachman thought. This unfortunate individual had a sudden vision of two horsemen bearing down upon him at a mad, run-away pace, and instinctively dragged his own startled horses up, and tried to get to the side of the road. On and on came the first horseman, nearer, and perilously nearer. Then, even as the frightened men on the box thought collision inevitable, the roan, held so far on a straight course by an iron hand and an insistent knee, swerved off to the right, and was forced back almost upon his haunches, and held rigidly.

The coach horses were plunging in fright; the coachman had all he could do to hold them. Seeing Sir Anthony swing to the right of the coach, John, all the time on his heels, wrenched the mare to the left. Sir Anthony's sword flourished horribly near the men on the box; instinctively the one nearest to it shrank from it, throwing himself sideways against his companion, who lurched, still pulling at his reins, towards John.

The vicious tug brought one of the horses up on its hind legs; confusion reigned between the traces; John brought the nervous mare in close, rose in his stirrups, and struck hard and true. The coachman crumpled where he sat, and came sliding to the floor of the box; his companion caught desperately at the loose rein as the horses plunged forward. The animal that had reared up became entangled in one of the traces, and the confusion was complete.

Inside the coach Prudence's two gaolers were taken entirely by surprise. Such an unheard of thing as an attack on a vehicle of the Law, in daylight, and only a few miles out of town did not occur to them as a reason for this sudden stop and commotion.

The apologetic man opposite Prudence, who had abstained carefully from looking at her till now, brought his eyes round to her, and said with inspiration: 'Ah! We've gone over a pig. That'll be it.'

Prudence said nothing at all, but her hand slid to that innocent-looking cane beside her, and closed round its head. She still leaned back in her corner, and there was nothing either in her pose or in her expression to tell her captors that every nerve and muscle in her body was taut and ready.

'That's no pig, Matthew!' said the leader of the two. 'We've run into another coach belike.' He got up as he spoke, and let down the window. Even as he thrust his head out a great roan horse seemed to spring up from nowhere, and a huge man astride it bent in the saddle and wrenched open the coach door. The result was inevitable. The officer of the law lost his balance, caught at the door frame to save himself, and received a blow from Mr Merriot which sent him sprawling head foremost down on to the road.

No sooner had she caught a glimpse of the large figure astride the roan than all Prudence's air of languor left her. The sword was out of the stick in a flash, and the carved handle caught the chief officer shrewdly between the shoulders. She did not pause to see what befell this unfortunate; she had given him all that was needed to send him tumbling out of the coach. She had one foot on the floor of the coach, and one knee on the seat, and swooped round upon poor Matthew almost before his companion's misfortunes had reached his intelligence. He gasped out 'Lordy, Lordy!' and clapped a hand to his pocket. And there it stayed, for as he turned his head to face his prisoner he found the point of a peculiarly murderous-looking sword about an inch from his nose. Mr Merriot's arm was drawn back in readiness to thrust; Mr Merriot's grey eyes were fixed on him with an expression in them which made Mr Matthew goggle with dismay.

'Put your hands up! Quick, or I thrust home through your gullet,' said Prudence tersely.

The apologetic gentleman had never had such an

experience in all his life. His arrests had never been interfered with in this unpleasant fashion, and he did not know what to do. There was a pistol in his pocket, but his hand had not reached it, and with that sword-point so close he had no intention of groping further for it.

The point touched his throat. 'Hands up!' Prudence said, and made as if to shorten her arm for the thrust.

Matthew's hands were raised in shaking haste; Matthew's eyes were riveted to Mr Merriot's face, and Matthew's lips formed the words: 'Don't now, sir! don't. It's—it's a hanging matter, and there was no offence meant to your worship. It was all dooty, sir!'

Sir Anthony's great bulk blocked the door as he sprang lightly up into the coach. He was a fearsome figure, with the muffler concealing the lower half of his face, his hat drawn over his eyes, and the heavy cloak making him to look even larger than he really was. Matthew began to tremble violently, and rolled a beseeching eye from him to Prudence.

'Right pocket. A pistol,' Prudence said, still holding the sword to Matthew's throat.

There was a deep low laugh, which sounded like a death-knell to poor Matthew; the gigantic newcomer bent and slipped a hand into the pocket indicated. The pistol was soon stowed away in that voluminous great-coat; to Matthew's relief the sword point was slightly withdrawn.

Sir Anthony's voice was full of amusement. 'Now,

fellow, I'm afraid we must truss you up a little,' he said. 'Your muffler's the very thing.' The shapely hand divested Matthew of his muffler and neckcloth without ceremony. He offered no resistance. He was twisted round, and in a trice his wrists were bound tightly behind his back with his own neckcloth, and Mr Merriot was winding the muffler round his ankles in a most efficient manner. He was dumped down upon the back seat, and the next moment both the giant and Mr Merriot had jumped down from the coach.

Prudence pushed the sword back into its stick and looked round wonderingly. The chief gaoler was lying bound at the side of the road; the coachman was groaning and swearing on the floor of the box, as he came to his senses; his mate was clinging desperately to the reins, with a noble attention to duty, and trying, unsuccessfully, to keep one eye on his horses and the other on John, who sat astride the mare, the roan's rein in his bridle hand, and a pistol in the other. The coach-horses appeared to be hopelessly entangled in the traces, and the coachman, by the looks of it, would be unable to do anything but hold his head for some time to come.

Sir Anthony hoisted his second captive into the coach and shut the door on him. Under the brim of his hat his eyes were dancing. The one unhurt and unbound man would have his hands full with the frightened horses for quite a considerable time.

Sir Anthony moved to the roan's side, and swung himself up, taking the bridle from John. He gathered it up short in his left hand, and reached down his right to Prudence. 'Put your foot on mine,' he said, 'and up with you!'

She flung her coat up first, sent her sword stick spinning into the ditch, and stretched up her hand to clasp Sir Anthony's. She came neatly up into the saddle before him, and got her leg over without fuss. A strong arm girdled her about, and the roan, stamping and sliding, was given his head. In a few minutes they were in the spinney, trotting briskly through, then out in the open fields, with the road lost to sight.

'My dear, my dear, you're surely mad!' she said, but her fingers clasped his. 'You should not—you should not, Tony—for me!'

Came only a little laugh from behind her, and a tightening of the hold about her waist.

'Lord, your unfortunate horse!' said Prudence. 'I believe I'm no featherweight.'

'He'll bear us both for as long as I need,' Sir Anthony said. 'We bear southwards, John, and leave you by Easterly Woods.'

'Ay, sir,' John answered, pulling the muffler down from his face.

Prudence turned her head, and smiled at his stolid countenance. 'Tell Robin, John. Oh, but how he would have delighted in this.'

'I'm like to find him bent on some madness,' grunted John.

Easterly Woods came into sight; in a few minutes they were under the spreading beeches, and the horses were pulled up.

Sir Anthony sprang down and lifted Prudence from the saddle. She had an odd delight in this masterful treatment of her, though she could have come down easily enough by herself. For a moment as he held her she looked down into his eyes, and saw them alight with laughter, and something else, more deep than that. She was set lightly on her feet, and for an instant caught his hands in hers. Then she turned and pulled her coat from the roan's saddle.

'You remember, John?'

'Yes, sir.' John was holding the mare in readiness for Prudence.

She came to him, and took the bridle. She had very little doubt of her destination now. 'You'll keep Robin safe, John?'

'Ay, trust me, mistress.'

The twinkle crept up. 'What, will you leave me to the large gentleman?'

'I will,' said John, and exerted himself to say more. 'And I'd not wish you in better hands, Miss Prue. You'll do as he says, and come to no harm. Up with you!'

She put her foot into his hand, and was flung up

into the saddle. Beside her Sir Anthony sat the roan again.

'Good luck to you, sir,' John said. 'You don't need to fret over Master Robin, mistress.'

'Get him away to-night,' Sir Anthony said, and reached down his hand. 'It was a good rough and tumble, John.'

John flushed unwontedly, and after a moment's hesitation gripped the outstretched hand. 'It was, sir. Good-bye, sir.'

The roan was pressed forward to the mare's side; together they moved forward through the wood.

CHAPTER TWENTY-EIGHT

Exit Miss Merriot

EASTERLY WOODS LAY but two miles, across country, from my Lady Lowestoft's house, and John covered the distance swiftly. He came to the house by the river as the lamps were lit, and found my lady waiting in the hall, and Sir Anthony's chaise in the drive outside. He pulled off his hat and spoke before my lady could open her mouth. 'I took Mr Merriot's message to Sir Anthony, my lady,' he said in a voice loud enough to carry to the listening lackeys by the door.

My lady's black eyes snapped. 'Yes?' she said. 'And he said?'

'I was to tell you, my lady, he would not think of troubling you by coming here since Mr Merriot was took off. I've a note for his man.'

'Bah, it is a mistake the most absurd!' cried my lady. 'Mr Merriot will return at once! Where does Sir Anthony go?'

'He did say, my lady, he would turn off to visit a friend,' John answered. He remembered the mare, and added apologetically: 'The mare cast a shoe, my lady, and I made bold to leave her with the smith.'

My lady nodded. Her eyes searched John's face, but could read nothing therein. 'Your mistress is in a sad way,' she informed him, with considerable meaning.

'Yes, my lady? Should I give the note to Sir Anthony's man?'

'Do so at once, of course. Then come to put up a change of clothes for Mr Merriot. You must take them to him on the instant. To snatch him away in that fashion with never a moment to pack a valise—*affreux!*' She swept round, and went off up the wide stairs.

John stayed but to give Sir Anthony's note to his man, and followed my lady to Robin's room. He entered without ceremony and found his young master in coat and breeches, pulling on his top boots.

'For the love of God, John, will you make him listen to reason?' besought my lady.

Robin's fair face was set in uncompromising lines. He threw my lady an impatient glance. 'Oh enough, ma'am, enough. Do you suppose I shall sit here while my sister's hailed off under escort?'

John shut the door behind him 'She's safe, sir.'

Robin's hands left tugging at his boot. 'What?'

'Sir Anthony has her, sir. He's ridden off with her into Hampshire, and he bid me tell you he would keep her safe.'

My lady gasped. Robin turned in his chair to face

John. 'Good gad!' he said. 'The mountain! But how, man, how?'

John became quite animated. 'Sir, you couldn't have done it better! No, nor my lord either. There's a coach well on the way to London with two men trussed up inside it, the horses kicked over the traces, and the whole in an uproar.' He laughed at the thought of it.

My lady sat down on the edge of the bed. 'Sir Anthony did this?' she said incredulously. 'Never!'

'We did it between us, my lady, but 'twas Sir Anthony planned it. Ay, there's a cool head to be sure! 'Deed I've not seen his equal with a horse, Master Robin. It's a wizard he is.'

'But tell!' ordered my lady, striking her hands together.

Robin's eyes were bright and questioning. 'Let's have it from the start, John, if you please.'

'Ay, sir. You've to know I was off to my lord the instant those two vultures had Miss Prue off into the coach. Well, I know a way over the fields, and I could get ahead fast enough. I came on Sir Anthony riding down here, and he had the tale out of me.' John smiled. 'He wouldn't have me go to his lordship; he said 'twas his affair. That's a man I don't care to cross, Master Robin. He planned it we were to hold the coach up and get Miss Prue safe away. He'd be off with her to his sister, so he said, and I was to get you away this very night, sir. And so I will,' he added, with a touch of truculence.

'Never mind that.' Robin brushed it aside. 'Do you tell me Sir Anthony planned to waylay this coach, and make off with a captive of the law?'

'Oh, he made nothing of that, sir! We was both muffled to the eyes, and Sir Anthony had his sword out. We waited in a bit of a spinney till the coach rounded a bend in the road. Sir Anthony, he said to me, ''Take them in a charge.'' But there was no doing it his way. Leastways, not for me, and I thought I could ride, so I did. He had the roan under him: you'll know the horse, sir. Great powerful quarters, and I'll warrant you he can cover the ground. Sir Anthony was out of the spinney, and thundering straight down upon the coach before I could know what he would be at. 'Deed, and I thought myself he would spear the roan on the shaft of the coach!'

My lady blinked. It all seemed so very unlike the indolent Sir Anthony Fanshawe.

'How many men?' demanded Robin.

'Four—if you could call them such, sir. Sir Anthony swerved to the right, and I got the mare round to the left of the coach. I'd a thick ash staff, and that accounted for the coachman. Sir Anthony planned it so that the horses were all startled and plunging; the other man on the box had his hands full with them. Sir Anthony wrenched open the coach door, and out comes one of the vultures, sprawling in the road. Sir Anthony was off the roan in a trice; I brought the mare round to him, and caught his bridle. I can tie up a man quickly and neat myself, sir, as you know, but Miss Prue's sleepy gentleman beats all, so he does! He had him bound, arms and legs, before you'd time to look round.'

'I make the mountain my compliments,' said Robin. 'Lord, I would I had been there! What did Prue do? You won't tell me she folded her hands.'

'I will not, sir. I'd seen to it she had her sword stick with her, and you may lay your life she made use of it. She had the point at the other man's throat till Sir Anthony jumped in to take his pistol from him, so I heard. There was no more to it. We were off, all three of us, with Miss Prue up before Sir Anthony on the roan. We made for Easterly Woods, and 'twas there I gave the mare up to Miss Prue.'

Robin slowly pulled off his boots again. 'Lord!' he said. 'And so farewell Peter Merriot! She went willingly?'

'Oh ay, she knew well enough there was no saying him nay then. He told me to bring her woman's clothes down to my Lady Enderby's as soon as may be. For, says he, ''she's done with this masquerade.'' But first, sir, I must have you away. We'll have a whole pack of the Watch down on us here when this is known.'

Robin bit one finger-tip. 'If the mountain—egad, what a man it is!—has borne Prue off there's naught for me to do. I'll slip away to-night.'

John nodded. 'Ay, but get you into your petticoats again now. I'm off to his lordship. It's odds he'll have something to say. I'll take the valise my lady spoke of, to seem as though I were off to Miss Prue in prison.'

'Drive the curricle,' my lady said.

'Ay, my lady. And you'll bide here, Master Robin, till I bring word from his lordship.'

Robin got up. 'Don't fear me. I make my escape when everyone's abed. I'll await your return safe enough.'

He and my lady had dinner in lonely state in the big dining-room. In the character of Miss Merriot he affected to be quite overcome; my lady, when dinner was over, insisted that poor Kate should lie down in her boudoir with the hartshorn. She led poor Kate thither, and summoned fat Marthe. Fat Marthe was told that my lady did not desire her servants to sit up late. It was to be understood both she and Miss Merriot had gone early to bed. Marthe signified complete understanding, and rolled out again. My lady and Robin sat and talked over the strange events of the day, and the gilt clock on the mantelpiece ticked over the minutes.

At ten o'clock Robin was restive, listening for John, and he began to tap an impatient foot. Why must he delay, a'God's name? Marthe came in with hot chocolate, and the news that old Williams had at last taken himself off to bed. The house was very still. Robin went softly away to his chamber, candlestick in hand, and was shut up there for nearly an hour. It was just on eleven when he came back into my lady's boudoir, and he was dressed in coat and breeches with shining top-boots on his feet, and a sword at his side. He went to the window, and stood looking down the moonlit road, listening.

My lady studied his profile, and when he turned, feeling her gaze upon him, nodded and said: '*Du vrai*, my child, I like you best as a man. I do not think anyone will ever know you for the bold Miss Merriot.'

'You don't, ma'am?' Robin glanced towards the mirror.

'No, never. I do not know what makes the so great change.' She pondered it. 'Miss Merriot was a fair height for a lady, but Master Robin—oh, we must not call him a little man, of course!'

'You spare my feelings, in fact. It may be the neckcloth, and the hair drawn back. I was careful always to affect a *dégagé* style as Miss Merriot.'

'We-ll,' said my lady slowly. 'Miss Merriot was a dainty piece, but you, my child—you look to be all muscle and—*je ne sais quoi*.'

'I have my fair share of muscle, ma'am, I believe,' Robin said modestly.

But my lady was right. With her petticoats he cast off all Miss Merriot's mannerisms. Kate had a tripping step: Robin a clean, swift stride; Kate was languorous: Robin never; Kate fell into charming attitudes: Robin's

every movement was alert and decisive; Kate could
adopt a melting siren's voice: Robin's speech was
crisp, just as his eyes was keen where Kate's was languishing. The truth was he was a consummate actor,
and if he played a part he became that part, heart and
soul. My Lady Lowestoft had often marvelled at the
perfection of his acting, the rigid attention to every
little feminine detail, but she doubted whether she had
ever appreciated him fully until now, when he threw
off his disguise and all its attendant mannerisms.

She was thinking of this when the sound of horses
came to her ear. In another minute or two the wheels
stopped by the porch.

Robin peered through the window-pane. 'This will
be John at last. Oh lord, ma'am, it's the old gentleman
himself!'

Marthe was evidently waiting to let in the travellers,
for a few seconds later the door of the boudoir opened,
and my Lord Barham walked in, point de vice as ever,
in a scarlet riding coat under his cloak, buff smallclothes, and high top-boots.

'Well, Robert!' said my lady.

My lord kissed her hand punctiliously, but without
his usual display of rapture. A severe gaze was bent
upon his son. 'The whole of this affair,' announced
my lord in an awful voice, 'is deplorable in the extreme. It has been botched and bungled in a manner
passing my comprehension.'

John, entering behind my lord, shut the door. 'He's

been like this all the way down,' he told Robin. 'We'd
ha' been here an hour since, but that he must needs
stop to change his clothes,' he added.

'It is not my habit to drive about the country in ball
dress,' said my lord crushingly.

It was quite evident that he was very much put out.
Lady Lowestoft patted the couch invitingly. 'But sit
down, my dear Robert!' she coaxed.

My lord came out of his cloak. 'Take it!' he said.
John obeyed with a wry smile at Robin. My lord gave
his ruffles a twitch, and bent to flick a speck of dust
from his shining boots. He then walked to the fireplace, and entirely ignoring my lady's invitation, stood
with his back to it, and proceeded to deliver himself
of a terrific denunciation. 'Botched and bungled!' he
repeated. He appeared to address no one in particular.
'Are my schemes so incomplete they need adjust-
ments? Do I leave aught to chance? Am I to be set
aside, disregarded, over-ruled? In a word, am I to be
disobeyed?'

His hearers felt that they were not expected to venture a reply. Robin sat down astride a chair, laid his
arms along the back of it, propped his chin on them,
and waited patiently. My lord's eyes swept the room.
'I am not!' he said, in a tone that made my lady jump
guiltily. 'At the start of this episode I made my plans.
They were beautifully complete. I do myself less than
justice: they were perfect! I issued my orders: a child
might have comprehended them. Not so my son. Did

I ordain that my Prudence should embroil herself in the affair? I did not. Did I inform my son that I desired him to escort Miss Grayson home when all was done? I did not. No one possessing but the smallest knowledge of me could have supposed it possible that I should meditate such a piece of folly! My children chose to set me at naught. They meddled in a plan of *my* making!' The penetrating eye flashed.

Robin sighed, and continued to watch his father; my lady blinked; John, standing still by the door, compressed his lips, and looked at my lord rather as an adult might look upon the tiresome tricks of a small child.

My lord's accusing gaze rested on each one in turn. 'I have a forbearance passing anything one could imagine,' he said amazingly. 'Did I, when this came to my astonished, my incredulous ears, give way to my very righteous indignation? I did not. Some slight reproof I may have allowed to pass my lips. Enough, one would say to warn my children that in future they must obey the very letter of my law. The thing was done; the crass error had been perpetrated. To what avail my censure? I held my peace. I said only: "Do nothing without word from me. Await my instructions!" When you came to this place—a measure of which I never approved—I said it. To John, my servant, I said more emphatically still: "If aught should befall my children apprise me instantly." By John no less than by my children have I been disregarded.'

'Ay, my lord, and I've been telling you for the past hour and more that I was on my way to you when I met Sir Anthony. If you would but listen—'

My lord flung up a hand. 'You interrupt me at every turn! Allow me to speak!' The tone was not that of a request; John looked helplessly at Robin, who held up a finger. It was quite plain to Robin that his father was greatly annoyed to think that anyone but himself had had a hand in the management of the affair.

'I have said I was disregarded,' my lord continued. 'It is very true! tragically true! Do you suppose that I had not foreseen the apprehension of my daughter? It is possible you could think I had not made my plans in preparation of this?' He paused a moment. Robin, who had thought precisely this, held his piece. My lord, satisfied that he was not going to venture to speak, swept on. 'It was, from the first moment of deviation from my original schemes a contingency to be expected. I expected it. It happens. My daughter is arrested; my servant, not yet lost to all sense of what is due to me, sets off to apprise me of it. He meets Sir Anthony Fanshawe. He should never have done such a thing!'

John was moved to answer. ''Deed, and how could I help it, my lord?' he said indignantly.

'Of course you could have helped it. In your place should I have fallen into the arms of Sir Anthony? Certainly not! Sir Anthony—I excuse him only because he has not had the inestimable advantage of being trained by me from childhood—must needs meddle—must needs put a clumsy finger into a pie of my making! And John! Does he inform Sir Anthony that it is unwise, nay, dangerous to meddle in my affairs?'

'Yes, my lord,' said John unexpectedly. 'I did.'

'You put me out with these senseless interruptions!' said his lordship tartly. 'You aided and abetted him in a flamboyant, noisy rescue! I—Tremaine of Barham—'

'I thought it would come,' murmured Robin.

My lord paid no heed. 'I—Tremaine of Barham—had a score of subtle schemes for Prue's release. I shall not divulge them now. They have been overset by folly and conceit!'

Robin straightened in his chair. 'By what, sir?'

'Conceit!' pronounced my lord. 'A vice I detest! You flatter yourselves that you could carry this through without my assistance. My daughter, as I understand, is riding all over the country like a hoyden with a man who has not yet obtained my consent to be affianced to her. The impropriety holds me speechless! The Honourable Prudence Tremaine is whisked off like a piece of baggage, smuggled away to the house of a woman of whom I know nothing, as though she were in sooth a criminal flying for her life!'

'Instead of which,' said Robin, inspecting the lacing of one of his great cuffs, 'she might be lying snug in gaol. Horrible, sir.'

'And why not?' my lord demanded. 'I had an alibi

for her—I should have intervened in a manner quiet, and convincing. All the dignity of my proceeding has been upset; my son is forced to escape at night, and in secrecy; a hue and cry for the Merriots must of course arise, and I—I must set all straight again! If I were not a man of infinite resource, and of resolution the most astounding, I might well cast up my hands, and abandon all. If I had not the patience of a saint I might be tempted to censure the whole of this affair as it deserves. But I say nothing. I bear all meekly. I am to set about the unravelling of a knot I had no hand in making. I have to adjust my plans to suit an entirely altered situation.' He stopped and took snuff.

My lady preserved her air of coaxing. But she felt shattered. 'It is all very dreadful, Robert,' she agreed. 'Give the *bon papa* a glass of Burgundy, Robin.'

Robin got up, and went to the table Marthe had set. He brought my lord a glass of the wine. My lord sipped it in austere silence, enjoying the bouquet. His manner underwent a sudden, bewildering change. With complete urbanity he said: 'A very good Burgundy, my dear Thérèse. I felicitate you.'

Robin judged it time to speak. 'You crush us, sir. Believe us all penitence. Doubtless we lack finesse. But I confess I applaud Sir Anthony's action. It seems to me masterly.'

'Of its kind,' said my lord affably, 'superb! Unworthy of me, clumsy beyond words, lacking entirely any forethought but—for any other man—worthy of applause. I applaud it. I smile to see such blundering methods, but I do not say what I think of them. Sir Anthony has my approbation.' The terrible frown was wiped from his face. He sat down beside my lady and became once more benign. 'We must now consider your case, my Robin. You have my forgiveness for what is past. I say nothing about it.'

'You can scarcely expect to find a brain like yours inside my poor head, sir,' said Robin dulcetly.

'I realise, it, my son. On that account alone I do condone all this folly. I even forgive John.'

John received this with a grunt not exactly expressive of gratitude. My lord looked affectionately across at him. 'You did very well, my John, from what I can discover. When I consider that you lacked my guiding hand, I am bound to acknowledge that you and Sir Anthony carried the affair through very creditably. But we have now to provide for Robin.' He put his finger-tips together, and smiled upon his son. 'I perceive you are in readiness to be gone. I do not entirely like the lacing of that coat, but let it pass. You will proceed at once to the coast with John. He knows the place. If Lawton—you do not know him, but I have had many dealings with him in my time—if Lawton, I say, keeps to the plans he had made when I was aboard his vessel last month, he should bring the *Pride o' Rye* in for cargo at about this time. If he has been already there will be others soon enough. You will show that ring. It is enough.' He handed a ring he wore on his little finger to his son. 'But John will be with you. I need have no anxieties. Once in France you will proceed to Dieppe. Your trunks are with Gaston still. You will collect them, and embark on the first packet to England—under your rightful name. Remember that! You may find me in Grosvenor Square by then. John will see you safe aboard the *Pride o' Rye*, and return then to me. I have need of him.'

'Good gad, sir, I don't need John to escort me to this mysterious place!' said Robin.

'Certainly you need John,' said my lord. 'He knows the ways of the Gentlemen. Do not presume to argue with me. I come now to you, Thérèse. To-morrow you will discover the flight of Miss Merriot. You will make an outcry; you will pronounce yourself to have been imposed upon. When questions are asked it will transpire that you made the acquaintance of the Merriots at the Wells, and knew no more of them than may be gathered from such a chance-met couple. Is it understood?'

My lady made a face. 'Oh, be sure! But I do not at all like to appear so foolish, Robert.'

'That cannot be helped,' said my lord.

Robin caught her hand, and kissed it. 'Ma'am, we treat you cavalierly, and you have been in truth our good angel. You know what I would say to you in thank: what Prue would say.'

'Ah, what is this?' She snatched her hand away. 'Do

not talk to me like that! Thank me for nothing, Robin. I will be the silly dupe. Eh, but how I will lament!'

'You will do it very well, my dear Thérèse,' my lord assured her. 'John, saddle the horses. Waste no more time, my son: it is time you were gone. I shall see you again very shortly. Thérèse, I shall drive back to town in your curricle, and if you send a man for it to-morrow you will find it in your own stables near Arlington Street. Naturally I shall have had nothing to do with this. I have not visited you to-night. Do not forget that! Robin, farewell! When you return, remember that you bear the name of Tremaine. John, have a care to my son!' My lord arose as he spoke, received his hat and cloak from John, and with a gesture that savoured strongly of a Pope's blessing, swept out of the room, and away.

CHAPTER TWENTY-NINE

The ride through the night

SHOULDER TO SHOULDER, galloping over silent fields in the light of the moon, Prudence and Sir Anthony passed through the country unseen and unheard. There was little said; the pace was too fast, and Prudence too content to talk. This then was the end, in spite of all. The large gentleman swept all before him, and faith, one could not be sorry. Several times she stole a look at that strong profile, pondering it; once he turned his head and met her eyes, and a smile passed between them, but no words.

It seemed she was very much the captive of his sword; there could be nothing more to say now, and, truth to tell, she had no mind to argue.

She supposed they were off to his sister, but the way was unfamiliar to her. The gentleman seemed to know the country like the back of his hand, as the saying was; he eschewed main roads and towns; kept to the solitary lanes, and ever and anon led her 'cross country, or turned off through some copse or meadow to avoid a village, or some lone cottage on the road.

There would be no one to tell of this mad flight through the dark hours; no man would have seen them pass, nor any hear the beat of the horses' hoofs racing by.

Sure, they seemed to be the only people awake in all England. The failing daylight had gone hours since; there had been a spell of darkness when they rested their horses in a walk along a deserted lane; and then the moon had risen, and there was a ghostly pale light to show them the way, and the trees threw weird shadows along the ground. There might be heard now and then the melancholy hoot of an owl, and the chirp and twitter of a nightjar, but all else was hushed: there was not so much as a breath of wind to rustle the leaves on the trees.

They saw squat villages lying darkly ahead, swung off to skirt them round, seeing occasionally the warm glow of a lamp-lit window, and reached the road again beyond. Once a dog barked in the distance and once a small animal ran across the road in front of them, and the mare shied and stumbled.

There was a quick hand ready to snatch at the bridle. Prudence laughed, and shook her head, bringing the mare up again. 'Don't fear for me, kind sir.'

'I need not, I know. Yet I can't help myself.'

The moon was high above them when they reined in to a walk again. Prudence was helped into her greatcoat; the horses drew close, and the riders' knees touched now and again.

'Tired, child?' Sir Anthony's free hand came to rest a moment on hers.

Faith, it was a fine thing to be so precious in a man's eyes. 'Not I, sir. Do you take me into Hampshire?'

'Be sure of it. I'll have you under my sister's wing at last.'

Prudence made a wry face. 'Egad, I wonder what she will say to me?'

There was a little laugh. 'Nothing, child. She's too indolent.'

'Oh, like Sir Anthony Fanshawe—upon occasion.'

'Worse. Beatrice is of too amble a girth to indulge even in surprise. Or so she says. I believe you will like her.'

'I am more concerned, sir, that she may be pleased to like me.'

'She will, don't fear it. She has a fondness for me.'

'I thank you for the pretty compliment, kind sir. You would say you may order her liking at your will.'

'You're a rogue. I would say she will be prepared to like you from the outset. Sir Thomas follows her lead in all things. It's a quaint couple.'

'Ay, and what are we? Egad, I believe I've fallen into a romantic venture, and I always thought I was not made for it. I lack the temperament of your true heroine.'

There was a smile hovering about Sir Anthony's mouth. 'Do you?' he said. 'Then who, pray tell me, might stand for a true heroine?'

'Oh, Letty Grayson, sir. She has a burning passion for romance and adventure.'

'Which Madam Prudence lacks. Dear me!'

'Entirely, sir. I was made for sobriety.'

'It looked excessively like it—back yonder in the coach,' said Sir Anthony, thinking of that shortened sword held to poor Matthew's throat.

'Needs must when the old gentleman drives,' said Prudence, smiling. 'I should like to breed pigs, Sir Anthony, I believe.'

'You shall,' he promised. 'I have several pigs down at Wych End.'

The chuckle came, but a grave look followed. 'Lud, sir, it's very well, but you lose your head over this.'

'An enlivening sensation, child.'

'Maybe. But I am not fit to be my Lady Fanshawe.'

The hand closed over her wrist; there was some sternness in the pressure. 'It is when you talk in that vein that I can find it in me to be angry with you, Prudence.'

'Behold me in a terror. But I speak only the truth, sir. I wish you would think on it. One day I will tell you the tale of my life.'

'I've no doubt I shall be vastly entertained,' said Sir Anthony.

'Oh, it's very edifying, sir, but it's not what the life of my Lady Fanshawe should be.'

'Who made you judge of that, child?'

She laughed. 'You're infatuated, sir. But I'm not

respectable, give you my word. In boy's clothes I've kept a gaming-house with my father; I've escaped out of windows and up chimneys; I've travelled in the tail of an army not English; I've played a dozen parts, and—well, it has been necessary for me often to carry a pistol in my pocket.'

Sir Anthony's head was turned towards her. 'My dear, will you never realise that I adore you?'

She looked down at her bridle hand; she was shaken and blushing like any silly chit, forsooth! 'It was not my ambition to make you admire me by telling you those things, sir.'

'No, egad, you hoped to make me draw back. I believe you don't appreciate yourself in the least.'

It was very true; she had none of her father's conceit; she had never troubled to think about herself at all. She raised puzzled eyes. 'I don't know how it is, Tony, but you seem to think me something wonderful, and indeed I am not.'

'I won't weary you with my reasons for holding to that opinion,' said Sir Anthony, amused. 'Two will suffice. I have never seen you betray fear; I have never seen you lose your head. I don't believe you've done so.'

Prudence accepted this; it seemed just. 'No, 'tis as Robin says: I've a maddening lack of imagination. The old gentleman tells me it is my mother in me, that I can never be in a flutter.'

Sir Anthony leaned forward, and took the mare's

bridle above the bit; the horses stopped, and stood still, very close together. An arm was round Prudence's shoulder; the roan's reins lay loose on his neck. Prudence turned a little towards Sir Anthony, and was gripped to rest against a broad shoulder. He bent his head over hers; she had a wild heart-beat, and put out a hand with a little murmur of agitation. It was taken in a firm clasp: for the first time Sir Anthony kissed her, and if that first kiss fell awry, as a first kiss must, the second was pressed ruthlessly on her quivering lips. She was held in a hard embrace; she flung up an arm round Sir Anthony's neck, and gave a little sob, half of protest, half of gladness.

The horses moved slowly on; the riders were hand-locked. 'Never?' Sir Anthony said softly.

She remembered she had said she could never be in a flutter. It seemed one was wrong. 'I thought not indeed.' Her fingers trembled in his. 'I had not before experienced—*that*, you see.'

He smiled, and raised her hand to his mouth. 'Do I not know it?' he said.

The grey eyes were honest, and looked gravely. 'You could not know it.'

The smiled deepened. 'Of course I could know it, my dear. Oh, foolish Prue!'

It was all very mysterious; the gentleman appeared to be omniscient. And what in the world was there to amuse him so? She gave a sigh of content. 'You give me the happy ending I never thought to have,' she said.

'I suppose you thought I was like to expose you in righteous wrath when I discovered the truth?'

'Something of the sort, sir,' she admitted.

'You're an amazing woman, my dear,' was all he said.

They rode on in silence, and quickened presently to a canter. 'I want to rest you awhile,' Sir Anthony said. 'Keep an eye for a likely barn.'

'The horses would be glad of it.' Prudence bent to pat the mare's neck.

They were in farm-land now; it was not long before they found such a barn. It lay by some tumbledown sheds across a paddock, where a little rippling stream separated field from field. The farm buildings were hidden from sight by a rise in the ground; they rode forward, past what was left of a haystack, and dismounted outside the barn.

It was not locked; the door hung on rusty hinges, and inside there was the sweet smell of hay.

Sir Anthony propped the door wide to let in the moonlight. 'Empty,' he said. 'Can you brave a possible rat?'

Prudence was unbuckling her saddle-girths. 'I've done so before now, but I confess I dislike 'em.' She lifted off the saddle and had it taken quickly from her.

'Learn, child, that I am here to wait on you.'

She shook her head, and went on to unbridle the

mare. 'Attend to Rufus, my lord. What, am I one of your frail, helpless creatures then?'

'You've a distressing independence, on the contrary.' Sir Anthony removed the saddle from the roan's back, and led him into the barn. For the next few minutes he was busy with a wisp of straw, rubbing the big horse down.

Prudence went expertly to work on her mare, and stood back at last. 'It's warm enough here,' she remarked. 'They'll take no hurt. When they've cooled we'd best take them down to the stream. Lord, but I'm thirsty myself!'

Sir Anthony threw away the wisp of straw. 'Come then. There's naught but my hands to make a cup for you, alack.'

But they served well enough. They came back at length to the barn, and found the horses lipping at a pile of hay in the corner. A bed was made for Prudence. 'Now sleep, my dear,' Sir Anthony said. 'You need it, God knows.'

She sank down on to the sweet-smelling couch. 'What of yourself, sir?'

'I'm going to take the horses down to the stream. Be at ease concerning me. What, must you be worrying still?'

She lay back with her head pillowed on her folded greatcoat, and smiled up at him. 'A pair of vagabonds,' she said. 'Faith, what have I done to the elegant Sir Anthony Fanshawe? It's scandalous, I protest, to set you at odds with the law.'

Sir Anthony led the horses to the door. 'Oh, you must always be thinking you had the ordering of this!' he said teasingly, and went out.

When he brought the horses back her eyes were closed, and she had a hand slipped under her cheek. Sir Anthony took off his greatcoat, and went down on his knee to lay it gently over her. She did not stir. For a moment he stayed, looking down at her, then he rose, and went softfooted to the door, and paced slowly up and down in the moonlight. Inside the barn the horses munched steadily at the armful of hay he had given them. There was silence over the fields; the world slept, but Sir Anthony Fanshawe stayed wakeful, guarding his lady's rest.

CHAPTER THIRTY

Triumph of Lord Barham

SPECULATION concerning the result of my Lord Barham's coming meeting in Grosvenor Square was in abeyance. The strange flight of the Merriots formed the topic of every conversation in Polite Circles. It was a seven-days' wonder, and society was greatly put out to think it had received this couple with open arms. It was felt that my Lady Lowestoft had been very much to blame, and quite a number of people who heard my lady's lamentation felt a glow of superiority. They had a comfortable conviction that they would never have been so foolish as to invite such a chance-met pair to stay. One or two persons had an odd idea that they had heard my lady say she was acquainted with the Merriots' father, but when they mentioned this my lady was positively indignant. *Voyons,* how could she have said anything of the sort she had never set eyes on the elder Mr Merriot? She had been most grossly deceived; no one could imagine how great was the kindness she had shown the couple; she had had no suspicion of foul play. When she heard that Mr

Merriot was taken by the law for the killing of Gregory Markham she was so shocked, so astonished, she
could scarcely speak. And then, next morning, to find
Kate flown, and a horse gone from her own stables—
oh, she was prostrated. The affair was terrible—she
believed she would never recover.

It seemed like it indeed. Society grew tired of hearing her on this subject, for she could talk of naught
else. And where had the Merriots gone? Who were the
men who snatched Peter from the coach? One had undoubtedly been the servant, John, but who was the
other? The unfortunate gaolers swore to a man of gigantic size, but no one paid much heed to that. It was
the sort of exaggeration one would have expected.

Sir Anthony Fanshawe heard of it down at Dartrey,
and took the trouble to write to his friend Molyneux.
He protested he could not believe young Merriot was
the villain this affair showed him to be. He was in-
expressibly shocked by the news, but he felt sure some
explanation must sooner or later be forthcoming. He
ended by telling his friend that he had some notion of
extending his stay with my Lady Enderby, since her
ladyship had with her a most charming visitor.

Molyneux chuckled over this, and told Mr Troubridge that Beatrice Enderby was once more trying to
foist an eligible bride on to poor Tony.

In the meantime there could be found no trace of
the fugitives. They had vanished, and no man saw the
way they went. Nor did any man see the way John

returned, for he came secretly and looked quite different. The black hair had changed to a grizzled brown crop; the black brows became sandy, and the ugly mole beside his nose had vanished. It was not to be expected that the Merriots' swarthy servant wore a wig, darkened his brows and lashes, and affixed a seeming mole to his face. Nor could it cross anyone's mind that an old servant of my lord's, who had been in waiting on the young Tremaines should have any connection with the Merriots' lackey. Such a notion occurred to no one, more especially since it appeared that more than once my lord had warned my Lady Lowestoft that she should not trust too much in her youthful visitors.

People could not help admiring my lord's perspicacity. He shook his head at my lady, and said only: 'Ah, Thérèse!'

Whereupon my lady put a handkerchief to her eyes, and confessed that she had been wrong in her estimation of the Merriots, and my lord right. It became known that my lord had warned her many times; he had suspected something to be amiss from the first.

For three days everyone had theories to put forward, and exclamations to make, but on the fourth day interest veered round again to my lord's claim.

My lord was to meet the lawyers and his cousin at Grosvenor Square, and he would give conclusive proof of his identity.

Mr Rensley, with his arm still in a sling, awaited

the issue with not unjustifiable impatience. The family lawyers, Clapperly and Brent, were the first to arrive: young Mr Clapperly brought old Mr Clapperly, long since retired from the lists; and Mr Brent brought a grave clerk, and many documents.

Mr Brent rubbed his hands together and murmured over a list he held. He desired to know whether a Mrs. Staines, and a Mr Samuel Burton had arrived.

Mr Rensley stared at that. 'Burton?' he echoed. 'Do you mean my lodge-keeper?'

Mr Brent coughed. 'Let us say, sir, the lodge-keeper at Barham. You know we said we would not be—er—controversial.'

Mr Rensley said something under his breath, at which Mr Clapperly frowned. 'Why should he arrive?' he asked brusquely.

'The claimant, sir, desired it. Also Mrs Staines, who is, I believe, Burton's sister.'

'I know nothing about her,' Rensley answered. 'Has that impostor bribed them to recognise him?'

Young Mr Clapperly, a man of some forty years, begged Mr Rensley to moderate his language. Mr Brent assured Rensley that my lord had not set eyes on either Burton or his sister since his arrival: both brother and sister were as mystified as he was himself.

Shortly after this the couple arrived, and were ushered into the big library.

Burton was a stockily-built man of middle age, sandy-haired and blue-eyed; his sister was rather older,

a respectable-looking woman, who dropped a shy curtsey to Rensley, and another to the lawyers. She was
given a chair by the table, and sat down on the extreme
edge of it, with her brother beside her.

'Three o'clock,' said young Mr Clapperly, consult-
ing a large watch. 'I think we said three, sir?'

A coach was heard to drive up, as though in answer.
In a few minutes the door opened to admit my Lord
Barham, my Lord Clevedale, and Mr Fontenoy.

My lord swept a magnificent leg to the assembled
company. 'I am late!' he exclaimed. 'I offer a thousand apologies!'

'No, sir, no, almost to the minute,' Mr Brent told
him.

Mr Rensley was looking with dislike upon my
lord's companions. My lord addressed him at once.
'You scowl upon my friends, cousin. But you must
remember that I have the right to bring whom I will
to this interview.' He turned to Mr Clapperly. 'Is that
not so?'

'Oh, perfectly, sir! There can be no objection. Pray,
will you not be seated, gentlemen?'

They were grouped about a table that stood in the
middle of the room. My lord sat at the end of the table,
with old Mr Clapperly opposite to him. My lord produced his snuff-box, and unfobbed it. 'And now my
cousin Rensley wants to put some questions to me,'
he said gently. 'There is no reason why I should answer any of them. I stand proved already Tremaine of

Barham. You have tried to find that I stole my papers, and you have failed, gentlemen. I condole with you. Let me hear your questions; I shall endeavour to satisfy you.'

There was an uncomfortable air of strain in the room; my lord was too much master of the situation. Rensley sat on Mr Clapperly's right hand, and scowled at the table. Mr Clapperly had begged him to leave all to his men of business, and he had agreed to hold his peace. He did not look at my lord; the sight of that smiling countenance enraged him to the point of desperation.

Mr Fontenoy preserved his prim severity; my Lord Clevedale lounged beside the old gentleman, and was frankly agog with curiosity. Burton and his sister sat together on one side of the table, and appeared to be rather bewildered.

Mr Brent signed to his clerk, who brought forward a leather case. Mr Brent opened this, and produced a slip of paper. It seemed to have been cut from a letter, for it was closely written over. 'Perhaps, sir, you would be good enough to tell us if you recognise this writing,' he said courteously, and gave the slip to the clerk, who carried it to my lord.

My lord put out a white hand to receive it. He glanced at it, smiled, and gave it back. 'Certainly,' he said. 'It is my father's hand.'

Mr Rensley shot a quick look at him, and bit his lip.

'Thank you, sir,' bowed Mr Brent. 'And these?'

My lord took three other such slips. One he handed back at once. 'My brother. Pray take it away.' He frowned over the second and shook his head. 'I have not the smallest notion,' he said calmly. 'I doubt whether I have ever seen it before.' He turned to the third, and spent some time over it. 'I am inclined to think that this must be my Aunt Susanna,' he said.

'Inclined, sir?'

'Inclined,' nodded my lord. 'I never received a letter from her in my life that I can remember. But I perceive the word Toto. My respected aunt, when I knew her— and I do trust she's dead?—had a small dog of that name. A yapping, petted little brute of a spaniel. Mr Fontenoy would remember.'

Mr Fontenoy nodded. The lawyers exchanged glances. If this were indeed an impostor he knew a deal about the family of Tremaine.

'But the second letter, sir?'

My lord raised his brows. 'I told you, did I not? I do not know the hand at all.' He put up his glass and looked at it again. 'Very ill-formed,' he remarked. 'No, I know no one with such an undistinguished hand.'

Mr Rensley reddened angrily and opened his mouth to speak. Mr Brent put up a hand to silence him. 'Is it not a little strange that you should not know the writing of the man you claim as cousin, sir?' he asked.

My lord was aghast. He looked at Rensley. 'Good

gad, cousin, is it yours indeed? I have been guilty of a breach of manners! I am desolated to have passed such a stricture on your hand.'

'You do not answer me, sir,' Mr Brent pointed out.

My lord turned to him. 'I crave your pardon. But does it need an answer? I thought I had made the situation between the Tremaines and the Rensleys clear to all. It is not in the least strange that I should not recognise the hand. I had never seen it before.'

Mr Brent bowed in a non-committal manner, and drew a miniature from the case before him. 'Do you know this face, sir?'

'I ought to,' said my lord. 'But do put it away again, dear sir! I've not the smallest wish to gaze upon my late brother's image.'

Old Mr Clapperly gave a dry cackle of laughter. Young Mr Clapperly looked reproachful, and said: 'I believe, gentlemen, we cannot regard that as conclusive. The late Viscount was well known. Show him the other one.'

My lord held a miniature of a dark lady at arm's length, and surveyed it critically. 'When was this done?' he inquired. 'It quite fails to convey an impression of her charm.'

'You know the face, sir?'

'Dorothea,' said my lord. 'At least, so I suppose, but it is very bad. More like my aunt Johanna. There is a far better portrait of her in the gallery of Barham.' He showed the miniature to Mr Fontenoy. 'You knew my sister, sir. Do you agree that this does her less than justice?'

'Miss Tremaine had certainly more animation than is shown here,' Mr Fontenoy answered.

My lord gave back the miniature. There was a gleam in his eye. 'But why not produce a picture of myself?' he suggested.

Mr Fontenoy, and old Mr Clapperly looked sharply. Rensley said triumphantly:—'You make a slip there, my clever gentleman! There is no picture of you!'

My lord smiled. 'No? And does my friend Mr Fontenoy agree with that?'

Mr Fontenoy said nothing. My lord tapped the lid of his snuff-box. 'What of the sketch that was taken of me when I was eighteen?' he asked softly.

It was plain Rensley knew nothing of this; equally plain was it that my lord had impressed the two eldest people present. 'It is true that there was once such a portrait, sir,' said old Mr Clapperly. 'But it exists no longer.'

'You may be right,' said my lord politely. 'It is a long time since I left England. But perhaps you have not looked for it in the right place.'

'We have searched both in this house, and at Barham, sir. It is not to be found.'

'It see that I must assist you,' smiled my lord.

There was an alert look in Mr Brent's face. 'Indeed, sir, and do you know where this likeness is to be found?'

'I hope so, Mr Brent. But do not let us be rash. If the likeness is still where I hid it, then I can find it.'

Mr Fontenoy lost some of his primness. Everyone was staring eagerly at my lord. 'Where you hid it, sir?'

'Where I hid it,' repeated my lord. 'Now I have overheard you to say, Mr Fontenoy, that young Robert Tremaine was a romantic youth. It is very true! Years have not dulled the edge of my romantic fervour.' He laid down his snuff-box on the table before him, and his strangely compelling eyes swept the room. 'They have only sharpened a brain that was always acute, gentlemen. You cannot fail to have observed a forethought in me that excites the admiration. I had it even as a boy.' He smiled benignantly. 'Such a contingency as the present one I dimly expected, even in those far off days. I saw that the day might come when I might desire to prove my identity. The romantic boy, Mr Fontenoy, hid a picture of himself in this very room, to serve as a proof if ever he should need one.'

'In this room!' ejaculated my Lord Clevedale, looking round.

'Certainly,' said my lord. 'That is why I chose this room to-day.' He rose. 'Tell me, cousin, are you a great reader?'

'No, I am not,' said Rensley curtly.

'Nor was my brother,' said his lordship. 'I thought of that at the time. My father was much addicted to the works of Shakespeare but I believe he had no Latin.'

'What's all this to do with it?' Rensley demanded uneasily.

My lord's glance travelled to the top shelf of the books that lined the room. 'Do you ever chance to take down the works of the poet Horace, cousin?'

'No, I do not, and I don't see—'

'Nor did my brother, I am convinced,' said my lord. 'I thought it was safe—wonderfully safe, and wonderfully neat. I admire my own astuteness.' He met the puzzled eyes of my Lord Clevedale. 'A great pity to have no knowledge of the humanities,' he said. 'It is an estimable advantage. Had you been familiar with the Odes of Horace, cousin—but you are not. But take them down now: it is never too late to begin. Over in that corner, on the top shelf you will find the first volume, elegantly bound in tooled leather, the covers clasped by wrought hasps.'

'Pray, sir, what's your meaning?' Mr Brent asked.

'Why, is it not plain?' said my lord. 'I ask my cousin to pull the steps to that corner, and to take down the Odes of Horace. Let him open the clasps, and turn to the Fifth Ode.'

'You speak in riddles, sir.'

'But the riddle will very soon be answered, sir, if my cousin will do as I say. The first volume and the Fifth Ode. It will be most enlightening.'

Rensley went impatiently to the shelves. 'Mountebank! What am I to find there?'

'The missing sketch, my dear Rensley, of course.'

'What!' Mr Clapperly looked up. 'You put it there, sir?'

'I don't believe it!' Rensley said, and went quickly up the ladder. He found the book, and pulled it out. A moment he fumbled with the clasps. The leaves parted naturally at the Fifth Ode. Mr Rensley stood staring down at the book.

Every head was turned his way. 'Is it there?' demanded Mr Clapperly.

'You were told of this!' Rensley burst out, and flung the book violently to the ground. A drawing fluttered across the room, and was pounced on by Mr Fontenoy.

Instantly everyone save my lord went to peep over Mr Fontenoy's shoulder. 'It is certainly Robert Tremaine,' Mr Fontenoy said. He looked from it to my lord. 'And there is—a likeness.'

'Why, damme, sir, the eyes and nose are exact!' cried Clevedale.

Mrs Staines ventured to speak. ''Deed, sir, but you have a look of Master Robert.'

'My good Maggie, you ought to know that I am Master Robert,' said his lordship. 'I perfectly remember you.'

She stared. 'You do know my name, sir. But your lordship will pardon me—it is so long ago, and you've changed, my lord.'

'So it would appear,' said his lordship. 'I said I should satisfy you, gentlemen.'

'Pardon, sir,' Mr Brent interposed. 'It seems a proof

certainly. But we must not forget that you might have been told of this.'

'How?' inquired my lord. 'No one but myself knew of it.'

'I am assuming, sir, for the moment, that you are not Tremaine.'

'An impertinence,' said my lord. 'But I suppose I must forgive it. Pray continue. The legal mind is very wonderful.'

'And if—I only say if, sir—you are not Tremaine, you might have heard this from the man himself.'

My lord looked at him in blank astonishment. It was Clevedale who spoke. 'Lord, what in the plague's name would Tremaine tell such a secret for?'

'It is a possibility, my lord: I do not say a probability.'

'This is all quite ridiculous,' said my Lord Barham. 'Moreover I am becoming weary of it. I bring you papers, and you say I stole them. I show you where I hid my own portrait, years ago, and you say I was told of it. I show you a ring, and you say I stole that. What a pity it is I have no birthmarks! Or would you say that I had stolen them as well? It is a very good thing that I brought my friend Mr Fontenoy. And here is Mr Clapperly as well may remember a little about me.'

'Vividly, sir.' Mr Clapperly inclined his head.

'Then I am sure you will remember the circumstances of my departure, all those years ago?'

'I do, sir.'

'Then I beg you will correct me if I should err in my tale. It is quite short.' He offered snuff to Clevedale. 'My own mixture, Clevedale. You will like it. Well, gentlemen, you know that I was never at one with my father: he could not appreciate the genius that was in me. I disliked my brother only less than he disliked me. He hated me, I believe, but he would *not* have chosen to set you in my shoes, cousin, in spite of it. He was, after all, a Tremaine. I was no doubt a wild youth. I can remember incidents here and there— but no matter. I overspent my allowance with amazing regularity. I shall be careful to put no limits to my son's income. Then I committed the indiscretion of falling in love with a lady called Maria Banstead. She was the daughter of a farmer.'

'Near Barham,' nodded Mr Clapperly.

My lord looked ironically across at him. 'Your memory fails you, sir. Not in the least near Barham. She lived at Culverly, on the estate of my aunt Johanna's husband. I was, I admit, young, and possibly hot-headed. But I have never regretted my marriage. An incomparable creature! I led her a sad dance I fear me. I eloped with her secretly, and went to France, just as soon as I heard that I had been thrown off by my indignant family. That is my story, gentlemen. Is it true?'

It was admitted to be true. My lord indicated the clerk with a wave of his hand. 'Tell your clerk, Brent, to call my man in. He is in the hall.'

'Certainly, my lord. Go, Fawley.' It is the first time he had addressed my lord by his title and Rensley flushed as he heard him.

The clerk went out, and a moment later John stood in the doorway.

Everyone looked towards him, since it seemed he had been called for some special purpose. But my lord's eyes were on Mrs Staines' face. 'He does not change much with the passing of time, I believe,' he said.

Mrs Staines was staring. The colour left her face, and she put up a hand to her ample bosom. 'Johnny!' she faltered. 'Oh, dearie, dearie, am I dreaming?'

Burton was incredulous. 'It's never our John!' he gasped. 'Bless my soul, but it is really yourself, John?'

'Ay, it's me,' John said grimly and sustained the shock of having his sister cast herself on his chest. 'Well, Maggie, how do you, eh? Remember where you are, lass!'

Mrs Staines was quite oblivious of her surroundings. 'Oh, Johnny, to think of you come back to us after all these years! Snakes, and I scarcely knew you, dearie, you've grown so grey! Sam, do you know your brother?'

Mr Samuel Burton gripped Mr John Burton's hand. 'Well, John!' was all he could find to say.

'Did you ever learn to master the bay mare?' John asked grinning.

It appeared to be an old jest. Samuel shook with

laughter. 'Lordy, John, to think you'd remember that! Ay, I was naught but a stripling then, and the mare the tricksiest piece—well, to think you'd remember!'

Surprise had held the others spellbound, but Mr Brent recovered himself. 'Mrs Staines, do you recognise this man?'

'Oh, the legal mind!' murmured my lord.

'Why, of course I do, sir! It's our John, who went off years ago soon after Master Robert.' She turned again to her brother. 'And you've been with him all the time! Eh, and we never thought of it! But you was always saying you'd be off to Americky to try your fortune, Johnny, and we made sure you'd gone there.'

Mr Brent put a question no one thought needful. 'Is this gentleman Viscount Barham?' he said.

John looked scornful. 'Ay, of course he is,' he answered. 'Is there ever another would have that nose but a Tremaine?'

'You have been with him all these years?'

'I have, sir, and a pretty dance he's led me.' John smiled grimly at my lord. 'Many's the time I've told his lordship I'd be off home again. But we Burtons have always served Tremaine.'

There was a long silence. Mr Brent was slowly putting his papers together; Mr Clapperly smiled knowingly at his son; Rensley stood staring at the floor.

'Cousin,' said my lord. 'I trust you are at last satisfied.'

'There is no more to be said, my lord,' said old Mr Clapperly.

My lord picked up his hat. 'In that case I will take my leave of you. I should like my house at the end of a week, if you please. Brent, you will make the arrangements necessary, and put my terms before Mr Rensley. I hope he will not find me ungenerous. Clevedale, your arm!'

CHAPTER THIRTY-ONE

The honourable Robin Tremaine

PEOPLE FLOCKED to offer their congratulations to my Lord Barham, and to tell him how delighted they were that his claim—which they had always felt to be true—had been successfully proved. He received these visitors with his usual smile, and deprecated the suggestion that he had made a most handsome settlement on his cousin Rensley. How this news got about no one knew, for certainly Rensley said nothing about it. Rensley went abroad almost immediately, for his health. He cherished no kind feelings whatsoever towards my lord: he even talked wildly of bringing an action against him. Mr Clapperly dissuaded him from so foolish a proceeding, and ventured to say that my lord had behaved towards the usurper with positive magnificence.

So my Lady Lowestoft thought, and wondered at it. My lord waved a lofty hand. 'I am Tremaine of Barham,' he said. 'A lesser man might have shown meanness.'

'You are superb, Robert,' she told him.

'Certainly,' he said.

In due course my lord took possession of his house in Grosvenor Square, and travelled down to Barham for a day or two, to warn the servants there of his coming later with guests. To his friends he announced that he did but await the advent of his children to proceed in state to the Court.

If he had been sought out before he was now inundated with invitations from all sides. He spent not a single evening alone: either he went out, or he gave select card parties in his own house. A great many mammas courted him blatantly in expectation of the arrival of his son; Mr Devereux told his friend Belfort that since that aunt of his showed every promise of being immortal he had a good mind to try his luck with the Honourable Prudence Tremaine. Charles Belfort opined that she would have a squint, or a face scarred by small-pox. He said that with the exception of Letty Grayson all heiresses were ill-favoured. Mr Belfort had been very much put out by the defection of Peter Merriot, and could still talk of little else. He had no interest, he said, in my Lord Barham's children.

It was not many days before a post-chaise, piled high with baggage, came to the house in Grosvenor Square, and drew up before the door. A slight young gentleman sprang out, followed by a French valet. One of my lord's servants opened the door to this young gentleman, and inquired politely who he might be. The young gentleman said briskly: 'My name's Tremaine. I must suppose I am expected.'

Indeed, it seemed so, for there was at once a bustle made. The numerous valises and boxes were brought into the house; a footman came bowing to inform Mr Tremaine that his lordship was unfortunately out, but should be sent for in a trice, to White's.

Mr Tremaine refused this offer. Having drunk a glass of excellent Burgundy, brought by yet another footman, he announced his intention of setting forth himself in search of his father. Faith, one must face everyone sooner or later; then a'God's name let it be at once!

One of the lackeys at White's escorted Mr Tremaine to the card room, and stood for a moment by the door looking round for my lord. Robin paused beside him, holding his hat under his arm, and his handkerchief and snuff-box in the other hand. Several people looked up, wondering who the handsome young stranger might be. Mr Belfort, dicing with Devereux and Orton, said:—'Gad, that's a devilish modish wig! Who is it?'

Sir Raymond looked round and met Robin's eyes. 'I don't think I know him,' he said hesitatingly. 'Yet— there's something faintly familiar in his face.'

Mr Devereux put up his glass. ''Pon my soul, Bel, that's a monstrous pretty fashion of lacing he has to his coat! A prodigiously modish young buck, I protest!'

At the next table Mr Troubridge said:—'Who's the

stranger? I seem to have seen that face before. A handsome boy, and carries himself well. A little arrogant, perhaps.'

Certain, Robin carried himself well, and had his trim figure well set off by a marvellously cut coat of dark blue cloth. He appeared to have been travelling, for he wore top boots, highly polished, on his small feet, and a sword at his side. His coat was heavily laced with gold, tight across the shoulders and at the waist, and spreading them into wide skirts, silk-lined, the cuffs very large and turned back almost to the elbow to show a profusion of Mechlin ruffles. His waistcoat, a dozen men of fashion noted at once, was of the very latest style; the lace at his throat was arranged to fall in cascades down his chest, and there was a sapphire pin glinting in it. His wig, at which Mr Belfort, an expert in these matters, had exclaimed, must have come direct from Paris; the hat under his arm was richly edged with finest point. His blue eyes were cool; his mouth, though delicately curved, was firm enough; when he turned that arrogant profile towards Mr Troubridge that gentleman said with greater emphasis than before:—'Gad, yes! A remarkably handsome boy. A pity he is not taller.'

The lackey had perceived my lord over by the window, and pointed him out now to Robin. Robin went forward between the tables, and stood at his father's elbow. 'Sir….'

My lord was playing picquet with my Lord March.

He looked round and exclaimed. 'My Robin!' He threw down his cards and sprang up. 'My son!' he said joyously.

Robin stood bowing deeply before his father. 'I've but this instant arrived, sir.' His lips brushed the back of my lord's hand punctiliously. 'I found you from home, and came to seek you here. You permit?'

My lord clasped his arm. 'And I am from home when my Robin arrives! My Lord March, you will allow me to present to you my son?'

'So this is your son, is it, Barham?' My lord nodded in a friendly fashion to the grave young gentleman bowing so gracefully before him. His lordship was not, after all, so very far removed from Robin's age, but he had the manner of a man of forty. 'A very pretty youth, Barham. And are you just come from France, Tremaine?'

'Just, sir.'

'I dare swear you have all the latest fashions at your finger-tips then. Is it true they are wearing ear-rings in Paris?'

'I have occasionally seen them, sir. At balls a single ear-ring is considered in some circles *de rigueur*.'

By this time nearly everyone in the card room had realised that the modish stranger must be my lord's long looked-for son. Sir Raymond Orton said that it accounted for the familiarity of his face, and went to be introduced.

My lord presented his son with justifiable pride, and

had the satisfaction of seeing him borne off to dice at Orton's table. Mr Belfort and Mr Devereux received him with kindness, and made him welcome. He protested that he had no right to be in the club at all, but was told that that was nonsense. In a day or two he would of course be made a member. He was found to be well-versed in the ways of the world, and could tell an entertaining tale. Mr Belfort enrolled him promptly in the numerous ranks of his intimates.

On his way out of the room Mr Troubridge paused to lay a hand on Robin's arm. 'Barham's son?' he said. 'To be sure, we have all been most anxious to see Robin Tremaine.'

Robin rose to his feet, a hand on the back of his chair. 'You are very kind, sir.'

'And have you brought your sister?' smiled Mr Troubridge.

Robin's brows rose. 'My sister came over some time before me, sir. She is the guest of my Lady Enderby, at Dartrey.'

Mr Molyneux, overhearing, gave a soundless whistle. So that was the charming visitor Tony had written about? Gad, but Tony had all the luck!

Robin very soon left the club in company with his father. My lord had presented him to everyone: several people said that they had thought his face vaguely familiar from the first, and were sure it must have been his likeness to his father. Robin bowed, and suppressed an inward smile.

Once outside the club my lord became more rapturous still. 'You are perfect, my Robin! Perfect! There is not a soul will suspect. You had no trouble?'

'None, sir. And you?'

'How should I, my son? Need you ask?'

'I suppose not. Am I to understand, sir, you are in very sooth Tremaine of Barham?'

My lord smiled. 'My Robin, confess you have doubted me!'

'Yes, sir. I do not know that I am to be blamed.'

'Certainly you are to be blamed. You who have known me from your cradle!'

'For that very reason, sir, I doubted.'

'Ah, you should have had faith in me, my Robin!'

'I had, sir—in your ingenuity.'

My lord shook a finger. 'I saw from the outset that you doubted. I might have convinced you. I chose rather to confound you, as I do now.'

Robin blinked. 'Let me have a plain answer, sir. Is this all a trick, or are you Tremaine?'

'Of course I am Tremaine,' said his lordship, with a calmness more convincing than all his heroics.

Robin turned his head to stare. He drew a deep breath. 'Give me time, sir. You have certainly confounded me. I confess, I thought it a trick.'

My lord laughed in gentle triumph. 'I am always an unknown quantity, my Robin. You should have thought of that. But if I were not in very truth Tremaine of Barham—which I am—I should stand precisely where I stand to-day. Therein lies my greatness. Believe it!'

'Oh, I do, sir. I'm of the opinion you might be King of England if you choose.'

My lord considered this. 'It is possible, my son,' he said seriously. 'I do not say that it would be altogether beyond my powers. But there would be difficulties— great difficulties.'

'Lord, let's remain content as we are!' said Robin, alarmed. 'I'm satisfied, sir.'

'I told you, and you would not believe it, that we had come to the end of our wanderings!'

'I doubt I shall wake up soon,' said Robin.

He was present at a dinner party my lord gave that night, and my lord's guests decided that he was a charmingly mannered young man. My lord said afterwards:—'You will be almost as great a success as your father, my Robin!'

'Impossible, sir,' said Robin, stirring the dregs of punch in the big silver bowl.

'I do not deny it,' said my lord. His eyes rested fondly on his son's fair face. 'To-morrow, Robin, you will go down to Dartrey and bring my Prudence to Barham.'

Came a slight frown. 'The next day, and it please you, sir. I've affairs of my own to-morrow.'

These affairs took him, on the next day, to the house of Sir Humphrey Grayson. Sir Humphrey received him in his library, and looked somewhat at a loss. 'Mr

Tremaine?' he said. Robin bowed. 'I have to suppose—my Lord Barham's son?' Again Robin bowed. 'Er—you have business with me?' Sir Humphrey was puzzled.

Robin looked straightly at him. 'Sir Humphrey, may I ask what you may perhaps think an impertinent question?—Are you in your daughter's confidence?'

'Fully, sir.' Sir Humphrey was a little stiff.

'She has perhaps mentioned to you a man calling himself *l'Inconnu?*'

Sir Humphrey started. 'Sir?'

'I am he,' said Robin quietly.

For a moment Sir Humphrey could find no words. This slim boy—that magic swordsman Letty raved about! No highwayman, no outlaw, as he had feared, but a Viscount's son and heir! 'You?' he gasped. 'You are the man who saved my daughter? Barham's son! You will excuse me, sir; I am completely taken aback! Are you indeed my daughter's mysterious champion?'

'A grander term than I should have chosen, sir. I am the Unknown who killed Markham, certainly. But I beg you won't mention it.'

'You are he! Sir, you must let me take your hand! I owe you more than I can ever hope to repay. Indeed, I scarcely know how to thank you, for words seem to be inadequate!'

Robin broke in, flushing. 'Sir Humphrey, you will agree that gratitude is out of place when I tell you that

I love your daughter. I am here to-day to ask you for your permission to pay my addresses to her in form.'

Sir Humphrey wrung his hand anew. His feelings were almost too much for him. At one moment he was under the gloomy conviction that the late appalling scandal had ruined his Letitia for ever; at the next a brilliant match for her was proposed to him. Her position in the world would be honourable beyond his wildest hopes, and no one would dare to talk scandal of the prospective Viscountess of Barham. He gave Robin to understand that he had a father's blessing and suggested that he should send Letty to him at once.

Robin begged him, with a dancing smile, to lose no time in so doing. Sir Humphrey went off with quite a jaunty step.

In a few moments the door opened again to admit Letty. She was dressed all in primrose taffety, with a riband through her curls. Her father had not told her who waited to see her; there was a wondering expression in the brown eyes, and she looked doubtfully at Robin.

He stood in the middle of the room, watching her, and said no word. The puzzled gaze ran over him slowly; a little hand stole to Letty's breast and her eyes widened. The slight, strong figure was surely familiar. She saw him put a hand to his pocket, and bring out a string of pearls. On his little finger was a gold ring cunningly wrought.

'It is you!' she said, little above a whisper. Then

she saw the fascinating smile, and the pearls held out to her, and she came forward in a stumbling run. 'Oh, you have come at last!' she said, on a sob, and found herself in his arms. The pearls dropped unheeded to the floor.

'I have come as I told you I should and you know what I demand,' he said in her ear. 'Letty, will you marry me?'

She breathed a shy yes; she was clinging to him, and she put up her face to be kissed. All dreams had come true for her.

The arms tightened about her. 'Ah, you wonderful girl!' Robin said. 'You do not even know my name!'

'I love you.'

'I worship you,' Robin said, and lifted one of her hands to his lips. 'Do you love me enough to forgive, Letitia?'

His voice sounded anxious. She pulled his hand to her own lips. 'Forgive you! I have nothing, nothing to forgive you!'

'Ah, but you have!' He put her gently from him. 'Look at me! Look at me well, Letty!'

She was blushingly rosily, and dropped shy eyelids. He said more insistently:—'Look into my face, Letitia, and tell me then if you have nothing to forgive.'

The long lashes fluttered upwards; the brown eyes were misty. 'What is it you mean?' Letty asked.

'You don't know me? You don't recognise me? Look at me well, child?'

She stared full into his face, blankly at first, and then with dawning astonishment. 'But—but—oh no, you could not be!'

'Could not be what?'

'Another brother—another brother of Kate Merriot's,' she ventured. 'You—it is the eyes—and the nose—and—'

'I am not her brother,' Robin said. 'Try again, Letty. You come near the truth.'

She fell back a pace. 'You are not—oh, you cannot be—no, no, how could you be?'

'I am Kate Merriot,' Robin said, and waited, his eyes on her face.

Letty was as pale now as she had been rosy. 'You—you? A woman? You acted— But it can't be! Kate *was* a woman!'

He shook his head; he was no longer smiling.

'Oh!' cried Letty. 'Oh, the things I must have said—' She broke off in distress.

'I swear on my honour you said naught to Kate you would not have said to a man!' he said quickly.

Letty was staring at him in amazement. 'It was not fair!' she said. 'You might have told me!'

'Will you let me explain?' he asked. 'Won't you hear me?'

Letty came nearer. 'Yes, please explain,' she said in a small tearful voice. 'But—but I wish you had trusted me!'

He held out his hand, and she put hers into it. 'I

wish I had, Letitia. But I had been schooled to tell no secrets. And this one had my life at stake.'

Her lips formed an O. 'Tell me!' she begged. 'You know I forgive you anything. And I would never, never betray you.'

'Beloved!' He caught her to him. 'I hardly dared to think that you could forgive so hateful a deception.'

She hung her head. 'You forget—you are the Unknown hero,' she confided shyly.

'There's very little of the hero about me, child; I'm an escaped Jacobite.'

Her head came up; her eyes sparkled. 'And I thought it romantic to elope with that odious Markham!' she cried. 'Tell me all about it, please!'

At that Robin went off into a peal of laughter. She was surprised. 'Why, you did not suppose I should mind, did you?' she inquired.

'I ought to have known,' Robin said, and swept her off her feet. 'My darling, my name is Robin, and I'm an adventurer! Will you still marry me?'

'I like your name, and I should love to be an adventuress,' said Letty. 'May I be one?'

'Alack, you are more like to be a Viscountess,' Robin said, and sat down with her on his knee.

The tale took some time in the telling, and it left Letty wide eyed and amazed. When she heard that Peter Merriot was Prudence Tremaine, she gasped, and gasped again. At the end for a while she could only bewail the fact that she had not known it all before.

'And Tony knew? *Tony*?'

'My dear, it was Fanshawe rescued her from the hands of the Law,' Robin said. 'He carried her off to his sister, and I'm off to fetch her to-morrow.'

Letty stammered a little. 'T—Tony tied up those m—men? T—Tony stopped the c—coach? Why—why—'

'He's not so stolid as you thought,' teased Robin. 'The truth is he has an ambition to marry her.'

'Oh, and I thought he wanted to marry you!' Letty cried. 'And all the while he knew, and—oh, 'tis the most amazing thing I ever heard! It is wonderful, Robin! I am very glad, for I like Tony vastly. But your sister to play the man— She must be monstrous brave and clever!'

'Like her brother,' bowed Robin. 'For myself I have a weakness for a fairy-like creature with brown eyes, but I confess Sir Anthony is fortunate. My Prue's a dear creature.'

'And—and you deceived me grossly!' Letty said, but she did not sound angry. 'Goodness, will your sister ever forgive me? 'Twas my fault she was taken by the Law for I told those odious men you had brown hair and were of medium height! But I never, never thought they would seize on Mr—I mean, on your sister. Robin, are you sure you are quite safe now?'

'Quite sure, child. Robin Lacey is no more. Here is only Robert Tremaine.'

'And no one would ever guess you were Kate,'

Letty said. 'Even I did not guess until you made me look at you, and then I could not credit it. Oh Robin, Robin, I knew you would come again, but I have been so miserable! There has been the horridest scandal and aunt is dreadfully cross.'

'But now,' Robin said, holding her close, 'it is for me to see that you are happy ever after. And I will see to it.'

'I am happy,' Letty said into his shoulder. A thought came to her; she lifted her head, and said in a voice of unholy glee:—'And aunt shall see that I am not in the least ruined for life! She will look very silly when she knows I am to be a Viscountess one day!'

CHAPTER THIRTY-TWO

Journey's end

ROBIN HAD INSTRUCTIONS to bring his sister to Barham Court, where my lord would await their coming. My lord wrote a beautiful letter to my Lady Enderby, thanking her for her kindness to his daughter, and begging her to honour his house with her company. He purposed to invite Sir Humphrey and Letty Grayson down too; my Lady Lowestoft, and of course Sir Anthony Fanshawe. He had begun to meditate nuptials: Robin felt sure that they were to be magnificent.

As for this unlooked for ending, it took Robin's breath away. It seemed there was no longer room for doubt: the old gentleman was Barham indeed, and the days of their adventuring were over. Faith, and it was like him to allow his children to doubt him to the end! It gave him the chance to make a gesture. It had been so, Robin reflected, all through this masquerade. Simplicity was abhorrent to his lordship; he revelled in a net-work of intrigue; he loved to accomplish the impossible. A less tortuous man might have established his identity in a way quieter and more direct; a less fantastic man might not perhaps have perceived the need for his son and daughter to be in town all this while. They could have escaped to France, and waited there. Robin understood the workings of that stupendous mind. The old gentleman wanted them to see his triumph; it would have lost half its savour if they had not been there to be mystified, aghast, and at the last thunderstruck. He liked also to make a dupe of the whole of Polite Society. He had thrown his son and daughter right into the lion's den, masquerading in a preposterous guise: Robin could imagine his delight. In fact, the old gentleman had once more shown himself to be too clever for the rest of the world, and for him that was the breath of life.

Robin wondered whether my lord would be content now, or whether thirty years of adventuring would not prove too strong for him. It was hard to imagine the old gentleman at rest.

Robin wondered too what Prue would have to say to it, if she did not already know of my lord's success. John, packing a valise for Robin, thought that Miss Prue would not be surprised. He said with a dry smile:—'She's taken up with her own affairs, Master Robin. Leastways, she was when I saw her.'

'Have you been down to Dartrey?' Robin asked.

'Ay, when I'd put you aboard the *Pride o' Rye* I was off post haste with all her gear.'

'How was she?'

'Well enough, but my Lady's Enderby's clothes hung on her. It's a merry, stout lady, that.'

Robin played with the hare's-foot. 'She wasn't married, I suppose?'

'She was not, sir, but I'd say it won't be long before she is.'

'Pleased, eh?'

'He's a fine man, Master Robin.'

'Oh ay, I dare swear he'll suit her. Egad, she'll turn respectable! I'm to be married myself, John.'

'No need to tell me that, sir.'

'You're mighty knowing, a'n't you?' Robin got up, and stretched himself. 'And so we all live happily ever after. Who'd ha' thought it?'

He journeyed to Dartrey in a luxurious chaise, which had the arms of the Tremaines blazoned on the doors, and enjoyed a silent laugh over it, remembering hand to mouth days abroad. He reached Dartrey on the afternoon of the next day, and was set down at an old white house that stood in well-timbered grounds, back from the road. A servant ushered him into the sunny withdrawing room, and went away to find his lady.

Robin took critical stock of his surroundings. Ay, here was an air of security, of comfort, and of tranquillity. It would suit Prue; she was made to live in just such a house. For himself—eh, but one wanted a spice to life, after all.

A pleasant voice broke into her reveries. 'Do you desire to see my Lady Enderby, sir?'

Robin turned quickly to face the long windows that gave on to the lawn. Sir Anthony Fanshawe stood there, sleepy as ever, smiling a little. 'She commissioned me to bring you out into the garden,' Sir Anthony said. His eyes ran over Robin, and narrowed. Gradually a look of recognition and of wonder came.

Robin had given no name to the servant. Now as he looked at Sir Anthony his lips quivered. 'I thank you, sir. And do I address Sir Anthony Fanshawe?'

'I am undoubtedly a fool,' Sir Anthony said, and came into the room. 'But I confess you had me baffled. How are you, my dear boy?'

Their hands clasped warmly. 'As you see, O mountain. I flourish. And you?'

'The same as ever. Prue's well, and will be overjoyed to see you. You must come out to her.' Sir Anthony stood back the better to survey Robin. 'Well, my little popinjay, you make a mighty pretty young man.'

'I do, don't I?' Robin retorted. 'One of these days my mammoth, I will cross foils with you, and maybe teach you a trick or two will make you respect me.'

'You are really very like your father,' sighed Sir Anthony.

They went out together on to the lawn. There was a cedar tree not far from the house, and chairs set under it. A lady of ample proportions sat in one: Robin had no difficulty in recognising Sir Anthony's sister. Beside her Prudence sat in a gown of white muslin.

She looked up as the two men crossed the lawn, and rose quickly. 'My dear!' she said, and held out her hands as she went to meet Robin.

He put an arm round her waist, and kissed her cheek. 'Well, child, does the gentleman like you in this guise?' Privately he thought he had never seen her look better. Handsome she was as a boy, but in her petticoats she was a beautiful, queenly creature: a big woman, perhaps, but not too big for the man she had chosen.

She gave her delightful chuckle. 'He says so, my dear, but I doubt he doesn't like to hurt my sensibilities. But I must make you known to my lady.' She led him forward. 'Beatrice, will you be kind to my little brother?'

My lady held out a plump hand. 'I'll be kind to anyone who doesn't want me to get up,' she said in a voice very like Sir Anthony's. She looked Robin over placidly. 'Of course, I begin to understand,' she said. 'You would make a charming girl.'

Robin bowed over her hand, and his eyes began to dance. 'Not near so charming a girl as a man, ma'am,' he assured her.

'Very, very like his lordship,' said Sir Anthony pensively.

Robin was made to sit down beside my lady. 'I feel sure you are going to entertain me,' she remarked. 'I've been driven to yawning point: I never could abide a pair of lovers.'

'Oh, I'm come to relieve you, ma'am. I'm to bear Prue off.' He gave her my lord's letter. 'I have this to deliver from my father.'

My lady opened the letter. Said Prudence twinkling:—'Is it true the old gentleman's Barham indeed?'

'So he says. I arrived to find him installed at the town house in some state.'

'Lord, it's a marvellous man!' Prudence said. 'We become persons of consequence, and Tony's denied his cherished rôle. He'd an ambition to play King Cophetua, Robin.'

'The poor mountain! All your hopes fall to the ground, sir. The old gentleman is like to demand a prince at the least for his daughter.'

'Remains only Gretna,' said Sir Anthony. 'Which reminds me—how did you leave Letty Grayson?'

'Reluctantly, my mammoth. Shall we be married all four together and delight the old gentleman with so much display?'

'Oh, we don't desire to dwarf you, little man!'

My lady looked up from her letter. 'I'm bid forth to Barham, Tony. You are all in league to disturb my peace. Well, we'll see what Thomas says.'

Sir Thomas came soon into sight round a corner of the hedge. He was as lean as his lady was stout, and his eye was as vague as hers was keen. He accepted Robin philosophically, but seemed to be exercised over his roses. 'I've a mind to move them,' he said. 'They don't thrive. Do you understand roses, sir?'

'Alack, sir, my education's been neglected.'

'A pity,' Sir Thomas said gravely.

His wife roused herself to inform him of my lord's invitation. 'Do we go, Sir Thomas?'

Sir Thomas considered it. 'He might understand roses,' he said hopefully.

It was not until later, after dinner, that Prudence had a word alone with her brother. She stepped out with him into the dim, scented garden, and walked with him beside a bed of lavender, her silken skirts hushing gently as she went. In the lamp-lit room they had left my lady said:—'That's a very pretty pair, Tony. I don't deny it. You must know you've to embrace the brother if you would embrace the sister.'

'My dear Beatrice, do you suppose I did not know it? It's a devoted couple. I wouldn't have it otherwise.'

'I shall have to come to Barham for your wedding,' decided my lady. 'I've an ambition to see the old gentleman.'

'He will fatigue you sadly, my dear.'

'A mad business from start to finish,' said my lady. 'I'll see it to the end.'

Beside the bed of lavender Prudence walked with a hand tucked in Robin's arm. 'So we come to the journey's end.'

'You're happy?'

'Egad, don't you think so?'

'To say truth, I thought it. You achieve respectability.'

'I make you my curtsey, child, for the compliment.'

Robin watched it critically. 'Not so prettily done as I can do it, my dear.'

'Oh, I always said I'd none of your graces. But think of my height. And you—what do you achieve?'

'Letty.' He laughed a little. 'She would not thank you for calling that respectability.'

'I don't, be sure. What for the old gentleman?'

'Faith, isn't a Viscounty enough? Do you look to see him turn respectable too?'

'Optimism falls short of it. In truth, we all achieve something more than our deserts. It's a quaint world.' She smiled and joined hands with him. 'Give you joy, Robin.'

'Certainly, child.' He pressed her long fingers. 'And you have it.'

'Yes, I have it.' She turned her head, for a large figure was coming towards them.

'Abundance of it,' Robin said wickedly.

BUT A WEEK LATER, at Barham, on the terrace, my lord looked over the lawns to where four people were throwing bread to the carp in the marble pond and waved a satisfied hand. 'I contrive!' he said.

My lady looked too at the pretty group. There was Prudence, blue-gowned, and stately, leaning on Sir Anthony's arm and beside them Robin seemed to be endeavouring to prevent an eager, laughing Letitia from overbalancing into the pond. It was a charming picture and my lady's bright eyes softened as she looked. 'What, all of it, Robert?'

'All of it,' said my lord. 'My plans are accomplished; I win—as ever. I have surpassed myself.'

'And when they are married—*Voilà,* your labours are ended at last.'

My lord wrinkled his brow. 'My Thérèse, you should know that I am a man of too powerful a character to fold my hands.' He looked meditative. 'I have too large a vision to be so easily satisfied.'

'La—la! What now?' cried my lady in some alarm.

My lord became impressive. 'It is not fitting that I should be no more than a Viscount,' he said. 'Our house must be enlarged. You may look to see it happen, Thérèse.'

'*Mon Dieu,* and will it?'

'Do not doubt it,' answered his lordship. 'I have made up my mind that my son must inherit an Earldom at the least. I shall once more contrive. Do not doubt that I shall contrive! I am a great man, Thérèse: I realise it at last. I am a very great man.'

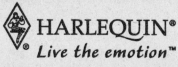

GEORGETTE
HEYER

83604	BEAUVALLET	___ $6.50 U.S.	___ $7.99 CAN.
83602	POWDER AND PATCH	___ $6.50 U.S.	___ $7.99 CAN.
83563	THE DEVIL'S CUB	___ $6.50 U.S.	___ $7.99 CAN.
83559	THESE OLD SHADES	___ $6.50 U.S.	___ $7.99 CAN.
83558	THE BLACK MOTH	___ $6.50 U.S.	___ $7.99 CAN.
83555	ARABELLA	___ $6.50 U.S.	___ $7.99 CAN.
83549	THE FOUNDLING	___ $6.50 U.S.	___ $7.99 CAN.
83548	THE GRAND SOPHY	___ $6.50 U.S.	___ $7.99 CAN.

(limited quantities available)

TOTAL AMOUNT $_____
POSTAGE & HANDLING $_____
($1.00 for 1 book, 50¢ for each additional)
APPLICABLE TAXES* $_____
<u>TOTAL PAYABLE</u> $_____

(Check or money order—please do not send cash)

To order, complete this form and send it, along with a check or money order for the total above, payable to Harlequin Books, to:
In the U.S.: 3010 Walden Avenue, P.O. Box 9077, Buffalo, NY 14269-9077;
In Canada: P.O. Box 636, Fort Erie, Ontario L2A 5X3.

Name:_____
Address:_____ City:_____
State/Prov.:_____ Zip/Postal Code:_____
Account Number (If Applicable):_____
075 CSAS

*New York residents remit applicable sales taxes.
   Canadian residents remit applicable GST and provincial taxes.

Visit us at www.eHarlequin.com

PHGH0404BL